WILD CHILD

T.C. BOYLE's novels include *World's End*, winner of the PEN/Faulkner Award for Fiction, *The Tortilla Curtain*, *Riven Rock*, *A Friend of the Earth*, *Drop City* (which was a finalist for the National Book Awards), *The Inner Circle* and, most recently, the highly acclaimed *The Women*. His short story collections include *After the Plague* and *Tooth and Claw*, and his stories appear regularly in most major magazines, including the *New Yorker*, *Esquire*, *Harper's*, *Granta* and *Paris Review*.

T.C. Boyle has been awarded the PEN/Malamud Award for lifetime achievement in the short story form and he was recently inducted into the Academy of Arts and Letters. He lives in California.

WILD CHILD

T.C. BOYLE

BLOOMSBURY
LONDON · BERLIN · NEW YORK · SYDNEY

First published in Great Britain 2010
This paperback edition published 2010

Bloomsbury Publishing Plc
36 Soho Square
London W1D 3QY

Bloomsbury Publishing, London, New York and Berlin

A CIP catalogue record for this book is available from the British Library

ISBN 978 1 4088 0949 5

10 9 8 7 6 5 4 3 2 1

Export ISBN 978 1 4088 1048 4

10 9 8 7 6 5 4 3 2 1

Printed in Great Britain by Clays Ltd, St Ives plc

MIX
Paper from
responsible sources
FSC® C018072
FSC
www.fsc.org

For Gordon and Cheryl Baptiste

ACKNOWLEDGMENTS

Grateful acknowledgment is made to the following magazines, in which these stories first appeared: *Best Life:* "Bulletproof"; *Harper's:* "Question 62" and "Admiral"; *The Kenyon Review:* "Hands On"; *McSweeney's:* "Wild Child"; *The New Yorker:* "La Conchita," "Sin Dolor," "The Lie," "Thirteen Hundred Rats" and "Ash Monday"; *The Paris Review:* "Balto"; *Playboy:* "The Unlucky Mother of Aquiles Maldonado" and "Three Quarters of the Way to Hell"; and *A Public Space:* "Anacapa."

"Balto" also appeared in *The Best American Stories, 2007,* edited by Stephen King (Boston: Houghton Mifflin, 2007), and "Admiral" in *The Best American Stories, 2008,* edited by Salman Rushdie (Boston: Houghton Mifflin, 2008).

The author would also like to acknowledge Harlan Lane's *The Wild Boy of Aveyron* and Roger Shattuck's *The Forbidden Experiment* as sources of certain factual details in "Wild Child."

In Wildness is the preservation of the world.

—Henry David Thoreau, "Walking"

CONTENTS

WILD CHILD

BALTO

There were two kinds of truths, good truths and hurtful ones. That was what her father's attorney was telling her, and she was listening, doing her best, her face a small glazed crescent of light where the sun glanced off the yellow kitchen wall to illuminate her, but it was hard. Hard because it was a weekday, after school, and this was her free time, her chance to breeze into the 7-Eleven or Instant Message her friends before dinner and homework closed the day down. Hard too because her father was there, sitting on a stool at the kitchen counter, sipping something out of a mug, not coffee, definitely not coffee. His face was soft, the lines at the corners of his eyes nearly erased in the gentle spill of light—his *crow's-feet,* and how she loved that word, as if the bird's scaly claws had taken hold there like something out of a horror story, Edgar Allan Poe, the Raven, Nevermore, but wasn't a raven different from a crow and why not call them raven's-feet? Or hawk's-feet? People could have a hawk's nose— they always did in stories—but they had crow's-feet, and that didn't make any sense at all.

"Angelle," the attorney said—*Mr. Apodaca*—and the sound of her own name startled her, "are you listening to me?"

She nodded her head. And because that didn't seem enough, she spoke up too. "Yes," she said, but her voice sounded strange in her ears, as if somebody else were speaking for her.

"Good," he said, "good," leaning into the table so that his big moist dog's eyes settled on her with a baleful look. "Because this is very important, I don't have to stress that—"

He waited for her to nod again before going on.

"There are two kinds of truths," he repeated, "just like lies. There are bad lies, we all know that, lies meant to cheat and deceive, and then there are white lies, little fibs that don't really hurt anybody"—he blew out a soft puff of air, as if he were just stepping into a hot tub—"and might actually do good. Do you understand what I'm saying?"

She held herself perfectly still. Of course she understood—he was treating her like a nine-year-old, like her sister, and she was twelve, almost thirteen, and this was an act of rebellion, to hold herself there, not answering, not nodding, not even blinking her eyes.

"Like in this case," he went on, "your father's case, I mean. You've seen TV, the movies. The judge asks you for the truth, the whole truth and nothing but the truth, and you'll swear to it, everybody does—your father, me, anybody before the court." He had a mug too, one she recognized from her mother's college days—B.U., it said in thick red letters, *Boston University*—but there was coffee in his, or there had been. Now he just pushed it around the table as if it were a chess piece and he couldn't decide where to play it. "All I want you to remember—and your father wants this too, or no, he needs it, needs you to pay attention—is that there are good truths and bad truths, that's all. And your memory only serves to a point; I mean, who's to say what really happened, because everybody has their own version, that woman jogger, the boy on the bike—and the D.A., the district attorney, he's the one who might ask you what happened that day, just him and me, that's all. Don't you worry about anything."

But she was worried, because Mr. Apodaca was there in the first place, with his perfect suit and perfect tie and his doggy eyes, and because her father had been handcuffed along the side of the road and taken to jail and the car had been impounded, which meant nobody could use it, not her father or her mother when she came back from France or Dolores the maid or Allie the au pair. There was all that, but there was something else too, something in her father's look and the attorney's sugary tones that hardened her: they were talking down to her. Talking down to her as if she had no more sense than her little sister. And she did. She did.

That day, the day of the incident—or accident, he'd have to call it an accident now—he'd met Marcy for lunch at a restaurant down by the marina where you could sit outside and watch the way the sun struck the masts of the ships as they rocked on the tide and the light shattered and regrouped and shattered again. It was one of his favorite spots in town— one of his favorite spots, period. No matter how overburdened he felt, no matter how life beat him down and every task and deadline seemed to swell up out of all proportion so that twenty people couldn't have dealt with it all—a team, an army—this place, this table in the far corner of the deck overlooking the jungle of masts, the bleached wooden catwalks, the glowing arc of the harbor and the mountains that framed it, always had a calming effect on him. That and the just-this-side-of-too-cold local char- donnay they served by the glass. He was working on his second when Marcy came up the stairs, swaying over her heels like a model on the run- way, and glided down the length of the deck to join him. She gave him an uncomplicated smile, a smile that lit her eyes and acknowledged every- thing—the day, the locale, the sun and the breeze and the clean pounded smell of the ocean and him perched there in the middle of it all—and bent to kiss him before easing herself into the chair beside him. "That looks nice," she said, referring to the wine dense as struck gold in the glass be- fore him, and held up a finger for the waiter.

And what did they talk about? Little things. Her work, the pair of shoes she'd bought and returned and then bought all over again, the movie they'd seen two nights ago—the last time they'd been together— and how she still couldn't believe he liked that ending. "It's not that it was cheesy," she said, and here was her wine and should they get a bottle, yeah, sure, a bottle, why not? "and it was, but just that I didn't believe it."

"Didn't believe what—that the husband would take her back?"

"No," she said. "Or yes. It's idiotic. But what do you expect from a French movie? They always have these slinky-looking heroines in their thirties—"

"Or forties."

"—with great legs and mascara out of, I don't know, a KISS revival, and then even though they're married to the greatest guy in the world they feel unfulfilled and they go out and fuck the whole village, starting with the butcher."

"Juliette Binoche," he said. He was feeling the wine. Feeling good.

"Yeah, right. Even though it wasn't her, it could have been. Should have been. Has been in every French movie but this one for the past what, twenty years?" She put down her glass and let out a short two-note laugh that was like birdsong, a laugh that entranced him, and he wasn't worried about work now, not work or anything else, and here was the bottle in the bucket, the wine cold as the cellar it came from. "And then the whole village comes out and applauds her at the end for staying true to her romantic ideals—and the *husband*, Jesus."

Nothing could irritate him. Nothing could touch him. He was in love, the pelicans were gliding over the belly of the bay and her eyes were lewd and beautiful and pleased with themselves, but he had to pull the stopper here for just a minute. "Martine's not like that," he said. "I'm not like that."

She looked over her shoulder before digging out a cigarette—this was California, after all—and when she bent to light it her hair fell across her face. She came up smiling, the smoke snatched away from her lips and neutralized on the breeze the moment she exhaled. Discussion over.

Marcy was twenty-eight, educated at Berkeley, and she and her sister had opened an artists' supply shop on a side street downtown. She'd been a double major in art and film. She rode a bike to work. She was Asian. Or Chinese, she corrected him. Of Chinese descent, anyway. Her family, as she'd informed him on the first date with enough irony in her voice to foreground and bury the topic at the same time, went back four generations to the honorable great-grandfather who'd smuggled himself across the Pacific inside a clichéd flour barrel hidden in the clichéd hold of a clichéd merchant ship. She'd grown up in Syracuse, in a suburban development, and her accent—the a's flattened so that his name came out *Eelan* rather than Alan—just killed him, so incongruous coming from someone, as, well—the words out of his mouth before he knew what he was saying— as *exotic*-looking as her. And then, because he couldn't read her expression—had he gone too far?—he told her he was impressed because he only went back three generations, his grandfather having come over from Cork, but if it was in a barrel it would have been full of whiskey. "And Martine's from Paris," he'd added. "But you knew that already, didn't you?"

The bottle was half-gone by the time they ordered—and there was no hurry, no hurry at all, because they were both taking the afternoon off, and no argument—and when the food came they looked at each other for just the briefest fleeting particle of a moment before he ordered a second bottle. And then they were eating and everything slowed down until all of creation seemed to come into focus in a new way. He sipped the wine, chewed, looked into her unparalleled eyes and felt the sun lay a hand across his shoulders, and in a sudden blaze of apprehension he glanced up at the gull that appeared on the railing behind her and saw the way the breeze touched its feathers and the sun whitened its breast till there was nothing brighter and more perfect in the world—this creature, his fellow creature, and he was here to see it. He wanted to tell Marcy about it, about the miracle of the moment, the layers peeled back, revelatory, joyous, but instead he reached over to top off her glass and said, "So tell me about the shoes."

Later, after Mr. Apodaca had backed out of the driveway in his little white convertible with the Mercedes sign emblazoned on the front of it and the afternoon melted away in a slurry of phone calls and messages—*OMG! Chilty likes Alex Turtieff, can you believe it?*—Dolores made them *chiles rellenos* with carrot and jícama sticks and ice cream for dessert. Then Allie quizzed her and Lisette over their homework until the house fell quiet and all she could hear was the faint pulse of her father's music from the family room. She'd done her math and was working on a report about Aaron Burr for her history teacher, Mr. Compson, when she got up and went to the kitchen for a glass of juice or maybe hot chocolate in the microwave—and she wouldn't know which till she was standing there in the kitchen with the recessed lights glowing over the stone countertops and the refrigerator door open wide. She wasn't thinking about anything in particular—Aaron Burr was behind her now, upstairs, on her desk—and when she passed the archway to the family room the flash of the TV screen caught her eye and she paused a moment. Her father was there still, stretched out on the couch with a book, the TV muted and some game on, football, baseball, and the low snarl of his music in the background. His face had that blank absorbed look he got while reading and sometimes when he was just sitting there staring across the room or out the window at nothing, and he had the mug cradled in one hand, balanced on his chest beside the book.

He'd sat with them over dinner, but he hadn't eaten—he was going out later, he told her. For dinner. A late dinner. He didn't say who with, but she knew it was the Asian woman. Marcy. She'd seen her exactly twice, behind the window of her car, and Marcy had waved at her both times, a little curl of the fingers and a flash of the palm. There was an Asian girl in her class—she was Chinese—and her name was Xuan. That seemed right for an Asian girl, Xuan. Different. A name that said who she was and where she was from, far away, a whole ocean away. But Marcy? She didn't think so.

"Hey," her father said, lifting his head to peer over the butt of the couch, and she realized she'd been standing there watching him, "what's up? Homework done? Need any help? How about that essay—want me to proof that essay for you? What's it on, Madison? Or Burr. Burr, right?"

"That's okay."

"You sure?" His voice was slow and compacted, as if it wasn't composed of vibrations of the vocal cords, the air passing through the larynx like in her science book, but made of something heavier, denser. He would be taking a taxi tonight, she could see that, and then maybe she—*Marcy*—would drive him back home. "Because I could do it, no problem. I've got"—and she watched him lift his watch to his face and rotate his wrist—"half an hour or so, forty-five minutes."

"That's okay," she said.

She was sipping her hot chocolate and reading a story for English by William Faulkner, the author's picture in her textbook a freeze-frame of furious eyes and conquered hair, when she heard her father's voice riding a current down the hall, now murmurous, now pinched and electric, then dense and sluggish all over again. It took her a minute: he was reading Lisette her bedtime story. The house was utterly still and she held her breath, listening, till all of a sudden she could make out the words. He was reading *Balto*, a story she'd loved when she was little, when she was

Lisette's age, and as his voice came to her down the hall she could picture the illustrations: Balto, the lead dog of the sled team, radiating light from a sunburst on his chest and the snowstorm like a monstrous hand closing over him, the team fighting through the Alaskan wind and ice and temperatures of forty below zero to deliver serum to the sick children in Nome—and those children would die if Balto didn't get through. Diphtheria. It was a diphtheria epidemic and the only plane available was broken down—or no, it had been dismantled for the winter. *What's diphtheria?* she'd asked her father, and he'd gone to the shelf and pulled down the encyclopedia to give her the answer, and that was heroic in itself, because as he settled back onto her bed, Lisette snuggled up beside her and rain at the windows and the bedside lamp the only thing between them and darkness absolute, he'd said, *You see, there's everything in books, everything you could ever want.*

Balto's paws were bleeding. The ice froze between his toes. The other dogs kept holding back, but he was the lead dog and he turned on them and snarled, fought them just to keep them in their traces, to keep them going. *Balto.* With his harnessed shoulders and shaggy head and the furious unconquerable will that drove him all through that day and into the night that was so black there was no way of telling if they were on the trail or not.

Now, as she sat poised at the edge of her bed, listening to Lisette's silence and her father's limping voice, she waited for her sister to pipe up in her breathy little baby squeak and frame the inevitable questions: *Dad, Dad, how cold is forty below?* And: *Dad, what's diphtheria?*

The sun had crept imperceptibly across the deck, fingering the cracks in the varnished floorboards and easing up the low brass rail Marcy was using as a backrest. She was leaning into it, the rail, her chair tipped back, her elbows splayed behind her and her legs stretched out to catch the sun, shapely legs, stunning legs, legs long and burnished and firm, legs that made him think of the rest of her and the way she was in bed. There was a scar just under the swell of her left kneecap, the flesh annealed in an irregular oval as if it had been burned or scarified, and he'd never noticed that before. Well, he was in a new place, half a glass each left of the second bottle and the world sprung to life in the fullness of its detail, everything sharpened, in focus, as if he'd needed glasses all these years and just clapped them on. The gull was gone but it had been special, a very special gull, and there were sparrows now, or wrens, hopping along the floor in little streaks of color, snatching up a crumb of this or that and then hurtling away over the rail as if they'd been launched. He was thinking he didn't want any more wine—two bottles was plenty—but maybe something to cap off the afternoon, a cognac maybe, just one.

She'd been talking about one of the girls who worked for her, a girl he'd seen a couple of times, nineteen, soft-faced and pretty, and how she—her name was Bettina—was living the party life, every night at the clubs, and how thin she was.

"Cocaine?" he wondered, and she shrugged. "Has it affected her work?"

"No," she said, "not yet, anyway." And then she went on to qualify that with a litany of lateness in the morning, hyper behavior after lunch and doctor's appointments, too many doctor's appointments. He waited a moment, watching her mouth and tongue, the beautiful unspooling way the words dropped from her lips, before he reached down and ran a finger over the blemish below her kneecap. "You have a scar," he said.

She looked at her knee as if she wasn't aware it was attached to her, then withdrew her leg momentarily to scrutinize it before giving it back to the sun and the deck and the waiting touch of his hand. "Oh, that?" she said. "That's from when I was a kid."

"A burn or what?"

"Bicycle." She teased the syllables out, slow and sure.

His hand was on her knee, the warmth of the contact, and he rubbed the spot a moment before straightening up in the chair and draining his glass. "Looks like a burn," he said.

"Nope. Just fell in the street." She let out that laugh again and he drank it in. "You should've seen my training wheels—or the one of them. It was as flat"—flaat—"as if a truck had run me over."

Her eyes flickered with the lingering seep of the memory and they both took a moment to picture it, the little girl with the wheel collapsed under her and the scraped knee—or it had to have been worse than that, punctured, shredded—and he didn't think of Lisette or Angelle, not yet, because he was deep into the drift of the day, so deep there was nothing else but this deck and this slow sweet sun and the gull that was gone now. "You want something else?" he heard himself say. "Maybe a Rémy, just to cap it off? I mean, I'm wined out, but just, I don't know, a taste of cognac?"

"Sure," she said, "why not?" and she didn't look at her watch and he didn't look at his either.

And then the waiter was there with two snifters and a little square of dark chocolate for each of them, compliments of the house. *Snifter,* he was thinking as he revolved the glass in his hand, what a perfect designation for the thing, a name that spoke to function, and he said it aloud, "Isn't it great that they have things like snifters, so you can stick your nose in it and sniff? And plus, it's named for what it is, unlike, say, a napkin or a fork. You don't nap napkins or fork forks, right?"

"Yeah," she said, and the sun had leveled on her hair now, picking out the highlights and illuminating the lobe of one ear, "I guess. But I was telling you about Bettina? Did you know that guy she picked up I told you about—not the boyfriend, but the one-night stand? He got her pregnant."

The waiter drifted by then, college kid, hair in his eyes, and asked if there'd be anything else. It was then that he thought to check his watch and the first little pulse of alarm began to make itself felt somewhere deep in the quiet lagoon of his brain: *Angelle,* the alarm said. *Lisette.* They had to be picked up at school after soccer practice every Wednesday because Wednesday was Allie's day off and Martine wasn't there to do it. Martine was in Paris, doing whatever she pleased. That much was clear. And today—today was Wednesday.

Angelle remembered waiting for him longer than usual that day. He'd been late before—he was almost always late, because of work, because he had such a hectic schedule—but this time she'd already got through half her homework, the blue backpack canted away from her and her notebook spread open across her knees as she sat at the curb, and still he wasn't there. The sun had sunk into the trees across the street and she felt a chill where she'd sweated through her shorts and T-shirt at soccer. Lisette's team had finished before hers and for a while her sister had sat beside her, drawing big x's and o's in two different colors on a sheet of loose-leaf paper, but she'd got bored and run off to play on the swings with two other kids whose parents were late.

Every few minutes a car would round the turn at the top of the street, and her eyes would jump to it, but it wasn't theirs. She watched a black SUV pull up in front of the school and saw Dani Mead and Sarah Schuster burst through the doors, laughing, their backpacks riding up off their shoulders and their hair swaying back and forth as they slid into the cavernous backseat and the door slammed shut. The car's brake lights flashed and then it rolled slowly out of the parking lot and into the street, and she watched it till it disappeared round the corner. He was always working, she knew that, trying to dig himself out from under all the work he had piled up—that was his phrase, *dig himself out,* and she pictured him in his office surrounded by towering stacks of papers, papers like the Leaning Tower of Pisa, and a shovel in his hands as if he were one of those men in the orange jackets bent over a hole in the road—but still, she felt impatient. Felt cold. Hungry. And where was he?

Finally, after the last two kids had been picked up by their mothers and the sun reduced to a streak that ran across the tile roof of the school and up into the crowns of the palms behind it, after Lisette had come back to sit on the curb and whine and pout and complain like the baby she was (*He's just drunk, I bet that's it, just drunk like Mom said*) and she had to tell her she didn't know what she was talking about, there he was. Lisette saw the car first. It appeared at the top of the street like a mirage, coming so slowly round the turn it might have been rolling under its own power, with nobody in it, and Angelle remembered what her father had told her about always setting the handbrake, always, no matter what. She hadn't really wanted a lesson—she'd have to be sixteen for that—but they were up in the mountains, at the summer cabin, just after her mother had left for France, and there was nobody around. "You're a big girl," he'd told her, and she was, tall for her age—people always mistook her for an eighth grader or even a freshman. "Go ahead, it's easy," he told her. "Like bumper cars. Only you don't bump anything." And she'd laughed and he laughed and she got behind the wheel with him guiding her and her heart was pounding till she thought she was going to lift right out of the seat. Everything looked different through the windshield, yellow spots and dirt, the world wrapped in a bubble. The sun was in her eyes. The road was a black river, oozing through the dried-out weeds, the trees looming and receding as if a wave had passed through them. And the car crept down the road the way it was creeping now. Too slow. Much too slow.

When her father pulled up to the curb, she saw right away that something was wrong. He was smiling at them, or trying to smile, but his face was too heavy, his face weighed a thousand tons, carved of rock like the faces of the presidents on Mount Rushmore, and it distorted the smile till it was more like a grimace. A flare of anger rose in her—Lisette was right—and then it died away and she was scared. Just scared.

"Sorry," he murmured, "sorry I'm late, I—" and he didn't finish the thought or excuse or whatever it was because he was pushing open the door now, the driver's door, and pulling himself out onto the pavement. He took a minute to remove his sunglasses and polish them on the tail of his shirt before leaning heavily against the side of the car. He gave her a weak smile—half a smile, not even half—and carefully fitted them back over his ears, though it was too dark for sunglasses, anybody could see that. Plus, these were his old sunglasses—two shining blue disks in wire frames that made his eyes disappear—which meant that he must have lost his good ones, the ones that had cost him two hundred and fifty dollars on sale at the Sunglass Hut. "Listen," he said, as Lisette pulled open the rear door and flung her backpack across the seat, "I just—I forgot the time, is all. I'm sorry. I am. I really am."

She gave him a look that was meant to burn into him, to make him feel what she was feeling, but she couldn't tell if he was looking at her or not. "We've been sitting here since four," she said, and she heard the hurt and accusation in her own voice. She pulled open the other door, the one right beside him, because she was going to sit in back as a demonstration of her disapproval—they'd both sit in back, she and Lisette, and nobody up front—when he stopped her with a gesture, reaching out suddenly to brush the hair away from her face.

"You've got to help me out here," he said, and a pleading tone had come into his voice. "Because"—the words were stalling, congealing, sticking in his throat—"because, hey, why lie, huh? I wouldn't lie to you."

The sun faded. A car went up the street. There was a boy on a bicycle, a boy she knew, and he gave her a look as he cruised past, the wheels a blur.

"I was, I had lunch with Marcy, because, well, you know how hard I've been—and I just needed to kick back, you know? Everybody does. It's no sin." A pause, his hand going to his pocket and then back to her hair again. "And we had some wine. Some wine with lunch." He gazed off down the street then, as if he were looking for the tapering long-necked green bottles the wine had come in, as if he were going to produce them for evidence.

She just stood there staring at him, her jaw set, but she let his hand fall to her shoulder and give her a squeeze, the sort of squeeze he gave her when he was proud of her, when she got an A on a test or cleaned up the dishes all by herself without anybody asking.

"I know this is terrible," he was saying, "I mean I hate to do this, I hate to . . . but Angelle, I'm asking you just this once, because the thing is?"—and here he tugged down the little blue discs so that she could see the dull sheen of his eyes focused on her—"I don't think I can drive."

When the valet brought the car round, the strangest thing happened, a little lapse, and it was because he wasn't paying attention. He was distracted by Marcy in her low-slung Miata with the top down, the redness of it, a sleek thing, pin your ears back and fly, Marcy wheeling out of the lot with a wave and two fingers kissed to her lips, her hair lifting on the breeze. And there was the attendant, another college kid, shorter and darker than the one upstairs frowning over the tip but with the same haircut, as if they'd both been to the same barber or stylist or whatever, and the attendant had said something to him—*Your car, sir; here's your car, sir*—and the strange thing was that for a second there he didn't recognize it. Thought the kid was trying to put something over on him. Was this his car? Was this the sort of thing he'd own? This mud-splattered charcoal-gray SUV with the seriously depleted tires? And that dent in the front fender, the knee-high scrape that ran the length of the body as if some metallic claw had caught hold of it? Was this some kind of trick?

"Sir?"

"Yeah," he'd said, staring up into the sky now, and where were his shades? "Yeah, what? What do you want?"

The smallest beat. "Your car. Sir."

And then it all came clear to him the way these things do, and he flipped open his wallet to extract two singles—finger-softened money, money as soft and pliable as felt—and the valet accepted them and he was in the car, looking to connect the male end of the seatbelt to the female, and where was the damned thing? There was still a sliver of sun cutting in low over the ocean and he dug into the glove compartment for his old sunglasses, the emergency pair, because the new ones were someplace else altogether, apparently, and not in his pocket and not on the cord round his neck, and then he had them fitted over his ears and the radio was playing something with some real thump to it and he was rolling on out of the lot, looking to merge with the traffic on the boulevard.

That was when everything turned hard-edged and he knew he was drunk. He waited too long to merge—too cautious, too tentative—and the driver behind him laid on the horn and he had no choice but to give him the finger and he might have leaned his head out the window and barked something too, but the car came to life beneath him and somebody swerved wide and he was out in traffic. If he was thinking anything at all it probably had to do with his last DUI, which had come out of nowhere when he wasn't even that drunk, or maybe not drunk at all. He'd been coming back from Johnny's Rib Shack after working late, gnawing at a rib, a beer open between his legs, and he came down the slope beneath the underpass where you make a left to turn onto the freeway ramp and he was watching the light and didn't see the mustard-colored Volvo stopped there in front of him until it was too late. And he was so upset with himself—and not just himself, but the world at large and the way it presented these problems to him, these impediments, the unforeseen and the unexpected just laid out there in front of him as if it were some kind of conspiracy—that he got out of the car, the radiator crushed and hissing and beer pissed all over his lap, and shouted, "All right, so sue me!" at the dazed woman behind the wheel of the other car. But that wasn't going to happen now. Nothing was going to happen now.

The trees rolled by, people crossed at the crosswalk, lights turned yellow and then red and then green, and he was doing fine, just sailing, thinking he'd take the girls out for burritos or In-N-Out burgers on the way home, when a cop passed him going in the other direction and his heart froze like a block of ice and then thawed instantaneously, hammering so hard he thought it would punch right through his chest. *Signal, signal,* he told himself, keeping his eyes on the rearview, and he did, he signaled and made the first turn, a road he'd never been on before, and then he made the next turn after that, and the next, and when he looked up again he had no idea where he was.

Which was another reason why he was late, and there was Angelle giving him that hard cold judgmental look—her mother's look exactly—because she was perfect, she was dutiful and put-upon and the single best kid in the world, in the history of the world, and he was a fuckup, pure and simple. It was wrong, what he asked her to do, but it happened nonetheless, and he guided her through each step, a straight shot on the way home, two and a half miles, that was all, and forget stopping at In-N-Out, they'd just go home and have a pizza delivered. He remembered going on in that vein, "Don't you girls want pizza tonight? Huh, Lisette? Peppers and onions? And those little roasted artichokes? Or maybe you'd prefer wormheads, mashed wormheads?"—leaning over the seat to cajole her, make it all right and take the tightness out of her face, and he didn't see the boy on the bicycle, didn't know anything about him until Angelle let out a choked little cry and there was the heart-stopping thump of something glancing off the fender.

. . . . .

The courtroom smelled of wax, the same kind of wax they used on the floors at school, sweet and acrid at the same time, a smell that was almost comforting in its familiarity. But she wasn't at school—she'd been excused for the morning—and she wasn't here to be comforted or to feel comfortable either. She was here to listen to Mr. Apodaca and the judge and the D.A. and the members of the jury decide her father's case and to testify in his behalf, tell what she knew, tell a kind of truth that wasn't maybe whole and pure but necessary, a necessary truth. That was what Mr. Apodaca was calling it now, *necessary,* and she'd sat with him and her father in one of the unused rooms off the main corridor—another courtroom—while he went over the whole business one more time for her, just to be sure she understood.

Her father had held her hand on the way in and he sat beside her on one of the wooden benches as his attorney went over the details of that day after school, because he wanted to make sure they were all on the same page. Those were his words exactly—"I want to make sure we're all on the same page on this"—as he loomed over her and her father, bracing himself on the gleaming wooden rail, his shoes competing with the floor for the brilliance of their shine, and she couldn't help picturing some Mexican boy, some dropout from the high school, laboring over those shoes while Mr. Apodaca sat high in a leatherbacked chair, his feet in the stainless steel stirrups. She pictured him behind his newspaper, looking stern, or going over his brief, the details, *these* details. When he was through, when he'd gone through everything, minute by minute, gesture by gesture, coaching her, quizzing her—"And what did he say? What did you say?"—he asked her father if he could have a minute alone with her.

That was when her father gave her hand a final squeeze and then dropped it and got up from the bench. He was wearing a new suit, a navy so dark and severe it made his skin look like raw dough, and he'd had his hair cut so tight round the ears it was as if a machine had been at work there, an edger or a riding mower like the one they used on the soccer field at school, only in miniature, and for an instant she imagined it, tiny people like in *Gulliver's Travels,* buzzing round her father's ears with their mowers and clippers and edgers. The tie he was wearing was the most boring one he owned, a blue fading to black, with no design, not even a stripe. His face was heavy, his crow's-feet right there for all the world to see—gouges, tears, slits, a butcher's shop of carved and abused skin—and for the first time she noticed the small gray dollop of loose flesh under his chin. It made him look old, worn-out, past his prime, as if he weren't the hero anymore but playing the hero's best friend, the one who never gets the girl and never gets the job. And what role was she playing? The star. She was the star here, and the more the attorney talked on and the heavier her father's face got, the more it came home to her.

Mr. Apodaca said nothing, just let the silence hang in the room till the memory of her father's footsteps had faded. Then he leaned over the back of the bench directly in front of her, the great seal of the State of California framed over the dais behind him, and he squeezed his eyes shut a moment so that when he opened them and fixed her with his gaze, there were tears there. Or the appearance of tears. His eyelashes were moist and the moistness picked each of them out individually until all she could think of was the stalks of cane against the fence in the back corner of the yard. "I want you to listen very carefully to what I'm about to say, Angelle," he breathed, his voice so soft and constricted it was like the sound of the air being let out of a tire. "Because this concerns you and your sister. It could affect your whole life."

Another pause. Her stomach was crawling. She didn't want to say anything but he held the pause so long she had to bow her head and say, "Yeah. Yeah, I know."

And then suddenly, without warning, his voice was lashing out at her: "But you don't know it. Do you know what's at stake here? Do you really?"

"No," she said, and it was a whisper.

"Your father is going to plead no contest to the charge of driving under the influence. He was wrong, he admits it. And they'll take away his driving privileges and he'll have to go to counseling and find someone to drive you and your sister to school, and I don't mean to minimize that, that's very serious, but here's the thing you may not know." He held her eyes, though she wanted to look away. "The second charge is child endangerment, not for the boy on the bike, who barely even scraped a knee, luckily, luckily, and whose parents have already agreed to a settlement, but for you, for allowing you to do what you did. And do you know what will happen if the jury finds him guilty on that charge?"

She didn't know what was coming, not exactly, but the tone of what he was conveying—dark, ominous, fulminating with anger and the threat about to be revealed in the very next breath—made her feel small. And scared. Definitely scared. She shook her head.

"They'll take you and Lisette away from him." He clenched both hands, pushed himself up from the rail and turned as if to pace off down the aisle in front of her, as if he was disgusted with the whole thing and had no more to say. But then, suddenly, he swung round on her with a furious twist of his shoulders and a hard accusatory stab of his balled-up right hand and a single rigid forefinger. "And no," he said, barely contained, barely able to keep his voice level, "in answer to your unasked question or objection or whatever you want to call it, your mother's not coming back for you, not now, maybe not ever."

Was he ashamed? Was he humiliated? Did he have to stop drinking and get his life in order? Yes, yes and yes. But as he sat there in the courtroom beside Jerry Apodaca at eleven-thirty in the morning, the high arched windows pregnant with light and his daughter, Marcy, Dolores and the solemn-faced au pair sitting shoulder-to-shoulder on the gleaming wooden bench behind him, there was a flask in his inside pocket and the faint burning pulse of single-malt scotch rode his veins. He'd taken a pull from it in the men's room not ten minutes ago, just to steady himself, and then he'd rinsed out his mouth and ground half a dozen Tic Tacs between his teeth to knock down any trace of alcohol on his breath. Jerry would have been furious with him if he so much as suspected . . . and it was a weak and cowardly thing to do, no excuse, no excuse at all, but he felt adrift, felt scared, and he needed an anchor to hold on to. Just for now. Just for today. And then he'd throw the thing away, because what was a flask for anyway except to provide a twenty-four-hour teat for the kind of drunk who wore a suit and brushed his teeth.

He began to jiggle one foot and tap his knees together beneath the table, a nervous twitch no amount of scotch would cure. The judge was taking his time, the assistant D.A. smirking over a sheaf of papers at her own table off to the right. She wore a permanent self-congratulatory look, this woman, as if she were queen of the court and the county too, and she'd really laid into him before the recess, and that was nasty, purely nasty. She was the prosecution's attack dog, that was what Jerry called her, her voice tuned to a perpetual note of sarcasm, disbelief and petulance, but he held to his story and never wavered. He was just glad Angelle hadn't had to see it.

She was here now, though, sitting right behind him, missing school— missing school because of him. And that was one more strike against him, he supposed, *because what kind of father would . . . ?*—but the thought was too depressing and he let it die. He resisted the urge to turn round and give her a look, a smile, a wink, the least gesture, anything. It was too painful to see her there, under constraint, his daughter dragged out of school for this, and then he didn't want anybody to think he was coaching her or coercing her in any way. Jerry had no such scruples, though. He'd drilled her over and over and he'd even gone to the extreme of asking her—or no, *instructing* her—to wear something that might conform to the court's idea of what a good, honest, straightforward child was like, something that would make her look younger than she was, too young to bend the truth and far too young even to think about getting behind the wheel of a car.

Three times Jerry had sent her back to change outfits until finally, with a little persuasion from the au pair (*Allie,* and he'd have to remember to slip her a twenty, a twenty at least, because she was gold, pure gold), she put on a lacy white high-collared dress she'd worn for some kind of pageant at school, with matching white tights and patent-leather shoes. There was something wrong there in the living room, he could see that, something in the way she held her shoulders and stamped up the stairs to her room, her face clenched and her eyes burning into him, and he should have recognized it, should have given her just a hair more of his attention, but Marcy was there and she had her opinion and Jerry was being an autocrat and he himself had his hands full—he couldn't eat or think or do anything other than maybe slip into the pantry and tip the bottle of Macallan over the flask. By the time he thought of it, they were in the car, and he tried, he did, leaning across the seat to ply her with little jokes about getting a free day off and what her teachers were going to think and what Aaron Burr might have done—he would've just shot somebody, right?— but Jerry was drilling her one last time and she was sunk into the seat beside Marcy, already clamped up.

The courtroom, this courtroom, the one she was in now, was a duplicate of the one in which her father's attorney had quizzed her an hour and a half ago, except that it was filled with people. They were all old, or older, anyway, except for one woman in a formfitting plaid jacket Angelle had seen in the window at Nordstrom who must have been in her twenties. She was in the jury box, looking bored. The other jurors were mostly men, businessmen, she supposed, with balding heads and recessed eyes and big meaty hands clasped in their laps or grasping the rail in front of them. One of them looked like the principal of her school, Dr. Damon, but he wasn't.

The judge sat up at his desk in the front of the room, which they called a bench but wasn't a bench at all, the flag of the State of California on one side of him and the American flag on the other. She was seated in the front row, between Dolores and Allie, and her father and Mr. Apodaca sat at a desk in front of her, the shoulders of their suits puffed up as if they were wearing football pads. Her father's suit was so dark she could see the dandruff there, a little spray of it like dust on the collar of his jacket, and she felt embarrassed for him. And sorry for him, sorry for him too—and for herself. And Lisette. She looked up at the judge and then the district attorney with his grim gray tight-shaven face and the scowling woman be-

side him, and couldn't help thinking about what Mr. Apodaca had told
her, and it made her shrink into herself when Mr. Apodaca called her
name and the judge, reading the look on her face, tried to give her a smile
of encouragement.

She wasn't aware of walking across the floor or of the hush that fell
over the courtroom or even the bailiff who asked her to hold up her right
hand and swear to tell the truth—all this, as if she were recalling a fragmented dream, would come to her later. But then she was seated in the
witness chair and everything was bright and loud suddenly, as if she'd just
switched channels on the TV. Mr. Apodaca was right there before her, his
voice rising sweetly, almost as if he were singing, and he was leading her
through the questions they'd rehearsed over and over again. Yes, she told
him, her father was late, and yes, it was getting dark, and no, she didn't
notice anything strange about him. He was her father and he always
picked her sister and her up on Wednesdays, she volunteered, because
Wednesdays were when Allie and Dolores both had their day off and there
was no one else to do it because her mother was in France.

They were all watching her now, the court gone absolutely silent, so
silent you would have thought everyone had tiptoed out the door, but
there they all were, hanging on her every word. She wanted to say more
about her mother, about how her mother was coming home soon—had
promised as much the last time she'd called long distance from her apartment in Saint-Germain-des-Prés—but Mr. Apodaca wouldn't let her. He
kept leading her along, using his sugary voice now, talking down to her,
and she wanted to speak up and tell him he didn't have to treat her like
that, tell him about her mother, Lisette, the school and the lawn and the
trees and the way the interior of the car smelled and the heat of the liquor
on her father's breath—anything that would forestall the inevitable, the
question that was tucked in just behind this last one, the question on the
point of which everything turned, because now she heard it, murmurous
and soft and sweet on her father's attorney's lips: "Who was driving?"

"I just wanted to say one thing," she said, lifting her eyes now to look
at Mr. Apodaca and only Mr. Apodaca, his dog's eyes, his pleading soft
baby-talking face, "just because, well, I wanted to say you're wrong about

my mother, because she *is* coming home—she told me so herself, on, on the phone—" She couldn't help herself. Her voice was cracking.

"Yes," he said too quickly, a hiss of breath, "yes, I understand that, Angelle, but we need to establish . . . you need to answer the question."

Oh, and now the silence went even deeper, the silence of the deep sea, of outer space, of the arctic night when you couldn't hear the runners of the sled or the feet of the dogs bleeding into the snow, and her eyes jumped to her father's then, the look on his face of hopefulness and fear and confusion, and she loved him in that moment more than she ever had.

"Angelle," Mr. Apodaca was saying, murmuring. "Angelle?"

She turned her face back to him, blotting out the judge, the D.A., the woman in the plaid jacket who was probably a college student, probably cool, and waited for the question to drop.

"Who," Mr. Apodaca repeated, slowing it down now, "was"—slower, slower still—"driving?"

She lifted her chin then to look at the judge and heard the words coming out of her mouth as if they'd been planted there, telling the truth, the hurtful truth, the truth no one would have guessed because she was almost thirteen now, almost a teenager, and she let them know it. "*I* was," she said, and the courtroom roared to life with so many people buzzing at once she thought at first they hadn't heard her. So she said it again, said it louder, much louder, so loud she might have been shouting it to the man with the camera at the back of the long churchy room with its sweat-burnished pews and the flags and emblems and all the rest. And then she looked away from the judge, away from the spectators and the man with the camera and the court recorder and the bank of windows so brilliant with light you would have thought a bomb had gone off there, and looked directly at her father.

LA CONCHITA

I n my business, where you put something like forty to forty-five thousand miles a year on your vehicle and the sweet suck of the engine at 3,500 rpm is like another kind of breathing, you can't afford distractions. Can't afford to get tired or lazy or lift your eyes from the road to appreciate the way the fog reshapes the palms on Ocean Avenue or the light slips down the flanks of the mountains on that mind-blowing stretch of Highway 1 between Malibu and Oxnard. Get distracted and you could wind up meat. I know that. The truckers know that. But just about everybody else—Honda drivers, especially, and I'm sorry—don't even know they're behind the wheel and conscious half the time. I've tried to analyze it, I have. They want value, the Honda drivers, value and reliability, but they don't want to pay for the real deal—German engineering is what I'm talking about here—and yet they still seem to think they're part of some secret society that allows them to cut people off at will, to take advantage because they're so in the know. So hip. So Honda. And yes, I carry a gun, a Glock 9 I keep in a special compartment I had built into the leather panel of the driver's side door, but that doesn't mean I want to use it. Or would use it again. Except in extremis.

The only time I did fire it, in fact, was during that rash of freeway shootings a few months back—a statistical bubble, the police called it—when people were getting popped at the rate of two a week in the greater L.A. area. I could never figure it, really. You see some jerk swerving in and out of traffic, tailgating, and maybe you give him the finger and maybe he comes up on you, but you're awake, aren't you? You've got an accelerator and a brake pedal, right? But most people, I guess, don't even know they're alive in the world or that they've just made the driver charging up alongside them homicidal or that their engine is on fire or the road is dropping off into a crater the size of the Sea of Tranquility because they've got the cell clamped to the side of their head and they're doing their nails or reading the paper. Don't laugh. I've seen them watching TV, gobbling kung pao out of the carton, doing crossword puzzles and talking on two cells at once—and all at eighty miles an hour. Anyway, I just fired two slugs—*blip blip.* Didn't even know my finger was on the trigger. Plus, of course, I was aiming low—just trying to perforate his rocker panels or the idiotic big-dick off-road Super Avenger tires that had him sitting about twelve feet up off the ground. I'm not proud of it. And I probably shouldn't have gone that far. But he cut me off—twice—and if he'd given me the finger it would have been one thing, but he didn't even know it, didn't even know he'd nearly run me into the median two times in the space of a minute.

On this particular day, though, everybody seemed to keep their distance. It was just past noon and raining, the ocean stretching out on my left like a big seething cauldron, the surface of the roadway slick beneath the wheels—so slick and soft and ill-defined I had to slow to seventy in places to keep from hydroplaning. But this wasn't just rain. This was one cell in a string of storms that had stalled over the coast for the past week, sucking load after load of moisture up out of the sea and dropping it on the hills that had burned clear of vegetation the winter before. I was already running late because of a slide at Topanga Canyon, boulders the size of SUVs in the middle of the road, cops in slickers waving their flashlights, down to two lanes, then one, and finally—I heard this on the radio after I got through, feeling stressed for time, but lucky I guess—down to none. Road closed. All she wrote.

I didn't like driving in the rain—it was just asking for disaster. My fellow drivers, riding their brakes and clinging to the wheel as if it were some kind of voodoo fetish that would protect them against drunks, curves, potholes, errant coyotes and sheet metal carved into knives, went to pieces the minute the first drop hit the windshield. As you might expect, the accident rate shot up something like three hundred percent every time it rained, and as I say, this wasn't just rain in the ordinary sense. But I had a delivery to make in Santa Barbara, an urgent delivery, and if I couldn't guarantee door-to-door faster than FedEx or Freddie Altamirano (my

major competitor, who rode a ProStreet FXR and moved like a spirit rap-
tured to heaven), then I was out of business. Plus, this wasn't just the
usual packet of bonds or stock certificates or the blockbuster screenplay
passing from writer to director and back again, this was the kind of thing
I handled maybe two or three times a month at most—and it never failed
to give me a thrill. In the trunk, anchored firmly between two big blocks
of Styrofoam, was a human liver packed in a bag of ice slurry inside a Bud
Light Fun-in-the-Sun cooler, and if that sounds ridiculous, I'm sorry.
That's how it's done. Simple fact. Ninety minutes earlier I'd picked it up at
LAX because the S.B. airport was closed due to flooding, and if you want
a definition of time sensitive, this was it. The recipient, a twenty-seven-
year-old mother of three, was on life support at University Hospital, and
I was running late and there wasn't much I could do about it.

At any rate, I was coming up on La Conchita, a little town no bigger
than a trailer court carved out of the hill where the freeway dips down to
the ocean, rounding the big curve at Mussel Shoals and dropping down to
fourth to blow past a U-Haul truck (the worst, the very worst, but that's
another story), when the hillside gave way. There was a series of sharp
cracks I at first took to be lightning hitting the hill, and then a deep rever-
berant concussion, as if all the air had been knocked out of the day. By
this point I was shifting down, hyper-aware of the chain of brake lights
flung up across the road in front of me and the U-Haul, piloted by a zombie on his way to Goleta or Lompoc with his zombie girlfriend at his side
and their little white dog in her lap, bearing down on me from behind. I
was able to stop. They weren't. They barely had time to flash their brake
lights before skidding past me and hammering the back end of a Mercedes
with its panic lights on, lifting the whole shimmering orange-and-white
truck up on two wheels before it crashed down on its side.

I'll say right up front I've never been much in an emergency—and
when you're behind the wheel as often as I am, you see plenty of emergencies, believe me. I don't know CPR, don't know how to stay calm or coun-
sel anybody else to stay calm either and I've been lucky because it's never
been me wrapped around the telephone pole or nodding over the windshield and nobody I know has ever choked at the dinner table or clutched

their heart or started hemorrhaging from the mouth and ears. I saw the dog lying there in the road like a heap of rags, saw the driver of the moving truck haul himself up out of the driver's side window like a pearl diver coming up for air, saw the rain eclipse him. And the first thing I did—for my own sake and for the sake of whoever else might be tooling up behind me—was pull the car off the road, as far up on the shoulder as I could take it without fear of getting stuck. I was just reaching for my cell to dial 911, the road blocked, the day shot, my mind churning and the donor organ sitting there undelivered and unincorporated and getting staler by the minute, when things got worse, a whole lot worse.

I don't know if the average person really has much of an idea of what a mudslide involves. I certainly didn't—not before I started driving for a living, anyway. You'd see footage on the six o'clock news, telephone poles down, trees knocked askew, a car or two flattened and a garage staved in, but it didn't seem like much. It wasn't hot lava, wasn't an earthquake or one of the firestorms that burned through this or that subdivision and incinerated a couple hundred homes every fall. Maybe it was the fault of the term itself—*mudslide*. It sounded innocuous, almost cozy, as if it might be one of the new attractions at Magic Mountain, or vaguely sexy, like the mud-wrestling that was all the rage when I was in high school and too young to get in the door. But that was the thinking of a limited imagination. A mudslide, as I now know, is nothing short of an avalanche, but instead of snow you've got 400,000 tons of liquefied dirt bristling with rock and tree trunks coming at you with the force of a tsunami. And it moves fast, faster than you would think.

The sound I'd heard, even through the rolled-up windows and the ready voice of the narrator of the book-on-tape I'd checked out of the library because I never go anywhere without a good story to take my mind off the raging idiots all around me, was the sudden angry shriek of the bulkhead in back of La Conchita giving way. Steel beams snapped like chicken bones, railroad ties went airborne. Up ahead of me, beyond the overturned U-Haul, a few of the cars had got through, but now a vanguard of boulders came sluicing across the freeway, followed by a soupy river of mud. A rock the size of a cannonball thumped into the underside of the U-Haul truck and a fistful of pellets—gravel, I guess—sprayed the side of my car, and that was going to mean a new paint job, I knew it, maybe even bodywork. The rain quickened. The mud spread out across the pavement, seething round the tires and underneath the car and beyond, and soon dark tongues of it had pushed across the southbound lanes too.

What did I do? I got out of the car, the normal reaction, and immediately my shoes filled with sludge. The mud was no more than a foot or so deep, and here, at the far verge of the slide, it was the consistency of pancake batter. But darker. And it smelled of something long buried and dug up again, damp and raw as an open grave, and for a moment there I flashed on my father's funeral, the squared-off edges of the hole with its fringe of roots, my mother trying to be stoic and my uncle putting an arm round my shoulders as if that could help. Let me say it wasn't a pleasant smell and leave it at that.

Doors slammed. Somebody was shouting. I turned my head to look up the road and there was the driver of the U-Haul, pulling his wife or girlfriend or whoever she was up out of the cab even as she reacted to the sight of the dog lying there on a clean stretch of pavement, and the mud, working to its own logic, flowed around it. Behind me were at least a hundred cars, bottled up and idling, their lights dully illuminating the scene, windshield wipers clapping in the way of a very tired audience. People were running up the street. A pickup just north of the overturned U-Haul began to float off, sustained on a wave of mud as if it were a dingy drifting away on the tide. My jacket was soaked through, the hair hanging in my face. The liver wasn't getting any fresher.

Suddenly, unaccountably, I found myself at the trunk of the car. I inserted the key and flipped it open, and I don't really know why—just to reassure myself, I guess. The lid of the cooler eased back and there it was, the liver, smooth and burnished, more pink than red—and it wasn't like meat, not at all, more like something sculpted out of very soft stone. But it was okay, it was fine, I told myself, and I should just stay calm. I figured we had an hour, more or less, before things began to get critical. It was then that the woman with the dog—she was bent over it in the rain, wailing, and the water dripping from the end of her nose was pink with the blood leaching out of her scalp—looked up and shouted something to me. She might have been asking if I knew anything about dogs. Or if she could use my cell to call the vet. Or if I had a knife, an oxygen mask, a GPS locater, a blanket. I don't know what she said, actually. She wanted something, but I couldn't hear her over the rattle of all those idling engines, the hiss of the rain, the shouts and curses, and in the next moment somebody else was there, some stranger, and he was taking care of it. I ducked back into the car, just to get out of the rain—mud everywhere, mud on the carpets, the doorframe, the console—and punched in the cell number of the assisting physician at the hospital.

"There's a problem," I said.

His voice came back at me in a thinly amplified yelp. "What do you mean? Where are you?"

"I'm maybe fifteen miles south, at La Conchita, that's what I mean, but I can't get through because there's some kind of slide—it just happened—and it's blocking the road. Totally." For the first time I looked up at the mountain outside the window and saw the scar there and the trail of displaced earth and the crushed houses. Everything was gray with the rain.

"How long before they clear it?"

"Actually? Could be a while."

He was silent and I tried to picture him, nobody I knew, an intern maybe, glasses, short hair because it was easier to maintain when your life wasn't your own, biting his lip and staring out the window into the pall of rain. "Is there any way I can get to *you*? I mean, if I jump in the car and—"

"Maybe," I said, and I wanted this to work in the worst way because my reputation was on the line here and that woman needed her liver she'd been waiting for for Christ knew how long, somebody freshly dead in Phoenix and this was the best match and I'd walk it there if I could, no doubt about it, walk till my feet turned to stumps, but I had to be honest with him. "You got to realize the traffic's already backed up in both directions," I said, and I wasn't calm, wasn't calm at all. "I mean nothing's going through, there's an accident just in front of me and there's mud and rocks all over the road. In both directions. Even if you leave now you're not going to be able to get within five miles of here, so you tell me. Tell me what you want me to do. Tell me."

Another silence. "All right," he said finally. His voice was pinched. "You know how urgent this is. How crucial. We'll get this done. We will. Just keep your cell on, all right? And don't do anything till I get back to you."

I must have sat there for five minutes at least, just staring out into the rain, the cell clutched in my hand. I was wet through and I'd begun to shiver, so I turned the engine over and got the heater going. The mud was still flowing, I could see that much, and the white dog had disappeared, along with the couple from the U-Haul. Apparently they'd found shelter somewhere, in the little gas station–cum–grocery that was La Conchita's sole commercial establishment, or maybe in one of the cars stalled behind me. There were people out on the pavement, hunched-over forms wading through the mud and shouting at one another, and I thought I heard the distant keening of a siren—police, fire, ambulance—and wondered how they expected to get through. You might find it hard to believe, but I really didn't think much about the danger, though if another section of the hillside were to let go we'd all be buried, no doubt about that—no, I was more concerned with the package in the trunk. Why hadn't they called me back? What were they waiting for? I could have been slogging down the road already, the cooler propped up on one shoulder, and somebody—I thought of an ambulance from the hospital—could have met me a couple miles up the freeway. But no, the ambulances would all be busy with the wreckage in front of me, with people trapped in their cars, bleeding from head wounds, their own organs ruptured, bones broken. Or in those houses. I turned my head to look out the passenger's side window at the ghost of La Conchita, a rectangular grid of split-level homes and trailers bereft of electricity and burdened by rain, and the ones up against the hillside, the ones that had been there ten minutes ago and were gone now.

Just then, just as I turned, a streaming dark figure surged up against the car and a woman's face appeared at the window. "Open up!" she demanded. "Open up!"

I was caught off-guard—startled, actually, the way she came up on me. It took a minute to react, but she didn't have a minute, because she was pounding at the window now, frantic, both hands in motion, her eyes cutting into me through the smeared-over glass. I hit the button for the window and that smell came at me, that graveyard stink, and there she was, a woman in her twenties with smudged makeup, mud in her hair and her hair wet and hanging loose like the frayed ends of a rope. Before the window was all the way down she thrust her head in and reached across the seat to grab hold of my wrist as if to tug me out of the car, going on about her husband, her husband and her little girl, her baby, her little girl, her little girl, her voice so strained and constricted I could barely make out what she was saying. "You've got to help," she said, jerking at my arm. "Help me. *Please*."

And then, before I knew what I was doing, I was out the driver's side door and into the mud again and I never even thought to crank the window back up, her urgency gone through me like an electric jolt, and why I thought to take the gun, to tuck it into my waistband, I'll never know. Maybe because panic is infectious and violence the only thing to soothe it. I don't know. Maybe I was thinking of looters—or of myself, of insulating myself from whatever was out there, good, bad or indifferent. I came round the front of the car, the mud to my knees, and without a word she grabbed hold of my hand and started pulling me forward. "Where're we going?" I shouted into the rain, but she just tugged at me and slashed through the debris until we were across the inundated railroad tracks— running now, both of us—and into La Conchita, where the mud flowed and the houses lay buried.

Though I must have passed by the place a hundred times, doing eighty, eighty-five, with one eye out for the CHP and the other for the inevitable moron blocking the fast lane, I don't think I'd actually stopped there more than once or twice—and then only to get gas and only in an emergency situation when I'd been so intent on a delivery I'd forgotten to check the

fuel gauge. What I knew of La Conchita was limited to what I'd heard—
that it was cheap, or relatively cheap, because the hillside had given way in
'95, obliterating a few houses and scaring off buyers and realtors alike,
and that people kept coming back to it because they had short memories
and the little community there, a hundred fifty houses or so and the store
I mentioned, exerted a real pull on the imagination. This was the last of
the Southern California beach towns anybody could afford, a throwback
to earlier, happier times before the freeways came and the megalopolis ate
everything up. I'd always meant to stop and look around and yet never
seemed to find the time—the whole place couldn't have been more than a
quarter mile from one end to the other, and that goes by in a heartbeat at
eighty-five.

But I was here now, right in the thick of it, skirting the tentacles of
mud and hurrying past houses that just sat there dark and untouched,
fumbling on up the street to where the slide had broken through, and this
woman, her bare legs mud-streaked and her shoulders pinched with urgency, never let go of my wrist. And that was strange, a strange feeling, as
if I were back in elementary school and bound to one of the other kids in
some weird variant of the three-legged race. Except that this woman was
a total stranger and this was no game. I moved without thinking, without
question, my legs heavy with the mud. By the time we reached the top of
the street, a long block and a half in, all of it uphill, I was out of breath—
heaving, actually—but whether my lungs burned or my shoes were ruined beyond salvage or repair or the finish on the car was damaged to the
tune of five hundred bucks or more didn't matter, because the whole thing
suddenly came clear to me. This was the real deal. This was affliction and
loss, horror unfolding, the houses crushed like eggshells, cars swallowed
up, sections of roof flung out across the street and nothing visible beneath
but tons of wet mud and a scatter of splintered beams. I was staggered. I
was in awe. I became aware of a dog barking somewhere, a muffled sound,
as if it were barking through a gag. "Help," the woman repeated, choking
on her own voice, "goddamnit, do something, *dig*," and only then did she
let go of my wrist. She gave me one frantic look and threw herself down in
the muck, flailing at the earth with her bare hands.

Again, as I said, I'm no hero—I'm barely capable of taking care of myself, if you want to know the truth—but I fell in beside her without a word. She was sobbing now, her face slack with shock and the futility of it all—we needed a shovel, a pick, a backhoe for christ's sake—but the tools were buried, everything was buried. "I was at the store," she kept saying, chanting it as her fingers raked and bled and her nails tore and the blouse clung wet to the hard frenetic muscles of her digging, "at the store, at the store," and my mind flew right out of my body. I snatched up a length of two-by-four and began to tear at the earth as if I'd been born to it. The dirt flew. I knew nothing. I was in a trench up to my knees, up to my waist, the mud sliding back in almost as fast as I could fling it out, and she was right there beside me with her martyred hands, looking like Alice, like my Alice when I first met her with her snaking hair and the smile that pulled you across the room, Alice before things went bad. And I wondered: Would Alice dig me out? Would she even care?

Back, shoulders, bending, flinging, gouging at the face of the earth: will it sound ridiculous if I say that in that hard labor, that digging, that sweat and panic and the headlong burning rush of adrenaline, I found my wife again? And that I saw something there, something in the fierceness of her need and the taint of her smeared limbs I found incredibly sexy? I didn't know the husband. I didn't know the little girl. I was digging, yes—in my place, the average person would have done the same—but I was no hero. I wasn't digging to save anybody. I was digging for her. And there came a point, ten, fifteen minutes into it, when I saw what was going to happen as clearly as if I could predict the future. Those people were dead down there, long dead, choked and asphyxiated, and she was going to grieve, this hot young woman, this girl in the muddy shorts and soaked-through top whose name I didn't even know, who kept saying over and over that she'd gone to the store for a can of tomato paste to add to the sauce, the sauce simmering on the stove while her husband set the table and the little girl bent over her coloring book. I saw that. The grief. The grief was only to be expected. And I saw that in time—six months, a year maybe—she was going to get over it, very gradually, in a tender and fragile way, and then I would be there for her, right there at her side, and she could cleave to me the way Alice couldn't and wouldn't. It was biblical, is what it was. And I was a seer—a fortune teller—for fifteen hard minutes. But let me tell you, digging for somebody's life is a desperate business, and you don't know your thoughts, you just don't.

At some point a neighbor appeared with a shovel, and I couldn't tell you whether this guy was thirty or eighty, ten feet tall or a hunchbacked dwarf, because in one unbroken motion I flung down the two-by-four, snatched the shovel from him, and started stabbing at the earth all on my own, feeling the kind of ecstasy only the saints must know. I was shoulder-deep, slamming at something—a window frame, shattered mullions and teeth of glass—when the cell in my right front pocket began to ring. It rang on and on, five times, six times, and I couldn't stop myself, the motion of pitching forward and heaving back all I knew, the dirt looser now, fragments of shingle appearing at the bottom of the hole like treasure. The ringing stopped. Shingle gave way to splintered wood, chicken wire and fragments of stucco, an interior wall—was that an interior wall? And then the cell began to ring again and I dropped the shovel, just for an instant, to pull the thing out of my pocket and shout into the receiver. "Yeah?" my voice boomed out, and all the while I was looking to the woman, to her hopeless eyes and bloodied hands, and there was the hillside poised above us like the face of death.

"It's Joe Liebowitz. Where are you?"

"Who?"

"Dr. Liebowitz. At the hospital."

It took a moment, shifting gears. "Yeah," I said. "I'm here."

"Good. All right. Now, listen: we found somebody and he's on his way to you, on a motorcycle, so we think—he thinks—he can get through, and all you have to do is hand the package over to him. Are you all right? You think you can do that?"

Yes, I was going to say, *of course I can do that,* but I didn't have the chance. Because at that moment, somebody—some guy in a blue windbreaker and a Dodgers cap gone black with the rain—made a grab for the shovel, and they're saying I brandished the gun, but I don't know, I truthfully don't. What I do know is that I dropped the cell and wrestled the shovel away from him and began to dig with everything I had, and I could have been made of steel and rivets, a digging machine, a robot, all sensation fled out of my limbs and hands and back. I dug. And the woman— the wife, the young mother—collapsed in the mud, giving up her grief in a chain of long shuddering sobs that fed me like an intravenous drip and people were gathering now to comfort her and some guy with a pick starting in beside me. The cell rang again. It was right there, at my feet, and I paused only to snatch it up and jam it down the front of my pants, mud and all.

I don't know how long it was after that—five minutes maybe, no more—until I broke through. I was stabbing at the bottom of the hole like a fencer parrying with an invisible opponent, thrusting away, when all at once the shovel plunged in all the way to my fist and everything went still. This was the miracle: he was in there, the husband, and the little girl with him, preserved in a pocket where the refrigerator and stove had gone down under a section of the wall and held it in place. As soon as I jerked the blade of the shovel back his arm came thrusting out of the hole, and it was a shock to see this grasping hand and the arm so small and white and unexpected in that sea of mud. I could hear him now—he was shouting his wife's name, *Julie! Julie!*—and the arm vanished to show a sliver of his face, one eye so intensely green it was as if all the vegetation of the hillside had been distilled and concentrated there underground, and then his hand thrust out again and she was there, the wife, clinging to it.

I stood back then and let the guy with the pick work at the hole, the rain settling into a thin drizzle and a long funnel of cloud clinging to the raw earth above us as if the mountain had begun to breathe. People were crowding around all of a sudden, and there must have been a dozen or more, wet as rats, looking shell-shocked, the hair glued to their heads. Their voices ran away like kites blown on the wind. Somebody had a movie camera. And my cell was ringing, had been ringing for I don't know how long. It took me a minute to wipe the scrim of mud from the face of it, then I pressed the talk button and held it to my ear.

"Gordon? Is this Gordon I'm talking to?"

"I'm here," I said.

"Where? Where are you, that's what I want to know. Because the man we got has been there for ten minutes now, looking for you. Don't you realize what's going on here? There's a woman's life at stake—"

"Yeah," I said, and I was already starting down the hill, my car up to the frame in mud and debris, the police there, lights revolving, somebody with a plow on the front of his pickup trying to make the smallest dent in the mudflow that stretched on as far as I could see, "yeah, I'm on it."

The doctor's voice ran at me, hard as a knife. "You know that, don't you? You know how much longer that organ's got? Till it's not viable? You know what that means?"

He didn't want an answer. He was venting, that was all, hyped-up on caffeine and frustrated and looking for somebody to take it out on. I said, "Yeah," very softly, more as an interjection than anything else, and then asked him who I was supposed to hand the package off to.

I could hear him breathing into the phone, ready to go off on another rant, but he managed to control himself long enough to say: "Altamirano. Freddie Altamirano. He's on a motorcycle and he says he's wearing a silver helmet."

Even before I could answer I saw Freddie, legging his way through the mud, the Harley looking more like a dirt bike in the motocross than a street machine. He gave me a thumbs-up sign and gestured to the trunk of my car, even as I waded through the muck and dug in my pocket for the keys. I was soaked through to the skin. My back began to signal its displeasure and my arms felt as if all the bone and sinew had been cored out of them. Did I mention that I don't have much respect for Freddie Altamirano? That I don't like him? That he lives to steal my clients?

"Hey, brother," he said, treating me to a big wet phony grin, "where you been keeping? I been here like fifteen minutes and they are *pissed* up there at the hospital. Come on, come on," he urged as I worked through the muddy keys, and the grin was gone now.

It took maybe three minutes, no more, before Freddie had the cooler secured—minutes that were ticking down till the donor organ was just a piece of meat you could have laid out on the stainless steel counter at the market—and then he was off, kicking up mud, the blast of his exhaust like the first salvo in a war of attrition. But I didn't care about any of that. I cared about the liver and where it was going. I cared about the woman who'd taken hold of my wrist and her husband and the little girl I never did get to lay eyes on. And though I was wet through and shivering and my car was stuck and my shoes ruined and my hands so blistered I couldn't make a fist with either one, I started back up the hill—and not, as you might think, to watch the lucky man emerge from the hole in the ground or to take a bow or anything like that, but just to see if anybody else needed digging out.

QUESTION 62

S he was out in the flower bed, crushing snails—and more on them later—when she happened to glance up into the burning eyes of an optical illusion. Without her glasses and given the looming obstruction of the brim of her straw gardener's hat, which kept slipping down the crest of her brow every time she bent forward, she couldn't be sure what she was seeing at first. She was wearing the hat even though it was overcast because the doctor had removed a basal cell carcinoma from the lobe of her left ear six months ago and she wasn't taking any chances, not with the hole in the ozone layer and the thinning—or was it thickening?—of the atmosphere. She was wearing sunblock too, though it had been raw and gray all week, grayer than she would have imagined last winter when she was living in Waunakee, Wisconsin, with her sister Anita and thinking of palm trees and a fat glowing postcard sun that melted everything away in its wake. It never rained in Southern California, except that it had been raining all week, all month, and the snails, sliding along on their freeways of slime, loved it. They were everywhere, chewing holes in her nasturtiums, yellowing the tips of her Kaffir lilies and sucking at the bright orange flowers till the delicate petals turned brown and dropped off.

Which was why she was out here this morning, early, before Doug was awake, while the mist clung like gauze to the ground and the *L.A. Times* landed with a resounding thump in the driveway, down on her hands and knees crushing snails with the garden trowel. She was a vegetarian, like her sister—they'd made a vow when they were in junior high—and she didn't like to kill anything, not even the flies that gathered in fumbling flotillas on the windowsill, but this was different, this was a kind of war. The snails were an invasive species, the very same escargot people paid fifteen dollars a plate for in the restaurant, brought here at the turn of the last century by a French chef who was a little lax in keeping them in their pens or cages or wherever. They were destroying her plants, so she was destroying them. The tip of the trowel closed over the whorl of the shell and then she pressed down and was rewarded by an audible pop as the shell gave way. She didn't want to look, didn't want to see the naked dollop of meat trying to follow its probing antennae out of the ruin of its shell, and so she pressed down again until the thing was buried, each snail following the next to its grave.

And then she looked up. And what she saw didn't compute, not at first. Right there, right behind the wrought-iron fence Doug had put up to keep the deer out of her garden, there seemed to be a big cat watching her, a big striped cat the size of a pony—a tiger, that was what it was, a tiger from India with a head as wide across as the pewter platter she trucked out each Thanksgiving for the veggie cornucopia. She was startled—who wouldn't be? She'd seen tigers at the zoo, on the Nature Channel, in cages at the circus, but not in her own backyard in Moorpark, California—might as well expect a polar bear in the Bahamas or a warthog at the Dorothy Chandler Pavilion. It took her a minute, staring into the yellow eyes and the blistered snout from thirty feet away, her vision blurred, the hat slipping down over her eyebrows, before she thought to be afraid. "Doug," she called in a low voice, as if he could hear her across the yard and through the pink stucco wall of the house, "Doug, Doug." She wondered if she should move, come out of her crouch and wave her arms and shout—wasn't that what you were supposed to do, wave your arms and shout? But the tiger, improbable as it was, didn't lift its lip in a snarl or leap over the fence or drift away into a corner of her imagination. No, it only twitched its tail and lifted its ears at the sound of her voice.

Two thousand miles away, under a sky of hammered granite, Anita Nordgarden was kicking across the frozen expanse of the drive, two bags of groceries clutched in her arms. She was on the midnight shift at the Page Center for Elder Care, midnight to eight a.m., and she'd had a few drinks after work with some of the other nurses, then sifted through the aisles at the supermarket for the things she'd forgotten she needed. Now, the wind in her face, her fingertips stinging with the cold, she wasn't thinking very clearly, but if she was thinking anything, it was the fish, Lean Cuisine, pop it in the microwave, wash it down with two glasses of chardonnay and then read till she fell away into the deeps of her midday sleep that was all but indistinguishable from a coma. Or maybe she'd watch a movie, because she was exhausted and a movie required less effort than a book, though she'd seen each of the twenty-three cassettes on the shelf over the TV so many times she could have stopped her ears and cinched a blindfold over her eyes and watched them all the same.

She was just mounting the steps to her trailer when a shadow detached itself from the gloom beneath the doorstep and presented a recognizable face to her. This was One-Eye, the feral tom that lived with his various paramours in the secret fastness beneath the trailer, an animal she neither encouraged nor discouraged. She'd never had a cat. Never especially liked them. And Robert, when he was alive, wouldn't have an animal in the house. Every once in a while, she'd toss a handful of kibble out in the yard, feeling charitable, but the cat was a bird killer—more than once she'd come home to find feathers scattered round the steps—and she probably would have got rid of it if it weren't for the mice. Since he'd moved in beneath the trailer she'd stopped finding the slick black mouse pellets in the cupboards and scattered across the kitchen counter and she didn't like to think of the disease they carried. At any rate, there he was, One-Eye, just staring at her as if she'd somehow intruded on him, and she was about to say something, to raise her voice in a soft, silly half-lubricated falsetto and murmur *Kitty, kitty,* when the cat suddenly darted back under the steps and she looked up to see a man coming round the corner of the trailer opposite hers.

He walked in a jaunty, almost demented way, closing quickly on her with a big artificial grin on his face—he was selling something, that was it—and before she could get her key in the door he was right there. "Good morning," he boomed, "lovely morning, huh? Don't you love the cold?" He was tall, she saw, nearly as tall as she was perched atop the third step, and he was wearing some sort of animal-skin hat with the ragged frizz of a tail dangling in back—coonskin, she wanted to call it, only she saw right away that this wasn't raccoon but something else. "Need a hand?"

"No," she said, and she would have closed out the scene right there, but for the look in his eyes: he wanted something, but he didn't want it desperately and he wasn't selling anything, she could see that now. There was a mystery here, and at this hour of the morning, with two Dewar's and sodas in her and nothing to look forward to but the fish and the chardonnay and the sleep of the dead, she felt the prick of it. "No, thanks," she added, "I can manage," and she was pushing open the door when he made his pitch.

"I was just wondering if you might have a minute to spare—? To talk. Just a minute, that's all?"

A Jesus freak, she was thinking. All I need. She was halfway through the door, looking back at him, down at him, but he must have been six-five, six-six, and his fixed blue eyes were nearly on a level with hers. "No," she said, "I don't think so. I work nights and—"

He lifted his eyebrows and the corners of his mouth went up a notch. "Oh, no, no, no," he said, "I'm not a Bible-thumper or anything like that. I'm not selling anything, nothing at all. I'm your neighbor, is all? Todd Gray? From over on Betts Street?"

The wind was at war with the heater and the soft warm slightly rancid smell of home that emanated from the pillows of the built-in couch and the cheap floorboards and the kitchen counter and the molded plastic strips of the ceiling. She was half-in and half-out and he was standing there on the frozen ground.

"No," he said, "no," as if she were protesting, "I just wanted to talk to you about Question 62, that's all. And I won't take a minute of your time."

She was down on her hands and knees for so long her back began to ache—her lower back, right at the base of the spine, where gravity tugged at the bunched muscles there and her stomach sagged beneath them—

and she could feel the burden of her torso in her shoulders and wrists. She was there so long the mist began to lift and an oblivious snail slid out from the furls of one of the plants and etched a trail across the knuckles of her right hand. But she didn't want to move. She couldn't move. She was beyond fear now and deep into the realm of fascination, of magic and wonder and the compelling strangeness of the moment. A tiger. A tiger in her garden. No one would believe it. No one, not Doug snoring in the bedroom or Anita locked away in her trailer with its frozen skirt of snow and the wind sitting in the north.

The tiger hadn't moved. It sat there on its haunches like a dog anticipating a treat, braced on its big buff paws, ears erect, tail twitching, watching her. She'd been talking to it in a low voice for some time now, offering up blandishments against the dwindling nugget of her fear, saying, *Good boy, good cat, that's right, yes*—and here her voice contracted to a syrupy chirp—*he just wants a little love, doesn't he? A little love, yeah?*

The animal made no sign it understood, but it stayed there, pressed to the fence, apparently as fascinated as she, and as the mist clotted round the smooth lanceolate leaves of the oleanders and steamed from the wet shingles of the Hortons' across the way, she understood that this was somebody's pet, the ward of some menagerie owner or private collector like that man in the Bronx or Brooklyn or wherever it was with the full-grown tiger in his apartment and the six-foot alligator in the bathtub. Of course it was. This wasn't Sumatra or the Sunderbans—aliens hadn't swooped down overnight in one of their radiant ships and set loose a plague of tigers across the land. The animal was a pet. And it had got loose. It was probably hungry. Bewildered. Tired. It was probably as surprised to see her in her straw hat and faded green overalls as she was to see it—or him. It was definitely a him—she could see the crease where his equipment lay against his groin and the twin bulbs of his testicles.

But she couldn't crouch like this forever—her back was killing her. And her wrists. Her wrists had gone numb. Very slowly, as if she were doing yoga to a tape running at half-speed, she lowered her bottom down in the damp soil and felt the pressure ease in her arms, and that was all right, except that her new posture seemed to confound the cat—or excite him.

He moved up off his haunches and slid silkily down the length of the iron fence, then swung round and came back again, the muscles tensed in his shoulders as he rubbed against the bars, and she was sure that he'd been in a cage, that he wanted a cage now—the security of it, the familiarity, probably the only environment he'd ever known—and all she could think of was how to get him in here, inside the fence and maybe into the garage, where she could lock the door and hide him away.

Since Robert died—was killed, that is—she hadn't had many visitors. There was Tricia, who lived with her boyfriend three trailers down—she sometimes came in for a cup of tea in the evening when Anita was just waking up and trying to consolidate her physical resources for the shift ahead, but her schedule kept her pretty much to herself. She was only thirty-five, widowed less than a year, the blood still ran in her veins and she liked a good time as much as anybody else. Still, it was hard to find people who wanted to make the rounds of the bars at eight a.m., other than congenital losers and pinch-faced retirees hunched over a double vodka as if it was going to give them back the key to their personalities, and the times she'd tried to go out at night on her days off she'd found herself drifting over her first beer while everybody else got up and danced. And so she invited him in, this man, Todd, and here he was sprawled on the couch in his faded cowboy boots with his legs that ran on forever, and she was offering him some stale Triscuits and a bright orange block of cheddar she'd surreptitiously shaved the mold off of and she was just wondering if he might like a glass of chardonnay.

He'd let his grin flag, but it came back now, a boy's grin, the grin that had no doubt got him whatever he wanted wherever he went. He pushed the hat back till the roots of his hair showed in front, squared his shoulders and gathered in his legs. She saw that he was her age, or close enough, and she saw too that he wasn't wearing a wedding ring. "A little early for me," he said, and his laugh was genuine. "But if you're going to have one—"

She was already pouring. "I told you," she said, "I work nights."

The wine was one of her few indulgences—it was from a little California vineyard in the Santa Ynez Valley. She and her sister Mae had gone wine-tasting when she was visiting over Christmas and she liked the faint dry echo of the chardonnay so much she had two cases shipped back to Wisconsin. Her impulse was to hoard it, but she was feeling generous this morning, expansive in a way that had nothing to do with the two scotches or the way the trailer ticked and hummed over its heating element and a feeble cone of rinsed-out sunshine poked through the blinds. "This is cocktail hour for me," she said, handing him the glass, "my chance to kick back before dinner."

"Right," he said, "just about the time everybody else is getting to work with crumbs in their lap and a cardboard cup of lukewarm coffee. I used to work nights," he said. "At a truck stop. I know how it is."

She'd eased into the chair opposite him, his legs snaking out again as if he couldn't contain them, boots crossed at the ankles, then uncrossed and crossed again. "So what do you do now?" she asked, wishing she'd had a chance to put on some lipstick, brush her hair. In time, though. In time she would. Especially if he stayed for a second glass.

His eyes, which had never strayed from hers since he hunched through the door, slipped away and then came back again. He shrugged. "This and that."

She had nothing to say to this and they were silent a moment as they sipped their wine and listened to the wind run at the trailer. "You like it?" she said finally.

"Hm?"

"The wine."

"Oh, sure, yeah. I'm not much of a connoisseur, I'd say . . . but yeah, definitely."

"It's a California wine. My sister lives out there. Got it right from the winery itself."

"Nice," he said, and she could see he was just being polite. Probably the next thing he would say was that he was more of a beer man himself.

She wanted to say more, wanted to tell him about the vineyard, the neat braided rows of grapevines curling round the hills and arcing down into the little valleys like the whorls of a shell, about the tasting room and the feel of the sun on her face as she and Mae sat outside at a redwood table and toasted each other and the power of healing and the beginning of a new life for them both, but she sensed he wouldn't be interested. So she leaned in then, elbows propped on the knees of the pale blue cotton scrubs she wore to work every night, his legs splayed out in front of her as if he'd been reclining there all his life, and said, "So what is this question you wanted to ask me about, anyway?"

The more she talked, the more the tiger seemed to settle down. Before long it stopped pacing, leaned into the rails of the fence and let its body melt away till it was lying there in the dirt and devil grass as if it had somehow found the one place in the world that suited it best. There was the sound of the birds—a jay calling harshly from the next yard over, a songbird swapping improvisations with its mate—and the soughing rumble of a car going up the street behind the house, and then she could hear the tiger's breathing as clearly as if she were sitting in the living room listening to it come through Doug's stereo speakers. It wasn't purring, not exactly, but there was a glottal sound there, deep and throaty, and after a moment she realized the animal was asleep and that what she was hearing was a kind of snore, a sucking wheeze, in and out, in and out. She was amazed. Struck dumb. How many people had heard a tiger snore? How many people in the world, in the history of the world, let alone Moorpark? What she felt then was grace, a grace that descended on her from the gray roof of the morning, a sense of privilege and intimacy no one on earth was feeling. This animal didn't belong to her, she knew that—it had an owner somewhere and he would be out looking for it, the police would be here soon, dogs, trackers, guns—but the moment did.

"Well, let me put it this way," he was saying, "I see you got some ferals living under your trailer . . ."

"Ferals?" At first she thought he'd meant ferrets and she gave his hat a closer scrutiny. Was that what that was, ferret fur?

"Cats. Stray cats."

He was studying her intently, challenging her with his eyes. She shrugged. "Three or four of them. They come and go."

"You're not feeding them, are you?"

"Not really."

"Good," he said, and then repeated himself with a kind of religious fervor, his voice echoing off the molded plastic of the ceiling. She saw that his glass was empty, clutched in one oversized hand and balanced delicately over the crotch of his jeans. "Because they're bird killers, you know. Big time. You ever notice feathers scattered around?"

"Not really." This was the moment to look at her own empty glass and hold it up to the light. "But hey, I'm going to have another—help me sleep. How about you?"

He waved his hand in a vague way, which she took to mean yes, and she lifted the bottle from the coffee table and held it aloft a moment so that the pale light through the window caught the label, then leaned forward, way out over the gulf of his parted thighs, to pour for him. He didn't thank her. Didn't even seem to notice. "I like birds," he said. "I love birds. I've been a member of the Audubon Society since I was in sixth grade, did you know that?"

She didn't know that, how could she?—she'd just met him ten minutes ago. But she'd always liked tall men and she liked the way he'd settled in, liked the way things were going. His brow furrowed, his eyes leapt out at her: he *was* a preacher, after all. So what did she do? She poured herself a glass of wine and shrugged again. *Let him talk.*

"Anyway," he said, and he drank off half the glass in a gulp, "anyway— this *is* good stuff, I see what you mean. But the cats. Did you know there are something like two million stray cats in this state alone and that they're responsible for killing between forty-seven million to a hundred and thirty-nine million native songbirds a year, depending on the estimate? A hundred and thirty-nine million." He drew up his legs, the boots sliding away from her and clapping lightly together as he sat up erect in the chair. "Now that's outrageous, don't you think?"

"Yeah," she said, sipping California, tasting the sun on her tongue, the earth, the trees, the vines that wove the hills into a big green fruit-hung tapestry. Robert had been five-eleven, an inch taller than she, and that was fine, that was all right, because she'd had her fill of blind dates and friends of friends who came up to her clavicle, but she'd always wondered what it would be like to date a man who made her feel short. And vulnerable. Somebody who could pull her head to his chest and just squeeze till she felt the weight go out of her legs.

"So that's why I'm here," he said, studying the pale gold of the wine in the clear crystal of the glass, before tilting his head to throw back what remained. "That's why I'm going house to house to drum up support for Question 62—for the birds. To save the birds."

She felt as if she were drifting, uncontained, floating right up and out through the ceiling of the trailer to blow off on the wind as if she were a bird herself—two scotches and two glasses of wine on a mostly empty stomach, the Lean Cuisine Salmon Gratin with Lemon & Dill sitting frozen on the counter. Still, she had the presence of mind to lean back in the chair, let out a deep breath and focus a smile on him. "All right," she said, "you got me—what's Question 62?"

The answer consumed the next ten minutes, during which she put on her listening expression and poured them each another half glass of wine and the presence of the sun grew firmer as it sliced the blinds into plainly delineated stripes that began ever so slowly to creep across the carpet. Question 62, he told her, was coming up for a vote in seventy-two counties on the twelfth of April and it was as simple as this: should cats be listed as an unprotected species like skunks and gophers and other nuisance animals? They were coldly efficient predators and they were interfering with the ecosystem. They were killing off birds and outcompeting native animals like hawks, owls and foxes for prey, and the long and short of it was that any cat found roaming without a collar could be hunted without a license or season or bag limit.

"Hunted?" she said. "You mean, with a gun? Like deer or something?"

"Like gophers," he said. "Like rats." His eyes were fierce and he leaned

over his empty glass as if he were about to snatch it up and grind it between his teeth. He was sweating, a translucent runnel of fluid leaching
out of his hairline and into the baffle of his right eyebrow; in a single
motion he shrugged out of his parka and pulled off the hat to reveal a
full head of russet hair streaked blond at the tips. He was staring right
into her.

"I don't like guns," she said.

"Guns're a fact of life."

"My husband was killed by a gun." As she said it, a flat statement of
fact, she saw Robert lying in the dirt not fifty feet from where they were
sitting now and she heard the sirens and the gunshots, and the face of
Tim Palko from the trailer across the way came back to her, Tim Palko,
drunk for a week after he lost his job and gone crazy with his deer rifle
till the SWAT team closed in and he put the barrel of it in his own mouth
and jerked the trigger one last time. But she'd seen death—she saw it
every week at the Page Center—and when she looked out the window of
the trailer after the first shot thumped through the afternoon like the
beat of a bass drum that never reverberated, she could see from the way
Robert was lying there that it had come for him and come instantly. Mae
had said, *How could you be sure?*, but she had two eyes and she knew absolutely and incontrovertibly, and that knowledge, cold as it was, grim as
it was, saved her. *If I'd run out there, Mae,* she told her, *we wouldn't be
sitting here now.*

The man—Todd—dropped his eyes, made a noise in the back of his
throat. They were silent a moment, just listening to the wind, and then the
clouds closed in and the sun failed and the room grew a shade darker, two
shades, and she reached for the pull on the lamp. "I'm sorry," he said. "It
must be hard."

She didn't answer. She studied his face, his hands, the nervous bounce
of his right heel. "What I was thinking," she said finally, "is maybe opening another bottle. Just one more glass. What do you say?"

He looked up at her with that grin, the grin resurrected in the space of
a heartbeat to make everything all right again. "I don't know," he sighed,

and he was watching her now, watching her as intently as he'd been a moment ago when he was delivering his speech, "but if I have another glass I'm going to want to lay down. How about you? You feel like laying down?"

For a long while Mae crouched there in the wet earth, toying with the idea of backing noiselessly across the lawn so she could slip next door to the Kaprielians' and see if she could maybe borrow or purchase some meat—steak, rump roast, whatever they had—and she'd pay them later because this was an emergency and she couldn't talk about it now. Meat, that was what she needed. Any kind of meat. She had a fantasy of dropping wet slabs of it across the lawn in a discontinuous path that snaked up the gravel walk and through the open door of the garage, the big cat lured inside where it would settle down to sleep over a full belly between the dryer and the Toyota. But no. She hardly knew the Kaprielians. And what she did know of them she didn't like, the husband a big-bellied inimical presence bent perpetually over the hood of his hot rod or whatever it was and the wife dressed like some sort of hooker even in the morning when she went out to the driveway to retrieve the newspaper . . .

She didn't believe in meat and neither did Doug. That was one of the things that had attracted her to him, one of the things they had in common, though there were other things—mountains of them, replete with ridges and declensions and towering heights—in which they were polar opposites. But Doug had worked two summers in a chicken plant in Tennessee, snatching the chickens up out of their cages to suspend them on a cable by their clamped feet so they could proceed to the pluckers and gutters, and he'd vowed never again to touch a piece of meat as long as he lived. He'd strung up tens of thousands of bewildered birds, their wings flapping in confusion amidst the chicken screech and the chicken stink, one after another heading down the line to have their heads removed and their innards ripped out. What did they ever do to us, he said, his face twisted with the memory of it, to deserve that?

She was still down on her knees, her eyes fixed on the swell of the tiger's ribs as they rose and fell in the decelerating rhythm of sleep, thinking maybe she could give it eggs, a stainless steel pan with raw egg and then a line of individual eggs just tapped enough to show the yolk, when the back door of the neighbors' house jerked open with a pneumatic wheeze and there was the Kaprielian woman, in her bathrobe and heels no less, letting the two yapping Pomeranians out into the yard. That was all it took to break the spell. The door wheezed shut, the dogs blew across the grass like down in a stiff wind, and the tiger was gone.

Later, after the dogs had got through sniffing and yapping and the neighborhood woke to the building clangor of a Saturday morning in March—doors slamming, voices rising and falling and engines of every conceivable bore and displacement screaming to life—she sat with Doug at the kitchen table and stared out into the gray vacancy of the backyard, where it had begun to rain. Doug was giving the paper his long squint. He'd lit a cigarette and he alternated puffs with delicate abbreviated sips of his second cup of overheated coffee. He was wearing his pajama bottoms and a sweatshirt stained with the redwood paint he'd used on the picnic table. At first he hadn't believed her. "What," he'd said, "it's not April Fools', not yet." But then, there it was in the paper—a picture of a leathery white-haired man, a tracker, bent over a pugmark in the mud near a dude ranch in Simi Valley, and then they turned on the TV and the reporter was standing there in the backwash of the helicopter's blades, warning people to stay inside and keep their pets with them because some sort of exotic cat had apparently got loose and could be a potential danger—and they'd both gone out back and studied the ground along the fence in silence.

There was nothing there, no sign, nothing. Just dirt. The first few spatters of rain feathered the brim of her hat, struck at her shoulders. For a moment she thought she could smell it, the odor released in a sprinkle of rain, the smell of litter, fur, the wild, but then she couldn't be sure.

Doug was staring at her, his eyes pale and wondering. "You really saw it?" he said. "Really? You're not shitting me, right?" In the next moment he went down on his heels and thrust his hand through the slats of the fence to pat the ground as if it were the striped hide of the animal itself.

She looked down at the top of his head, the hair matted and poorly cut, his bald spot spinning in a whorl of its own, galactic, a whole cosmos there. She didn't bother to answer.

Todd barely fit the bed, which occupied its own snug little cubbyhole off the wall of the master bedroom, and twice, in his passion, he sat up abruptly and cracked his head on the low-slung ceiling, and she had to laugh, lying there naked beneath him, because he was so earnest, so eager in his application. But he was tender too, and patient with her—it had been a long time, too long, and she'd almost forgotten what a man could make her feel like, a man other than Robert, a stranger with a new body, new hands and tongue and groin. New rhythm. New smell. Robert had smelled of his mother, of the sad damp house he'd grown up in, carpet slippers and menthol, the old dog and the mold under the kitchen sink and the saccharine spice of the aftershave he tried to cover it all up with. Todd's smell was different, fresher somehow, as if he'd just come back from a roll in the snow, but there was something else too, something darker and denser, and she held him a long while, her face pressed to the back of his head, before she understood what it was: the lingering scent of the fur hat that was lying now on the couch in the other room. She thought of that and then she was gone, deep in her coma, the whole world closing down on her cubbyhole in the wall.

He left her a note on the kitchen table. She saw it there when she got up for work, the windows dark and the heater ticking away like a Geiger counter. His hand was free-flowing, shapely, and that pleased her, the care that went into it, what it said about him as an individual. The words were pretty special too. He said that she was the most beautiful woman he'd ever met in his life and that he was going to take her out to breakfast in the morning, make it a date, if that was all right with her, and he signed his full name, Todd Jefferson Gray, and wrote out his address and phone number beneath it.

Next morning, when her shift was over, she walked across the snow-scabbed lot to her car, her spirits rising with every step. She never doubted he'd be there, not for a minute, but she couldn't help craning her neck to sweep the lot, expecting him to emerge from one car or another, tall and quick-striding, his smile widening. As it was, she didn't notice him until she was nearly on him—he wasn't in a car; he didn't have a car. He was standing just beyond the front bumper of her Saturn with a solemn look on his face, rooted to the ground like one of the trees that rose up behind him in a black tangle. When she was right there, right at the door of the car with the keys in her hand and he still hadn't moved, she felt confused. "Todd?" she heard herself say. "Is everything all right?"

He smiled then and swept the fur hat from his head with a mock bow. "I believe we have a date, don't we?" he said, and without waiting for an answer he moved forward to hold the door for her before sliding into the passenger's seat.

At the diner—already busy with the Sunday-morning church crowd—they ordered two large orange juices, which Todd discreetly reinforced with vodka from the bottle he produced from the inside pocket of his parka. She drained the first one all the way to the bottom before she lit her first cigarette of the day and ordered another. Only then did she look at the menu.

"Go on," Todd told her, "it's on me. Order anything you want. Have a steak, anything. Steak and eggs—"

She was feeling the vodka, the way it seemed to contract her insides and take the lingering chill out of her fingers and toes. She took another sip of her screwdriver, threw back her head to shake out her hair. "I'm a vegetarian," she said.

It took him a minute. She watched his eyes narrow, as if he were trying for a better perspective. The waitress stalked by, decaf in one hand, regular in the other, giving them a look. "So what does that mean?"

"It means I don't eat any meat."

"Dairy?"

She shrugged. "Not much. I take a calcium supplement."

A change seemed to come over him. Where a moment ago he'd been loose and supple, sunk into the cushion of the fake-leather banquette as if his spine had gone to sleep, now suddenly he went rigid. "What," he said, his voice saturated with irony, "you feel sorry for the cows, is that it? Because they have to have their poor little teats pulled? Well, I'll tell you, I was raised on a dairy farm and if you didn't milk those cows every morning they'd explode—and that's cruelty, if you want to know."

She didn't say anything, didn't really want to get into it. Whether she drank milk or ate sloppy joes and pig's feet was nobody's business but hers and it was a decision she'd made so long ago it was just part of her now, like the shape of her eyes and her hair color. She picked up the menu, just to do something.

"So what," he said. "I'm just wasting my time here, is that it? You're one of these save the animals people? You hate hunting, isn't that right?" He drew in a breath. "And hunters."

"I don't know," she said, and she felt a spark of irritation rising in her, "what difference does it make?"

She saw him clench his fist, and he almost brought it down on the table before he caught himself. He was struggling to control his voice: "What *difference* does it make? Have you been listening to me? I've had *death* threats over Question 62—from your cat lovers, the pacifists themselves."

"Right," she said. "Like the cats under my trailer are some big threat, aren't they? Invasive species, right? Well, we're an invasive species. Mrs. Merker I was telling you about, the one that gets up twenty times a night to find the bathroom and twenty times a night asks me who I am and what I think I'm doing in her house? She's part of the problem, isn't she? Why not hunt old ladies too?"

His eyes jumped round the room before they came back to her, exasperated eyes, irritated, angry. "I don't know. I'm not into that. I mean, that's people."

She told herself to shut it down, to pick up the menu and order something innocuous—waffles, with fake maple syrup that spared even the maple trees—but she couldn't. Maybe it was the drinks, maybe that was it. "But don't people kill birds? Habitat destruction and whatever, minimalls, diesel engines and what, plastics. Plastics kill birds, don't they?"

"Don't get crazy on me. Because that's nuts. Just nuts."

"Just asking."

"Just *asking*?" Now the fist did come down on the table, a single propulsive thump that set the silverware rattling and heads turning. "We're talking death threats and you think this is some kind of game?" He was on his feet suddenly, the tallest man in the world, the jacket riding up over his belt, his face soaring, all that displacement of air and light. He bent for his hat, then straightened up again, his face contorted. "Some date," he said, and then he was gone.

The night of the tiger, a night that collapsed across the hills like a wet sack under the weight of yet another storm, Mae kept the television on late, hoping for news. Earlier, she and Doug had thought of going out to dinner and then maybe a movie, but with the rain showing no sign of letting up Doug didn't think he wanted to risk it and so she'd got creative with some leftover marinara sauce, zucchini and rice and they'd wound up watching an old pastel movie on the classic channel. The movie—they missed the first ten minutes and she never did catch the title—featured Gene Kelly in a sailor suit. Doug, who was working on the last beer of his six-pack, said it should have been *Singin' in the Rain*.

That was funny, and though she was distracted—had been distracted all day—she laughed. There was a silence then and they both listened to the rain hammering at the roof—it was so loud, so persistent, that for a moment it drowned out the dialogue on the TV.

"I guess this is it," Doug said, leaning back in his recliner with a sigh, "—the monsoon. The real deal, huh?" He gestured to the ceiling with the can of beer.

"Yeah," she said, watching the bright figures glide across the screen, "but I just hope it doesn't float us away. You think the car's going to be all right in the driveway?"

He gave her a look of irritation. "It's only rain."

"It seems so strange, though, because there's no thunder, no lightning. It just keeps coming as if somebody'd turned on a big spigot in the sky." She made a face. "I don't know. I don't like it. I don't think I'll ever get used to it—even the word, *monsoon*. It's so bizarre, like something out of some jungle someplace."

He just shrugged. They'd looked to his career and chosen California—Moorpark—over Atlanta, because, and they were both in absolute agreement here, they didn't want to live in the South. And while she loved the idea of year-round gardening—flowers in February and trees that never lost their leaves—she was still feeling her way around the way the seasons seemed to stall and the earth hardened to clay under the unblinking summer sun till it was like brick and nothing would grow along the fence but devil grass and tumbleweeds. *Tumbleweeds*. She might as well have been in the Wild West.

She'd had two beers herself and her attention was drifting—she couldn't really focus on the movie, all that movement, singing, dancing, the earnest plot, as if any of this meant anything—and when Doug got up without a word and steadied himself against the arm of the chair before moving off toward the bedroom, she picked up the remote and began flicking through the channels. She was looking for something, anything that might bring her back to what she'd felt that morning, on her knees in the garden with the mist rising round her. The tiger was out there, in the black of the night, the rain steaming round it. That was a thing she could hold on to, an image that grew inside her like something that had been planted there. And they wouldn't be able to track it, she realized, not now, not in this. After a while she muted the sound and just sat there listening to the rain, hoping it would never stop.

A week went by. The temperature took a nosedive and then it began to snow, off and on, until Saturday, when Anita came out of work to the smell of diesel and the flashing lights of the snowplow and had to struggle through a foot of fresh snow to her car. Her mood was desolate. Mrs. Merker had torn off her Depends and squatted to pee right in front of the nurses' station and Mr. Pohnert ("Call me Alvin") kept pressing his buzzer every five minutes to complain that his feet were cold despite the fact that both his legs had been removed five years ago due to complications from diabetes. And there were the usual aggravations, the moans and whimpers and the gagging and retching and people crying out in the dark—the strangeness of the place, insulated and overheated, with its ticking machines and dying bodies and her at the center of it. And now this. The sky was dark and roiled, the snow flung on the wind in sharp stinging pellets. It took her fifteen minutes to get her car out. And she drove home like a zombie, both hands clenching the wheel even as the tires floated and shimmied over the patches of ice.

There were tracks punched in the snow around her doorstep, cat tracks, amidst a scattering of blue feathers tipped with black. And a flyer, creased down the middle and shoved into the crack of the door. NO ON 62, it said, SAVE OUR PETS. She didn't have the heart to open a bottle of chardonnay—that she would save for brighter times—but she did make herself a cup of tea and spike it with a shot of Dewar's while she thought about what she wanted to eat, soup maybe, just a can of Chunky Vegetable and some wheat toast to dip in it. She had the TV on and her feet up before she noticed the blinking light on her message machine. There were two messages. The first was from Mae—"Call me," delivered in a tragic voice—and the second, the one she'd been waiting all week for, was from Todd. He was sorry about the blowup, but he'd been under a lot of pressure lately and he hoped they could get together again—soon, real soon—despite their differences, because they really did have a lot in common and she was the most beautiful woman he'd ever met and he'd really like to make it up to her. If she would let him. *Please*.

She was wondering about that—what exactly they had in common aside from two semi-drunken go-arounds on her bed and the fact that they were both tall and both lived in Waunakee—when the phone rang. She picked it up on the first ring, thinking it was him. "Hello?" she whispered.

"Anita?" It was Mae. Her voice was cored out and empty, beyond tragic, beyond tears. "Oh, Anita, Anita." She broke off, gathered herself. "They shot the tiger."

"Who? What tiger?"

"It didn't even have claws. This beautiful animal, somebody's pet, and it couldn't have—"

"Couldn't have what? What tiger? What are you talking about?"

But the conversation ended there. The connection was broken, either on Mae's end or hers—she couldn't be sure until she tried to dial her sister and the phone gave back nothing but static. Somebody had skidded into a telephone pole, that was it, and she wondered how much longer the lights would be on—that would be next, no power—and she got up out of the chair to pull open the tab on the top of the soup can, disgorge the contents into a ceramic bowl and flag the mircrowave while she could. She punched in the three digits and was rewarded by the mechanical roar of the thing starting up, the bowl rotating inside and the visual display of the numbers counting down, 3:30, 3:29, 3:28, until suddenly, in the space of the next second, the microwave choked off and the TV died and the fluorescent strip under the cabinet flickered once and buried its light in a dark tube.

For a long while she sat there in the shadows, sipping her tea, which had already crossed the threshold from hot to lukewarm, and then she got up and dumped a handful of ice in it and filled it to the rim with Dewar's. She was sipping her drink and thinking vaguely about food, a sandwich, she'd make a sandwich when she felt like it, cheese, lettuce, wheat bread— that she could do with or without power—when a sound from beneath the trailer brought her back, a scrabbling there, as of an animal, on its four paws, making a quiet meal.

She'd have to sacrifice the cats, she could see that now, because as soon as they hooked the phones back up she was going to call Todd. She wished he were here now, wished they were in bed together, under the quilt, drinking chardonnay and listening to the snow sift down on the aluminum roof of the trailer. She didn't care about the cats. They were nothing to her. And she wanted to please him, she did, but she couldn't help wondering—and she'd ask him too, she'd put it to him—What had Question 61 been, or Question 50, Question 29? Pave over the land? Pollute the streams? Kill the buffalo? Or what about Question 1, for that matter. Question 1—and she pictured it now, written on a slate in chalk and carried from village to village in a time of want and weather just like this, the snow coming down and people peering out from behind heavy wooden doors with a look of suspicion and irritation—Question 1 must have been something really momentous, the kick start of the whole program of the Department of Natural Resources. And what could it have been? Cut down the trees, flay the hides, pull the fish from the rivers? Or no, she thought, tipping back the mug, it would have been even more basic than that: Kill off the Indians. Yeah. Sure. That must have been it: Kill off the Indians.

She got up then and made herself a sandwich, then poured herself another little drop of scotch and took the plate and the mug with her to the cubbyhole of her bed, where she sat cross-legged against the pillow that still smelled of him and chewed and drank and listened to the cold message of the snow.

SIN DOLOR

He came into the world like all the rest of them—like us, that is—brown as an iguana and flecked with the detritus of after-birth, no more remarkable than the date stamped on the morning's newspaper, but when I cleared his throat and slapped his infant buttocks, he didn't make a sound. Quite the contrary. His eyes snapped open with that searching myopia of the newborn and he began to breathe, calmly and quietly, with none of the squalling or fuss of the others. My nurse, Elvira Fuentes, who had spent fifteen years working on the cancer ward at the hospital in Guadalajara before coming home to devote herself to me, both as lover and helpmeet, frowned as I handed the infant to his mother. She was thinking exactly the same thing I was: there must have been some constriction or deformation of the child's vocal apparatus. Or perhaps he'd been born without it. We've seen stranger things, all manner of defects and mutations, especially among the offspring of the migrant workers, what with the devil's brew of herbicides, pesticides and geneti-cally engineered foodstuffs to which they've been routinely exposed. There was one man I won't name here who came back from the cotton fields of Arizona looking like one of Elvira's oncological ghosts, and whose wife gave birth nine months later to a monster without a face—no eyes, ears, mouth or nose, just a web of translucent skin stretched tight over a head the size of an avocado. Officially, we labeled it a stillbirth. The corpse—if you could call it that—was disposed of with the rest of the medical waste.

But that's neither here nor there. What I mean to say is that we were wrong. Happily, at least as it appeared. The child—he was born to Fran-cisco and Mercedes Funes, street vendors whose *tacos de chivo* are abso-lutely poisonous to the digestive tract, and I advise all who read this to avoid their stall at the corner of Independencia and Constitución if you value your equilibrium—was soon groping at his mother's breast and making the usual gurgling and sucking noises. Mercedes Funes, twenty-seven years old at the time, with six children already to her credit, a pair of bow legs, the shoulders of a fullback and one continuous eyebrow that made you think of Frida Kahlo (stripped of artistry and elegance, that is), was back at her stall that evening, searing goat over a charcoal grill for the entertainment of the unwary, and, as far as Elvira and I were concerned, that was that. One more soul had entered the world. I don't remember what we did that night, but I suppose it was nothing special. Usually, after we closed the clinic, we would sit in the courtyard, exhausted, and watch the doves settle on the wires while the serving girl put together a green salad and a *caldereta de verduras* or a platter of fried artichoke hearts, Elvira's favorite.

Four years slipped by before I next saw the child or gave more than a glancing thought to the Funes clan except when I was treating cases of vomiting and diarrhea, and as a matter of course questioning my patients as to what and where they'd eaten. "It was the oysters, Doctor," they'd tell me, looking penitent. "Onions, definitely the onions—they've never agreed with me." "Mayonnaise, I'll never eat mayonnaise again." And, my favorite: "The meat hardly smelled at all." They'd blame the Chinese restaurant, the Mennonites and their dairy, their own wives and uncles and dogs, but more often than not I was able to trace the source of the problem to the Funes stall. My patients would look at me with astonishment. "But that can't be, Doctor—the Funes make the best tacos in town."

At any rate, Mercedes Funes appeared at the clinic one sun-racked morning with her son in tow. She came through the door tugging him awkwardly by the wrist (they'd named the boy Dámaso, after her husband's twin brother, who sent small packets of chocolate and the occasional twenty-dollar bill from Los Angeles when the mood took him), and settled into a chair in the waiting room while Elvira's parrot gnawed at the wicker bars of its cage and the little air conditioner I keep in the front window churned out its hyperborean drafts. I was feeling especially good that morning, at the top of my game, certain real estate investments having turned out rather well for me, and Elvira keeping her eye on a modest little cottage at the seashore, which we hoped to purchase as a getaway and perhaps, in the future, as a place of retirement. After all, I was no longer as young as I once was and the Hippocratic *frisson* of healing the lame and curing the incurable had been replaced by a sort of repetitious drudgery, nothing a surprise anymore and every patient who walked through the door diagnosed before they even pulled up a chair. I'd seen it all. I was bored. Impatient. Fed up. But, as I say, on this particular day, my mood was buoyant, my whole being filled with an inchoate joy over the prospect of that little frame cottage at the seashore. I believe I may even have been whistling as I entered the examining room.

"And what seems to be the problem?" I asked.

Mercedes Funes was wrapped in a shawl despite the heat. She'd done up her hair and was wearing the shoes she reserved for mass on Sundays. In her lap was the child, gazing up at me out of his father's eyes, eyes that were perfectly round, as if they'd been created on an assembly line, and which never seemed to blink. "It's his hands, Doctor," Mercedes said in a whisper. "He's burned them."

Before I could say "Let's have a look" in my paternal and reassuring tones, the boy held out his hands, palms up, and I saw the wounds there. The burns were third degree, right in the center of each palm, and involved several fingers as well. Leathery scabs—eschars—had replaced the destroyed tissue and were seeping a deep wine-colored fluid around the margins. I'd seen such burns before, of course, on innumerable occasions, the result of a house fire, smoking in bed, a child blundering against a stove, but these seemed odd, as if they'd been deliberately inflicted. I glanced up sharply at the mother and asked what had happened.

"I was busy with a customer," she said, dropping her eyes as if to summon the image, "a big order, a family of seven, and I wasn't watching him—and Francisco wasn't there; he's out selling bicycle tires now, you know, just so we can make ends meet. Dámaso must have reached into the brazier when my back was turned. He took out two hot coals, Doctor, one in each hand. I only discovered what he'd done when I smelled the flesh burning." She gave me a glance from beneath the continuous eyebrow that made her look as if she were perpetually scowling. "It smelled just like goat. Only different."

"But how—?" I exclaimed, unable to finish the question. I didn't credit her for a minute. No one, not even the fakirs of India (and they are fakers), could hold on to a burning coal long enough to suffer third-degree burns.

"He's not normal, Doctor. He doesn't feel pain the way others do. "Look here"—and she lifted the child's right leg as if it weren't even attached to him, rolling up his miniature trousers to show me a dark raised scar the size of an adult's spread hand—"do you see this? This is where that filthy pit bull Isabel Briceño keeps came through the fence and bit him, and we've gone to the lawyer over it too, believe me, but he never cried out or said a word. The dog had him down in the dirt, chewing on him like he was a bone, and if my husband hadn't gone out into the yard to throw his shaving water on the rosebushes I think he would have been torn to pieces."

She looked out the window a moment, as if to collect herself. The boy stared at me out of his unblinking eyes. Very slowly, as if he were in some perverse way proud of what had befallen him or of how stoically he'd endured, he began to smile, and I couldn't help thinking he'd make a first-rate soldier in whatever war we were prosecuting when he grew up.

"And do you see this?" she went on, tracing her index finger over the boy's lips. "These scars here?" I saw a tracery of pale jagged lines radiating out from his mouth. "This is where he's bitten himself—bitten himself without knowing it."

"Señora Funes," I said in my most caustic tone, the tone I reserve for inebriates with swollen livers and smokers who cough up blood while lighting yet another cigarette, and right there in my office, no less, "I don't think you're telling me the whole truth here. This boy has been abused. I've never seen a more egregious case. You should be ashamed of yourself. Worse: you should be reported to the authorities."

She rolled her eyes. The boy sat like a mannequin in her lap, as if he were made of wood. "You don't understand: he doesn't feel pain. Nothing.

Go ahead. Prick him with your needle—you can push it right through his arm and he wouldn't know the difference."

Angry now—what sort of dupe did she take me for?—I went straight to the cabinet, removed a disposable syringe, prepared an injection (a half-dose of the B_{12} I keep on hand for the elderly and anemic) and dabbed a spot on his stick of an arm with alcohol. They both watched indifferently as the needle slid in. The boy never flinched. Never gave any indication that anything was happening at all. But that proved nothing. One child out of a hundred would steel himself when I presented the needle (though the other ninety-nine would shriek as if their fingernails were being pulled out, one by one).

"Do you see?" she said.

"I see nothing," I replied. "He didn't flinch, that's all. Many children—some, anyway—are real little soldiers about their injections." I hovered over him, looking into his face. "You're a real little solider, aren't you, Dámaso?" I said.

From the mother, in a weary voice: "We call him Sin Dolor, Doctor. That's his nickname. That's what his father calls him when he misbehaves, because no amount of spanking or pinching or twisting his arm will even begin to touch him. Sin Dolor, Doctor. The Painless One."

The next time I saw him he must have been seven or eight, I don't really recall exactly, but he'd grown into a reedy, solemn boy with great, devouring eyes and his father's Indian hair, still as thin as a puppet and still looking anemic. This time the father brought him in, carrying the boy in his arms. My first thought was worms, and I made a mental note to dose him before he left, but then it occurred to me that it must only have been his mother's cooking and I dismissed the idea. A stool sample would do. But of course we'd need to draw blood to assess hemoglobin levels—if the parents were willing, that is. Both of them were notoriously tightfisted and I rarely saw any of the Funes clan in my offices unless something were seriously amiss.

"What seems to be the problem?" I asked, rising to take Francisco Funes' hand in my own.

With a grunt, he bent down to set the boy on his feet. "Go ahead, Dámaso," he said, "walk for the doctor."

I noticed that the boy stood unevenly, favoring his right leg. He glanced first at his father, then at me, dipped his shoulder in resignation and walked to the door and back, limping as if he'd dislocated his knee. He looked up with a smile. "I think something's wrong with my leg," he said in a voice as reduced and apologetic as a confessor's.

I cupped him beneath his arms and swung him up onto the examining table, giving the father a look—if this wasn't child abuse, then what was?—and asked, "Did you have an accident?"

His father answered for him. "He's broken his leg, can't you see that? Jumping from the roof of the shed when he should know better—" Francisco Funes was a big man, powerfully built, with a low but penetrating voice, and he leveled a look of wrath on his son, as if to say that the truth of the matter was evident and the boy would have a whipping when he got home, broken leg or no.

I ignored him. "Can you stretch out here for me on your back?" I said to the boy, patting the examining table. The boy complied, lifting both his legs to the table without apparent effort, and the first thing I noticed were the scars there, a constellation of burns and slashes uncountable running from his ankles to his thighs, and I felt the outrage come up in me all over again. Abuse! The indictment flared in my head. I was about to call for Elvira to come in and evict the father from my offices so that I could treat the son—and quiz him too—when I ran my hand over the boy's left shin and discovered the swelling there. He did indeed have a broken leg—a fractured tibia, from the feel of it. "Does this hurt?" I asked, putting pressure on the spot.

The boy shook his head.

"Nothing hurts him," the father put in. He was hovering over me, looking impatient, expecting to be cheated and wanting only to extract the pesos from his wallet as if his son's injury were a sort of tax and then get on with the rest of his life.

"We'll need X-rays," I said.

"No X-rays," he growled. "I knew I should have taken him to the *curandero*, I knew it. Just set the damn bone and get it over with."

I felt the boy's gaze on me. He was absolutely calm, his eyes like the motionless pools of the rill that brought the water down out of the mountains and into the cistern behind our new cottage at the seashore. For the first time it occurred to me that something extraordinary was going on here, a kind of medical miracle: the boy had fractured his tibia and should have been writhing on the table and crying out with the pain of it, but he looked as if there were nothing at all the matter, as if he'd come into the friendly avuncular doctor's office just to have a look around at the skeleton on its stand and the framed diplomas on the whitewashed walls and to bask in the metallic glow of the equipment Elvira polished every morning before the patients started lining up outside the door.

It hit me like a thunderclap: he'd walked on a broken leg. Walked on it and didn't know the difference but for the fact that he was somehow mysteriously limping. I couldn't help myself. I gripped his leg to feel the alignment of the bone at the site of the fracture. "Does this hurt?" I asked. I felt the bone slip into place. The light outside the window faded and then came up again as an unseen cloud passed overhead. "This?" I asked. "This?"

After that day, after I'd set and splinted the bone, put the boy in a cast and lent him a couple of old mismatched crutches before going out to the anteroom and telling Francisco Funes to forget the bill—"Free of charge," I said—I felt my life expand. I realized that I was staring a miracle in the face, and who could blame me for wanting to change the course of my life, to make my mark as one of the giants of the profession to be studied and revered down through the ages instead of fading away into the terminal ennui of a small-town practice, of the doves on the wire, the *caldereta* in the pot and the cottage at the seaside? The fact was that Dámaso Funes must have harbored a mutation in his genes, a positive mutation, superior, progressive, nothing at all like the ones that had given us the faceless infant and all the other horrors that paraded through the door of the clinic day in and day out. If that mutation could be isolated—if the genetic sequence could be discovered—then the boon for our poor suffering species would be immeasurable. Imagine a pain-free old age. Painless childbirth, surgery, dentistry. Imagine Elvira's patients in the oncology ward, racing round in their wheelchairs, grinning and joking to the last. What freedom! What joy! What an insuperable coup over the afflictions that twist and maim us and haunt us to the grave!

I began to frequent the Funes stall in the hour before siesta, hoping to catch a glimpse of the boy, to befriend him, take him into my confidence, perhaps even have him move into the house and take the place of the child Elvira and I had never had because of the grinding sadness of the world. I tried to be casual. *"Buenas tardes,"* I would say in my heartiest voice as Mercedes Funes raised her careworn face from the grill. "How are you? And how are those mouthwatering tacos? Yes, yes, I'll take two. Make it three." I even counterfeited eating them, though it was only a nibble and only of the tortilla itself, while whole legions of my patients past and present lined up for their foil-wrapped offerings. Two months must have gone by in this way before I caught sight of Dámaso. I ordered, stepped aside, and there he was, standing isolated behind the grill, even as his younger siblings—there were three new additions to the clan—scrabbled over their toys in the dirt.

His eyes brightened when he saw me and I suppose I said something obvious like "I see that leg has healed up well. Still no pain, eh?"

He was polite, well-bred. He came out from behind the stall and took my hand in a formal way. "I'm fine," he said, and paused. "But for this." He lifted his dirty T-shirt (imprinted with the logo of some North American pop band, three sneering faces and a corona of ragged hair) and showed me an open wound the size of a fried egg. Another burn.

"Ooh," I exclaimed, wincing. "Would you like to come back to the office and I'll treat that for you?" He just looked at me. The moment hovered. The smoke rose from the grill. "Gratis?"

He shrugged. It didn't matter to him one way or the other—he must have felt himself immortal, as all children do until they become sufficiently acquainted with death and all the miseries that precede and attend it, but of course he was subject to infection, loss of digits, limbs, the sloughing of the flesh and corruption of the internal organs, just like anyone else. Though he couldn't feel any of it. Mercifully. He shrugged again. Looked to his mother, who was shifting chunks of goat around the cheap screen over the brazier as the customers called out their orders. "I need to help my mother," he said. I was losing him.

It was then that I hit on a stratagem, the sort of thing that comes on a synaptical flutter like the beating of internal wings: "Do you want to see my scorpions?"

I watched his face change, the image of a foreshortened arachnid with its claws and pendent stinger rising miasmic before him. He gave a quick glance to where his mother was making change for Señora Padilla, an enormous woman of well over three hundred pounds whom I've treated for hypertension, adult-onset diabetes and a virulent genital rash no standard medication seemed able to eradicate, and then he ducked behind the brazier, only to emerge a moment later just up the street from where I was standing. He signaled impatiently with his right hand and I gave up the ruse of lunching on his mother's wares, turned my back on the stall and fell into step with him.

"I keep one in a jar," he said, and it took me a moment to realize he was talking of scorpions. "A brown one."

"Probably *Vaejovis spinigeris,* very common in these parts. Does it show dark stripes on its tail?"

He nodded in a vague way, which led me to believe he hadn't looked all that closely. It was a scorpion—that was enough for him. "How many do you have?" he asked, striding along without the slightest suggestion of a limp.

I should say, incidentally, that I'm an amateur entomologist—or, more specifically, arachnologist—and that scorpions are my specialty. I collect them in the way a lepidopterist collects butterflies, though my specimens are very much alive. In those days, I kept them in terraria in the back room of the clinic, where they clung contentedly to the undersides of the rocks and pottery shards I'd arranged there for their benefit.

"Oh, I don't know," I said. We were just then passing a group of ur-chins goggling at us from an alleyway, and they all, as one, called out his name—and not in mockery or play, but reverentially, in homage. He was, I was soon to discover, a kind of hero amongst them.

"Ten?" he guessed. He was wearing sandals. His feet shone in the glare of the sunlight, kicking out ahead of him on the paving stones. It was very hot.

"Oh, a hundred or more, I'd say. Of some twenty-six species." And then, slyly: "If you have the time, I'll show you them all."

Of course, I insisted on first treating the burn as a kind of quid pro quo. It wouldn't do to have him dying of a bacterial infection, or of anything else for that matter—for humanitarian reasons certainly, but also with re-spect to the treasure he was carrying for all of mankind. His excitement was palpable as I led him into the moist, dim back room, with its concrete floor and its smell of turned earth and vinegar. The first specimen I showed him—*Hadrurus arizonensis pallidus,* the giant desert scorpion, some five inches long and nearly indistinguishable in color from the sand it rested on—was clutching a cricket in its pedipalps as I lifted the screen at the top of the terrarium. "This is the largest scorpion in North America," I told him, "though its venom is rather weak compared to what *Centruroides ex-ilicauda* delivers. The bark scorpion, that is. They live around here too and they can be very dangerous."

All he said was, "I want to see the poison one."

I had several specimens in a terrarium set against the back wall and I shut down the lights, pulled the shades and used a black light to show him how they glowed with their own natural phosphorescence. As soon as I flicked on the black light and he'd had a moment to distinguish the crea-tures' forms as they crawled round their home, he let out a whoop of de-light and insisted on shining it in each of the terraria in succession until he finally led me back to *Centruroides.* "Would they sting me?" he asked. "If I reached in, I mean?"

I shrugged. "They might. But they're shy creatures and like most ani-mals want to avoid any sort of confrontation—and they don't want to waste their venom. You know, it takes a great deal of caloric resources to make the toxin—they need it for their prey. So they can eat."

He turned his face to me in the dark, the glow of the black light erasing his features and lending a strange blue cast to his eyes. "Would I die?" he asked.

I didn't like where this was leading—and I'm sure you've already guessed what was to come, the boy who feels no pain and the creatures who come so well equipped to inflict it—and so I played up the danger. "If one were to sting you, you might become ill, might vomit, might even froth at the mouth. You know what that is, frothing?"

He shook his head.

"Well, no matter. The fact is, a sting of this species might kill someone very susceptible, an infant maybe, a very old person, but probably not a boy of your age, though it would make you very, very sick—"

"Would it kill my grandfather?"

I pictured the grandfather. I'd seen him dozing behind the stall on occasion, an aggregation of bones and skin lesions who must have been in his nineties. "Yes," I said, "it's possible—if he was unlucky enough to step on one on his way to the bathroom one night . . ."

It was then that the bell sounded in the clinic, though we were closed, except for emergencies, during the afternoon. I called for Elvira, but she must have been taking her lunch in the garden or dozing in the apartment upstairs. "Come with me," I said to the boy and I led him out of the back room, through the examining room and into the office, where I found one of the men of the neighborhood, Dagoberto Domínguez, standing at the counter, his left hand wrapped in a bloody rag and a small slick gobbet of meat, which proved to be the tip of his left index finger, clutched in the other. I forgot all about Dámaso.

When I'd finished bandaging Señor Domínguez's wound and sent him off in a taxi to the hospital with the tip of his finger packed in ice, I noticed that the door to the back room stood open. There, in the dark, with the black light glowing in its lunar way, stood little Dámaso, his shirt fluorescing with the forms of my scorpions—half a dozen at least—as they climbed across his back and up and down the avenues of his arms. I didn't say a word. Didn't move. Just watched as he casually raised a hand to his neck where my *Hadrurus*—the giant—had just emerged from the collar of his shirt, and I watched as it stung him, repeatedly, while he held it between two fingers and then tenderly eased it back into its cage.

Was I irresponsible? Had I somehow, in the back of my mind, hoped for just such an outcome—as a kind of perverse experiment? Perhaps so. Perhaps there was that part of me that couldn't help collapsing the boundary between detachment and sadism, but then did the term even apply? How could one be sadistic if the victim felt nothing? At any rate, from that day on, even as I wrote up my observations and sent them off to Boise State University, where Jerry Lemongello, one of the world's premier geneticists and an old friend from my days at medical school in Guadalajara, had his state-of-the-art research lab, Dámaso became my constant companion. He seemed to revel in the attention Elvira and I gave him, coming as he did from a large and poor family, and over the course of time he began to dine with us frequently, and even, on occasion, to spend the night on a cot in the guest bedroom. I taught him everything I knew about scorpions and their tarantula cousins too and began to instruct him in the natural sciences in general and medicine in particular, a subject for which he seemed to have a special affinity. In return he did odd jobs about the place, sweeping and mopping the floors of the clinic, seeing that the scorpions had sufficient crickets to dine on and the parrot its seed and water and bits of fruit.

In the meantime, Jerry Lemongello pressed for a DNA sample and I took some scrapings from inside the boy's mouth (which had been burned many times over—while he could distinguish hot and cold, he had no way of registering what was *too* hot or *too* cold) and continued my own dilatory experiments, simple things like reflex tests, pinpricks to various parts of the anatomy, even tickling (to which he proved susceptible). One afternoon—and I regret this still—I casually remarked to him that the paper wasps that had chosen to build a massive nest just under the eaves of the clinic had become a real nuisance. They were strafing my patients as they ducked through the screen door and had twice stung poor Señora Padilla in a very tender spot when she came in for her medication. I sighed and wished aloud that someone would do something about it.

When I glanced out the window fifteen minutes later, there he was, perched on a ladder and shredding the nest with his bare hands while the wasps swarmed him in a roiling black cloud. I should have interfered. Should have stopped him. But I didn't. I simply watched as he methodically crushed the combs full of pupae underfoot and slapped the adults dead as they futilely stung him. I treated the stings, of course—each of them an angry swollen red welt—and cautioned him against ever doing anything so foolish again, lecturing him on the nervous system and the efficacy of pain as a warning signal that something is amiss in the body. I told him of the lepers whose fingers and toes abrade away to nothing because of the loss of feeling in the extremities, but he didn't seem to understand what I was driving at. "You mean pain is good?" he asked.

"Well, no," I said. "Pain is bad, of course, and what we do in my profession is try to combat it so people can go on with their lives and be productive and so on . . ."

"My mother has pain," he said, running a finger over the bumps on his forearm as if they were nothing more than a novelty. "In her back. From bending over the grill all day, she says."

"Yes," I said—she suffered from a herniated disk—"I know."

He was quiet a moment. "Will she die?"

I told him that everyone would die. But not today and not from back pain.

A slow smile bloomed on his lips. "Then may I stay for dinner?"

It was shortly after this that the father came in again and this time he came alone, and whether his visit had anything to do with the wasp adventure or not, I can't say. But he was adamant in his demands, almost rude. "I don't know what you're doing with my boy—or what you think you're doing—but I want him back."

I was sitting at my desk. It was eleven in the morning and beyond the window the hummingbirds were suspended over the roseate flowers of the trumpet vine as if sculpted out of air. Clouds bunched on the horizon. The sun was like butter. Elvira was across the room, at her own desk, typing into the new computer while the radio played so softly I could distinguish it only as a current in the background. The man refused to take a seat.

"Your son has a great gift," I said after a moment. And though I'm an agnostic with regard to the question of God and a supernatural Jesus, I employed a religious image to reinforce the statement, thinking it might move a man like Francisco Funes, imbued as he was with the impoverished piety of his class: "He can redeem mankind—redeem us from all the pain of the ages. I only want to help."

"Bullshit," he snarled, and Elvira looked up from her typing, dipping her head to see over her glasses, which slipped down the incline of her nose.

"It's the truth," I said.

"Bullshit," he repeated, and I reflected on how unoriginal he was, how limited and ignorant and borne down under the weight of the superstition and greed that afflicts all the suffering hordes like him. "He's *my* son," he said, his voice touching bottom, "not yours. And if I ever catch him here again, I'll give him such a whipping—" He caught himself even as I flashed my bitterest smile. "You don't know, but I have my ways. And if I can't beat him, I can beat you, Doctor, with all respect. And you'll feel it like any other man."

"Are you threatening me? Elvira"—I turned to her—"take note."

"You bet your ass I am," he said.

And then, quite simply, the boy disappeared. He didn't come into the clinic the following morning or the morning after that. I asked Elvira about it and she shrugged as if to say, "It's just as well." But it wasn't. I found that I missed having him around, and not simply for selfish reasons (Jerry Lemongello had written to say that the DNA sample was unusable

and to implore me to take another), but because I'd developed a genuine
affection for him. I enjoyed explaining things to him, lifting him up out
of the stew of misinformation and illiteracy into which he'd been born,
and if I saw him as following in my footsteps as a naturalist or even a
physician, I really didn't think I was deluding myself. He was bright,
quick-witted, with a ready apprehension of the things around him and an
ability to observe closely, so that, for instance, when I placed a crab, a
scorpion and a spider on a tray before him he was able instantly to discern
the relationship between them and apply the correct family, genus and
species names I'd taught him. And all this at nine years of age.

On the third morning, when there was still no sign of him, I went to
the Funes stall in the marketplace, hoping to find him there. It was early
yet and Mercedes Funes was just laying the kindling on the brazier while
half a dozen slabs of freshly (or at least recently) slaughtered goat hung
from a rack behind her (coated, I might add, in flies). I called out a greeting and began, in a circuitous way, to ask about her health, the weather
and the quality of her goat, when at some point she winced with pain and
put her hand to her back, slowly straightening up to shoot me what I can
only call a hostile look. "He's gone off to live with his grandmother," she
said. "In Guadalajara."

And that was that. No matter how hard I pressed, Mercedes Funes
would say no more, nor would her donkey of a husband, and when they
had the odd medical emergency they went all the way to the other side of
the village to the clinic of my rival, Dr. Octavio Díaz, whom I detest heart-
ily, though that's another story. Suffice to say that some years went by
before I saw Dámaso again, though I heard the rumors—we all did—that
his father was forcing him to travel from town to town like a freak in a
sideshow, shamelessly exploiting his gift for the benefit of every gaping
rube with a few pesos in his pocket. It was a pity. It was criminal. But there
was nothing that I or Jerry Lemongello or all the regents of Boise State
University could do about it. He was gone and we remained.

Another generation of doves came to sit on the wires, Elvira put on
weight around the middle and in the hollow beneath her chin, and as I
shaved each morning I watched the inevitable progress of the white hairs

as they crept up along the slope of my jowls and into my sideburns and finally colonized the crown of my head. I got up from bed, ran the water in the sink and saw a stranger staring back at me in the mirror, an old man with a blunted look in his reconstituted eyes. I diagnosed measles and mumps and gonorrhea, kneaded the flesh of the infirm, plied oto-scope, syringe and tongue depressor as if the whole business were some rarefied form of punishment in a Sophoclean drama. And then one after-noon, coming back from the pet shop with a plastic sack of crickets for my brood, I turned a corner and there he was.

A crowd of perhaps forty or fifty people had gathered on the sidewalk outside the Gómez bakery, shifting from foot to foot in the aspiring heat. They seemed entranced—none of them so much as glanced at me as I worked my way to the front, wondering what it was all about. When I spotted Francisco Funes, the blood rushed to my face. He was standing to one side of a makeshift stage—half a dozen stacked wooden pallets— gazing out on the crowd with a calculating look, as if he were already counting up his gains, and on the stage itself, Dámaso, shirtless, shoeless, dressed only in a pair of clinging shorts that did little to hide any part of his anatomy, was heating the blade of a pearl-handled knife over a char-coal brazier till it glowed red. He was stuck all over like a kind of hedge-hog with perhaps twenty of those stainless steel skewers people use for making shish kebab, including one that projected through both his cheeks, and I watched in morbid fascination as he lifted the knife from the brazier and laid the blade flat against the back of his hand so that you could hear the sizzling of the flesh. A gasp went up from the crowd. A woman beside me fainted into the arms of her husband. I did nothing. I only watched as Dámaso, his body a patchwork of scars, found a pinch of skin over his breastbone and thrust the knife through it.

I wanted to cry out the shame of it, but I held myself in check. At the climactic moment I turned and faded away into the crowd, waiting my chance. The boy—he was an adolescent now, thirteen or fourteen, I cal-culated—performed other feats of senseless torture I won't name here, and then the hat went round, the pesos were collected, and father and son headed off in the direction of their house. I followed at a discreet distance, the crickets rasping against the sides of the bag. I watched the father enter the house—it was grander now, with several new rooms already framed and awaiting the roofer's tar paper and tiles—as the boy went to a yellow plastic cooler propped up against the front steps, extracted a bottle of Coca-Cola and lowered himself into the battered armchair on the porch as if he were a hundred and fifty years old.

I waited a moment, till he'd finished his poor reward and set the bottle down between his feet, and then I strolled casually past the house as if I just happened to be in the neighborhood. When I drew even with him— when I was sure he'd seen me—I stopped in my tracks and gave him an elaborate look of surprise, a double take, as it were. "Dámaso?" I exclaimed. "Can it really be you?"

I saw something light up in his eyes, but only the eyes—he seemed incapable of forming a smile with his lips. In the next moment he was out of the chair and striding across the yard to me, holding out his hand in greeting. "Doctor," he said, and I saw the discoloration of the lips, the twin pinpoints of dried blood on either cheek amidst a battlefield of annealed scars, and I couldn't have felt more shock and pity if he were indeed my own son.

"It's been a long time," I said.

"Yes," he agreed.

My mind was racing. All I could think of was how to get him out of there before Francisco Funes stepped through the door. "Would you like to come over to the clinic with me—for dinner? For old times' sake? Elvira's making an eggplant lasagna tonight, with a nice crisp salad and fried artichokes, and look"—I held up the bag of crickets and gave it a shake—"we can feed the scorpions. Did you know that I've got one nearly twice as big as *Hadrurus*—an African variety? Oh, it's a beauty, a real beauty—"

And there it was, the glance over the shoulder, the very same gesture he'd produced that day at the stall when he was just a child, and in the next moment we were off, side by side, and the house was behind us. He seemed to walk more deliberately than he had in the past, as if the years had weighed on him in some unfathomable way (or fathomable, absolutely fathomable, right down to the corrosive depths of his father's heart), and I slowed my pace to accommodate him, worrying over the thought that he'd done some irreparable damage to muscle, ligament, cartilage, even to the nervous system itself. We passed the slaughterhouse where his mother's first cousin, Refugio, sacrificed goats for the good of the family business, continued through the desiccated, lizard-haunted remains of what the city fathers had once intended as a park, and on up the long sloping hill that separates our village by class, income and, not least, education.

The holy aroma of Elvira's lasagna bathed the entire block as we turned the corner to the clinic. We'd been talking of inconsequential things, my practice, the parrot—yes, she was well, thank you—the gossip of the village, the weather, but nothing of his life, his travels, his feelings. It wasn't till I'd got him in the back room under the black light, with a glass of iced and sweetened tea in his hand and a plate of *dulces* in his lap, that he began to open up to me. "Dámaso," I said at one point, the scorpions glowing like apparitions in the vestibules of their cages, "you don't seem to be in very high spirits—tell me, what's the matter? Is it—your travels?"

In the dark, with the vinegary odor of the arachnids in our nostrils and the promise of Elvira's cuisine wafting in the wings, he carefully set down his glass and brushed the crumbs from his lap before looking up at me. "Yes," he said softly. And then with more emphasis, "*Yes.*"

I was silent a moment. Out of the corner of my eye I saw my *Hadrurus* probing the boundaries of its cage. I waited for him to go on.

"I have no friends, Doctor, not a single one. Even my brothers and sisters look at me like I'm a stranger. And the boys all over the district, in the smallest towns, they try to imitate me." His voice was strained, the tones of the adult, of his father, at war with the cracked breathy piping of a child. "They do what I do. And it hurts them."

"You don't have to do this anymore, Dámaso." I felt the heat of my own emotions. "It's wrong, deeply wrong, can't you see that?"

He shrugged. "I have no choice. I owe it to my family. To my mother."

"No," I said, "you owe them nothing. Or not that. Not your own self, your own body, your heart—"

"She brought me into the world."

Absurdly, I said, "So did I."

There was a silence. After a moment, I went on, "You've been given a great gift, Dámaso, and I can help you with it—you can live here, with us, with Elvira and me, and never have to go out on the street and, and *damage* yourself again, because what your father is doing is evil, Dámaso, *evil*, and there's no other word for it."

He raised a wounded hand and let it fall again. "My family comes first," he said. "They'll always come first. I know my duty. But what they'll never understand, what you don't understand, is that I do hurt, I do feel it, I *do*." And he lifted that same hand and tapped his breastbone, right over the place where his heart constricted and dilated and shot the blood through his veins. "Here," he said. "Here's where I hurt."

He was dead a week later.

I didn't even hear of it till he was already in the ground and Jerry Lemongello buckled in for the long flight down from Boise with the hope of collecting the DNA sample himself, too late now, Mercedes Funes inhaling smoke and tears and pinning one hopeless hand to her lower back as she bent over the grill while her husband wandered the streets in a dirty *guayabera*, as drunk as any derelict. They say the boy was showing off for the urchins who followed him around as if he were some sort of divinity, the kind of boys who thrive on pain, who live to inflict and extract it as if it could be measured and held, as if it were precious, the kind of boys who carve hieroglyphs into their skin with razor blades and call it fashion. It was a three-story building. "Jump!" they shouted. "Sin Dolor! Sin Dolor!" He jumped, and he never felt a thing.

But what I wonder—and God, if He exists, have mercy on Francisco Funes and the mother too—is if he really knew what he was doing, if it was a matter not so much of bravado but of grief. We will never know. And we will never see another like him, though Jerry Lemongello tells me he's heard of a boy in Pakistan with the same mutation, another boy who stands in the town square and mutilates himself to hear the gasps and the applause and gather up the money at his feet.

Within a year, Dámaso was forgotten. His family's house had burned to ashes around the remains of a kerosene heater, the goats died and the brazier flared without him, and I closed up the clinic and moved permanently, with Elvira and her parrot, to our cottage by the sea. I pass my days now in the sunshine, tending our modest garden, walking the sugar-white beach to see what the tide has brought in. I no longer practice medicine, but of course I'm known here as *El Estimado Doctor,* and on occasion, in an emergency, a patient will show up on my doorstep. Just the other day a little girl of three or four came in, swaddled in her mother's arms. She'd been playing in the tide pools down by the lava cliffs that rise up out of the sand like dense distant loaves and had stepped on a sea urchin. One of the long black spikes the animal uses for defense had broken off under the child's weight and embedded itself in the sole of her foot.

I soothed her as best I could, speaking softly to distract her, speaking nonsense really—all that matters in such circumstances is the intonation. I murmured. The sea murmured along the shore. As delicately as I could, I held her miniature heel in my hand, took hold of the slick black fragment with the grip of my forceps and pulled it cleanly from the flesh, and I have to tell you, that little girl shrieked till the very glass in the windows rattled, shrieked as if there were no other pain in the world.

BULLETPROOF

The Sticker

I don't have any children—I'm not even married, not anymore—but last month, though I was fried from my commute and looking forward to nothing more complicated than the bar, the TV and the microwave dinner, in that order, I made a point of attending the Thursday-evening meeting of the Smithstown School Board. On an empty stomach. Sans alcohol. Why? Because of Melanie Albert's ninth-grade biology textbook— or, actually, the sticker affixed to the cover of it. This is the book with the close-up of the swallowtail butterfly against a field of pure environmental green, standard issue, used in ten thousand schools across the land, and it came to my attention when her father, Dave, and I were unwinding after work at the Granite Grill a week earlier.

The Granite is our local watering hole, and it doesn't have much to recommend it, beyond the fact that it's there. Its virtues reside mainly in what it doesn't offer, I suppose—no waiters wrestling with their consciences, no chef striving to demonstrate his ability to fuse the Ethiopian and Korean culinary traditions, no music other than the hits of the eighties, piped in through a service that plumbs the deep cuts so that you get to hear The Clash doing "Wrong 'Em Boyo" and David Byrne's "Swamp," from his days with Talking Heads, instead of the same unvarying eternal crap you get on the radio. And it's dimly lighted. Very dimly lighted. All you see, really, beyond the shifting colors of the TV, is the soft backlit glow of the bottles on display behind the bar dissolving into a hundred soothing glints of gold and copper. It's relaxing—so relaxing I've found myself drifting off to dreamland right there in the grip of my barstool, one hand clenched round the stem of the glass, the other bracing up a chin as heavy as all the slag heaps of the earth combined. You could say it's my second home. Or maybe my first.

We'd just settled into our stools, my right hand going instinctively to the bowl of artificial bar snacks while the Mets careened round the bases on the wide-screen TV and Rick, the bartender, stirred and strained my first Sidecar of the evening, when I became aware of Dave, off to my left, digging something out of his briefcase. There was a thump beside me and I turned my head. "What's that?" I said. The title, in fluorescent orange, leapt out at me: *An Introduction to Biology.* "A little light reading?"

Dave—he was my age, forty-three, and he didn't bother to dye his hair or counteract the wrinkles eroding his forehead and chewing away at the corners of his eyes because he accepted who he was and he had no qualms about letting the world in on it—just stared at me. He'd given up tennis. Given up poker. And when I called him on a Saturday morning to go out for a hike or a spin up the river in my speedboat with the twin Merc 575s that'll shear the hair right off your head, he was always busy.

"What?" I said.

He tapped the cover of the book. "Don't you notice anything?"

My drink had come, iced, sugared, as necessary as oxygen. The Mets scored again. I took a sip.

"The sticker," he said. "Don't you see the sticker?"

Prodded, I took notice of it, a lemon-yellow circle the size of a silver dollar, inside of which was a disclaimer printed in sober black letters. *The theory of evolution as put forth in this text,* it read, *is just that, a theory, and should not be confused with fact.* "Yeah," I said. "So?"

He clenched his jaw. Gave me a long hard look. "Don't you know what this means?"

I thought about that a moment, turning the book over in one hand before setting it back down on the bar. I worked at the sticker with my thumbnail. It was immovable, as if it had been fused to the cover using a revolutionary new process. "Sucker's really on there," I said. I gave him a grin. "You wouldn't happen to have any sandpaper on you, would you?"

"It's not fucking funny, Cal. You can laugh—you haven't got a kid in school. But if you believe in anything, if you believe in what's happening

to this country, what's happening right here in our own community—"
He broke off, so wrought up he couldn't go on. His face was flushed. He
picked up his beer and set it down again.

"You're talking about the fact that we're living in a theocracy now,
right? A theocracy at war with another theocracy?"

"Why do you always have to make a joke out of everything?"

"Bible-thumpers," I said, but without conviction. I was in a bar. It had
been a long day. I wanted to talk about nothing, sports, women, the subtle
manipulations of the commercials for beer, cars, Palm Pilots. I didn't
want to delve beneath the surface. It was too cold down there, too dark
and claustrophobic. "You can't be serious," I said finally, giving ground.
"Here? Thirty-five miles up the river from Manhattan?"

He was nodding, his eyes fixed on mine. "I don't pay that much attention, I guess," he said finally. "Or Katie either. I don't even think we voted
in the last school board election . . . I mean, it's our own fault. It was just
a slate of names, you know. Like the judges. Does anybody ever know the
slightest thing about any of the judges on the ballot that comes round
every November? Or the town supervisors? Shit. You'd have to devote
your life to it, know what I'm saying?"

Feelings were stirring in me—anger, resentment, helplessness. My
drink had gone warm. I said the only thing I could think to say: "So what
are you going to do?"

Jesus, and Where He Resides

It was raining that Thursday night, though the air was warm still, a last
breath of summer before September gave way to October and the days
began to wind down till the leaves littered the streets and the boat would
have to come out of the water. I had a little trouble finding the place where
they were holding the meeting—they've built a whole city's worth of new
buildings since I went to school, the population ratcheting up relentlessly
even around here where there are zero jobs to be had and all everybody
talks about is preserving the semi-rural feel, as if we were all dipping our

own candles and greasing the wheels of our buggies. Which is another reason why I couldn't find the place. It's dark. The streetlights give out within a block of the junction of the state road and Main Street, and the big old black-barked oaks and elms everybody seems to love soak up the light till the roads might as well be tunnels in a coal mine. And I admit it: my eyes aren't what they used to be. I've put off getting glasses because of the kind of statement they make—weakness, that is—and I've heard that once you begin to rely on them you can never go back to the naked eye, that's it, and here's your crutch forever. The next thing is reading glasses, and then you're pottering around with those pathetic lanyards looped round your neck, murmuring, *Has anybody seen my glasses?*

Anyway, it was the cars that clued me. There must have been a hundred or more of them jamming every space in the parking lot behind the new elementary school, with the overflow parked on a lawn that was just a wet black void sucked out of the shadows. I pulled up within inches of the last car squeezed in on the grass—a cobalt-blue Suburban, humped and mountainous—and felt the wheels give ever so slightly before I shut down the ignition, figuring I'd worry about it later. I pulled up the collar of my coat and hurried along the walk toward the lights glowing in the distance.

The auditorium was packed, standing room only, and everybody looked angry—from the six school board members seated behind a collapsible table up onstage to the reporter from the local paper and the concerned parents and students warming the chairs and lining the walls like extras on a movie set. I caught a nostalgic whiff of floor wax, finger paint and formaldehyde, but it was short-lived, overwhelmed by the working odor of all that crush of humanity. The fact that everybody was wet to one degree or another didn't help matters, the women's hair hanging limp, the men's jackets clinging at the shoulders and under the arms, umbrellas drooling, smears of wet black mud striping the linoleum underfoot. I could smell myself—what I was adding to the mix—in the bad cheese of my underarms and the sweet reek of mango-pineapple rising from the dissolved gel in my hair. It was very hot.

The door closed softly behind me and I found myself squeezed in between a gaunt leathery woman with a starburst of shellacked hair and a pock-faced man who looked as if he'd had a very bad day made worse by the dawning awareness that he was going to have to stand here amidst all these people, in this stink and this heat, till the last word was spoken and the doors opened to deliver him back out into the rain. I hunched my shoulders to make room and let my eyes roam over the crowd in the hope of spotting Dave and his wife. Not that it would matter—even if they'd saved a seat for me I couldn't have got to them. But still, it gave me the smallest uptick of satisfaction to see them sitting there in the third row left, Katie's head shrouded in a black scarf, as if she were attending a funeral, and Dave's bald spot glowing like a poached egg in the graying nest of his hair.

What can I say? This was the most normal scene in the world, a scene replicated through the generations and across the continent, the flag drooping to one side of the podium, red velvet curtains disclosing the stage beyond, student art buckling away from the freshly painted walls while parents, teachers and students gathered in a civic forum to weigh all the pedagogical nuances of the curriculum. Standing there, the fluorescent lights glaring in my eyes and the steam of my fellow humans rising round me, I was plunged into a deep pool of nostalgia, thinking of my own parents, now dead, my own teachers, mostly dead, and myself, very much alive and well though in need of a drink. On some level it was strangely moving. I shifted my feet. Looked to the tiles of the ceiling as a way of neutering my emotions. It was then that I felt the door open behind me—a cold draft, the sizzle of rain—as a newcomer even tardier than I slipped in to join the gathering. A female. Young, pretty, with an overload of perfume. I gave her a glance as she edged in beside me. "Sorry," she whispered. "No problem," I said under my breath, and because I felt awkward and didn't want to stare, I turned my attention back to the stage.

There was a general coughing and rustling, and then one of the school board members—a sour-looking woman with reading glasses dangling from her throat—leaned forward and reached for the microphone perched at the edge of the table. There was a thump followed by the hiss of static as she wrestled the thing away from its stand, and then her amplified voice came at us as if it had been there all along, just under the surface: "And since that concludes the formal business for the evening, we're prepared to take your questions and comments at this point. One person at a time, please, and please come to the center aisle and use the microphone there so everybody can hear."

The first speaker—a man in his thirties, narrow eyes, narrow shoulders, a cheap sportcoat and a turquoise bola tie he must have worn in the hope somebody would think him hip—rose to a spatter of applause and a cascade of hoots from the students against the wall. "Ba-oom!" they chanted. "Ba-oom!" In an instant the mood had been transformed from nervous anticipation to a kind of ecstasy. "Ba-oom!"

He took hold of the microphone, glanced over his shoulder at the students behind him and snapped, "That'll be enough now, and I *mean* it," until the chant died away. Then he half-turned to the audience—and this was awkward because he was addressing the board up onstage as well—and began by introducing himself. "My name is Robert Tannenbaum"—a burst of *Ba-oom, Ba-oom!*—"and as many of you know, I teach ninth-grade biology at Smithstown High. And I have a statement here, signed not only by the entire science department—with one notable exception—but the majority of the rest of the faculty as well."

It was just a paragraph or so—he knew to keep it short—and as he read I couldn't help watching the faces of the board members. They were four men and two women, with the usual hairstyles and appurtenances, dressed in shades of brown and gray. They held themselves so stiffly their bones might have been fused, and they gazed out over the crowd while the teacher read his statement, their eyes barely registering him. The statement said simply that the faculty rejected the warning label the board had imposed on *An Introduction to Biology* as a violation of the Constitution's separation of church and state. "No reputable scientist anywhere in the world," the teacher went on, lifting his head to stare directly at the woman with the microphone, "subscribes to the notion of Intelligent Design—or let's call it by its real name, *Creationism*—as a viable scientific theory." And now he swung round on the crowd and spread his arms wide: "Get real, people. There's no debate here—just science and anti-science."

A few members of the audience began stamping their feet. The man beside me pulled his lips back and hissed.

"And that's the key phrase here, *scientific* theory—that is, testable, subject to peer review—and not a theological one, because that's exactly what this is, trying to force religion into the classroom—"

"Atheist!" a woman cried out, but the teacher waved her off. "No theory is bulletproof," he said, raising his voice now, "and we in the scientific community welcome debate—legitimate, scientific debate—and certainly theories mutate and evolve just like life on this planet, but—"

"Ba-oom, Ba-oom!"

There was a building ferment, a muted undercurrent of dissent and anger, the students chanting, people shouting out, until the sour-looking woman—the chairwoman, or was she the superintendent?—slammed the flat of her hand down on the table. "You'll all get your chance," she said, pinching her voice so that it shot splinters of steel through the microphone and out into the audience on a blast of feedback, "because everybody's got the right to an opinion." She glared down at the teacher, then lifted the reading glasses to the bridge of her nose and squinted at a sheet of paper she held up before her in an attempt to catch the light. "Thank you, Mr. Tannenbaum," she said. "We'll hear now from the Reverend Doctor Micah Stiller, of the First Baptist Church. Reverend Stiller?"

I was transfixed. I'd had no idea. Here I'd taken the train into the city every day and slogged on back every night, lingered at the Granite, hiked the trails and rocketed my way up the river to feel the wind in my face and impress whatever woman I'd managed to cajole along with me, and all the while this Manichean struggle had been going on right up the street. The reverend (beard, off-the-rack suit, big black shoes the size of andirons) invoked God, Jesus and the Bible as the ultimate authorities on matters of creation, and then a whole snaking line of people trooped up to the microphone one after another to voice their opinions on everything from the Great Flood to the age of the earth (*Ten thousand years! Are you out of your mind?* the biology teacher shouted as he slammed out the side exit to a contrapuntal chorus of cheers and jeers), to recent advancements in space travel and the unraveling of the human genome and how close it was to the chimpanzee's. And the garden slug's.

At one point, Dave even got into the act. He stood abruptly, his face frozen in outrage, stalked up to the microphone and blurted, "If there's no evolution, how come we all have to get a new flu shot each year?" Before anyone could answer him he was back in his seat and the chairwoman was clapping her hands for order. How much time had gone by I couldn't say—an hour, an hour at least. My left leg seemed to have gone dead at the hip. I breathed perfume. Stole a look at the woman beside me and saw that she had beautiful hands and feet and a smile that sought out my own. She was thirty-five or so, blond, no hat, no coat, in a blue flocked dress cut just above her knees, and we were complicit. Or so I thought.

Finally, when things seemed to be winding down, a girl dressed in a white sweater and plaid skirt, with her hair cut close and her arms folded palm to elbow, came down the aisle as if she were walking a bed of hot coals and took hold of the microphone. Her hands trembled as she tried to adjust it to her height, but she couldn't seem to loosen the catch. She stood there a moment, working at it, and when she saw that no one was going to help her, she went up on her tiptoes. "I just wanted to say," she breathed, clutching the mike as if it were a wall she was trying to climb, "that my name is Mary-Louise Mohler and I'm a freshman at Smithstown High—"

Hoots, catcalls, two raw-faced kids in baseball hats leering from the far side of the auditorium, adult faces swiveling angrily, the clatter of the rain beyond the windows.

She stood there patiently till the noise died down and the sour-faced woman, attempting a smile, gestured for her to go ahead. "I want everyone to know that the theory of evolution is only a theory, just like the sticker says—"

"What about Intelligent Design?" someone called out, and I was startled to see that it was Dave, half-risen from his seat. "I suppose that's fact?" I couldn't help laughing, but softly, softly, and turned to the woman beside me—the blonde. "To all the Jesus freaks, maybe," I whispered, and gave her an unequivocal grin. Which she ignored. Her gaze was fixed on the girl. The auditorium had grown quiet. I raised my hand to my mouth to suppress an imaginary cough, shifted my weight and looked back down the aisle.

"It is," the girl said quietly, dropping her eyes so she wouldn't have to look Dave in the face. "It *is* fact and I'm the one to know it." She clenched her hands in front of her, rocked back on her heels and then rose up once more on point to let her soft feathery voice inhabit the microphone: "I know it because Jesus lives in my heart."

The Weak

I was the first one out the door. The rain had let up, nothing more than a persistent drizzle now, the shrubs along the walk black with moisture and the air dense with the smell of it—the smell of nature, that is, wet, fungal, chaotic. And sweet. Infinitely sweet after the reek of that auditorium. I hurried down the walk and across the lot, thinking to get out ahead of the traffic. I was meeting Dave and Katie at the Granite for burgers and a drink or two and I could hardly wait for the postmortem, because I'd wanted to flag my hand and put a question to the girl in the plaid skirt, wanted to ask her just how provable her contention was. Could we thread one of those surgical mini-cameras up through the vein in her thigh and into her left ventricle just to see if we could find the Redeemer there? And what would He be doing? Sitting down to dinner? Frying up fish in a pan? At least Jonah had some elbow room. But then I guessed Jesus was capable of making himself very, very small—sub-microscopic even.

High comedy—Dave and I would have a real laugh over this one. My feet sailed on down the walk, across the lot and through the drizzle of the world, and I was thinking cold beer, medium-rare burger with extra cheese and two slices of Bermuda onion, until I reached my car and saw that I wasn't going anywhere. The rear tires had sunk maybe half an inch into the grass-turned-to-mud, but that wasn't the problem, or not the immediate problem. The immediate problem was the Mini Cooper (two-tone, red and black) backed up against my bumper and blocking me as effectively as if a wall had been erected round my car while the meeting was going down.

I was wearing a tan leather three-quarter-length overcoat that had caught my eye in the window of a shop on Fifth Avenue a month back and for which I'd paid too much, and it was on its way to being ruined. I didn't have an umbrella. And I'd ignored the salesgirl, who'd given me a four-ounce plastic bottle of some waterproofing agent and made me swear to spray the coat with it the minute I got home. I could feel the coat drinking up the wet. A thin trickle, smelling of mango-pineapple, began to drip from the tip of my nose. I looked round me, thinking of the blond woman—this was her car, I was sure of it, and where in hell was she and how could she just block me in like that?—and then I opened the door of my car and slid in to wait.

Twenty of the longest minutes of my life crumbled round me as I sat there in the dark, smoking one of the cigarettes I'd promised myself to give up while the radio whispered and the windshield fogged over. Head-lights illuminated me as one car after another backed out, swung round and rolled on out of the lot to freedom. I reminded myself, not for the first time, that patience, far from being a virtue, was just weakness in disguise. A mosquito beat itself up out of nowhere to settle on the back of my neck so I could put an end to its existence before it had its opportunity to pro-duce more mosquitoes to send out into a world of exposed necks, arms and midriffs. Midriffs. I began to think about midriffs and then the blond woman and what hers might look like if she were wearing something less formal than a flocked blue dress that buttoned all the way up to the collar and I pulled on my cigarette and drummed my fingers on the dash and felt my lids grow heavy.

Finally—and it was my bad luck that the last two cars left in the whole place were the ones blocking me in—I heard voices and glanced in the rearview mirror to see three figures emerging from the gloom. Women. "All right, then," one of them called out, and here she was—the chair-woman, her big white block of a face looming up on the passenger side of my car like a calving glacier as the Suburban flashed its lights and gurgled in appreciation of her—"you have a good night. And feel good. You did real well tonight, honey."

The door slammed. The Suburban roared. Red brake lights, a great powerful churning of tires and the song of the steering mechanism, and then she was gone. I shifted my eyes to the other side, and there she was, the blonde, framed in the driver's side mirror. Right next to her daughter, in the plaid skirt and damp white sweater.

I froze. Absolutely. I was motionless. I didn't draw breath. The girl and her mother climbed into the Mini Cooper and I wanted to shrink down in my seat, crawl into the well under the steering wheel, vanish altogether, but I couldn't do a thing. I heard the engine start up—they were on their way; in a second they'd be gone—and for all I'd been through, for all the rumbling of my stomach and the craving for alcohol that was almost like a need and the strangeness of that overstuffed auditorium and the testimony I'd witnessed, I felt a yearning so powerful it took me out of myself till I didn't know where I was. And then I heard the harsh message of the wheels slipping and then an accelerating whine as they fought for purchase in the mud. She had no idea, this woman—not the faintest notion— of how to rock a car out of a hole in a yielding surface. She accelerated. The wheels spun. Then she did it again. And again.

I watched the door swing open, watched her legs emerge from the car as she reached down to remove her shoes and step out onto the grass to assess the situation while her daughter's torso faded in soft focus behind the fogged-over windshield. And because I was weak, because I hadn't dated anybody in a month and more and couldn't stand to see those shining bare legs and glistening feet stained with mud and didn't care whether Jesus and all the saints in heaven were involved in the equation or not, I got out of my car, looked her full in the face over the glare of the headlights and said, "Can I help?"

The Fit

I never did get to the Granite that night. I called Dave on my cell and he sounded annoyed—wound up from the meeting and eager to take it out on somebody—but the Mini Cooper was in deeper than it looked and by the time we were able to free it I was in no shape for anything but bed. My coat was ruined. Ditto my shoes. Both pantlegs were greased with mud, my hands dense with it, my fingernails blackened. I should have given up, the term *lost cause* hammered like a spike into the back of my brain, but I was feeling demonstrative—and maybe just a little bit ashamed of myself over the Jesus freak comment. We were ten minutes into it, the drizzle thickening to rain, the miniature wheels digging deeper and the daughter and I straining against the rear bumper, when the woman behind the wheel—the blonde, the mother—stuck her head out the window and gave me my out. "You know," she called over the ticking of the engine and the soft beat of the rain, "maybe I should just call Triple A?"

I came up alongside the car so I could see the pale node of her face wrapped in her shining hair and her eyes like liquid fire. The interior of the car sank away into the shadows beyond her. I couldn't see her shoulders or her torso or her legs. Just her face, like a picture in a frame. "No," I said, "no need. We can get it out."

The daughter chimed in then—Mary-Louise. She was standing on the far side of the car, hands on hips. There was a spatter of mud on her sweater. "Come on, Mom," she said with an edge of exasperation. "Try it again." She looked to me, then bent to brace herself against the bumper. "Come on," she said, "one more time."

I watched the mother's face. She squeezed her eyes shut a moment so that a little hieroglyph of flesh appeared over the bridge of her nose, then she gave me the full benefit of her gaze and it came to me that she hadn't heard what I'd said back in the auditorium, that there was no animosity, none at all. I wasn't on trial. I was just a helpful stranger, the Good Samaritan himself. "I'm Lynnese Mohler," she said, and here was her hand, the nails done in a metallic shade of blue or lavender, slipping free of the darkness to take hold of my own. "And this is my daughter, Mary-Louise."

"Calvin Jessup." I leaned toward her, toward the smell of her, her perfume and what lay beneath it. "But people call me Cal. My friends, anyway." I was smiling. Broadly. Stupidly. The rain quickened.

"Come on, Mom."

"I want to thank you for your help—you're really sweet. I mean it. But are you sure I shouldn't call Triple A? It's nothing. I mean, they don't even charge—"

I straightened up and gave her an elaborate shrug, feeling the accumulated weight of every cell and fiber of my one hundred and eighty-seven pounds. I didn't need alcohol. Didn't need a burger. All I needed was to push this car out of the ditch. "If you want to wait here in the dark," I said. "But I really think we can get you out if you just—"

"You have to rock the car, Mom." The girl—what was she, fourteen, fifteen? Was that ninth grade? I couldn't remember—slapped the side of the car with her open palm. "We almost had it there that last time, so just, come on, start it up and then you go back and forth—you know, the way Dad showed us."

Lynnese glanced up at me, then ducked her head and shook it side to side so that her hair, dense with moisture, fell loose to screen her face. "I'm divorced," she said.

Behind us, across the lot, the lights of the auditorium faded briefly and then blinked out. "Yeah," I said. "So am I."

The Fittest

A week later I was sitting with Dave at the Granite, enjoying my second Sidecar of the evening and watching the first round of the playoffs that wouldn't feature the Mets (this year, anyway), thinking about Lynnese while Dave went on about the lawsuit he and twelve of the other parents were filing against the school district. I liked Dave. He was one of my oldest friends. And I agreed with him both in principle and fact, but when he got on his high horse, when he got *Serious* with a capital *S,* he tended to repeat himself to the point of stupefaction. I was listening to him, feeding him the appropriate responses ("Uh-huh, uh-huh—really?") at the appropriate junctures, yet I was tuning him out too.

I wanted to talk about Lynnese and what had happened between us in the past week, but I couldn't. I'd never been comfortable exposing my feelings, which was why people like Dave accused me of making a joke of everything, and I couldn't even mention her—not to Dave—without feeling like a traitor to the cause. "I'm a Christian," she told me on the occasion of our first date, before I'd even had a chance to ice the beer or rev up the engines or ask her if she'd like to release the stern line and help cast us off (which was a simple way to involve anybody in the process of what we were about to do, because there's no pretense in boating and the thrill of being out on the water takes you right back to your childhood, automatically—boom—just like that). The sun was high, Indian summer, a Saturday delivered from the heavens, and I was planning to take her up the river to a floating restaurant–cum–club where we could have cocktails on the deck, listen to reggae (and dance, maybe dance, if she was up for it) and get dinner too. She was wearing shorts. Her hair was its own kind of rapture. "Hi," I said. "Hi," she said back. "Where's Mary-Louise?" I asked, secretly thrilled that she'd come alone and all the while dreading the intrusion of that child with Jesus in her heart, half-expecting her to pop up out of the backseat of the Mini Cooper or come strolling out of the bushes, and she told me that Mary-Louise was out in the woods hiking—"Up Breakneck Ridge? Where that trail loops behind the mountain to where those lakes are? She loves nature," she said. "Every least thing, the way she focuses on it—it's just a shame they won't let her alone in school, in biology. She could be a scientist, a doctor, anything." I didn't have much to say to that. I held out a hand to help her into the boat. She anchored her legs, the hull rocking beneath us, and leveled her eyes on me. "I'm a Christian," she said.

Well, all right. I'd seen her twice since, and she was as lively, smart and well-informed as anybody I knew—and if I'd expected some sort of sackcloth-and-ashes approach to the intimate moments of an exploratory relationship, well, there went another prejudice. She was hot. And I was intrigued. Really intrigued. (Though I wouldn't want to call it love or infatuation or anything more specific than that after what I'd gone through with my ex-wife and the three or four women who came after her.)

"We're going to break them," Dave was saying. "I swear to you. There was that case in Pennsylvania and before that in Kansas, but these people just don't learn. And they've got bucks behind them. Big bucks."

"You want to call them fanatics," was what I said.

"That's right," he said. "They're fanatics."

The Petitions

Before the trial, there were the petitions. Trials require a whole lot of steam, time to maneuver for position, war chests, thrusts and counter-thrusts, but petitions require nothing more than footwork and a filing fee. Within a week of the meeting, petitioners were everywhere. You couldn't go into the grocery, the post office or the library without sidestepping a fold-up table with two or three clench-jawed women sitting behind it in a welter of pens, Styrofoam cups, ledgers and homemade signs. And men, men too. Men like Dave, and on the other side of the issue, men like the reverend and the pock-marked man who'd stood beside me in the auditorium distending his lips and puffing up his cheeks to express his opinion of the proceedings. I'd taken a lot of things for granted. Some of us might have lived at the end of long driveways and maybe we didn't get involved in community issues because that sort of rah-rah business didn't mesh with our personalities, but as far as I knew we'd always been a community in agreement—save the trees, confine the tourists, preserve the old houses on Main Street, clean up the river and educate the kids to keep them from becoming a drag on society. Now I saw how wrong I was.

Of course, Dave came into the Granite and laid his petition right out on the bar and I was one of the first to sign it—and not just out of social pressure, Rick and half a dozen of the regulars looking over my shoulder while Elvis Costello sang "My Aim Is True" and my burger sizzled on the grill and the late sun melted across the wall, but because it was the right thing to do. "People can believe what they want," Dave said, giving a little speech for the bar, "but that doesn't make it the truth. And it sure as shit doesn't make it science." I signed. Sure, I signed. He would have killed me if I didn't.

And then I was coming up the hill from the station, the trees fired with the season and dusk coming down over the river behind me, everything so changeless and pure it was as if I'd stepped back in time, when I remembered I needed to pick up a few things at the deli. I didn't cook much—I let Tom Scoville, the chef at the Granite, take care of that—but I ate cereal for breakfast, slipped the odd frozen dinner into the microwave or went through the elaborate ritual of slicing Swiss and folding it between two slices of rye. I was out of milk, butter, bread. And as I'd walked down the hill to the train that morning I'd reminded myself to remind myself when I came back up.

I was deep in my post-work oblivion, thinking nothing, and the pockmarked man took me by surprise. Suddenly he was standing there, right in front of the door of Gravenites' Deli, not exactly blocking my access, but taking up space in a way I didn't like. Up close, I saw that the pockmarks were a remnant of an epidermal war he was fighting not only on his face but his scalp and throat as well. He smelled like roast beef. "Hello, brother," he said, thrusting a clipboard at me.

I was in no mood. "I'm an only child," I said.

Unfazed—I don't even think he heard me—he just kept talking, "There's a battle going on here for the souls of our children. And we all have to get involved."

"Not me," I said, trying to maneuver past him. "What I have to get is a quart of milk."

"I saw you at the meeting," he said, and now he was blocking my way. "You know damn well what this is all about." Behind him, in the depths of the store, I could see people lined up waiting for cold cuts, sandwiches, a slice of pizza. Thirty seconds had gone by, thirty seconds out of my life.

I moved for the door and the clipboard flew up like a bird. "What side you on?" he said. "Because there's only one side to this—God's side."

"Get the fuck out of my way."

His eyes jumped and steadied and something hard settled into his face. "Don't use that language with me."

The whole world dissolved in that instant, as if the movie had slipped off the reel, and a long sorrow opened up inside me. What was going on here had nothing to do with Dave or school boards or Lynnese or her daughter either—it was just some stranger getting in my face, and nobody gets in my face. Some redneck. Some yahoo with a complexion like a cheese grater and bad breath on top of it. So I shoved him and he lurched back against the window and everybody in Gravenites' Deli looked up at the concussion as the plate glass contracted and snapped back again. He came at me before I could get a second shove in, his hands at the collar of my shirt, bunching the material there, and he was the one cursing now, "Jesus, Jesus, Jesus!"

It was over in a minute, the way most fights are. I grabbed both his hands and flung them away from me even as my shirt—green Tencel, in a banana-leaf pattern, eighty-seven bucks on sale—ripped down the front and I gave him a parting shove that sent him into the empty steel frame-work of the bicycle rack, where his legs got tangled up and he went down hard on the sidewalk. Then I was stalking up the street, the blood scream-ing in my ears and everything so distorted I thought I was losing my sight.

I felt contaminated. Angry with myself but more angry with him and everybody like him, the narrow, the bigoted, the *fanatics,* because that was what they were, their hope masquerading as certainty, desperation pluck-ing at your sleeve, plucking, always plucking and pushing. In college—I think it was my sophomore year—I took a course called "Philosophy of Religion" by way of fulfilling an elective requirement, but also because I wanted ammunition against my Catholic mother and the fraud the priests and rabbis and mullahs were perpetrating on people too ignorant and scared to know better. Throughout my childhood I'd been the victim of a scam, of the panoply of God and His angels, of goodness everlasting and the answer to the mystery Mary-Louise carried in her heart and laid out for all to see, and I wanted this certified college course and this middle-aged professor with a pouf of discolored hair and a birthmark in the shape of Lake Erie on his forehead to confirm it. I knew Paley's argument from design, knew about the watch and the watchmaker, and I knew now that these people—these Jesus freaks—were trundling out the same old argument dressed in new clothes. Intricacy requires design, that was what they said. And design requires a designer. That was as far as they could see, that was it, case closed: God exists. And the earth is ten thousand years old, just like the Bible says.

I went up the sidewalk, my legs churning against the grade with the fierce regularity of my rage, my quadriceps muscles flexing and releasing, the anterior cruciate ligaments aligning and realigning themselves in my knees, the chambers of my Jesus-less heart pumping like the slick-working intricate parts of the intricate machine they were, and the whole debate reduced to a naked clipboard and a torn shirt. I was two blocks from the Granite. I couldn't see. I couldn't think. I crossed one street, then the next, and the hill sank ahead of me until the familiar yellow awning of the bar came into view, cars parked out front, lights glowing against the twilight and all the trees down the block masked in shadow.

That was when my vision suddenly came clear and I spotted Lynnese. She was sitting behind a card table in front of the bookstore, Mary-Louise perched on a folding chair beside her with her back arched so perfectly she might have been auditioning for junior cotillion. They were fifty feet from me. I saw a mug imprinted with the hopeful yellow slash of a smiley face, front and center, right in the middle of the table, saw Mary-Louise's pink backpack at her feet and the sprawl of her books and homework. And I saw the clipboard. Cheap dun plastic, the shining metallic clip. Saw it all at the very moment Lynnese lifted her eyes and flashed me a smile with wings on it.

My reaction? Truthfully? I made as if I didn't see her. Suddenly I had to cross the street—this was very compelling, an absolute necessity, because even though crossing the street would take me away from the Gran-

ite and I'd have to walk a block in the opposite direction and then double
back, I had an urgent errand over there on the other side of the street, in
that antique shop I'd passed a hundred times and never yet set foot in.

Mutation, and How It Operates in Nature

And then it was a Sunday toward the end of the month, warmer than it
should have been at this time of year, and I was out in the woods on the
trail behind Breakneck Ridge, enjoying the weight of my daypack and the
way the trees caught the wind and shook out their colors. I had two hot
dog buns with me, two all-beef wieners, yellow mustard in a disposable
packet and a bottle of red wine I'd decanted into my bota bag, and I was
planning on a good six- or seven-mile loop and lunch beside a creek I
liked to visit, especially in the fall when the bugs were down. The World
Series was on, but it featured two teams that didn't excite me all that much
and I figured the Granite could do without me, at least for the afternoon—
I'd been in and out all week anyway, mostly when Dave wasn't there.
Nothing against Dave—I just needed a little time to myself. Nights were
getting cold. The season was almost gone.

I felt the climb as a burn in my lungs and I realized I wasn't in the kind
of shape I should have been—the walk up from the train was one thing,
but the ridge was another thing altogether. I was thinking about the philosophy of religion professor and a trick he'd played on the class one Friday afternoon when all we wanted, collectively, was to get out the door
and head downtown for beer, loud music and whatever association we
could make with the opposite sex. He put a drawing up on the black-
board, nothing very elaborate, just lines and shadings, that appeared to be
a scene out of nature, a crag, a pine tree, a scattering of boulders. He didn't
identify it as a trompe l'oeil, but that was what it was, a trick of the eye, a
deception, sweet and simple. *There's a hidden figure here,* he told us, *and
when you see it—and please don't reveal it to anyone else—you're welcome
to leave. Just concentrate. That's all it takes.* One by one, my classmates

gave out with expressions of surprise, wondered a moment over the sub-
tlety of the lesson, packed up their books and left. I was the last one. I
stared at that crag, that pine tree, till they were imprinted on my brain,
increasingly frustrated—there was nothing there, I was sure of it, and the
others were faking it in order to curry favor and not least to get out of the
classroom and into the sunlit arena of that Friday afternoon. When finally I did see it—a representation of Jesus leaping clear of the background, his halo a pine bough, a boulder for his cheek—all I felt was
disappointment. It was a cheap trick, that was all. What did it prove? That
anybody can be fooled? That we can't trust the evidence of our five senses
when five senses are all we've got?

It had rained the night before and the path was slick beneath my feet.
I came within an ace of losing my balance on a switchback with a considerable drop to it and that drove the professor and his drawing right out of
my head. There was the sound of running water everywhere, a thousand
little streams sprung up overnight to churn away at the side of the mountain, and the wind picked up so that the branches of the trees rattled overhead and the leaves came down like confetti. I was almost to the creek
where I was planning to gather up some damp twigs and get a fire going
so I could roast my wieners and take in the glory of the day from a new
perspective, when I came around a bend in the trail and saw a figure up
ahead. A girl. Dressed in khaki shorts and a denim jacket. Her back was to
me and she was bent at the waist in a patch of sun just off the trail, as if she
were looking for something.

I stopped where I was. It was always awkward meeting people on the
trail—they'd come for solitude and so had I, and a woman alone would
always view a man with suspicion, and rightfully so. There'd been attacks,
even out here. It took me a moment, poised there with my feet still in their
tracks, before I recognized her, Mary-Louise, bent over in a column of
sunlight with her blond hair clipped short and the back of her neck so
white it was like an ache. For a moment, I didn't know what to do—I was
about to turn away and tiptoe back down the trail, but she turned her
face to me as if she'd known all along that I was there and I scuffed my
hiking boots on the dirt just to make some noise, and said, "Hi. Hi, Mary-

Louise." And then a joke, lame, admittedly, but the best I could manage under the circumstances: "I see you've stepped up in the world."

She'd turned back to whatever it was that had caught her attention and when she looked at me again she put a single finger to her lips and then gestured for me to come closer. I moved up the path as stealthily as I could, one slow step at a time. When I reached her, when I was standing over her and seeing what she was seeing—a snake, a blacksnake stretched out across a fallen log in the full glare of the sun, its scales trapping the light like a fresh coat of paint—she gave me such a look of pride you'd think she'd created it herself. "It's a blacksnake," I said. "A big one too. They can get to be ten feet long, you know."

"Eight feet," she said. "Maximum. The record's a hundred and one inches."

"And you didn't have to shush me—I mean, it's not as if they can hear."

"They feel the vibrations. And they can see."

We both looked down at it. Its eyes were open, its tongue flicking. There was no hurry in it because the sun was a thing it needed and the season was going fast and soon it would be underground. Or dead. "You know," I said, "it's really a black racer—"

"*Coluber constrictor,*" she said without turning her head. "That's the scientific name."

The wind beat at the trees and a shadow chased violently across the ground, but the snake never moved. "Yeah," I said, out of my league now. "It's amazing how fast they can move if they want to. I saw one once, when I was a kid, and it was in this swamp. A couple of inches of water, anyway, and it went after a frog like you couldn't believe."

"They move by contracting the muscles of their ribs. All snakes have at least a hundred vertebrae and some as many as four hundred, did you know that?"

"But no legs. Their lizard cousins have legs, though, and how do you think they got them? And out west—I saw one once in the Sierras—they have a legless lizard, just like a snake, but it's not." I should have left it, but I couldn't. "Why do you suppose that is? I think—no, I know—it's because of evolution, and that legless lizard is a link between the snakes, who don't need legs to crawl into tight spaces, and the lizards that can get up and run. Like us." She didn't say anything. The trees dipped and rose again. The snake lay still.

"Once," she said, turning all the way round to stare at me as if I were the wonder of nature and the snake no more than incidental, "in the spring? I was with my mother and we were standing outside my friend Sarah's house, a farmhouse, but it's not a farm really, just an old stone place with a barn. Right there, while we were saying goodbye and getting ready to walk to our car, these snakes began to come out of a hole in the ground right where we were standing. Garter snakes."

I wanted to tell her that they balled up like a skein of yarn to survive the winter, hundreds of them sometimes, that they gave birth to live young and that the babies were on their own after that, but I didn't. "Red and yellow stripes," I said. "And black."

She nodded. Her eyes went distant at the memory. "They were like ribbons," she said. "Ribbons of God."

HANDS ON

S he liked his hands. His eyes. The way he looked at her as if he could see beneath the skin, as if he were modeling her from clay, his fingers there at her jawline, at the orbits of her eyes, feeling their way across her brow. She'd stepped in out of the hard clean light of early summer, announced herself to the receptionist and barely had time to leaf through one of the magazines on the end table before she'd been ushered into this room, with its quiet shadows and the big black-leather reclining chair in the middle of the floor—it was like a dentist's chair, that was her impression, only without all the rest of the paraphernalia. And that was good, because she hated the dentist, but then who didn't? Pain, necessary pain, pain in the service of improvement and health, that was what the dentist gave you, and she wondered about this—what would this give her? The recliner said nothing to her, but it intimidated her all the same, and so she'd taken a seat in a straight-backed chair just under the single shaded window. And then he was there, soft-voiced and smiling, and he pulled up a second chair and sat close, studying her face.

"It was the Botox I was interested in," she heard herself say, the walls soaking up her words as if she were in a confessional. "These frown marks, right here?"—she lifted a hand to run two fingers along the rift between her eyes—"and maybe my eyes too, underneath them? I thought—well, looking in the mirror I thought they looked a little tired or saggy or something. Right here? Right along here? And maybe you could—if there's some procedure, nothing radical, just some smoothing out there? Is that possible?" She couldn't help herself: she laughed then, a laugh of nerves, yes, because all this was strange to her and he hadn't said a word beyond that first soft hello, just fixed those eyes of his on the lines of her face and hadn't let go even to blink. "I guess it's because I'm coming up on my birthday—next week, I mean. I'll be thirty-five, if you can believe it, so I just—"

"Yes," he said, rising, "why don't you have a seat here"—indicating the leather recliner—"and we'll have a look?"

On the way out, she stopped at the desk to make an appointment for the Botox treatment. Both secretaries—or no, one was a nurse flipping through files in the far corner—had flawless faces, not a line or wrinkle visible, and she wondered about that. Did they get a discount? Was that one of the perks of the job? There was a color brochure to take home and study, forms to sign. The Botox was nothing, he'd assured her—simplest thing in the world, and it wouldn't take more than fifteen minutes—and the procedure on her eyes was very routine too, a snip of the excess skin and removal of the fat pads, the whole thing done in-office, though she'd be under sedation. It would take a month to heal, two to three months till it was perfect. He had run his fingers under her chin, stroked the flesh below her ears and pressed his thumbs into the hollows there. "You've got beautiful skin," he said. "Stay out of the sun and you won't need anything major for fifteen, twenty years."

"I was just wondering," she said to the secretary, feeling bright now, hopeful, "Dr. Mellors' wife—did he work on her? I mean, the kind of procedure we're talking about for me?" She pushed her credit card across the counter. "It's no big deal, I was just wondering if he would, you know, on his own wife . . . ?"

The secretary—*Maggie,* her nametag read—was in her thirties, or maybe forties, it was hard to say. She'd put her hair up in a bun and she wore a low-cut blouse over a pair of suspiciously full breasts, but then she was an advertisement, wasn't she? Her smile—the complicitous sunny smile that had beamed out continuously to this point—faded suddenly. The eyes—too round, too tight at the corners—dodged away. "I wouldn't know," she said. "He got a divorce five years ago and I've only been here three. But I don't see why not."

.   .   .   .   .

The procedure—the injection of the botulin toxin under the skin between her eyes and then creeping on up to her hairline, one needle prick after another—hurt more than she thought it would. He numbed the area first with a packet of ice, but the ice gave her an instant headache and still she felt the sting of the needle. On the second or third prick she must have flinched. "Are you comfortable?" he asked, inches from her, his pale gray eyes probing hers, and she said, "Yes," and tried to nod, but that only made it worse. "I guess I don't handle pain well." She tried to compose herself, tried to keep it light, because she wasn't a whiner—that wasn't her image of herself. Not at all. "Too sensitive, I guess," she said, and she meant it as a joke.

The purpose of the toxin, as he'd explained to her in his sacerdotal tones, was to paralyze the muscles between her eyes and the ones that lifted her brow too, so that when she squinted in the bright sun or frowned over her checkbook, the skin wouldn't crease—it wouldn't move at all. She could be angry, raging, as furious as she'd ever been in her life, and certainly her body language would show that—her mouth, her eyes—but her brow would remain as smooth and untroubled as if she were asleep and dreaming of a boat drifting across a placid lake. Of course, the effect would last an average of three months or so and then she'd have to undergo the procedure all over again. And he had to warn her that a small percentage of patients reported side effects—headaches, nausea, that sort of thing. A very small percentage, negligible really. This was the safest thing in the world—in the right hands, that is. These Botox parties she'd read about? Not a good idea.

Now he took her hand to lift it to her forehead and the patch of gauze she was to hold there, just till the pinpricks closed up. "There," he was saying, "that wasn't so bad, was it?"

Lying back in the chair, staring into his eyes, she felt something give way inside her, the thin tissue of susceptibility, of surrender: she was in his hands now. This was his domain, this darkened room with its examining chair, the framed degrees on the wall, the glint of polished metal. How old was he? she wondered. She couldn't say, and she realized with a jolt that he wore the same expression as the nurse and the secretary, that his brow was immobile and his eyes rounded as if they'd been shaped out of dough. Forty, she guessed. Forty-five, maybe. But he had a spread to his shoulders—and those hands. His hands were like electric blankets on a cold night in a cabin deep in the woods. "No," she lied. "No, not bad at all."

"All right, good," he said, rising from the chair though he hadn't shifted his gaze from her. "Any problems, you call me right away, day or night, okay?" He drifted to the table in the corner and came back with a card imprinted with his name, the number of the office and an after-hours number. "And let's get a date set up for that blepharoplasty—we'll plan it around your schedule."

She was about to get up too, but before she could move he reached forward to take the pad of gauze from her and she saw that it was flecked with minuscule spots of blood. "Here," he said, handing her a mirror. "You see, there's nothing there—if you want, you can cover up with a dab of makeup. And you should expect results within a day or two."

"Wonderful," she said, giving him a smile. In the background—and she'd been faintly aware of it all along, even through her minor assault of nerves—a familiar piano piece was sifting through speakers hidden somewhere in the walls, as orderly and precise as the beating of a young heart. Bach. The partitas for keyboard, and she could hear the pianist—what was his name?—humming over them. She rose and stood there a moment in the still, shadowy room with the bright light focused on the chair in the middle of the floor, absorbing the music as if she'd just awakened to it. "Do you like classical music?" she murmured.

He gave her a smile. "Yes, sure."

"Bach?"

"Is that what this is? I never know—it's the music service. But they're good and I think it helps the patients relax—soothing, you know? Hey, better than heavy metal, right?"

She made a leap here, and everything to come was the result of it, as inevitable and indisputable as if she'd planned it all out beforehand: "The reason I ask is because I have two tickets for Saturday night—at the Music

Academy? It's an all-Bach program, and"—she lifted her eyebrows, she could still do that—"my girlfriend just told me this morning she can't make it. She was—she had to go out of town unexpectedly—and I was wondering: would you like to go?"

After the concert—he'd begged off, said he'd love to go but had to check with Maggie, the secretary, to see if he was free, and then he wasn't—she went into Andalusia, a restaurant she liked because it had a good feel and a long bar where people gathered to have tapas and drinks while a guitarist worked his way through the flamenco catalogue in a nook by the fireplace. She knew people here—the bartender, Enrique, especially—and she didn't feel out of place coming in alone. Or she did, but not to the extent she felt elsewhere. Enrique took care of her, made sure nobody crowded her. He was protective, maybe a little obsessive even, and if he had a thing for her, well, she could use that to her advantage. A little mutual flirtation, that was all, but she wasn't seriously looking—or she hadn't been, not since she'd got her divorce. She had a house, money in the bank, the freedom to eat when and where she liked, to travel, make her own schedule, and she was enjoying it, that was what she kept telling herself.

She was having ceviche and a salad, sipping a glass of Chilean red and looking through the local newspaper—she couldn't resist the Personals: they were so tacky, so dishonest and nakedly self-serving, and how pathetic could people be?—when she felt a tap at her shoulder and there he was, Dr. Mellors, in a pale gold sportcoat and a black silk shirt open at the collar. "Hello," he said, "or should I say *buenas noches*," and there was nothing even faintly medicinal in his tone.

"Oh, hi," she said, taken by surprise. Here he was, looming over her again, and though she'd been thinking of him all through the concert, trying to fit him into the empty seat beside her, for one flustered second she couldn't summon his name. "How are you?"

He just smiled in answer. A beat went by, Enrique giving her a sidelong glance from the near end of the bar. "You look terrific," he said finally. "All dressed up, huh?"

"The concert," she said.

"Oh, right, yeah—how was that?"

"All right, I guess." It had served its purpose, giving her an excuse to put on some makeup and leave the house, to do something, anything. "A little dreary, actually. Organ music." She let her smile bloom. "I left at the intermission."

His smile opened up now too. "So what do I say—I'm glad I couldn't make it? But you look great, you do. No complications, right? The headache's gone away? No visual problems?"

"No," she said, "no, I'm fine," and then she saw Maggie, with her hair down and a pair of silver chandelier earrings dangling above her bare shoulders, watching them from a table in the dining room.

"Good," he said, "good. Well, listen, nice to see you—and I guess we'll be seeing you next week, then?"

The first thing she did when she got home was put on some music, because she couldn't stand the silence of an empty house, and it wasn't Bach, anything but Bach, her hand going to the first disc on the shelf, which turned out to be a reggae compilation her husband had left behind. She poured herself a glass of wine as the chords fell like debris into the steadily receding sea of the bass line, a menace there, menace in the vocals and the unshakable rhetoric of the dispossessed. Reggae. She'd never much liked it, but here it was, background music to her own awakening drama of confusion and disappointment. And anger, anger too. He'd blown her off. Dr. Mellors. Said he was busy, too busy to sit beside her in a dim auditorium and listen to a professor from the local college sweat over the keyboard, but not in the least embarrassed to be caught out in a lie. Or even contrite. He'd tried to make a joke of it, as if she were nobody, as if her invitation counted for nothing—and for what? So he could fuck his secretary?

The windows were black with the accumulation of the night and she went around pulling the shades, too many shades, too many windows.

The house—it was what she'd wanted, or thought she wanted, new construction, walk-in closets, three-car garage and six thousand square feet of views opening out to the hills and the ocean beyond—was too big for her. Way too big. Even when Rick was around, when she was wound up twenty-four/seven with selecting carpets and furniture and poring over catalogues and landscaping books, the place had seemed desolate. There were no nooks—it was nookless, a nookless house that might as well have been a barn in Nebraska—no intimate corners, no place where she could feel safe and enclosed. She went through the dining room to the kitchen and then back round again to what the architect called "the grand room," turning on all the lights, then she poured herself another glass of wine, went into the bathroom and closed and locked the door.

For a long while she stared at herself in the mirror. The lines—the two vertical furrows between her eyes—didn't seem appreciably different, but maybe they were shallower, maybe that was it. She put a finger there, ran it over the skin. Then she smiled, seductively at first—"Hello, Dr. Mellors," she said to her reflection, "and what do I call you, Ed? Eddie? Ted?"—and then goofily, making faces at herself the way she used to when she was growing up with her three sisters and they'd pull at their lips and nostrils and ears, giggling and screeching till their mother had to come in and scoot them out of the bathroom. It didn't do any good. She snatched the glass up off the marble countertop, drained it and looked at herself the way she really was, a not-so-young woman wearing a permanent scowl, her nose too big, her chin too narrow, her eyes crystallizing in wariness and suspicion. But she was interesting. She was. Interesting and pretty too, in her own way. Prettier than the secretary or the nurse or half the other women in town. At least she looked real.

Or did she? And what was real worth, anyway?

She shrugged out of her clothes then and for a long while studied herself in the full-length mirror on the door. In profile her stomach swelled out and away from her hips, a hard little ball of fat—but she'd just eaten, that was it—and her buttocks seemed to be sagging, from this angle, anyway. Her breasts—they weren't like the breasts of the women in the porn videos her ex-husband seemed so turned on by—and she wondered about that, about the procedure there, about liposuction, a tummy tuck, maybe even a nose job. She didn't want to look like the secretary, like Maggie, because she didn't care about Maggie, Maggie was beneath her, Maggie wasn't even pretty, but the more she looked in the mirror the less she liked what she was seeing.

On Tuesday, the day of her pre-op appointment, she woke early and for a long while lay in bed watching the sun search out the leaves of the flowering plum beyond the window. She made herself two cups of coffee but no eggs or toast or anything else because she'd resolved to eat less and she didn't even lighten the coffee with a splash of non-fat milk. She took her time dressing. The night before she'd laid out a beige pantsuit she thought he might like, but when she saw it there folded over the chair like a vacated skin, she knew it wasn't right. After trying on half the things in the closet she decided finally on a black skirt, a cobalt-blue blouse that buttoned up the back and a pair of matching heels. She looked fine, she really did. But she spent so much time on her makeup she had to speed down the narrow twisting roads to the town spread out below and she ran a couple of lights on the yellow and still she was ten minutes late for her appointment.

Maggie greeted her with a plastic smile. She was wearing another revealing top—borderline tacky for business dress—and she seemed to have lightened her hair, or no, she'd streaked it, that was it. "If you'll just follow me," she chirped, and came out from behind the counter to lead her down the hallway in a slow hip-grinding sashay and then she was in the examining room again, and the door closed softly behind her. *Awaiting an audience,* she thought, and this was part of the mystique doctors cultivated, wasn't it, and why couldn't they just be there in the flesh instead of lurking somewhere down the corridor in another hushed room identical to this one? She set her purse down on the chair in the corner and settled herself into the recliner. She resisted the impulse to lift the hand mirror from the table and touch up her eyes.

"So," he was saying, gliding through the doorway on noiseless feet, "how are we today?"

"Okay, I guess."

"Okay? Just okay?"

"Listen," she said, ignoring the question, "before we go any further I just wanted to ask you something—"

"Sure," he said, and he pulled up a stool on wheels, the sort of thing dentists use, so he could sit beside her, "anything you want. Any concerns you have, that's what I'm here for."

"I just wanted to ask you, do you think I'm pretty?"

The question seemed to confound him and it took him a moment to recover himself. "Of course," he said. "Very pretty."

She said nothing and he moved into her then, his hands on her face, under her eyes, probing along the occipital bone, kneading, weighing the flesh while she blinked into his unwavering gaze. "Which is not to say that we can't improve on it," he said, "because it was your perception, and I agree with you, that right here"—his fingers tightened—"there's maybe just a few millimeters of excess skin. And—"

"I don't care about my eyes," she said abruptly, cutting him off. "I want you to look at my breasts. And my hips, and, and"—the formal term ran in and out of her head—"my tummy. It's fat. I'm fat."

She watched his eyes drop away. "I don't, uh," he began, fumbling now for the right words. "You appear to be fine, maybe a pound or two—but if you're interested, of course, we can consult on that too, and I've got brochures—"

"I don't want brochures," she said, and she began to unbutton her blouse. "I want you to tell me, right here, right now, face to face, because I don't believe you. You say I'm pretty but when I asked you to—to what, accompany me to hear Bach of all people?— you said you were busy, too busy, and then I see you out on the town. How am I supposed to feel?"

"Whoa," he said, "let's just back up a minute—and don't do anything, don't unbutton your . . . because I have to ask Maggie into the room. For legal reasons." He was at the door suddenly, the door swinging open, and he was calling down the hall for his secretary.

"I don't want Maggie," she said, and she had her brassiere off now and was working at the hook of her skirt. "I want to look real, not like some mannequin, not like her. Leave her out of this."

She was looking over her shoulder at him as he stood at the door, the skirt easing down her thighs, and she hadn't worn any stockings because they were just an encumbrance and she was here to be examined, to feel his hands on her, to set the conditions and know what it would take to improve. That was what this was all about, wasn't it? Improvement?

THE LIE

'd used up all my sick days and the two personal days they allowed us, but when the alarm went off and the baby started squalling and my wife threw back the covers to totter off to the bathroom in a hobbled two-legged trot, I knew I wasn't going in to work. It was as if a black shroud had been pulled over my face: my eyes were open but I couldn't see. Or no, I could see—the pulsing LED display on the clock radio, the mounds of laundry and discarded clothes humped round the room like the tumuli of the dead, a hard-driving rain drooling down the dark vacancy of the window—but everything seemed to have a film over it, a world coated in Vaseline. The baby let out a series of scaled-back cries. The toilet flushed. The overhead light flicked on.

Clover was back in the room, the baby flung over one shoulder. She was wearing an old Cramps T-shirt she liked to sleep in and nothing else. I might have found this sexy to one degree or another but for the fact that I wasn't at my best in the morning and I'd seen her naked save for one rock-and-roll memento T-shirt for something like a thousand consecutive mornings now. "It's six-fifteen," she said. I said nothing. My eyes eased shut. I heard her at the closet, and in the dream that crashed down on me in that instant she metamorphosed from a rippling human female with a baby slung over one shoulder to a great shining bird springing from the brink of a precipice and sailing on great shining wings into the void. I woke to the baby. On the bed. Beside me. "You change her," my wife said. "You feed her. I'm late as it is."

We'd had some people over the night before, friends from the pre-baby days, and we'd made margaritas in the blender, watched a movie and stayed up late talking about nothing and everything. Clover had shown off the baby—Xana, we'd named her Xana, after a character in one of the movies I'd edited, or actually, logged—and I'd felt a rush of pride. Here was this baby, perfect in every way, beautiful because her parents were beautiful, and that was all right. Tank—he'd been in my band, co-leader, co-founder, and we'd written songs together till that went sour—said she was fat enough to eat and I'd said, "Yeah, just let me fire up the barbie," and Clover had given me her little drawn-down pout of disgust because I was being juvenile. We stayed up till the rain started. I poured one more round of margaritas and then Tank's girlfriend opened her maw in a yawn that could have sucked in the whole condo and the street out front too and the party broke up. Now I was in bed and the baby was crawling up my right leg, giving off a powerful reek of shit.

The clock inched forward. Clover got dressed, put on her makeup and took her coffee mug out to the car and was gone. There was nothing heroic in what I did next, dealing with the baby and my own car and the stalled nose-to-tail traffic that made the three miles to the babysitter's seem like a trek across the wastelands of the earth—it was just life, that was all. But as soon as I handed Xana over to Violeta at the door of her apartment that threw up a wall of cooking smells, tearful Telemundo dialogue and the diachronic yapping of her four Chihuahuas, I slammed myself into the car and called in sick. Or no: not sick. My sick days were gone, I reminded myself. And my personal days too. My boss picked up the phone. "Iron House Productions," he said, his voice digging out from under the *r*'s. He had trouble with *r*'s. He had trouble with English, for that matter.

"Hello, Radko?"

"Yes, it is he—who is it now?"

"It's me, Lonnie."

"Let me guess—you are sick."

Radko was one of that select group of hard chargers in the production business who kept morning hours, and that was good for me because with Clover working days and going to law school at night—and the baby, the baby, of course—my own availability was restricted to the daylight hours when Violeta's own children were at school and her husband at work operating one of the cranes that lifted the beams to build the city out till there was nothing green left for fifty miles around. But Radko had promised me career advancement, moving up from logging footage to actual editing, and that hadn't happened. On this particular morning, as on too many mornings in the past, I felt I just couldn't face the editing bay, the computer screen, the eternal idiocy of the dialogue repeated over and over through take after take, frame after frame, "No, Jim, stop/No—Jim, stop!/No! Jim, Jim: *stop!!*" I used to be in a band. I had a college degree. I was no drudge. Before I could think, it was out: "It's the baby," I said.

There was a silence I might have read too much into. Then Radko, dicing the interrogative, said, "What baby?"

"Mine. My baby. Remember the pictures Clover e-mailed everybody?" My brain was doing cartwheels. "Nine months ago? When she was born?"

Another long pause. Finally, he said, "Yes?"

"She's sick. Very sick. With a fever and all that. We don't know what's wrong with her." The wheel of internal calculus spun one more time and I made another leap, the one that would prove to be fatal: "I'm at the hospital now."

As soon as I hung up I felt as if I'd been pumped full of helium, giddy with it, rising right out of my seat, but then the slow seepage of guilt, dread and fear started in, drip by drip, like bile drained out of a liver gone bad. A delivery truck pulled up next to me. Rain beat at the windshield. Two cholos rolled out of the apartment next to Violeta's, the green block tattoos they wore like collars glistening in the light trapped beneath the clouds. I had the whole day in front of me. I could do anything. Go anywhere. An hour ago it was sleep I wanted. Now it was something else. A pulse of excitement, the promise of illicit thrills, started up in my stomach.

I drove down Ventura Boulevard in the opposite direction from the bulk of the commuters. They were stalled at the lights, a single driver in every car, the cars themselves like steel shells they'd extruded to contain their resentments. They were going to work. I wasn't. After a mile or so I came to a diner where I sometimes took Clover for breakfast on Sundays, especially if we'd been out the night before, and on an impulse, I pulled into the lot. I bought a newspaper from the machine out front and then I took a copy of the free paper too and went on in and settled into a seat by the window. The smell of fresh coffee and home fries made me realize how hungry I was and I ordered the kind of breakfast I used to have in college after a night of excess—salt, sugar and grease, in quantity—just to open my pores. While I ate, I made my way through both newspapers, item by item, because this was luxurious, kingly, the tables clean, the place brightly lit and warm to the point of steaming with the bustle of the waitresses and the rain at the windows like a plague. Nobody said a word to me. Nobody even looked at me, but for my waitress. She was middle-aged, wedded to her uniform, her hair dyed shoe-polish black. "More coffee?" she asked for the third or fourth time, no hurry, no rush, just an invitation. I glanced at my watch and couldn't believe it was only nine-thirty.

That was the thing about taking a day off, the way the time reconfigured itself and how you couldn't help comparing any given moment with what you'd be doing at work. At work, I wouldn't have eaten yet, wouldn't even have reached the coffee break—*Jim, stop! No, no!*—and my eyelids would have weighed a hundred tons each. I thought about driving down to the ocean to see what the surf looked like under the pressure of the storm—not that I was thinking about surfing; I hadn't been surfing more than a handful of times since the baby was born. It was just that the day was mine and I wanted to fill it. I made my way down through Topanga Canyon, the commuter traffic dissipated by now, and I saw how the creek was tearing at the banks and there were two or three places where there was water on the road and the soft red dough of the mud was like something that had come out of a mold. There was nobody on the beach but me. I walked along the shore till the brim of my baseball cap was sodden and the legs of my jeans as heavy as if they'd just come out of the washing machine.

I drove back up the canyon, the rain a little worse, the flooding more obvious and intense, but it wasn't anything really, not like when the road washes out and you could be driving one minute and the next flailing for your life in a chute full of piss-yellow water. There was a movie at two I was interested in, but since it was only just past twelve and I couldn't even think about lunch after the Lumberjack's Special I'd had for breakfast, I went back to the condo, parked the car and walked down the street, getting wetter and wetter and enjoying every minute of it, to a bar I knew. The door swung in on a denseness of purpose, eight or nine losers lined up on their barstools, the smell of cut lime and the sunshine of the rum, a straight shot of Lysol from the toilet in back. It was warm. Dark. A college basketball game hovered on the screen over the cash register. "A beer," I said, and then clarified by specifying the brand.

I didn't get drunk. That would have been usual, and I didn't want to be usual. But I did have three beers before I went to the movie and after the movie I felt a vacancy in my lower reaches where lunch should have been and so I stopped at a fast-food place on my way to pick up the baby. They got my order wrong. The employees were glassy-eyed. The manager was nowhere to be seen. And I was thirty-five minutes late for the baby. Still, I'd had my day, and when I got home I fed the baby her Cream of Wheat, opened a beer, put on some music and began chopping garlic and dicing onions with the notion of concocting a marinara sauce for my wife when she got home. Thoughts of the following morning, of Radko and what he might think or expect, never entered my mind. Not yet.

All was well, the baby in her crib batting at the little figurines in the mobile over her head (the figurines personally welded to the wires by Clover's hippie mother so that there wasn't even the faintest possibility the baby could get them lodged in her throat), the sauce bubbling on the stove, the rain tapping at the windows. I heard Clover's key in the door. And then she was there with her hair kinked from the rain and smelling like everything I'd ever wanted and she was asking me how my day had gone and I said, "Fine, just fine."

Then it was morning again and the same scene played itself out—Clover stutter-stepping to the bathroom, the baby mewling, rain whispering under the soundtrack—and I began to calculate all over again. It was Thursday. Two more days to the weekend. If I could make it to the weekend, I was sure that by Monday, Monday at the latest, whatever was wrong with me, this feeling of anger, hopelessness, turmoil, whatever it was, would be gone. Just a break. I just needed a break, that was all. And Radko. The thought of facing him, of the way he would mold the drooping dog-like folds of his Slavic flesh around the suspicion in his eyes while he told me he was docking me a day's pay and expected me to work overtime to make up for yesterday, was too much to hold on to. Not in bed. Not now. But then the toilet flushed, the baby squalled and the overhead light went on. "It's six-fifteen," my wife informed me.

The evening before, after we'd dined on my marinara sauce with porcini mushrooms and Italian-style turkey sausage over penne pasta, in the interval before she put the baby down for the night, while the dishwasher murmured from the kitchen and we lingered over a second glass of Chianti, she told me she was thinking of changing her name. "What do you mean?" I was more surprised than angry, but I felt the anger come up in me all the same. "My name's not good enough for you? Like it was my idea to get married in the first place?"

She had the baby in her lap. The baby was in high spirits, grinning her toothless baby grin and snatching for the wineglass my wife held just out of reach. "You don't have to get nasty about it. It's not your name that's the problem—it's mine. My first name."

"What's wrong with Clover?" I said, and even as I said it, I knew how stupid I sounded. She was Clover. I could close my eyes and she was Clover, go to Africa and bury myself in mud and she'd still be Clover. Fine. But the name was a hippie affectation of her hippie parents—they were glassblowers, with their own gallery—and it was insipid, I knew that, down deep. They might as well have named her Dandelion or Fescue.

"I was thinking of changing it to Cloris." She was watching me, her eyes defiant and insecure at the same time. "Legally."

I saw her point—she was a legal secretary, studying to be a lawyer, and Clover just wouldn't fly on a masthead—but I hated the name, hated the idea. "Sounds like something you clean the toilet with," I said.

She shot me a look of hate.

"With bleach in it," I said. "With real scrubbing power."

But now, though I felt as if I'd been crucified and wanted only to sleep for a week, or till Monday, just till Monday, I sat up before she could lift the baby from the crib and drop her on the bed, and in the next moment I was in the bathroom myself, staring into the mirror. As soon as she left I was going to call Radko. I would tell him the baby was worse, that we'd been in the hospital all night. And if he asked what was wrong with her I wasn't going to equivocate because equivocation—any kind of uncertainty, a tremor in the voice, a tonal shift, playacting—is the surest lie detector. Leukemia, that was what I was going to tell him. "The baby has leukemia."

This time I waited till I was settled into the booth at the diner and the waitress with the shoe-polish hair had got done fussing over me, the light of recognition in her eyes and a maternal smile creasing her lips—I was a regular, two days in a row—before I called in. And when Radko answered, the deepest consonant-battering pall of suspicion lodged somewhere between his glottis and adenoids, I couldn't help myself. "The baby," I said, holding it a beat, "the baby . . . passed." Another beat. The waitress poured. Radko breathed fumes through the receiver. "Last night. At—at four a.m. There was nothing they could do."

"Past?" his voice came back at me. "What is this *past*?"

"The baby's dead," I said. "She died." And then, in my grief, I broke the connection.

I spent the entire day at the movies. The first show was at eleven and I killed time pacing round the parking lot at the mall till they opened the doors, and then I was inside, in the anonymous dark. Images flashed by on the screen. The sound was amplified to a killing roar. The smell of melted butter hung over everything. When the lights came up I ducked into the men's room and then slipped into the next theater and the next one after that. I emerged at quarter of four, feeling shaky.

I told myself I was hungry, that was all, but when I wandered into the food court and saw what they had arrayed there, from chapattis to corn dogs to twice-cooked machaca, pretzels and Szechuan eggplant in a sauce of liquid fire, I pushed through the door of a bar instead. It was one of those oversanitized, too-bright, echoing spaces the mall designers, in their wisdom, stuck in the back of their plastic restaurants so that the average moron, accompanying his wife on a shopping expedition, wouldn't have to kill himself. There was a basketball game on the three TVs encircling the bar. The waitresses were teenagers, the bartender had acne. I was the only customer and I knew I had to pick up the baby, that was a given, that was a fact of life, but I ordered a Captain and Coke, just for the smell of it.

I was on my second, or maybe my third, when the place began to fill up and I realized, with a stab of happiness, that this must have been an after-work hangout, with a prescribed happy hour and some sort of comestibles served up gratis on a heated tray. I'd been wrapped up in my grief, a grief that was all for myself, for the fact that I was twenty-six years old and going nowhere, with a baby to take care of and a wife in the process of flogging a law degree and changing her name because she wasn't who she used to be, and now suddenly I'd come awake. There were women everywhere, women my age and older, leaning into the bar with their earrings swaying, lined up at the door, sitting at tables, legs crossed, feet tapping rhythmically to the canned music. Me? I had to pick up the baby. I checked my watch and saw that I was already late, late for the second day running, but I was hungry all of a sudden and I thought I'd just maybe have a couple of the taquitos everybody else was shoving into their mouths while I finished my drink, and then I'd get in the car, take the back streets to Violeta's and be home just before my wife and see if we could get another meal out of the marinara sauce. With porcini mushrooms. And turkey sausage.

That was when I felt a pressure on my arm, my left arm, and I lifted my chin to glance over my shoulder into the face of Joel Chinowski, who occupied the bay next to mine at Iron House Productions. At first, I didn't recognize him—one of those tricks of the mind, the inebriated mind, especially, in which you can't place people out of context, though you know them absolutely. "Joel," I said.

He was shaking his head, very slowly, as if he were tolling a bell, as if his eyes were the clappers and his skull the ringing shell of it. He had a big head, huge—he was big all around, one of those people who aren't obese, or not exactly, but just overgrown to the extent that his clothes seemed inflated, his pants, his jacket, even his socks. He was wearing a tie—the only one of the seventy-six employees at Iron House to dress in shirt and tie—and it looked like a toy trailing away from his supersized collar. "Shit, man," he said, squeezing tighter. "Shit."

"Yeah," I said, and my head was tolling too. I felt caught out. Felt like the very essence he was naming—like shit, that is.

"We all heard," he said. He removed his hand from my arm, peered into his palm as if trying to divine what to say next. "It sucks," he said. "It really sucks."

"Yeah," I said.

And then, though his face never changed expression, he seemed to brighten around the eyes for just an instant. "Hey," he said, "can I buy you a drink? I mean, to drown the sorrow—I mean, that's what you're doing, right? And I don't blame you. Not at all. If it was me . . ." He let the thought trail off. There was a girl two stools down from me, her hair pulled up in a long trailing ponytail, and she was wearing a knit jumper over a little black skirt and red leggings. She glanced up at me, two green swimming eyes above a pair of lips pursed at the straw of her drink. "Or maybe," Joel said, "you'd rather be alone?"

I dragged my eyes away from the girl. "The truth is," I said, "I mean, I really appreciate it, but like I'm meeting Clover at the—well, the funeral parlor. You know, to make the arrangements? And it's—I just stopped in for a drink, that's all."

"Oh, man"—Joel was practically erupting from his shoes, his face drawn down like a curtain and every blood vessel in his eyes gone to waste—"I understand. I understand completely."

On the way out the door I flipped open my cell and dialed Violeta to tell her my wife would be picking up the baby tonight because I was working late, and then I left a message to the same effect at my wife's law office. Then I went looking for a bar where I could find something to eat and maybe one last drink before I went home to lie some more.

.   .   .   .   .

The next day—Friday—I didn't even bother to call in, but I was feeling marginally better. I had a mild hangover, my head still clanging dully and my stomach shriveled up around a little nugget of nothing so that after I dropped the baby off I wasn't able to take anything more than dry toast and black coffee at the diner that was fast becoming my second home, and yet the force of the lie, the enormity of it, was behind me, and here, outside the windows, the sun was shining for the first time in days. I'd been listening to the surf report in the car on the way over—we were getting six-foot swells as a result of the storm—and after breakfast I dug out my wetsuit and my board and let the Pacific roll on under me until I forgot everything in the world but the taste of salt and the smell of the breeze and the weird, strangled cries of the gulls. I was home by three and I vacuumed, washed the dishes, scrubbed the counters. I was twenty minutes early to pick up Xana and while dinner was cooking—meat loaf with boiled potatoes in their skins and asparagus vinaigrette—I took her to the park and listened to her screech with baby joy as I held her in my lap and rocked higher and higher on the swings.

When Clover came home she was too tired to fight and she accepted the meat loaf and the wine I'd picked out as the peace offerings they were and after the baby was asleep we listened to music, smoked a joint and made love in a slow deep plunge that was like paddling out on a wave of flesh for what seemed like hours. We took a drive up the coast on Saturday and on Sunday afternoon we went over to Tank's for lunch and saw how sad his apartment was with its brick-and-board bookcases, the faded band posters curling away from the walls and the deep-pile rug that was once off-white and was now just plain dirty. In the car on the way home, Clover said she never could understand people who treated their dog as if they'd given birth to it and I shook my head—tolling it, but easily now, thankfully—and said I couldn't agree more.

I woke on Monday before the alarm went off and I was showered and shaved and in the car before my wife left for work, and when I pulled up in front of the long windowless gray stucco edifice that housed Iron House Productions, I was so early Radko himself hadn't showed up yet. I took off my watch and stuffed it deep in my pocket, letting the monotony of work drag me down till I was conscious of nothing, not my fingers at the key-board or the image on the screen or the dialogue I was capturing frame by frozen frame. Log and capture, that was what I was doing, hour, minute, second, frame, transcribing everything that had been shot so the film's editor could locate what he wanted without going through the soul-crushing drudgery of transcribing it himself.

At some point—it might have been an hour in, two hours, I don't know—I became aware of the intense gland-clenching aroma of vanilla chai, hot, spiced, blended, the very thing I wanted, caffeine to drive a stake into the boredom. Vanilla chai, available at the coffeehouse down the street, but a real indulgence because of the cost—usually I made do with the acidic black coffee and artificial creamer Radko provided on a stained cart set up against the back wall. I lifted my head to search out the aroma and there was Jeannie, the secretary from the front office, holding a pa-perboard Venti in one hand and a platter of what turned out to be home-made cannoli in the other. "What?" I said, thinking Radko had sent her to tell me he wanted to see me in his office. But she didn't say anything for a long excruciating moment, her eyes full, her face white as a mask, and then she shoved the chai into my hand and set the tray down on the desk beside me. "I'm so sorry for your loss," she said, and then I felt her hand on my shoulder and she was dipping forward in a typhoon of perfume to plant a lugubrious kiss just beneath my left ear.

What can I say? I felt bad about the whole business, felt low and despi-cable, but I cracked the plastic lid and sipped the chai, and as if I weren't even conscious of what my fingers were doing, I started in on the cannoli, one by one, till the platter was bare. I was just sucking the last of the sugar from my fingertips when Steve Bartholomew, a guy of thirty or so who worked in special effects, a guy I barely knew, came up to me and without a word pressed a tin of butter cookies into my hand. "Hey," I said, ad-dressing his retreating shoulders, "thanks, man, thanks. It means a lot." By noon my desk was piled high with foodstuffs—sandwiches, sweets, a dry salami as long as my forearm—and at least a dozen gray-jacketed sympathy cards inscribed by one co-worker or another. I wanted to hide. Wanted to quit. Wanted to go home, tear the phone out of the wall, get into bed and never leave. But I didn't. I just sat there, trying to work, giving one person after another a zombie smile and my best impression of the thousand-yard stare.

Just before quitting time, Radko appeared, his face like an old paper bag left out in the rain. He was flanked by Joel Chinowski. I glanced up at them out of wary eyes and in a flash of intuition I realized how much I hated them both, how much I wanted only to jump to my feet like a cornered animal and punch them out, both of them. Radko said nothing. He just stood there gazing down at me and then, after a moment, he pressed one hand to my shoulder in Slavic commiseration, turned and walked away. "Listen, man," Joel said, shifting his eyes away from mine, "we all wanted to . . . Well, we got together, me and some of the others, and I know it isn't much, but—"

I saw now that he was holding a plastic grocery sack in one hand. I knew what was in the sack. I tried to wave it away, but he thrust it at me and I had no choice but to take it. Later, when I got home and the baby was in her high chair smearing her face with Cream of Wheat and I'd slipped the microwave pizza out of its box, I sat down and emptied the contents of the bag on the kitchen table. It was mainly cash, but there were maybe half a dozen checks too. I saw one for twenty-five dollars, another for fifty. The baby made one of those expressions of baby joy, sharp and sudden, as if the impulse had seized her before she could process it. It was five-thirty and the sinking sun was pasted over the windows. I sifted the bills through my hands, tens and twenties, fives—a lot of fives—and surprisingly few singles, thinking how generous my co-workers were, how good and real and giving, but I was grieving all the same, grieving beyond any measure I could ever have imagined or contained. I was in the process of counting the money, thinking I'd give it back—or donate it to some charity—when I heard Clover's key in the lock and I swept it all back into the bag and tucked that bag in the deep recess under the sink where the water persistently dripped from the crusted-over pipe and the old sponge there smelled of mold.

. . . . .

The minute my wife left the next morning I called Radko and told him I wasn't coming in. He didn't ask for an excuse, but I gave him one anyway. "The funeral," I said. "It's at eleven a.m., just family, very private. My wife's taking it hard." He made some sort of noise on the other end of the line—a sigh, a belch, the faintest cracking of his knuckles. "Tomorrow," I said. "I'll be in tomorrow without fail."

And then the day began, but it wasn't like that first day, not at all. I didn't feel giddy, didn't feel liberated or even relieved—all I felt was regret and the cold drop of doom. I deposited the baby at Violeta's and went straight home to bed, wanting only to clear some space for myself and think things out. There was no way I could return the money—I wasn't that good an actor—and I couldn't spend it either, even to make up for the loss of pay. That would have been low, lower than anything I'd ever done in my life. I thought of Clover then, how furious she'd be when she found out my pay had been docked. If it had been docked. There was still a chance Radko would let it slide, given the magnitude of my tragedy, a chance that he was human after all. A good chance.

No, the only thing to do was bury the money someplace. I'd burn the checks first—I couldn't run the risk of anybody uncovering them; that would really be a disaster, magnitude 10. Nobody could explain that, though various scenarios were already suggesting themselves—a thief had stolen the bag from the glove box of my car; it had blown out the window on the freeway while I was on my way to the mortuary; the neighbor's pet macaque had come in through the open bathroom window and made off with it, wadding the checks and chewing up the money till it was just monkey feces now. *Monkey feces*. I found myself repeating the phrase, over and over, as if it were a prayer. It was a little past nine when I had my first beer. And for the rest of the day, till I had to pick up the baby, I never moved from the couch.

I tried to gauge Clover's mood when she came in the door, dressed like a lawyer in her gray herringbone jacket and matching skirt, her hair pinned up and her eyes in traffic mode. The place was a mess. I hadn't picked up. Hadn't put on anything for dinner. The baby, asleep in her molded plastic carrier, gave off a stink you could smell all the way across the room. I looked up from my beer. "I thought we'd go out tonight," I told her. "My treat." And then, because I couldn't help myself, I added: "I'm just trashed from work."

She wasn't happy about it, I could see that, lawyerly calculations trans-figuring her face as she weighed the hassle of running up the boulevard with her husband and baby in tow before leaving for her eight o'clock class. I watched her reach back to remove the clip from her hair and shake it loose. "I guess," she said. "But no Italian." She'd set down her briefcase in the entry hall, where the phone was, and she put a thumb in her mouth a moment—a habit of hers; she was a fingernail chewer—before she said, "What about Chinese?" She shrugged before I could. "As long as it's quick, I don't really care."

I was about to agree with her, about to rise up out of the grip of the couch and do my best to minister to the baby and get us out the door, en famille, when the phone rang. Clover answered. "Hello? Uh-huh, this is she."

My right knee cracked as I stood, a reminder of the torn ACL I'd suf-fered in high school when I'd made the slightest miscalculation regarding the drop off the backside of a boulder while snowboarding at Mammoth.

"Jeannie?" my wife said, her eyebrows lifting in two perfect arches. "Yes," she said. "Yes, *Jeannie*—how are you?"

There was a long pause as Jeannie said what she was going to say and then my wife said, "Oh, no, there must be some mistake. The baby's fine. She's right here in her carrier, fast asleep." And her voice grew heartier, surprise and confusion riding the cusp of the joke, "She could use a fresh diaper, judging from the smell of her, but that's her daddy's job, or it's go-ing to be if we ever expect to—"

And then there was another pause, longer this time, and I watched my wife's gaze shift from the form of the sleeping baby in her terry-cloth jumpsuit to where I was standing beside the couch. Her eyes, in soft focus for the baby, hardened as they climbed from my shoetops to my face, where they rested like two balls of granite.

. . . . .

Anybody would have melted under that kind of scrutiny. My wife, the lawyer. It would be a long night, I could see that. There would be no Chinese, no food of any kind. I found myself denying everything, telling her how scattered Jeannie was and how she must have mixed us up with the Lovetts—she remembered Tony Lovett, worked in sfx? Yeah, they'd just lost their baby, a little girl, yeah. No, it was awful. I told her we'd all chipped in—"Me too, I put in a fifty, and that was excessive, I know it, but I felt I had to, you know? Because of the baby. Because what if it happened to us?" I went on in that vein till I ran out of breath and when I tried to be nonchalant about it and go to the refrigerator for another beer, she blocked my way. "Where's the money?" she said.

We were two feet apart. I didn't like the look she was giving me because it spared nothing. I could have kept it up, could have said, "What money?" injecting all the trampled innocence I could summon into my voice, but I didn't. I merely bent to the cabinet under the sink, extracted the white plastic bag and handed it to her. She took it as if it were the bleeding corpse of our daughter—or no, of our relationship that went back three years to the time when I was up onstage, gilded in light, my message elided under the hammer of the guitar and the thump of the bass. She didn't look inside. She just held my eyes. "You know this is fraud, don't you?" she said. "A felony offense. They can lock you up for this. You know that."

She wasn't asking a question, she was making a demand. And I wasn't about to answer her because the baby *was* dead and she was dead too. Radko was dead, Jeannie the secretary whose last name I didn't even know and Joel Chinowski and all the rest of them. Very slowly, button by button, I did up my shirt. Then I set my empty beer bottle down on the counter as carefully as if it were full to the lip and went on out the door and into the night, looking for somebody I could tell all about it.

THE UNLUCKY MOTHER
OF AQUILES MALDONADO

When they took Aquiles Maldonado's mother, on a morning so hot it all but seared the hide off the hundred and twenty thousand stray dogs in Caracas, give or take a few, no one would have guessed they would keep her as long as they did. Her husband was dead, murdered in a robbery attempt six years earlier, and he would remain unconcerned and uncommunicative. But there were the household servants and the employees of the machine shop ready to run through the compound beating their breasts, and while her own mother was as feeble as a dandelion gone to seed, she was supremely capable of worry. As were Marita's four grown sons and Aquiles' six children by five different *aficionadas*, whom she looked after, fed, scolded and sent off to school each morning. There was concern, plenty of concern, and it rose up and raced through the community the minute the news hit the streets. "They took Marita Villalba," people shouted from window to window while others shouted back, "Who?"

"Who?" voices cried out in outrage and astonishment. "Who? Aquiles Maldonado's mother, that's who!"

At that time, Aquiles was playing for Baltimore, in the American League, away from home from the start of spring training in late February to the conclusion of the regular season in the first week of October. He was thirty years old and had worked his way through four teams with a fierce determination to reach the zenith of his profession—he was now the Birds' closer, pitching with grit and fluidity at the end of the first year of his two-year, eleven-point-five-million-dollar contract, despite the sharp burn he felt up under the rotator cuff of his pitching arm every time he changed his release point, about which he had told no one. There were three weeks left in the season, and the team, which had already been eliminated from playoff contention by the aggressive play of the Red Sox and Yankees, was just going through the motions. But not Aquiles. Every time he was handed the ball with a lead to protect, however infrequently, he bore down with a fury so uncompromising you would have thought every cent of his eleven-point-five-million U.S. guaranteed dollars rode on each and every pitch.

He was doing his pre-game stretching and joking with the team's other Venezuelan player, Chucho Rangel, about the two tattooed *güeras* they'd taken back to the hotel the night before, when the call came through. It was from his brother Néstor, and the moment he heard his brother's voice, he knew the news was bad.

"They got Mamí," Néstor sobbed into the receiver.

"Who did?"

There was a pause, as if his brother were calling from beneath the sea and needed to surface to catch his breath. "I don't know," he said, "the gangsters, the FARC, whoever."

The field was the green of dreams, the stands spotted with fans come early for batting practice and autographs. He turned away from Chucho and the rest of them, hunched over his cell. "For what?" And then, because the word slipped into his mouth: "For ransom?"

Another pause, and when his brother came back to him his voice was as pinched and hollow as if he were talking through his snorkel: "What do you think, *pendejo*?"

"It just shouldn't be so hot this time of year," she'd been saying to Rómulo Cordero, foreman of the machine shop her son had bought her when he signed his first big league contract. "I've never seen it like this—have you? Maybe in my mother's time . . ."

The children were at school, under supervision of the nuns and the watchful eye of Christ in heaven, the lathes were turning with their insectoid drone and she was in the back office, both fans going full speed and directed at her face and the three buttons of cleavage she allowed herself on the hottest days. Marita Villalba was forty-seven years old, thirty pounds heavier than she'd like to be, but pretty still and so full of life (and, let's face it, money and respectability) that half the bachelors of the neighborhood—and all the widowers—were mad for the sight of her. Rómulo Cordero, a married man and father of nine, wasn't immune to her charms, but he was an employee first and never allowed himself to forget it. "In the nineteen sixties, when I was a boy," he said, pausing to sweeten his voice, "—but you would have been too young to remember—it was a hundred nineteen degrees by eleven in the morning every day for a week and people were placing bets on when it would break a hundred and twenty—"

He never got to finish the story. At that moment, four men in the uniform of the federal police strode sweating into the office to crowd the little dirt-floored room with its walls of unpainted plywood and the rusting filing cabinets and the oversized Steelcase desk on which Marita Villalba did her accounts. "I've already paid," she said, barely glancing up at them.

Their leader, a tall stoop-shouldered man with a congenitally deformed eye and a reek of the barrio who didn't look anything like a policeman, casually unholstered his gun. "We don't know anything about that. My instructions are to bring you to the station for questioning."

And so it began.

When they got outside, to the courtyard, where the shop stood adjacent to the two-story frame house with its hardwood floors and tile roof, the tall one, who was referred to variously as "Capitán" and "El Ojo" by the others, held open the door of a blistered pale purple Honda with yellow racing stripes that was like no police vehicle Marita Villalba or Rómulo Cordero had ever seen. Marita balked. "Are you sure we have to go through with this?" she said, gesturing to the dusty backseat of the car, to the open gate of the compound and the city festering beyond it. "Can't we settle this right here?" She was digging in her purse for her checkbook, when the tall one said abruptly, "I'll call headquarters." Then he turned to Rómulo Cordero. "Hand me your cell phone."

Alarm signals began to go off in Marita Villalba's head. She sized up the three other men—boys, they were boys, street urchins dressed up in stolen uniforms with automatic pistols worth more than their own lives

and the lives of all their ancestors combined clutched in nervous hands—
even as Rómulo Cordero unhooked the cell phone from his belt and
handed it to the tall man with the drooping eye.

"Hello?" the man said into the phone. "District headquarters? Yes,
this is"—and he gave a name he invented out of the scorched air of the
swollen morning—"and we have the Villalba woman." He paused. "Yes,"
he said, "yes, I see: she must come in in person."

Marita glanced at her foreman and they shared a look: the phone was
dead, had been dead for two weeks and more, the batteries corroded in the
shell of the housing and new ones on order, endlessly on order, and they
both broke for the open door of the shop at the same instant. It was hopeless. The weapons spoke their rapid language, dust clawed at her face and
Rómulo Cordero went down with two red flowers blooming against the
scuffed leather of the tooled boot on his right foot, and the teenagers—the
boys who should have been in school, should have been working at some
honest trade under an honest master—seized Aquiles Maldonado's
mother by the loose flesh of her upper arms, about which she was very
sensitive, and forced her into the car. It took a minute, no more. And then
they were gone.

Accompanied by a bodyguard and his brother Néstor, Aquiles mounted
the five flights of listing stairs at the Central Police Headquarters and found
his way, by trial and error, through a dim dripping congeries of hallways to
the offices of the Anti-Extortion and Kidnap Division. The door was open.
Commissioner Diosado Salas, Chief of the Division, was sitting behind his
desk. "It's an honor," he said, rising to greet them and waving a hand to
indicate the two chairs set before the desk. "Please, please," he said, and
Aquiles and Néstor, with a glance for the bodyguard, who positioned
himself just outside the door, eased tentatively into the chairs.

The office looked like any other, bookshelves collapsing under the
weight of papers curling at the edges, sagging venetian blinds, a poor pale
yellowish light descending from the fixtures in the ceiling, but the desk,
nearly as massive as the one Aquiles' mother kept in her office at the ma-

chine shop, had been purged of the usual accoutrements—there were no papers, no files, no staplers or pens, not even a telephone or computer. Instead, a white cloth had been spread neatly over the surface, and aside from the two pale blue cuffs of the Chief's shirtsleeves and the *pelota* of his clenched brown hands, there were but four objects on the table: three newspaper clippings and a single sheet of white paper with something inscribed across it in what looked to be twenty-point type.

All the way up the stairs, his brother and the bodyguard wheezing behind him, Aquiles had been preparing a speech—"I'll pay anything, do anything they say, just so long as they release her unharmed and as soon as possible, or expeditiously, I mean expeditiously, isn't that the legal term?"—but now, before he could open his mouth, the Chief leaned back in the chair and snapped his fingers in the direction of the door at the rear of the room. Instantly, the door flew open and a waiter from the Fundador Café whirled across the floor with his tray held high, bowing briefly to each of them before setting down three white ceramic plates and three Coca-Colas in their sculpted greenish bottles designed to fit the hand like the waist of a woman. In the center of each plate was a steaming *reina pepeada*—a maize cake stuffed with avocado, chicken, potatoes, carrots and mayonnaise, Aquiles' favorite, the very thing he hungered for during all those months of exile in the north. "Please, please," the Chief said. "We eat. Then we talk."

Aquiles was fresh off the plane. There was no question of finishing the season, of worrying about bills, paychecks, the bachelor apartment he shared with Chucho Rangel in a high-rise within sight of Camden Yards or the milk-white Porsche in the parking garage beneath it, and the Orioles' manager, Frank Bowden, had given him his consent immediately. Not that it was anything more than a formality. Aquiles would have been on the next plane no matter what anyone said, even if they were in the playoffs, even the World Series. His mother was in danger. And he had come to save her. But he hadn't eaten since breakfast the previous day, and before he knew what he was doing, the sandwich was gone.

The room became very quiet. There was no sound but for the whirring of the fans and the faint mastication of the Chief, a small-boned man with an overlarge head and a crown of dark snaking hair that pulled away from his scalp as if an invisible hand were eternally tugging at it. Into the silence came the first reminder of the gravity of the situation: Néstor, his face clasped in both hands, had begun to sob in a quiet soughing way. "Our mother," he choked, "she used to cook *reinas* for us, all her life she used to cook. And now, now—"

"Hush," the Chief said, his voice soft and expressive. "We'll get her back, don't you worry." And then, to Aquiles, in a different voice altogether, an official voice, hard with overuse, he said: "So you've heard from them."

"Yes. A man called my cell—and I don't know how he got the number—"

The Chief gave him a bitter smile, as if to say *Don't be naïve.*

Aquiles flushed. "He didn't say hello or anything, just 'We have the package,' that was all, and then he hung up."

Néstor lifted his head. They both looked to the Chief.

"Typical," he said. "You won't hear from them for another week, maybe two. Maybe more."

Aquiles was stunned. "A week? But don't they want the money?"

The Chief leaned into the desk, the black pits of his eyes locked on Aquiles. "What money? Did anybody say anything about money?"

"No, but that's what this is all about, isn't it? They wouldn't"—and here an inadmissible thought invaded his head—"they're not sadists, are they? They're not . . . ," but he couldn't go on. Finally, gathering himself, he said, "They don't kidnap mothers just for the amusement of it, do they?"

Smiling his bitter smile, the Chief boxed the slip of white paper so that it was facing Aquiles and pushed it across the table with the tips of two fingers. On it, in those outsized letters, was written a single figure: ELEVEN-POINT-FIVE MILLION DOLLARS. In the next moment he was brandishing the newspaper clippings, shaking them so that the paper crackled with the violence of it, and Aquiles could see what they were: articles in the local press proclaiming the *beisbol* star Aquiles Maldonado a national hero second only to Simón Bolívar and Hugo Chávez. In each of them, the figure of eleven-point-five million dollars had been underlined in red ink. "This is what they want," the Chief said finally, "money, yes. And now that they have your attention they will come back to you with a figure, maybe five million or so—they'd demand it all and more, except that they know you will not pay them a cent, not now or ever."

"What do you mean?'

"I mean we do not negotiate with criminals."

"But what about my mother?"

He sighed. "We will get her back, don't you worry. It may take time and perhaps even a certain degree of pain"—here he reached down beneath the desk and with some effort set a two-quart pickle jar on the table before him—"but have no fear."

Aquiles stole a look at his brother. Néstor had jammed his forefinger into his mouth and was biting down as if to snap it in two, a habit he'd developed in childhood and had been unable to break. These were not pickles floating in the clear astringent liquid.

"Yes," the Chief said, "this is the next step. It is called proof of life."

It took a moment for the horror to settle in.

"But these fingers—there are four of them here, plus two small toes, one great toe and a left ear—represent cases we have resolved. Happily resolved. What I'm telling you is be prepared. First you will receive the proof of life, then the demand for money." He paused. And then his fist came down, hard, on the desktop. "But you will not pay them, no matter what."

"I will," Aquiles insisted. "I'll pay them anything."

"You won't. You can't. Because if you do, then every ballplayer's family will be at risk, don't you understand that? And, I hate to say this, but you've brought it on yourself. I mean, please—driving a vermilion Hummer through the streets of this town? Parading around with your gold necklaces and these disgraceful women, these *putas* with their great inflated tits and swollen behinds? Did you really have to go and paint your compound the color of a ripe tangerine?"

Aquiles felt the anger coming up in him, but as soon as he detected it, it was gone: the man was right. He should have left his mother where she was, left her to the respectability of poverty, should have changed his name and come home in rags wearing a beard and a false nose. He should never in his life have picked up a baseball.

"All right," the Chief was saying, and he stood to conclude the meeting. "They call you, you call me."

Both brothers rose awkwardly, the empty plate staring up at Aquiles like the blanched unblinking eye of accusation, the jar of horrors grinning beside it. The bodyguard poked his head in the door.

"Oh, but wait, wait, I almost forgot." The Chief snapped his fingers once again and an assistant strode through the rear door with a cellophane package of crisp white baseballs in one hand and a Magic Marker in the other. "If you wouldn't mind," the Chief said. "For my son Aldo, with Best Wishes."

She was wedged between two of the boys in the cramped backseat of the car, the heat oppressive, the stink of confinement unbearable. El Ojo sat up front beside the other boy, who drove with an utter disregard for life. At first she tried to shout out the window at pedestrians, shrieking till she thought the glass of the windshield would shatter, but the boy to her right—pinch-faced, with two rotted teeth like fangs and a pair of lifeless black eyes—slapped her and she slapped him right back, the guttersnipe, the little hoodlum, and who did he think he was? How dare he? Beyond that she remembered nothing, because the boy punched her then, punched her with all the coiled fury of his pipestem arm and balled fist and the car jolted on its springs and the tires screamed and she passed into unconsciousness.

When she came back to the world she was in a skiff on a river she'd never seen before, its waters thick as paste, all the birds and insects in the universe screaming in unison. Her wrists had been tied behind her and her ankles bound with a loop of frayed plastic cord. The ache in her jaw stole up on her, her tongue probing the teeth there and tasting her own blood, and that made her angry, furious, and she focused all her rage on the boy who'd hit her—there he was, sitting athwart the seat in the bow, crushed beneath the weight of his sloped shoulders and the insolent wedge of the back of his head. She wanted to cry out and accuse him, but she caught herself, because what if the boat tipped, what then? She was help-less. No one, not even the Olympic butterfly champion, could swim with all four limbs bound. So she lay there on the rocking floor of the boat, soaked through with the bilge, the sun lashing her as she breathed the fumes of the engine and stared up into a seared fragment of the sky, wait-ing her chance.

Finally, and it seemed as if they'd been on that river for days, though that was an impossibility, the engine choked on its own fumes and they cut across the current to the far bank. El Ojo—she saw now that he had been the one at the tiller—sprang out and seized a rope trailing from the branch of a jutting tree, and then the boy, the one who'd assaulted her, reached back to cut the cord at her ankles with a flick of his knife and he too was in the murky water, hauling the skiff ashore. She endured the thumps and bumps and the helpless feeling they gave her and then, when he thrust a hand under her arm to lead her up onto the bank, the best she could do was mutter, "You stink. All of you. Don't you have any pride? Can't you even wash yourselves? Do you wear your clothes till they rot, is that it?" And then, when that got no response: "What about your mothers—what would they think?"

They were on the bank now, El Ojo and the others taking pains to se-crete the boat in the undergrowth, where they piled sticks and river-run debris atop it. The boy who had hold of her just gave her his cold vampire's smile, the two stubs of his teeth stabbing at his lower lip. "We don't got no mothers," he said softly. "We're guerrillas."

"Hoodlums, you mean," she snapped back at him. "Criminals, *nar-cotraficantes*, kidnappers, cowards."

It came so quickly she had no time to react, the arm snaking out, the wrist uncoiling to bring the flat of his hand across her face, right where it had begun to bruise. And then, for good measure, he slapped her again.

"Hey, Eduardo, shithead," El Ojo rasped, "get your ass over here and give us a hand. What do you think this is, a nightclub?"

The others laughed. Her face stung and already the flies and mosqui-toes were probing at the place where it had swelled along the line of her jaw. She dropped her chin to her shoulder for protection, but she didn't say anything. To this point she'd been too indignant to be scared, but now, with the light fading into the trees and the mud sucking at her shoes and the ugly nameless things of the jungle creeping from their holes and dens to lay siege to the night, she began to feel the dread spread its wings inside her. This was about Aquiles. About her son, the major leaguer, the pride of her life. They wanted him, wanted his money he'd worked so hard to acquire since he was a barefoot boy molding a glove out of old milk cartons and firing rocks at a target nailed to a tree, the money he'd earned by his sweat and talent—and the fame, the glory, the pride that came with it. They had no pride themselves, no human decency, but they would do anything to corrupt it—she'd heard the stories of the abductions, the mutilations, the families who'd paid ransom for their daughters, sons, parents, grandparents, even the family dog, only to pay again and again until hope gave way to despair.

But then, even as they took hold of her and began to march her through the jungle, she saw her son's face rise before her, his portrait just as it appeared on his Topps card, one leg lifted in the windup and that little half-smile he gave when he was embarrassed because the photographer was there and the photographer had posed him. *He'll come for me,* she said to herself. *I know he will.*

For Aquiles, the next three weeks were purgatorial. Each day he awoke sweating in the silence of dawn and performed his stretching exercises on the Turkish carpet until the maid brought him his orange juice and the protein drink into which he mixed the contents of three raw eggs, two ounces of wheatgrass and a tablespoon of brewer's yeast. Then he sat dazed in front of the high-definition plasma TV he'd bought his mother for her forty-fifth birthday, surrounded by his children (withdrawn from school for their own protection), and the unforgivably homely but capable girl from the provinces, Suspira Salvatoros, who'd been brought in to see after their welfare in the absence of his mother. In the corner, muttering darkly, sat his *abuela,* the electric ghost of his mother's features flitting across her face as she rattled her rosary and picked at the wart under her right eye till a thin line of serum ran down her cheek. The TV gave him nothing, not joy or even release, each show more stupefyingly banal than the last—how could people go about the business of winning prizes, putting on costumes and spouting dialogue, singing, dancing, stirring soft-shell crabs and cilantro in a fry pan for christ's sake, when his mother, Marita Villalba, was in the hands of criminals who refused even to communicate let alone negotiate? Even baseball, even the playoffs, came to mean nothing to him.

And then, one bleak changeless morning, the sun like a firebrick tossed in the window and all Caracas up in arms over the abduction—*Free Marita* was scrawled in white soap on the windows of half the cars in town—he was cracking the eggs over his protein drink when Suspira Salvatoros knocked at the door. "Don Aquiles," she murmured, sidling into the room in her shy fumbling way, her eyes downcast, "something has come for you. A missive." In her hand—bitten fingernails, a swell of fat—there was a single dirty white envelope, too thick for a letter and stained with a smear of something he couldn't name. He felt as if his chest had been torn open, as if his still-beating heart had been snatched out of him and flung down on the carpet with the letter that dropped from his ineffectual fingers. Suspira Salvatoros began to cry. And gradually, painfully, as if he were bending for the rosin bag in a nightmare defeat in which he could get no one out and the fans were jeering and the manager frozen in the dugout, he bent for the envelope and clutched it to him, hating the feel of it, the weight of it, the guilt and horror and accusation it carried.

Inside was a human finger, the little finger of the left hand, two inches of bone, cartilage and flesh gone the color of old meat, and at the tip of it, a manicured nail, painted red. For a long while he stood there, weak-kneed, the finger cold in the palm of his hand, and then he reverently folded it back into the envelope, secreted it in the inside pocket of his shirt, closest to his heart, and flung himself out the door. In the next moment he sprang into the car—the Hummer, and so what if it was the color of poppies and arterial blood, so much the worse for them, the desecrators, the criminals, the punks, and he was going to track them down if it was the last thing he did. Within minutes he'd reached the police head-quarters and pounded up the five flights of stairs, the ashen-faced body-guard plodding along behind him. Without a word for anyone he burst into the Chief's office and laid the envelope on the desk before him.

The Chief had been arrested in the act of biting into a sweet cake while simultaneously blowing the steam off a cup of coffee, the morning news-paper propped up in front of him. He gave Aquiles a knowing look, set down the cake and extracted the finger from the envelope.

"I'll pay," Aquiles said. "Just let me pay. Please, God. She's all I care about."

The Chief held the finger out before him, studying it as if it were the most pedestrian thing in the world, a new sort of pen he'd been pre-sented by the Boys' Auxiliary, a stick of that dried-out bread the Italians serve with their antipasto. "You will not pay them," he said without glancing up.

"I will." Aquiles couldn't help raising his voice. "The minute they call, I swear I'll give them anything, I don't care—"

Now the Chief raised his eyes. "Your presumption is that this is your mother's finger?"

Aquiles just stared at him.

"She uses this shade of nail polish?"

"Yes, I—I assume . . ."

"Amateurs," the Chief spat. "We're onto them. We'll have them, be-lieve me. And you—*assume* nothing."

The office seemed to quaver then, as if the walls were closing in. Aquiles had begun to take deep breaths as he did on the mound when the situation was perilous, runner on first, no outs, a one-run ballgame. "My mother's in pain," he said.

"Your mother is not in pain. Not physical pain, at any rate." The Chief had set the severed finger down on the napkin that cradled the sweet bun and brought the mug to his lips. He took a sip of the coffee and then set the mug down too. "This is not your mother's finger," he said finally. "This is not, in fact, even the finger of a female. Look at it. Look closely. This," he pronounced, again lifting the mug to his lips, "is the finger of a man, a young man, maybe even a boy playing revolutionary. They like that, the boys. Dressing up, hiding out in the jungle. Calling themselves"—and here he let out his bitter laugh—"guerrillas."

She was a week in the jungle, huddled over a filthy stewpot thick with chunks of *carpincho,* some with the hide still on it, her digestion in turmoil, the insects burrowing into her, her dress—the shift she'd been wearing when they came for her—so foul it was like a layer of grease applied to her body. Then they took her farther into the jungle, to a crude airstrip—the kind the *narcotraficantes* employ in their evil trade—and she was forced into a Cessna airplane with El Ojo, the boy with the pitiless eyes and an older man, the pilot, and they sailed high over the broken spine of the countryside and up into the mountains. At first she was afraid they were taking her across the border to Colombia to trade her to the FARC rebels there, but she could see by the sun that they were heading southeast, and that was small comfort because every minute they were in the air she was that many more miles from her home and rescue. Their destination—it appeared as a cluster of frame cottages with thatched roofs and the splotched yawning mouth of a dried-up swimming pool— gave up nothing, not a road or even a path, to connect it with the outside world.

The landing was rough, very rough, the little plane lurching and pitching like one of those infernal rides at the fair, and when she climbed down out of the cockpit she had to bend at the waist and release the contents of her stomach in the grass no one had thought to cut. The boy, her tormentor, the one they called Eduardo, gave her a shove from behind so that she fell to her knees in her own mess, so hurt and confused and angry she had to fight to keep from crying in front of him. And then there were other boys there, a host of them, teenagers in dirty camouflage fatigues with the machine rifles slung over their shoulders, their faces blooming as they greeted Eduardo and El Ojo and then narrowing in suspicion as they regarded her. No one said a word to her. They unloaded the plane—beer, rum, cigarettes, pornographic magazines, sacks of rice and three cartons of noodles in a cup—and then ambled over to a crude table set up in the shade of the trees at the edge of the clearing, talking and joking all the while. She heard the hiss of the first beer and then a chorus of hisses as one after another they popped the aluminum tabs and pressed the cans to their lips, and she stood and gazed up at the barren sky and then let her eyes drop to the palisade of the jungle that went on unbroken as far as she could see.

Within a week, they'd accepted her. There was always one assigned to guard her, though for the life of her she couldn't imagine why—unless she could sprout wings like a *turpial* and soar out over the trees she was a prisoner here just as surely as if she'd been locked away in a cell—but aside from that, they gave her free rein. Once she'd recovered from the shock of that inhuman flight, she began to poke through the dilapidated buildings, just to do something, just to keep occupied, and the first thing she found was a tin washtub. It was nothing to collect fragments of wood at the edge of the clearing and to build a fire-ring of loose stone. She heated water in the tub, shaved a bar of soap she found in the latrine, wrapped herself in the blanket they gave her and washed first her hair, then her dress. The boys were drunk on the yeasty warm beer, sporadically shooting at something in the woods until El Ojo rose in a rage from his nap and cursed them, but soon they gathered round and solemnly stripped down to their underwear and handed her their filth-stiffened garments, murmuring, "Please, *señora*" and "Would you mind?" and "Me too, me too." All except Eduardo, that is. He just sneered and lived in his dirt.

Ultimately, she knew these boys better than they knew themselves, boys playing soldier in the mornings, *beisbol* and *fútbol* in the afternoons, gathering to drink and boast and lie as the sun fell into the trees. They were the spawn of prostitutes and addicts, uneducated, unwanted, unloved, raised by grandmothers, raised by no one. They knew nothing but cruelty. Their teeth were bad. They'd be dead by thirty. As the days accumulated she began to gather herbs at the edge of the jungle and sort through the store of cans and rice and dried meat and beans, sweetening the clearing on the hilltop with the ambrosial smell of her cooking. She found a garden hose and ran it from the creek that gave them their water to the lip of the empty swimming pool and soon the boys were cannon-balling into the water, their shrieks of joy echoing through the trees even as the cool clear water cleansed and firmed their flesh and took the rank-ness out of their hair. Even El Ojo began to come round to hold out his tin plate or have his shirt washed and before long he took to sitting in the shade beside her just to pass the time of day. "These kids," he would say, and shake his head in a slow portentous way, and she could only cluck her tongue in agreement. "You're a good mother," he told her one night in his cat's tongue of a voice, "and I'm sorry we had to take you." He paused to lick the ends of the cigarette he'd rolled and then he passed it to her. "But this is life."

And then one morning as she was pressing out the corn cakes to bake on a tin sheet over the fire for the *arepas* she planned to serve for breakfast and dinner too, there was a stir among the boys—a knot of them gathered round the table and El Ojo there, brandishing a pair of metal shears. "You," he was saying, pointing the shears at Eduardo, "you're the tough guy. Make the sacrifice."

She was thirty feet from them, crouched over a stump, both hands thick with corn meal. Eduardo fastened his eyes on her. "She's the hos-tage," he spat. "Not me."

"She's a good person," El Ojo said, "a saint, better than you'll ever be. I won't touch her—no one will. Now hold out your hand."

The boy never flinched. Even when the shears bit, even when metal contacted metal and the blood drained from his face. And all the while he never took his eyes from her.

By the time the call came, the one Aquiles had been awaiting breathlessly through five and a half months of sleepless nights and paralyzed days, spring training was well under way. Twice the kidnappers had called to name their price—the first time it was five million, just as the Chief had predicted, and the next, inexplicably, it had dropped to two—but the voice on the other end of the phone, as hoarse and buzzing as the rattle of an inflamed serpent, never gave directions as to where to deliver it. Aquiles fell into despair, his children turned on one another like demons so that their disputations rang through the courtyard in a continual clangor, his *abuela*'s face was an open sore and Suspira Salvatoros cleaned and cooked with a vengeance even as she waded in amongst the children like the referee of an eternal wrestling match. And then the call came. From the Chief. Aquiles pressed the cell to his ear and murmured, *"Bueno?"* and the Chief's voice roared back at him: "We've found her!"

"Where?"

"My informants tell me they have her at an abandoned tourist camp in Estado Bolívar."

"But that's hundreds of miles from here."

"Yes," the Chief said. "The amateurs."

"I'm coming with you," Aquiles said.

"No. Absolutely no. Too dangerous. You'll just be in the way."

"I'm coming."

"No," the Chief said.

"I give you my solemn pledge that I will sign one truckload of baseballs for the sons and daughters of every man in the federal police district of Caracas and I will give to your son, Aldo, my complete 2003, 2004 and 2005 sets of Topps baseball cards direct from the U.S.A."

There was a pause, then the Chief's voice came back at him: "We leave in one hour. Bring a pair of boots."

They flew south in a commercial airliner, the Chief and ten of his men in camouflage fatigues with the patch of the Federal Police on the right shoulder and Aquiles in gum boots, blue jeans and an old baseball jersey from his days with the Caracas Lions, and then they took a commandeered produce truck to the end of the last stretch of the last road on the map and got down to hike through the jungle. The terrain was difficult. Insects thickened the air. No sooner did they cross one foaming yellow cataract than they had to cross another, the ground underfoot as slippery as if it had been oiled, the trees alive with the continuous screech of birds and monkeys. And they were going uphill, always uphill, gaining altitude with each uncertain step.

Though the Chief had insisted that Aquiles stay to the rear—"That's all we need," he said, "you getting shot, and I can see the headlines already: 'Venezuelan Baseball Star Killed in Attempt to Save His Sainted Mother'"—Aquiles' training regimen had made him a man of iron and time and again he found himself well out in front of the squad. Repeatedly the Chief had to call him back in a terse whisper and he slowed to let the others catch up. It was vital that they stay together, the Chief maintained, because there were no trails here and they didn't know what they were looking for except that it was up ahead somewhere, high up through the mass of vegetation that barely gave up the light, and that it would reveal itself when they came close enough.

Then, some four hours later, when the men had gone gray in the face and they were all of them as soaked through as if they'd been standing fully clothed under the barracks shower, the strangest thing happened. The Chief had called a halt to check his compass reading and allow the men to collapse in the vegetation and squeeze the blood, pus and excess water from their boots, and Aquiles, though he could barely brook the delay, paused to slap mosquitoes on the back of his neck and raise the canteen of Gatorade to his mouth. That was when the scent came to him, a faint odor of cooking that insinuated itself along the narrow olfactory avenue between the reeking perfume of jungle blooms and the fecal stench of the mud. But this was no ordinary smell, no generic scent you might encounter in the alley out back of a restaurant or drifting from a barrio window—this was his mother's cooking! His mother's! He could even name the dish: tripe stew! *"Jefe,"* he said, taking hold of the Chief's arm and pulling him to his feet, "do you smell that?"

They approached the camp warily, the Chief's men fanning out with their weapons held rigidly before them. Surprise was of the essence, the Chief had insisted, adding, chillingly, that the guerrillas were known to slit the throats of their captives rather than give them up, and so they must be eliminated before they knew what hit them. Aquiles felt the moment acutely. He'd never been so tense, so unnerved, in all his life. But he

was a closer and a closer lived on the naked edge of catastrophe every time
he touched the ball, and as he moved forward with the rest of them, he felt
the strength infuse him and knew he would be ready when the moment
came.

There were sounds now—shouts and curses and cries of rapture amid
a great splash and heave of water in motion—and then Aquiles parted the
fronds of a palm and the whole scene was made visible. He saw rough huts
under a diamond sky, a swimming pool exploding with slashing limbs
and ecstatic faces, and there, not thirty feet away, the cookfire and the
stooping form of a woman, white-haired, thin as bone. It took him a moment to understand that this was his mother, work-hardened and deprived
of her makeup and the Clairol Nice 'n Easy he sent her by the cardboard
case from the north. His first emotion, and he hated himself for it, was
shame, shame for her and for himself too. And then, as the voices car-
omed round the pool—*Oaf! Fool! Get off me, Humberto, you ass!*—he felt
nothing but anger.

He would never know who started the shooting, whether it was one of
the guerrillas or the Chief and his men, but the noise of it, the lethal stutter that saw the naked figures jolted out of the pool and the water bloom
with color, started him forward. He stepped from the bushes, oblivious to
danger, stopping only to snatch a rock from the ground and mold it to his
hand in the way he'd done ten thousand times when he was a boy. That
was when the skinny kid with the dead eyes sprang up out of nowhere to
put a knife to his mother's throat, and what was the point of that? Aquiles
couldn't understand. One night there was victory, another night defeat.
But you played the game just the same—you didn't blow up the ballpark
or shoot the opposing batter. You didn't extort money from the people
who'd earned it through God-given talent and hard work. You didn't
threaten mothers. That wasn't right. That was impermissible. And so he
cocked his arm and let fly with his fastball that had been clocked at ninety-
eight miles an hour on the radar gun at Camden Yards while forty-five
thousand people stamped and shouted and chanted his name—*High and
inside,* he was thinking, *high and inside*—and, without complicating matters, let's just say that his aim was true.

. . . . .

Unfortunately, Marita Villalba never fully recovered from her ordeal. She would awaken in the night, smelling game roasting over a campfire— smelling *carpincho* with its rodent's hide intact—and she seemed lost in her own kitchen. She gave up dyeing her hair, rarely wore makeup or jewelry. The machine shop was nothing to her and when Rómulo Cordero, hobbled by his wounds, had to step down, she didn't even come downstairs to attend his retirement party, though the smell of the *arepas, empanadas* and *chivo en coco* radiated through the windows and up out of the yard and into the streets for blocks around. More and more she was content to let Suspira Salvatoros look after the kitchen and the children while she sat in the sun with her own mother, their collective fingers, all twenty of them, busy with the intricate needlepoint designs for which they became modestly famous in the immediate neighborhood.

Aquiles went back to the major leagues midway through the season, but after that moment of truth on the hilltop in the jungle of Estado Bolívar, he just couldn't summon the fire anymore. That, combined with the injury to his rotator cuff, spelled disaster. He was shelled each time he went to the mound, the boos rising in chorus till the manager took the ball from him for the last time and he cleared waivers and came home to stay, his glory gone but the contract guaranteed. The first thing he did was take Suspira Salvatoros to the altar, defeating the ambitions of any number of young and not-so-young women whose curses and lamentations could be heard echoing through the streets for weeks to come. Then he hired a team of painters to whitewash every corner of the compound, even to the tiles of the roof. And finally—and this was perhaps the hardest thing of all—he sold the vermilion Hummer to a TV actor known for his sensitive eyes and hyperactive jaw, replacing it with a used van of uncertain provenance and a color indistinguishable from the dirt of the streets.

ADMIRAL

She knew in her heart it was a mistake, but she'd been laid off and needed the cash and her memories of the Strikers were mostly on the favorable side, so when Mrs. Striker called—*Gretchen, this is Gretchen? Mrs. Striker?*—she'd said yes, she'd love to come over and hear what they had to say. First, though, she had to listen to her car cough as she drove across town (fuel pump, that was her father's opinion, offered in a flat voice that said it was none of his problem, not anymore, not now that she was grown and living back at home after a failed attempt at life), and she nearly stalled the thing turning into the Strikers' block. And then did stall it as she tried, against any reasonable expectation of success, to parallel park in front of their great rearing fortress of a house. It felt strange punching in the code at the gate and seeing how things were different and the same, how the trees had grown while the flowerbeds remained in a state of suspended animation, everything in perpetual bloom and clipped to within a millimeter of perfection. The gardeners saw to that. A whole battalion of them that swarmed over the place twice a week with their blowers and edgers and trimmers, at war with the weeds, the insects, the gophers and ground squirrels and the very tendency of the display plants to want to grow outside the box. At least that was how she remembered it. The gardeners. And how Admiral would rage at the windows, showing his teeth and scrabbling with his claws—and if he could have chewed through glass he would have done it. "That's right, boy," she'd say, "that's right—don't let those bad men steal all your dead leaves and dirt. You go, boy. You go. That's right."

She rang the bell at the front door and it wasn't Mrs. Striker who answered it but another version of herself in a white maid's apron and a little white maid's cap perched atop her head, and she was so surprised she had to double-clutch to keep from dropping her purse. *A woman of color does not clean house,* that was what her mother always told her, and it had become a kind of mantra when she was growing up, a way of reinforcing core values, of promoting education and the life of the mind, but she couldn't help wondering how much higher a dogsitter was on the socio-economic scale than a maid. Or a sous-chef, waitress, aerobics instructor, ticket puncher and tortilla maker, all of which she'd been at one time or another. About the only thing she hadn't tried was leech gathering. There was a poem on the subject in her college text by William Wordsworth, the poet of daffodils and leeches, and she could summon it up whenever she needed a good laugh. She developed a quick picture of an old long-nosed white man rolling up his pantlegs and wading into the murk, then squeezed out a miniature smile and said, "Hi, I'm Nisha? I came to see Mrs. Striker? And Mr. Striker?"

The maid—she wasn't much older than Nisha herself, with a placid expression that might have been described as self-satisfied or just plain vacant—held open the door. "I'll tell them you're here," she said.

Nisha murmured a thank-you and stepped into the tiled foyer, thinking of the snake brain and the olfactory memories that lay coiled there. She smelled dog—smelled Admiral—with an overlay of old sock and furniture polish. The great room rose up before her like something transposed from a cathedral. It was a cold room, echoing and hollow, and she'd never liked it. "You mind if I wait in the family room?" she asked.

The maid—or rather the girl, the young woman, the young woman in the demeaning and stereotypical maid's costume—had already started off in the direction of the kitchen, but she swung round now to give her a look of surprise and irritation. For a moment it seemed as if she might snap at her, but then, finally, she just shrugged and said, "Whatever."

Nothing had changed in the paneled room that gave onto the garden, not as far as Nisha could see. There were the immense old high-backed leather armchairs and the antique Stickley sofa rescued from the law offices of Striker and Striker, the mahogany bar with the wine rack and the backlit shrine Mr. Striker had created in homage to the spirits of single-malt scotch whiskey, and overseeing it all, the oil portrait of Admiral with its dark heroic hues and golden patina of varnish. She remembered the day the painter had come to the house and posed the dog for the preliminary snapshots, Admiral uncooperative, Mrs. Striker strung tight as a wire and the inevitable squirrel bounding across the lawn at the crucial moment. The painter had labored mightily in his studio to make his subject look noble, snout elevated, eyes fixed on some distant, presumably worthy, object, but to Nisha's mind an Afghan—any Afghan—looked inherently ridiculous, like some escapee from *Sesame Street,* and Admiral seemed a kind of concentrate of the absurd. He looked goofy, just that.

When she turned round, both the Strikers were there, as if they'd floated in out of the ether. As far as she could see, they hadn't aged at all. Their skin was flawless, they held themselves as stiff and erect as the Ituri carvings they'd picked up on their trip to Africa and they tried hard to make small talk and avoid any appearance of briskness. In Mrs. Striker's arms—*Call me Gretchen, please*—was an Afghan pup, and after the initial exchange of pleasantries, Nisha, her hand extended to rub the silk of the ears and feel the wet probe of the tiny snout on her wrist, began to get the idea. She restrained herself from asking after Admiral. "Is this his pup?" she asked instead. "Is this little Admiral?"

The Strikers exchanged a glance. The husband hadn't said, *Call me Cliff,* hadn't said much of anything, but now his lips compressed. "Didn't you read about it in the papers?"

There was an awkward pause. The pup began to squirm. "Admiral passed," Gretchen breathed. "It was an accident. We had him—well, we were in the park, the dog park . . . you know, the one where the dogs run free? You used to take him there, you remember, up off Sycamore? Well, you know how exuberant he was . . ."

"You really didn't read about it?" There was incredulity in the husband's voice.

"Well, I—I was away at college and then I took the first job I could find. Back here, I mean. Because of my mother. She's been sick."

Neither of them commented on this, not even to be polite.

"It was all over the press," the husband said, and he sounded offended now. He adjusted his oversized glasses and cocked his head to look down at her in a way that brought the past rushing back. "*Newsweek* did a story, *USA Today*—we were on *Good Morning America,* both of us."

She was at a loss, the three of them standing there, the dog taking its spiked dentition to the underside of her wrist now, just the way Admiral used to when he was a pup. "For what?" she was about to say, when Gretchen came to the rescue.

"This *is* little Admiral. Admiral II, actually," she said, ruffling the blond shag over the pup's eyes.

The husband looked past her, out the window and into the yard, an ironic grin pressed to his lips. "Two hundred and fifty thousand dollars," he said, "and it's too bad he wasn't a cat."

Gretchen gave him a sharp look. "You make a joke of it," she said, her eyes suddenly filling, "but it was worth every penny and you know it." She mustered a long-suffering smile for Nisha. "Cats are simpler—their eggs are more mature at ovulation than dogs' are."

"I can get you a cat for thirty-two thou."

"Oh, Cliff, stop. Stop it."

He moved to his wife and put an arm round her shoulders. "But we didn't want to clone a cat, did we, honey?" He bent his face to the dog's, touched noses with him and let his voice rise to a falsetto, "Did we now, Admiral? Did we?"

At seven-thirty the next morning, Nisha pulled up in front of the Strikers' house and let her car wheeze and shudder a moment before killing the engine. She flicked the radio back on to catch the last fading chorus of a tune she liked, singing along with the sexy low rasp of the lead vocalist, feeling good about things—or better, anyway. The Strikers were giving her twenty-five dollars an hour, plus the same dental and health care package they offered the staff at their law firm, which was a whole solid towering brick wall of improvement over what she'd been making as a waitress at Johnny's Rib Shack, sans health care, sans dental and sans any tip she could remember above ten percent over the pre-tax total because the people who came out to gnaw ribs were just plain cheap and no two ways about it. When she stepped out of the car, there was Gretchen coming down the front steps of the house with the pup in her arms, just as she had nine years ago when Nisha was a high school freshman taking on what she assumed was going to be a breeze of a summer job.

Nisha took the initiative of punching in the code herself and slipping through the gate to hustle up the walk and save Gretchen the trouble, because Gretchen was in a hurry, always in a hurry. She was dressed in a navy-blue suit with a double string of pearls and an antique silver pin in the shape of a bounding borzoi that seemed eerily familiar—it might have been the exact ensemble she'd been wearing when Nisha had told her she'd be quitting to go off to college. *I'm sorry, Mrs. Striker, and I've really enjoyed the opportunity to work for you and Mr. Striker,* she'd said, hardly able to contain the swell of her heart, *but I'm going to college. On a scholarship.* She'd had the acceptance letter in her hand to show her, thinking how proud of her Mrs. Striker would be, how she'd take her in her arms for a hug and congratulate her, but the first thing she'd said was, *What about Admiral?*

As Gretchen closed on her now, the pup wriggling in her arms, Nisha could see her smile flutter and die. No doubt she was already envisioning the cream-leather interior of her BMW (a 750i in Don't-Even-Think-About-It Black) and the commute to the office and whatever was going down there, court sessions, the piles of documents, contention at every turn. Mr. Striker—Nisha would never be able to call him Cliff, even if she lived to be eighty, but then he'd have to be a hundred and ten and probably wouldn't hear her, anyway—was already gone, in his matching Beemer, his and hers. Gretchen didn't say *good morning* or *hi* or *how are you?* or *thanks for coming,* but just enfolded her in the umbrella of her perfume and handed her the dog. Which went immediately heavy in Nisha's arms, fighting for the ground with four flailing paws and the little white ghoul's teeth that fastened on the top button of her jacket. Nisha held on. Gave Gretchen a big grateful-for-the-job-and-the-health-care smile, no worries, no worries at all.

"Those jeans," Gretchen said, narrowing her eyes. "Are they new?"

The dog squirming, squirming. "I, well—I'm going to set him down a minute, okay?"

"Of course, of course. Do what you do, what you normally do." An impatient wave. "Or what you used to do, I mean."

They both watched as the pup fell back on its haunches, rolled briefly in the grass and sprang up to clutch Nisha's right leg in a clumsy embrace. "I just couldn't find any of my old jeans—my mother probably threw them all out long ago. Plus"—a laugh—"I don't think I could fit into them anymore." She gave Gretchen a moment to ruminate on the deeper implications here—time passing, adolescents grown into womanhood, flesh expanding, that sort of thing—then gently pushed the dog down and murmured, "But I *am* wearing—right here, under the jacket?—this T-shirt I know I used to wear back then."

Nothing. Gretchen just stood there, looking distracted.

"It's been washed, of course, and sitting in the back of the top drawer of my dresser where my mother left it, so I don't know if there'll be any scent or anything, but I'm sure I used to wear it because Tupac really used to drive my engine back then, if you know what I mean." She gave it a beat. "But hey, we were all fourteen once, huh?"

Gretchen made no sign that she'd heard her—either that or she denied the proposition outright. "You're going to be all right with this, aren't you?" she said, looking her in the eye. "Is there anything we didn't cover?"

The afternoon before, during her interview—but it wasn't really an interview because the Strikers had already made up their minds and if she'd refused them they would have kept raising the hourly till she capitulated—the two of them, Gretchen and Cliff, had positioned themselves on either side of her and leaned into the bar over caramel-colored scotches and a platter of *ebi* and *maguro* sushi to explain the situation. Just so that she was clear on it. "You know what cloning is, right?" Gretchen said. "Or what it involves? You remember Dolly?"

Nisha was holding fast to her drink, her left elbow pressed to the brass rail of the bar in the family room. She'd just reached out her twinned chopsticks for a second piece of the shrimp, but withdrew her hand. "You mean the country singer?"

"The sheep," the husband said.

"The first cloned mammal," Gretchen put in. "Or larger mammal."

"Yeah," she said, nodding. "Sure. I guess."

What followed was a short course in genetics and the method of somatic cell nuclear transplant that had given the world Dolly, various replicated cattle, pigs and hamsters, and now Admiral II, the first cloned dog made available commercially through SalvaPet, Inc., the genetic engineering firm with offices in Seoul, San Juan and Cleveland. Gretchen's voice constricted as she described how they'd taken a cell from the lining of Admiral's ear just after the accident and inserted it into a donor egg, which had had its nucleus removed, stimulated the cell to divide through the application of an electric current, and then inserted the developing embryo into the uterus of a host mother—"The sweetest golden retriever you ever saw. What was her name, Cliff? Some flower, wasn't it?"

"Peony."

"Peony? Are you sure?"

"Of course I'm sure."

"I thought it was—oh, I don't know. You sure it wasn't Iris?"

"The point is," he said, setting his glass down and leveling his gaze on Nisha, "you can get a genetic copy of the animal, a kind of three-dimensional Xerox, but that doesn't guarantee it'll be like the one you, well, the one you lost."

"It was so sad," Gretchen said.

"It's nurture that counts. You've got to reproduce the animal's experiences, as nearly as possible." He gave a shrug, reached for the bottle. "You want another?" he asked, and she held out her glass. "Of course we're both older now—and so are you, we realize that—but we want to come as close as possible to replicating the exact conditions that made Admiral what he was, right down to the toys we gave him, the food, the schedule of walks and play and all the rest. Which is where you come in—"

"We need a commitment here, Nisha," Gretchen breathed, leaning in

so close Nisha could smell the scotch coming back at her. "Four years. That's how long you were with him last time. Or with Admiral, I mean. The original Admiral."

The focus of all this deliberation had fallen asleep in Gretchen's lap. A single probing finger of sunlight stabbed through the window to illuminate the pale fluff over the dog's eyes. At that moment, in that light, little Admiral looked like some strange conjunction of ostrich and ape. Nisha couldn't help thinking of *The Island of Dr. Moreau,* the cheesy version with Marlon Brando looking as if he'd been genetically manipulated himself, and she would have grinned a private grin, fueled by the scotch and the thundering absurdity of the moment, but she had to hide everything she thought or felt behind a mask of impassivity. She wasn't committing to anything for four years—four years? If she was still living here in this craphole of a town four years from now she promised herself she'd go out and buy a gun and eliminate all her problems with a single, very personal squeeze of the trigger.

That was what she was thinking when Gretchen said, "We'll pay you twenty dollars an hour," and the husband said, "With health care—and dental," and they both stared at her so fiercely she had to look down into her glass before she found her voice. "Twenty-five," she said.

And oh, how they loved that dog, because they never hesitated. "Twenty-five it is," the husband said, and Gretchen, a closer's smile blooming on her face, produced a contract from the folder at her elbow. "Just sign here," she said.

After Gretchen had climbed into her car and the car had slid through the gate and vanished down the street, Nisha sprawled out on the grass and lifted her face to the sun. She was feeling the bliss of déjà vu—or no, not déjà vu, but a virtual return to the past, when life was just a construct and there was nothing she couldn't have done or been and nothing beyond the thought of clothes and boys and the occasional term paper to hamper her. Here she was, gone back in time, lying on the grass at quarter of eight in the morning on a sunstruck June day, playing with a puppy while everybody else was going to work—it was hilarious, that's what it was. Like something you'd read about in the paper—a behest from some crazed millionaire. Or in this case, two crazed millionaires. She felt so good she let out a laugh, even as the pup came charging across the lawn to slam headfirst into her, all feet and pink panting tongue, and he was Admiral all right, Admiral in the flesh, born and made and resurrected for the mere little pittance of a quarter million dollars.

For a long while she wrestled with him, flipping him over on his back each time he charged, scratching his belly and baby-talking him, enjoying the novelty of it, but by quarter past eight she was bored and she pushed herself up to go on into the house and find something to eat. *Do what you used to do,* Gretchen had told her, but what she used to do, summers especially, was nap and read and watch TV and sneak her friends in to tip a bottle of the husband's forty-year-old scotch to their adolescent lips and make faces at one another before descending into giggles. Twice a day she'd take the dog to the doggie park and watch him squat and crap and run wild with the other mutts till his muzzle was streaked with drool and he dodged at her feet to snatch up mouthfuls of the Evian the Strikers insisted he drink. Now, though, she just wanted to feel the weight of the past a bit, and she went in the back door, the dog at her heels, thinking to make herself a sandwich—the Strikers always had cold cuts in the fridge, mounds of pastrami, capicolla, smoked turkey and Swiss, individual slices of which went to Admiral each time he did his business outside where he was supposed to or barked in the right cadence or just stuck his goofy head in the door. She could already see the sandwich she was going to make—a whole deli's worth of meat and cheese piled up on Jewish rye; they always had Jewish rye—and she was halfway to the refrigerator before she remembered the maid.

There she was, in her maid's outfit, sitting at the kitchen table with her feet up and the newspaper spread out before her, spooning something out of a cup. "Don't you bring that filthy animal in here," she said, glancing up sharply.

Nisha was startled. There didn't used to be a maid. There was no one in the house, in fact, till Mrs. Yamashita, the cook, came in around four, and that was part of the beauty of it. "Oh, hi," she said, "hi, I didn't know you were going to be—I just . . . I was going to make a sandwich, I guess." There was a silence. The dog slunk around the kitchen, looking wary. "What was your name again?"

"Frankie," the maid said, swallowing the syllables as if she weren't ready to give them up, "and I'm the one has to clean up all these paw marks off the floor—and did you see what he did to that throw pillow in the guest room?"

"No," Nisha said, "I didn't," and she was at the refrigerator now, sliding back the tray of the meat compartment. This would go easier if they were friends, no doubt about it, and she was willing, more than willing. "You want anything?" she said. "A sandwich—or, or something?"

Frankie just stared at her. "I don't know what they're paying you," she said, "but to me? This is the craziest shit I ever heard of in my life. You think I couldn't let the dog out the door a couple times a day? Or what, take him to the park—that's what you do, right, take him to the doggie park over on Sycamore?"

The refrigerator door swung shut, the little light blinking out, the heft of the meat satisfying in her hand. "It's insane, I admit it—hey, I'm with you. You think I wanted to grow up to be a dogsitter?"

"I don't know. I don't know anything about you. Except you got your degree—you need a degree for that, dogsitting, I mean?" She hadn't moved, not a muscle, her feet propped up, the cup in one hand, spoon in the other.

"No," Nisha said, feeling the blood rise to her face, "no, you don't. But what about you—you need a degree to be a maid?"

That hit home. For a moment, Frankie said nothing, just looked from her to the dog—which was begging now, clawing at Nisha's leg with his forepaws—and back again. "This is just temporary," she said finally.

"Yeah, me too." Nisha gave her a smile, no harm done, just establishing a little turf, that was all. "Totally."

For the first time, Frankie's expression changed: she almost looked as if she were going to laugh. "Yeah, that's right," she said, "temporary help,

ADMIRAL 157

that's all we are. We're the temps. And Mr. and Mrs. Striker—dog crazy, plain crazy, two-hundred-and-fifty-thousand-dollar crazy—they're permanent."

And now Nisha laughed, and so did Frankie—a low rumble of amusement that made the dog turn its head. The meat was on the counter now, the cellophane wrapper pulled back. Nisha selected a slice of Black Forest ham and held it out to him. "Sit!" she said. "Go ahead, sit!" And the dog, just like his father or progenitor or donor or whatever he was, looked at her stupidly till she dropped the meat on the tile and the wet plop of its arrival made him understand that here was something to eat.

"You're going to spoil that dog," Frankie said.

Nisha went unerringly to the cabinet where the bread was kept, and there it was, Jewish rye, a fresh loaf, springy to the touch. She gave Frankie a glance over her shoulder. "Yeah," she said. "I think that's the idea."

A month drifted by, as serene a month as Nisha could remember. She was making good money, putting in ten-hour days during the week and half days on the weekends, reading through all the books she hadn't had time for in college, exhausting the Strikers' DVD collection and opening her own account at the local video store, walking, lazing, napping the time away. She gained five pounds and vowed to start swimming regularly in the Strikers' pool, but hadn't got round to it yet. Some days she'd help Frankie with the cleaning and the laundry so the two of them could sit out on the back deck with their feet up, sharing a bottle of sweet wine or a joint. As for the dog, she tried to be conscientious about the whole business of imprinting it with the past—or *a* past—though she felt ridiculous. Four years of college for this? Wars were being fought, people were starving, there were diseases to conquer, children to educate, good to do in the world, and here she was reliving her adolescence in the company of an inbred semi-retarded clown of a cloned Afghan hound because two childless rich people decreed it should be so. All right. She knew she'd have to move on. Knew it was temporary. Swore that she'd work up a new résumé

and start sending it out—but then the face of her mother, sick from vomiting and with her scalp as smooth and slick as an eggplant, would rise up
to shame her. She threw the ball to the dog. Took him to the park. Let the
days fall round her like leaves from a dying tree.

And then one afternoon, on the way back from the dog park, Admiral
jerking at the leash beside her and the sky opening up to a dazzle of sun
and pure white tufts of cloud that made her feel as if she were floating
untethered through the universe along with them, she noticed a figure
stationed outside the gate of the Strikers' house. As she got closer, she saw
that it was a young man dressed in baggy jeans and a T-shirt, his hair fanning out in rusty blond dreads and a goatee of the same color clinging to
his chin. He was peering over the fence. Her first thought was that he'd
come to rob the place, but she dismissed it—he was harmless; you could
see that a hundred yards off. Then she saw the paint smears on his jeans
and wondered if he was a painting contractor come to put in a bid on the
house, but that wasn't it either. He looked more like an amateur artist—
and here she had to laugh to herself—the kind who specializes in dog
portraits. But she was nearly on him now, thinking to brush by him and
slip through the gate before he could accost her, whatever he wanted,
when he turned suddenly and his face caught fire. "Wow!" he said. "Wow,
I can't believe it! You're her, aren't you, the famous dog sitter? And this"—
he went down on one knee and made a chirping sound deep in his throat—
"this is Admiral. Right? Am I right?"

Admiral went straight to him, lurching against the leash, and in the
next instant he was flopping himself down on the hot pavement, submit-
ting to the man's caresses. The rope of a tail whapped and thrashed, the
paws gyrated, the puppy teeth came into play. "Good boy," the man
crooned, his dreads riding a wave across his brow. "He likes that, doesn't
he? Doesn't he, boy?"

Nisha didn't say anything. She just watched, the smallest hole dug out
of the canyon of her boredom, till the man rose to his feet and held out his
hand even as Admiral sprang up to hump his leg with fresh enthusiasm.
"I'm Erhard," he said, grinning wide. "And you're Nisha, right?"

"Yes," she said, taking his hand despite herself. She was on the verge of asking how he knew her name, but there was no point: she already understood. He was from the press. In the past month there must have been a dozen reporters on the property, the Strikers stroking their vanity and posing for pictures and answering the same idiotic questions over and over—*A quarter million dollars: that's a lot for a dog, isn't it?*—and she herself had been interviewed twice already. Her mother had even found a fuzzy color photo of her and Admiral (couchant, lap) on the Web under the semi-hilarious rubric CLONE-SITTER. So this guy was a reporter—a foreign reporter, judging from the faint trace of an accent and the blue-eyed rearing height of him, German, she supposed. Or Austrian. And he wanted some of her time.

"Yes," he said, as if reading her thoughts. "I am from *Die Weltwoche*, and I wanted to ask of you—prevail upon you, beg you—for a few moments? Is that possible? For me? Just now?"

She gave him a long slow appraisal, flirting with him, yes, definitely flirting. "I've got nothing but time," she said. And then, watching his grin widen: "You want a sandwich?"

They ate on the patio overlooking the pool. She was dressed casually in shorts and flip-flops and her old Tupac tee, and that wasn't necessarily a bad thing because the shirt—too small by half—lifted away from her hips when she leaned back in the chair, showing off her navel and the onyx ring she wore there. He was watching her, chattering on about the dog, lifting the sandwich to his lips and putting it down again, fooling with the lens on the battered old Hasselblad he extracted from the backpack at his feet. The sun made sequins on the surface of the pool. Admiral lounged beneath the table, worrying a rawhide bone. She was feeling good, better than good, sipping a beer and watching him back.

They had a little conversation about the beer. "Sorry to offer you Miller, but that's all we have—or the Strikers have, I mean."

"Miller High Life," he said, lifting the bottle to his mouth. "Great name. What person would not want to live the high life? Even a dog. Even Admiral. He lives the high life, no?"

"I thought you'd want a German beer, something like Beck's or something."

He set down the bottle, picked up the camera and let the lens wander down the length of her legs. "I'm Swiss, actually," he said. "But I live here now. And I like American beer. I like everything American."

There was no mistaking the implication and she wanted to return the sentiment, but she didn't know the first thing about Switzerland, so she just smiled and tipped her beer to him.

"So," he said, cradling the camera in his lap and referring to the note-pad he'd laid on the table when she'd served him the sandwich, "this is the most interesting for me, this idea that Mr. and Mrs. Striker would hire you for the dog? This is very strange, no?"

She agreed that it was.

He gave her a smile she could have fallen into. "Do you mind if I should ask what are they paying you?"

"Yes," she said. "I do."

Another smile. "But it is good—worth your while, as they say?"

"I thought this was about Admiral," she said, and then, because she wanted to try it out on her tongue, she added, "Erhard."

"Oh, it is, it is—but I find you interesting too. More interesting, really, than the dog." As if on cue, Admiral backed out from under the table and squatted on the concrete to deposit a glistening yellow turd, which he examined briefly and then promptly ate.

"Bad dog," she said reflexively.

Erhard studied the dog a moment, then shifted his eyes back to her. "But how do you feel about the situation, this concept of cloning a pet? Do you know anything about this process, the cruelty involved?"

"You know, frankly, Erhard, I haven't thought much about it. I don't know really what it involves. I don't really care. The Strikers love their dog, that's all, and if they want to, I don't know, bring him back—"

"Cheat death, you mean."

She shrugged. "It's their money."

He leaned across the table now, his eyes locked on hers. "Yes, but they must artificially stimulate so many bitches to come into heat and then they must take the eggs from the tubes of these bitches, what they call 'surgically harvesting,' if you can make a guess as to what that implies for

the poor animals"—she began to object but he held up a peremptory finger—"and that is nothing when you think of the numbers involved. Do
you know about Snuppy?"

She thought she hadn't heard him right. "Snuppy? What's that?"

"The dog, the first one ever cloned—it was two years ago, in Korea?
Well, this dog, this one dog—an Afghan like your dog here—was the
result of over a thousand embryos created in the laboratory from donor
skin cells. And they put these embryos into one hundred and twenty-
three bitches and only three clones resulted—and two died. So: all that
torture of the animals, all that money—and for what?" He glanced down
at Admiral, the flowing fur, the blunted eyes. "For this?"

A sudden thought came to her: "You're not really a journalist, are
you?"

He slowly shook his head, as if he couldn't bear the weight of it.

"You're what—one of these animal people, these animal liberators or
whatever they are. Isn't that right? Isn't that what you are?" She felt frightened suddenly, for herself, for Admiral, for the Strikers and Frankie and
the whole carefully constructed edifice of getting and wanting, of supply
and demand and all that it implied.

"And do you know why they clone the Afghan hound," he went on,
ignoring her, "—the very stupidest of all the dogs on this earth? You don't?
Breeding, that is why. This is what they call an uncomplicated genetic
line, a pure line all the way back to the wolf ancestor. Breeding," he said,
and he'd raised his voice so that Admiral looked up at the vehemence of it,
"so that we can have this purity, this stupid hound, this *replica* of nature."

Nisha tugged down her T-shirt, drew up her legs. The sun glared up
off the water so that she had to squint to see him. "You haven't answered
my question," she said, "Erhard. If that's even your name."

Again, the slow rolling of the head on his shoulders, back and forth in
rhythmic contrition. "Yes," he said finally, drawing in a breath, "I am one
of 'these animal people.'" His eyes went distant a moment and then came
back to her. "But I am also a journalist, a journalist first. And I want you
to help me."

· · · · ·

That night, when the Strikers came home—in convoy, her car following his through the gate, Admiral lurching across the lawn to bark furiously at the shimmering irresistible disks of the wheels of first one car, then the other—Nisha was feeling conflicted. Her loyalties were with the Strikers, of course. And with Admiral too, because no matter how brainless and ungainly the dog was, no matter how many times he wet the rug or ravaged the flowerbed or scrambled up onto the kitchen table to choke down anything anyone had been foolish enough to leave untended even for thirty seconds, she'd bonded with him—she would have been pretty cold if she hadn't. And she wasn't cold. She was as susceptible as anyone else. She loved animals, loved dogs, loved the way Admiral sprang to life when he saw her walk through the door, loved the dance of his fur, his joyous full-throated bark, the feel of his wet whiskered snout in the cupped palm of her hand. But Erhard had made her feel something else altogether.

What was it? A sexual stirring, yes, absolutely—after the third beer, she'd found herself leaning into him for the first of a series of deep, languid, adhesive kisses—but it was more than that. There was something transgressive in what he wanted her to do, something that appealed to her sense of rebellion, of anarchy, of applying the pin to the swollen balloon . . . but here were the Strikers, emerging separately from their cars as Admiral bounced between them, yapping out his ecstasy. And now Gretchen was addressing her, trying to shout over the dog's sharp vocalizations, but without success. In the next moment, she was coming across the lawn, her face set.

"Don't let him chase the car like that," she called, even as Admiral tore round her like a dust devil, nipping at her ankles and dodging away again. "It's a bad habit."

"But Admiral—I mean, the first Admiral—used to chase cars all the time, remember?"

Gretchen had pinned her hair up so that all the contours of her face stood out in sharp relief. There were lines everywhere suddenly, creases and gouges, frown marks, little embellishments round her eyes, and how could Nisha have missed them? Gretchen was old—fifty, at least—and the realization came home to Nisha now, under the harsh sun, with the taste of the beer and of Erhard still tingling on her lips. "I don't care," Gretchen was saying, and she was standing beside Nisha now, like a figurine the gardeners had set down amid that perfect landscape.

"But I thought we were going to go for everything, the complete behavior, good or bad, right? Because otherwise—"

"That was how the accident happened. At the dog park. He got through the gate before Cliff or I could stop him and just ran out into the street after some idiot on a motorcycle . . ." She looked past Nisha a moment, to where Admiral was bent over the pool, slurping up water as if his pinched triangular head worked on a piston. "So no," she said, "no, we're going to have to modify some behavior. I don't want him drinking that pool water, for one thing. Too many chemicals."

"Okay, sure," Nisha said, shrugging. "I'll try." She raised her voice and sang out "Bad dog, bad dog," but it was halfhearted and Admiral ignored her.

The cool green eyes shifted to meet hers again. "And I don't want him eating his own"—she paused to search for the proper word for the context, running through various euphemisms before giving it up—"shit."

Another shrug.

"I'm serious on this. Are you with me?"

Nisha couldn't help herself, and so what if she was pushing it? So what? "Admiral did," she said. "Maybe you didn't know that."

Gretchen just waved her hand in dismissal. "But *this* Admiral," she said. "He's not going to do it. Is he?"

Over the course of the next two weeks, as summer settled in with a succession of cloudless, high-arching days and Admiral steadily grew into the promise of his limbs, Erhard became a fixture at the house. Every morning, when Nisha came through the gate with the dog on his leash, he was there waiting for her, shining and tall and beautiful, with a joke on his lips and always some little treat for Admiral secreted in one pocket or another. The dog worshipped him. Went crazy for him. Pranced on the leash, spun in circles, nosed at his sleeves and pockets till he got his treat, then rolled over on his back in blissful submission. And then it was the dog park, and instead of sitting there wrapped up in the cocoon of herself, she had Erhard to sustain her, to lean into her so that she could feel the heat of him through the thin cotton of his shirt, to kiss her, and later, after lunch and the rising tide of the beer, to make love to her on the divan in the cool shadows of the pool house. They swam in the afternoons—he didn't mind the five pounds she'd put on; he praised her for them—and sometimes Frankie would join them, shedding the maid's habit for a white two-piece and careering through a slashing backstroke with a bottle of beer her reward, because she was part of the family too, Mama and Papa and Aunt Frankie, all there to nurture little Admiral under the beneficent gaze of the sun.

Of course, Nisha was no fool. She knew there was a quid pro quo involved here, knew that Erhard had his agenda, but she was in no hurry, she'd committed to nothing, and as she lay there on the divan smoothing her hands over his back, tasting him, enjoying him, taking him inside her, she felt hope, real hope, for the first time since she'd come back home. It got so that she looked forward to each day, even the mornings that had been so hard on her, having to take a tray up to the ghost of her mother while her father trudged off to work, the whole house like a turned grave, because now she had Admiral, now she had Erhard, and she could shrug off anything. Yes. Sure. That was the way it was. Until the day he called her on it.

Cloudless sky, steady sun, every flower at its peak. She came down the walk with Admiral on his leash at the appointed hour, pulled back the gate, and there he was—but this time he wasn't alone. Beside him, already straining at the leash, was a gangling overgrown Afghan pup that could have been the twin of Admiral, and though she'd known it was coming, known the plan since the very first day, she was awestruck. "Jesus," she said, even as Admiral jerked her forward and the two dogs began to romp round her legs in a tangle of limbs and leashes, "how did you—? I mean, he's the exact, he's totally—"

"That's the idea, isn't it?"

"But where did you find him?"

Erhard gave her a look of appraisal, then his eyes jumped past her to sweep the street. "Let's go inside, no? I don't want that they should see us here, anyone—not right in the front of the house."

He hadn't talked her into it, not yet, not exactly, but now that the moment had come she numbly punched in the code and held the gate open for him. What he wanted to do, what he was in the process of doing with her unspoken complicity, was to switch the dogs—just for a day, two at the most—by way of experiment. His contention was that the Strikers would never know the difference, that they were arrogant exemplars of bourgeois excess, even to the point of violating the laws of nature—and God, God too—simply to satisfy their own solipsistic desires. Admiral wouldn't be harmed—he'd enjoy himself, the change of scenery, all that. And certainly she knew how much the dog had come to mean to him. "But these people will not recognize their own animal," he'd insisted, his voice gone hard with conviction, "and so I will have my story and the world will know it."

Once inside the gate, they let the dogs off their leashes and went round back of the house where they'd be out of sight. They walked hand-in-hand, his fingers entwined with hers, and for a long while, as the sun rode high overhead and a breeze slipped in off the ocean to stir the trees, they watched as the two dogs streaked back and forth, leaping and nipping and tumbling in doggy rhapsody. Admiral's great combed-out spill of fur whipped round him in a frenzy of motion, and the new dog, Erhard's dog—the imposter—matched him step for step, hair for glorious hair. "You took him to the groomer, didn't you?" she said.

Erhard gave a stiff nod. "Yes, sure: what do you think? He must be exact."

She watched, bemused, for another minute, her misgivings buried deep under the pressure of his fingers, bone, sinew, the wedded flesh, and why shouldn't she go along with him? What was the harm? His article, or exposé or whatever it was, would appear in Switzerland, in German, and the Strikers would never know the difference. Or even if they did, even if it was translated into English and grabbed headlines all over the country, they had it coming to them. Erhard was right. She knew it. She'd known it all along. "So what's his name?" she asked, the dogs shooting past her in a moil of fur and flashing feet. "Does he have a name?"

"Fred."

"Fred? What kind of name is that for a pedigree dog?"

"What kind of name is Admiral?"

She was about to tell him the story of the original Admiral, how he'd earned his sobriquet because of his enthusiasm for the Strikers' yacht and how they were planning on taking Admiral II out on the water as soon as they could, when the familiar rumble of the driveway gate drawing back on its runners startled her. In the next moment, she was in motion, making for the near corner of the house where she could see down the long macadam strip of the drive. Her heart skipped a beat: it was Gretchen. Gretchen home early, some crisis compelling her, mislaid papers, her blouse stained, the flu, Gretchen in her black Beemer, waiting for the gate to slide back so she could roll up the drive and exert dominion over her house and property, her piss-stained carpets and her insuperable dog. "Quick!" Nisha shouted, whirling round, "grab them. Grab the dogs!"

She saw Erhard plunge forward and snatch at them, the grass rising up to meet him and both dogs tearing free. "Admiral!" he called, scrambling to his knees. "Here, boy. Come!" The moment thundered in her ears. The dogs hesitated, the ridiculous sea of fur smoothing and settling momentarily, and then one of them—it was Admiral, it had to be—came to him and he got hold of it even as the other pricked up its ears at the sound of the car and bolted round the corner of the house.

"I'll stall her," she called.

Erhard, all six feet and five inches of him, was already humping across the grass in the direction of the pool house, the dog writhing in his arms.

But the other dog—it was Fred, it had to be—was chasing the car up the drive now, nipping at the wheels, and as Nisha came round the corner she could read the look on her employer's face. A moment and she was there, grabbing for the dog as the car rolled to a stop and the engine died. Gretchen stepped out of the car, heels coming down squarely on the pavement, her shoulders thrust back tightly against the grip of her jacket. "I thought I told you. . . ," she began, her voice high and querulous, but then she faltered and her expression changed. "But where's Admiral?" she said. "And whose dog is *that*?"

In the course of her life, short though it had been, she'd known her share of embittered people—her father, for one; her mother, for another—and she'd promised herself she'd never go there, never descend to that hopeless state of despair and regret that ground you down till you were nothing but raw animus, but increasingly now everything she thought or felt or tasted was bitter to the root. Erhard was gone. The Strikers were inflexible. Her mother lingered. Admiral reigned supreme. When the car had come up the drive and Gretchen had stood there confronting her, she'd never felt lower in her life. Until Admiral began howling in the distance and then broke free of Erhard to come careening round the corner of the house and launch himself in one wholly coordinated and mighty leap right into the arms of his protector. And then Erhard appeared, head bowed and shoulders slumped, looking abashed.

"I don't think I've had the pleasure," Gretchen said, setting down the dog (which sprang right up again, this time at Erhard) and at the same time shooting Nisha a look before stepping forward and extending her hand.

"Oh, this is, uh, Erhard," she heard herself say. "He's from Switzerland, and I, well, I just met him in the dog park and since he had an Afghan too—"

Erhard was miserable, as miserable as she'd ever seen him, but he mustered a counterfeit of his smile and said, "Nice to meet you," even as Gretchen dropped his hand and turned to Nisha.

"Well, it's a nice idea," she said, looking down at the dogs, comparing them, "—good for you for taking the initiative, Nisha . . . but really, you have to know that Admiral didn't have any—*playmates*—here on the property, Afghans or no, and I'm sure he wasn't exposed to anybody from *Switzerland,* if you catch my drift?"

There was nothing Nisha could do but nod her acquiescence.

"So," Gretchen said, squaring her shoulders and turning back to Erhard. "Nice to meet you," she said, "but I'm going to have to ask that you take your dog—what's his name?"

Erhard ducked his head. "Fred."

"Fred? What an odd name. For a dog, I mean. His does have papers, doesn't he?"

"Oh, yes, he's of the highest order, very well-bred."

Gretchen glanced dubiously down at the dog, then back at Erhard. "Yes, well, he looks it," she said, "and they do make great dogs, Afghans— we ought to know. I don't know if Nisha told you, but Admiral is very special, very, very special, and we can't have any other dogs on the property. And I don't mean to be abrupt"—a sharp look for Nisha—"but strangers of any sort, or species, just cannot be part of this, this . . ." she trailed off, fighting, at the end, to recover the cold impress of her smile. "Nice meeting you," she repeated, and there was nowhere to go from there.

It had taken Nisha a while to put it all behind her. She kept thinking Erhard was lying low, that he'd be back, that there had been something between them after all, but by the end of the second week she no longer looked for him at the gate or at the dog park or anywhere else. And very slowly, as the days beat on, she began to understand what her role was, her true role. Admiral chased his tail and she encouraged him. When he did his business along the street, she nudged the hard little bolus with the tip of her shoe till he stooped to take it up in his mouth. Yes, she was living in the past and her mother was dying and she'd gone to college for nothing, but she was determined to create a new future—for herself and Admiral— and when she took him to the dog park she lingered outside the gate, to let him run free where he really wanted to be, out there on the street where the cars shunted by and the wheels spun and stalled and caught the light till there was nothing else in the world. "Good boy," she'd say. "Good boy."

ASH MONDAY

He'd always loved the smell of gasoline. It reminded him of when he was little, when he was seven or eight and Grady came to live with them. When Grady moved in he'd brought his yellow Chevy Super Sport with him, backing it into the weeds by the side of the garage on a sleek black trailer he must have rented for the day because it was gone in the morning. That first night had fallen over Dill like an absence, like all the nights then and most of the days too, a whole tumble of nothing that sparked with a particle of memory here and there. But he remembered the trailer, and Grady—of course he remembered Grady because Grady was here in this house till he was eleven years old—and he remembered seeing the car mounted on cement blocks the next morning as if it had gone through a wall at a hundred miles an hour and got hung up on the rubble. And he remembered the smell of gasoline. Grady wore it like perfume.

Now Dill was thirteen, with a car of his own, or at least the one he'd have when he was old enough to get his learner's permit, and when he tried to picture Grady, what Grady looked like, he could see Grady's hat, the grease-feathered baseball cap that had a #4 and a star sign on it in a little silver box in front, and he could see Grady's silver shades beneath the bill of that cap, and below that there must have been a nose and a mouth but all he could remember was the mustache that hooked down over the corners of Grady's lips, making him look like the sad face Billy Bottoms used to draw on every available surface when they were in fifth grade.

At the moment, he was in the yard, smelling gasoline, thinking of Grady, looking at his own piece-of-shit car parked there by the garage where the Super Sport had sunk into its cement blocks till his mother had it towed away to the junkyard. He felt the weight of the gas can in his

hand, lifted his face to the sun and the hot breath sifting through the canyon, but for just a fraction of a second he forgot what he was doing there,
as if he'd gone outside of himself. This was a thing that happened to him,
that had always happened to him, another kind of absence that was so
usual he hardly noticed it. It irritated his mother. Baffled his teachers. He
wished it wouldn't happen or happen so often, but there it was. He was a
dreamer, he guessed. That was what his mother called him. A dreamer.

And here came her voice through the kitchen window, her caught-
high-in-the-throat voice that snapped like the braided tail of a whip: "Dill,
what are you doing standing there? The potatoes are almost done. I need
you to light the fire and put up the meat *right this minute!*"

His mother was a teacher. His father didn't exist. His grandmother
was dead. And this house, high in the canyon with bleached boulders all
around it like the big toes of a hundred buried giants, was his grandmother's house. And his piece-of-shit '97 Toyota Camry with no front
bumper, two seriously rearranged fenders and the sun-blistered paint that
used to be metallic gold but had turned the color of a fresh dog turd, was
his grandmother's car. But then she didn't need a car, not where she was
now. And where was that? he'd asked his mother in the hush of the back
room at the funeral parlor where they'd burned up his grandmother and
made her fit into a squared-off cardboard box. "You know," his mother
said. "You know where she is." And he'd said, "Yeah, I know where she
is—in that box right there."

So he felt a little thrill. He had a can of gasoline in his hand. He was
the man of the house—"You're my man now," his mother had told him
when he was eleven years old and Grady's face swelled up like a soccer ball
from all the screaming and fuck-you's and fuck-you-too's before he
slammed out the door and disappeared for good—and it was his job to
light the fire and grill the meat. Every night. Even in winter when the
rains came and it was cold and he had to wear his hoodie and watch the
flames from under the overhang on the garage. That was all right. He had
nothing better to do. And he liked the way the charcoal went up in a flash
that sucked the life out of the air after he'd soaked it with gasoline, a thing
his mother had expressly forbidden him to do (*It could explode, you know*

that, don't you?), but they were out of charcoal lighter and the store was way down the snaking road at the bottom of the canyon and for the past week this was the way he'd done it.

The grill was an old iron gas thing shaped like a question mark with the dot cut off the bottom. The tank was still attached, but it had been empty for years and they just dumped briquettes in on top of the chunks of ancient pumice that were like little burned-up asteroids sent down from space and went ahead and cooked that way. He set down the can, patted the front pocket of his jeans to feel the matches there. Then he lifted the iron lid and let it rest back on its hinges, and he was just bending to the bag of charcoal when he saw something move beneath the slats of the grill. He was startled, his first thought for the snakes coming down out of the chaparral because of the drought, but this was no snake—it was a rat. A stupid dun-colored little thing with a wet black eye and cat's whiskers peering up at him from the gap between two slats, and what was it thinking? That it would be safe in a cooking grill? That it could build a nest in there? He slammed the lid down hard and heard the thing scrambling around in the ashes.

He could feel a quick pulse of excitement coming up in him. He glanced over his shoulder to make sure his mother wasn't watching through the screen door, and he snatched one quick look at the blank stucco wall and sun-glazed windows of the house next door—Itchy-goro's house, Itchy-goro, with his gook face and gook eyes and his big liar's mouth—and then he cracked the lid of the grill just enough to slosh some gasoline inside before slamming it shut. He started counting off the seconds, *one-a-thousand, two-a-thousand,* and there was no sound now, nothing but silence. And when he struck the match and flung it in he felt the way he did when he was alone in his room watching the videos he hid from his mother, making himself hard and then soft and then hard again.

Sanjuro Ichiguro was standing at the picture window, admiring the way the light sifted through the pale yellow-green leaves of the bamboo he'd planted along the pathway to the front door and down the slope to the neighbors' yard. This was a variety of bamboo called Buddha's Belly, for the plump swellings between its joints, perfect for poor soils and dry climates, and he fed and watered it sparingly, so as to produce the maximal swelling. He'd planted other varieties too—the yellow groove, the marbled, the golden—but Buddha's Belly was his favorite because his father had prized it and it reminded him of home. He didn't care so much about the cherry trees on the east side of the house—they were almost a cliché—but Setsuko had insisted on them. If they were going to have to live so far away from home—*Six thousand miles!* she'd kept repeating, riding a tide of woe as they packed and shipped their things and said goodbye to their families in Okutama nearly a decade ago—then she wanted at least to make this house and this sun-blasted yard into something beautiful, something *Japanese* set down amidst the scrub oak and manzanita. He'd hired a carpenter to erect the *torii* to frame her view of the cherry trees and a pair of Mexican laborers to dig a little jigsaw pond out front so she could rest there in the late afternoon and watch the koi break the surface while the lily pads revealed their flowers and the dragonflies hovered and he sat entombed in the steel box of the car, stuck in traffic.

From the kitchen came the smell of dinner—garlic, green onions, sesame oil. His commute from Pasadena had been murder, nearly two hours when it should have been half of that, but some idiot had plowed into the back end of another idiot and then a whole line of cars joined in the fun and the freeway was down to one lane by the time he got there. But he was home now and the light was exquisite, the air was rich with whatever it was Setsuko was preparing and in his hand he held a glass of Onikoroshi, chilled to perfection. He was remembering the pond, the old one, the one he'd made too shallow so that the raccoons had wallowed in it at night and made sashimi of the koi that had cost him a small fortune because he wanted to establish a breeding stock and his salary at JPL allowed him the freedom to purchase the very best of everything.

The raccoons. They were a hazard of living up here, he supposed. Like the coyotes that had made off with Setsuko's cat while she was standing right in front of the house, not ten feet away, watering the begonias. And that bird. A great long-legged thing that might have been a stork but for the pewter glaze of its feathers. He'd come out one morning at dawn to get a head start on the traffic, his car keys dangling from one hand, his lucky ceramic mug and a thermos of green tea in the other, only to see it there up to its knees in the pond, his marble-white *purachina ogon* clasped between the twin levers of its bill as neatly as if the bird were an animated pair of chopsticks, *hashi* with legs and wings. That was his metaphor. His joke. And he used it on his colleagues at work, the whole story, from the snatching of the fish to his outraged shout to the bird's startled flapping as it wrote its way across the sky, refining it in the telling till the fact that the fish had cost him sixteen hundred dollars only underscored the hilarity— he even called Setsuko from his cell on the way home and told her too: *Hashi with wings.*

Suddenly his eyes were drawn to the neighboring yard, to a drift of movement there, and he felt the smallest tick of irritation. It was that kid, that boy, the one who'd insulted him to his face. And what was he up to now? The grill, the nightly ritual with the grill, and why couldn't the mother cook in the oven like anyone else? These weren't feudal times. They weren't cavemen, were they? He raised the glass to his nose to feel the cold rim of it there and inhale the scent of his sake. He took a sip, then another long sniff, and it calmed him. This was the scent of pleasure, of unwinding after work, of civility, the scent of a country where people would never dream of calling their next-door neighbor a gook motherfucker or anything else for that matter. And while he understood perfectly well the term motherfucker, its significance escaped him, unless it had to do with incest or some infantile fixation with marital sex, in which case the preponderance of men were indeed motherfuckers. But it was the gook part of the equation that truly mystified him. Colin Andrews, at work, had flinched when Sanjuro had asked him its meaning, but then put on the bland frozen-eyed look Americans assumed when confronting racial issues and explained that it was a derogatory term for the Vietnamese deriving from the war there in the sixties, but that had only further confused him. How could this boy, even if he was mentally deficient—and he was, he was sure of it—ever confuse him, a Japanese, with one of those spindly little underfed peasants from Vietnam?

Angry now, angry all at once, he called over his shoulder to Setsuko. "He's at it again."

Her face appeared in the kitchen doorway, round as the moon. He saw that she'd had her hair done, two waves cresting on either side of her brow and an elevated dome built up on top of it. She looked almost like an American, like a *gaijin,* and he didn't know whether he liked that or not. "Who?" she asked in Japanese—they always spoke Japanese at home.

"The kid next door. The delinquent. The little shit. Now he's using gasoline to cook his hot dogs or hamburgers or whatever it is, can you imagine?"

She glanced at the window, but from where she was standing the angle was wrong so that she must have seen only the sky and the tips of the bamboo waving in the breeze. If she'd taken five steps forward, she could have seen what he was talking about, the kid dancing round the rusted grill with the red-and-yellow gas can and his box of kitchen matches, but she didn't. "Do you like my hair?" she said. "I went to Mrs. Yamamura at the beauty parlor today and she thought we would try something different. Just for a change. Do you like it?"

"Maybe I should donate a box of lighter fluid—just leave it on the front porch. Because if he keeps this up he's going to burn the whole canyon down, I tell you that."

"It's nothing. Don't let it worry you."

"Nothing? You call this nothing? Wait till your cherry trees go up in smoke, the house, the cars, wait till the fish boil in the pond like it's a pot on the stove, then tell me it's nothing."

The kid struck the match, pulled back the lid and flung it in. There was the muffled concussion of the gasoline going up, flames leaping high off the grill in a jagged corona before sucking themselves back in, and something else, something shooting out like the tail of a rocket and jerking across the ground in a skirt of fire.

It was the coolest thing he'd ever seen. The rat came flying out of there squealing like the brakes on the Camry and before he had a chance to react it was rolling in the dirt, and then, still aflame, trying to bury itself in the high weeds in back of the garage. And then the weeds caught fire. Which was intense. And he was running after the thing with the vague intent of crushing its skull under the heel of his shoe or maybe watching to see how long it would take before it died on its own, when here came Itchy-goro flying down the hill like he was on drugs, screaming, "You crazy? You crazy outta your mind?"

The weeds hissed and popped, burrs and stickers mainly, a few tumbleweeds that were all air, the fire already burning itself out because there was nothing to feed it but dirt and gravel. And the rat was just lying there now, blackened and steaming like a marshmallow that's fallen off the stick and into the coals. But Itchy-goro—he was in his bathrobe and slippers and he had a rake in his hand—jumped over the fence and started beating at the weeds as if he was trying to kill a whole field full of rattlesnakes. Dill just stood there while Itchy-goro cursed in his own language and snatched up the hose that was lying by the side of the garage and sprayed water all over everything like it was some big deal. Then he heard the door slam behind him and he looked over his shoulder to see his mother running toward them in her bare feet and he had a fleeting image of the harsh deep lines that dug in around her toes that were swollen and red from where her shoes pinched her because she was on her feet all day long. "Can't you get up and get the milk?" she'd say. Or "I'm too exhausted to set the table, can't you do it?" And then the kicker: "I've been on my feet all day long."

Itchy-goro's face was twisted out of shape. He looked like one of the dupes in a ninja movie, one of the ten thousand anonymous grimacing fools who rush Jet Li with a two-by-four or tire iron only to be whacked in the throat or the knee and laid out on the ground. "You see?" he was shouting. "You see what he does? Your boy?" Itchy-goro's hands were trembling. He couldn't seem to get the hose right, the water arcing up to spatter the wall of the garage, then drooling down to puddle in the dust. The air stank of incinerated weed.

Before his mother could put on her own version of Itchy-goro's face and say "What on earth are you doing now?" Dill kicked at a stone in the dirt, put his hands on his hips and said, "How was I supposed to know a rat was in there? A rat, Mom. A rat in our cooking grill."

But she took Itchy-goro's side, the two of them yelling back and forth— "Dry tinder!" Itchy-goro kept saying—and pretty soon they were both yelling at him. So he gave his mother a look that could peel hide and stalked off around the corner of the garage and didn't even bother to answer when she called his name out in her shrillest voice three times in a row.

He kept going till he came to the shed where Grady used to keep the chinchillas, and then he went round that too and pushed his way through the door that was hanging by one hinge and into the superheated shadows within. She could cook her own pork chops, that was what he was thinking. Let her give them to Itchy-goro. She always took his side, anyway. Why didn't she just go ahead and marry him? That's what he'd say to her later when he was good and ready to come in and eat something and listen to her rag on him about his homework: "Marry Itchy-goro if you love him so much."

It took him a moment, standing slumped in the half-light and breathing in the shit smell of the chinchillas that would probably linger there forever like the smell of the bandages they wrapped the mummies in, before he felt his heartbeat begin to slow. He was sweating. It must have been twenty degrees hotter in there than outside, but he didn't care. This was where he came when he was upset or when he wanted to think or remember what it had been like when Grady was raising the chinchillas and they'd had to work side by side to keep the cages clean and make sure there was enough food and water for each and every one of them. You needed between eighty and a hundred pelts to make one coat, so Grady would always go on about how they had to keep breeding them to get more and more or they'd never turn a profit. That was his phrase, turn a profit. And Dill remembered how his mother would throw it back at him because he wasn't turning a profit and never would, the cost of feed and the animals themselves a constant drain—and that was her phrase—but nothing compared to what they were spending on air-conditioning.

"They've got to be kept cool," Grady insisted.

"What about us?" his mother would say. "We can't afford to run the air-conditioning in the house—you jump down my throat every time I switch it on as if it was some kind of crime—but god forbid your precious rodents should do without it."

"You've got to have patience, Gloria. Any business—"

"Business? You call sitting around in an air-conditioned shed all day a business? How many coats have you made, tell me that? How many pelts have you sold? How many have you even harvested? Tell me that."

Dill was on Grady's side and he never even thought twice about it. His mother didn't know anything. Chinchillas were from South America, high in the Andes Mountains where the temperature was in the cool range and never went over eighty degrees, not even on the hottest day in history. At eighty degrees they'd die of heatstroke. She didn't know that. Or she didn't care. But Dill knew it. And he knew how to feed them their chin-chilla pellets and the little cubes of hay, but no cabbage or corn or lettuce because it would give them gas and they would bloat up and die. He knew how to kill them too. Grady showed him. What you did was pull the chin-chilla out of its cage by the tail and then take hold of its head in one hand and give the back legs a jerk to break the neck. Then it twitched for a while. Then you skinned it out. Grady didn't like to kill them—they were cute, they were harmless, he didn't like to kill anything—but it was a business and you had to keep sight of that.

That fall, the Santa Ana winds had begun to blow. Dill's science teacher, Mr. Shields, had explained it to them—how, when a high-pressure system built up inland and low pressure settled in over the ocean, all the air got sucked down from the deserts and squeezed through the canyons in gusts of wind that were clocked at as much as a hundred miles an hour, drying everything to the bone—but Dill knew the wind as something more im-mediate. He felt it in the grit between his teeth, the ring of dirt in his nostrils in the morning. And he could taste it when he was out in the backyard, the whole world baking like the pizza ovens at Giovanni's, only instead of pizza it was sage they were baking, it was the leaves from the sycamore trees along the dried-up streambed and the oil of the poison oak that was everywhere. He came home from school one afternoon and the wind was so strong it shook the bus when he stepped off it. Immediately a fistful of sand raked his face just as if it had been blasted out of a shotgun, and somebody—Billy Bottoms, most likely—shouted "Sucker!" as the doors wheezed shut.

He turned his head to keep the dirt out of his eyes. Tumbleweeds catapulted across the yard. Scraps of paper and plastic bottles spewed from the trash can in a discontinuous stream, like water blown out of a sprinkler, and he could already hear his mother going on about how somebody had been too lazy and too careless to take one extra second to fasten the raccoon clamps on the lid. He pulled down the brim of his cap, the one Grady had given him, with the silver-and-black F-14 Tomcat on the crown, hiked up his backpack to get the weight off his spine, and went on up the walk and into the house.

In the kitchen, he poured himself a tall glass of root beer and drank it down in a gulp, never so thirsty in his life, then poured another one and took his time with it while his Hot Pocket sizzled in the microwave. He was planning on going out to the shed to see what Grady was doing, but first he flicked on the TV in the kitchen just to have something to do while he was eating, and there was nothing but news on. The news was on because everything was burning everywhere, from Malibu through the San Fernando Valley and into L.A. and Orange County too. On every channel there was a woman with a microphone and some seriously blowing hair standing in front of a burning house and trees gone up like candles— change the channel and all you did was change the color of the woman, blond, black, Mexican, Chinese. Mr. Shields had told them a wildfire could come at you faster than you could run and that was why firemen sometimes burned to death and homeowners too—which was why you had to evacuate when the police came round and told you to. But nobody believed him. How could fire go faster than somebody running all out? He thought of Daylon James, the fastest kid in the school—how nobody could even touch him in flag football, let alone swipe the flag—and the idea seemed preposterous. But there were helicopters on the screen now, the camera jumping from one angle to another, and then just the flames, sheets of them rippling from red to orange to yellow and back, and the black crown of the smoke.

He was picturing himself running as hard as he could through a field of burning bushes and trees as a whole mountain of fire came down on him, and he must have zoned out a minute because when he looked up the TV screen was blank and the LED display on the microwave had switched off. That was when Grady burst through the back door. "Quick," he said, and he was panting as if he couldn't catch his breath and his face wasn't Grady's face but the face of some crazy person in a horror flick in the instant before the monster catches up to him. "Grab all the ice you can. Quick! Quick!"

They ran out the back door with every scrap of ice from the ice maker in two black plastic bags and the bags rippled and sang with the wind and the dirt blew in their eyes and the door to the shed didn't want to open and when it did it tore back and slammed against the bleached-out boards like a giant fist. The shed was still cool inside, but the air-conditioning was down—the power was out, through the whole canyon—and already the chinchillas were looking stressed. He and Grady went down all four rows of cages, cages stacked three high with newspapers spread out on top of each row to catch the turds from the cages above, tossing ice cubes inside. Half an hour later, it was up to seventy-eight in the shed and Grady, his eyes jumping in his face like two yellow jackets on a piece of meat, said, "I'm going to make a run down the canyon for ice. You stay here and, I don't know, take off your shirt and fan them, anything to work up some breeze, and maybe run the hose over the roof and the walls, you know? Just to cool it a little. All we need is a little till the sun goes down and we'll be all right."

But they weren't all right. Even though Grady came back with the trunk of the Camry packed full of ice, thirty bags or more, and they filled the cages with the little blue-white machine-made cubes and draped wet sheets over everything, the heat kept rising. Till it was too hot. Till the chinchillas got heatstroke, one after another. First the standard grays started to die, then the mosaics and the black velvets that were worth twice as much. Grady kept reviving them with ice packs he squeezed around their heads till they came to and wobbled across their cages, but the electricity didn't come back on and the ice melted and the sun didn't seem to want to go down that day because it was a sci-fi sun, big and fat and red, and it wanted only to dry out everything in creation. By the time Dill's mother got back from school—"Sorry I'm late; the meeting just dragged on and on"—the chinchillas were dead, all dead, two hundred and seventeen of them. And the shed smelled the way it still smelled now. Like piss. And shit. And death.

It was a thing they did on Fridays, after work, he and some of his colleagues who tracked CloudSat, the satellite that collected data on global cloud formations for the benefit of meteorologists worldwide, not to mention the local weatherman. They met at a sushi bar in Pasadena, one of those novelty places for *gaijin* featuring a long oval bar with the chefs in the middle and a flotilla of little wooden boats circling around in a canal of fresh-flowing water from which you plucked one plate or another from the passing boats till the saucers mounted up and the Filipino busboy slid them into his wet plastic tub. It wasn't authentic. And it wasn't good, or not particularly. But you could special-order if you liked (which he always did, depending on what the head chef told him was best that day), and, of course, the beer and sake never stopped coming. Sanjuro had already put away two sakes and he was thinking about ordering a beer—or splitting one with Colin, because he was going to have to switch to tea eventually, to straighten himself out for the drive home. He gazed absently down the bar, past his co-workers and the mob of other people crowding in to ply their chopsticks and drip cheap sake into their little ceramic cups as if it were some exotic rite, and saw how the sun took the color out of everything beyond the windows. The cars were white with it, the trees black. What was he doing here?

Colin turned to him then and said, "Isn't that right, Sange?"

They'd been discussing sports, the usual topic, before they moved on to women, and, inevitably, work. Sanjuro hated sports. And he hated to be called Sange. But he liked Colin and Dick Wurzengreist and Bill Chen, good fellows all, and he liked being here with them, even if he was feeling the effects of the sake on a mostly empty stomach—or maybe because he was. "What?" he heard himself say. "Isn't what right?"

Colin's face hung there above half a dozen saucers smeared with soya and a bottle of Asahi with a quarter inch of beer left in it. He was grinning. His eyes looked blunted. "SC," he said. "They're thirty-five-point favorites over Stanford, can you believe it? I mean, how clueless do you have to be not to bet against the spread—am I right?"

There was something like merriment in the drawn-down slits of Dick Wurzengreist's eyes—Dick was drunk—but Bill Chen was involved in a conversation about alternate-side-of-the-street parking with the woman seated beside him and everyone knew the question was for show only, part of a long-standing joke at Sanjuro's expense. They were all what the average person would call nerds, but it seemed that Sanjuro was the prince of the nerds simply because he didn't care two pennies for sports. "Yes," he said, and he wanted to flash a smile but couldn't seem to summon the energy, "you're absolutely right."

Everyone had a laugh over that, and he didn't mind—it was part of the routine—and then the beer came and things quieted down and Colin began to talk about work. Or not work, so much as gossip revolving around work, how so-and-so kept a bottle in his desk and how another had tested positive for marijuana and then slammed into a deer right out front of the gate, that sort of thing. Sanjuro listened in silence. He was a good listener. But he was bored with gossip and shoptalk too, and when Colin paused to top off both their glasses, he said, "You know that kid I was telling you about? The one that called me a gook?"

"A gook motherfucker," Colin corrected.

"Well, you know how the wind's been blowing, especially in the canyon—and I told you how the mother sends the kid out there every night to start up the grill?"

Colin nodded. His eyes were like the lenses of a camera, the pupils narrowing and then dilating: click. He was drunk. He'd have to call his wife to drive him home again, Sanjuro could see that. And he himself would soon have to push the beer aside and gear himself up for the freeway.

"You know it's been gasoline all week, as if they couldn't afford char-coal lighter, and I tell you last night he nearly blew the thing up."

Colin let out a short bark of a laugh before he seemed to realize that it wasn't funny, that Sanjuro hadn't meant to be funny, not at all—that he was worried, deeply concerned, nearly hysterical over it and right on the verge of calling the police. Or the fire department, Sanjuro was thinking. The fire marshal. Wasn't there a fire marshal?

"And there was a rat in it, in the grill, and he set the rat on fire."

"A rat? You're joking, right?"

"No joke. The rat was like this flaming ball shooting across the drive-way and right on into the weeds behind the garage."

"No," Colin said, because that was the required response. And then he grinned: "Let me guess," he said. "Then the weeds caught fire."

Sanjuro felt weary suddenly, as if an invisible force, cupped to fit round his back and his shoulders and arms like a custom-made suit, were press-ing down on him with a weight he couldn't sustain. He was living at the top of a canyon, far from the city, in a high-risk area, because of Setsuko, because Setsuko was afraid of Americans, black Americans, Mexicans, whites too—all the people crowding the streets of Pasadena and Altadena and everyplace else. She watched the TV news, trying to learn the lan-guage, and it made her crazy. "I won't live in an apartment," she'd in-sisted. "I won't live with that kind of people. I want nature. I want to live where it's safe." She'd sacrificed for him in coming here, to this country, for his career, and so he'd sacrificed for her and they bought the house at the end of the road at the very top of a wild canyon and tried to make it just like a house in Mitaka or Okutama.

He paused to give Colin a long look, staring into the weed-green shut-ters of his eyes—Colin, his friend, his amigo, the man who understood him best of anyone on the team—and he let out a sigh that was deeper and moister and more self-pitying than he'd intended, because he never showed emotion, or never meant to. That wasn't the Japanese way. He looked down. Made his face conform. "Yeah," he said. "That's just what happened."

.   .   .   .   .

So tonight it was chicken—and three of those hot Italian sausages he liked, and a piece of fish, salmon with the skin still on it his mother had paid twelve dollars for because they were having a guest for dinner. One of the teachers who worked with her at the elementary school. "His name's Scott," she said. "He's a vegetarian."

It took him a moment to register the information: guest for dinner, teacher, vegetarian. "So what does he eat—spinach? Brussels sprouts? Bean burritos?"

She was busy at the stove. Her wineglass stood half-full on the baked enamel surface between the snow peas sautéing in the pan and the pot where she was boiling potatoes for her homemade potato salad. He could see the smudge of her lipstick on the near side of the glass and he could see through it to the broken clock set in its display above the burners and the shining chrome-framed window on the door of the oven that didn't work anymore because the handle had broken off and there was no way to turn it on, even with a pair of pliers. "Fish," she said, swiveling to give him a look over her shoulder, "he eats fish."

She'd come straight home from school that afternoon, showered, changed her clothes and run the vacuum over the rug in the living room. Then she'd set the table and stuck an empty vase in the middle of it— "He'll bring flowers, you wait and see: that's the kind of person he is, very thoughtful"—and then she'd started chopping things up for a green salad and rinsing the potatoes. Dill was afraid she was going to add, "You're really going to like him," but she didn't and so he didn't say anything either, though after the fish comment he'd thought about pitching his voice into the range of sarcasm and asking, "So is this a date?"

Her last words to him as he slammed out the door with the platter of meat, the matches and the plastic squeeze bottle of lighter fluid that had appeared magically on the doorstep that morning, were, "Don't burn the fish. And don't overcook it either."

He was in the yard. The wind had died, but now it came up again, rattling things, chasing leaves across the driveway and up against the piece-of-shit Toyota, where they gathered with yesterday's leaves and the leaves from last week and the week before that. For a long moment he just stood there, halfway to the grill, feeling the wind, smelling it, watching the way the sun pushed through the air one layer after another and the big bald rock at the top of the canyon seemed to ripple and come clear again. Then he went to the grill, set down the platter of chicken and sausage and the fat red oblong slab of fish, and lifted the heavy iron lid, half-hoping there'd be another rat in there—or a snake, a snake would be even better. But of course there was nothing inside. It was just a grill, not a rat condo. Ash, that was all that was there, just ash.

The wind jumped over the garage then and the ash came to life, sifting out like the sand in *The Mummy Returns,* and that was cool and he let it happen because here was the grill, cleaning itself. And while that was happening and the meat sat there on its platter and the plastic container squeezed in and out like a cold nipple in his hand, he was back in school, last spring, and Billy Bottoms, who wasn't scared of anybody or ever showed any weakness or even a flaw—not a single zit, nothing—had a black thumbprint right in the middle of his forehead. It was an amazing thing, as if Billy had turned Hindu overnight, and Dill couldn't resist calling him out on it. Or no, he didn't call him out on it. He came up behind him and wrestled one arm around his neck, and before Billy knew what was happening Dill had touched his own thumb to the mark there and his thumb came away black. Billy punched him in the side of the head and he punched back and they both got sent to the office and his mother had to come pick him up after detention because there was no late bus and it was your hard luck—part of your punishment—to have to have your mother come for you. Or your father.

Her face was set. She didn't ask, not right away. She was trying to be understanding, trying to make small talk so as not to start in on him before they could both have a minute to calm themselves, so he just came out and said, "He had this spot of ash on his forehead. Like a Hindu, like in *Indiana Jones and the Temple of Doom.* I wanted to see what it was, that was all."

"So? A lot of kids in my class had it too. It's Ash Wednesday." She gave him a glance over the steering wheel. "They're Catholic. It's a Catholic thing."

"But we're not Catholic," he said. There were only seven cars left in the parking lot. He counted them.

"No," she said, shaking her head but keeping her face locked up all the same.

"We're not anything, are we?"

She was busy with the steering wheel, maneuvering her own car, her Nissan Sentra that was only slightly better than the piece-of-shit Toyota, around the elevated islands that divided the parking lot. The radio gave up a soft hum and a weak voice bleated out one of the easy-listening songs she was always playing. She shook her head again. Let out an audible breath. Shrugged her shoulders. "I don't know. I believe in God, if that's what you're asking." He said nothing. "Your grandparents, my parents, I mean, were Presbyterian, but we didn't go to church much. Christmas, Easter. In name only, I guess."

"So what does that make me?"

Another shrug. "You can be anything you want. Why? Are you interested in religion?"

"I don't know."

"Well, you're a Protestant, then. That's all. Just a Protestant."

He was dumping more briquettes into the grill now, the wind teasing the black powder that wasn't ash off the hard-baked stony little things that weren't really charcoal at all. Then he was squirting them with the clear dry-smelling fluid that was nothing like gasoline with its heavy rich petroleum sweetness, soaking them down, thinking every day was made out of ash, Ash Monday, Ash Tuesday, Ash Saturday and Sunday too. He glanced up to see a car pulling into the driveway at the front of the house. The car door slammed, and a man his mother's age stepped out into the wind with an armload of flowers and a bottle that was probably wine or maybe whiskey. Dill looked to Itchy-goro's house, the windows painted over with sun so that he couldn't see whether Itchy-goro was watching or not, and then he lit the match.

. . . . .

It was a Monday and she hated Mondays most of all because on Mondays Sanjuro always went to work early to set an example for the others, stealing out of the house while it was dark yet and the little thieves of the night, the raccoons, coyotes and rats, were just crawling back into their holes. She'd awaken with the first colorless stirrings of light and lie there in the still room, thinking of her parents and the house she'd grown up in, and feel as if the ground had gone out from under her. This morning was no different. She woke to grayness and for a long while stared up at the ceiling as the color crept back into things, and then she pushed herself up and went down the hallway to the kitchen and lit the stove under the kettle. It wasn't till she was blowing softly into her second cup of tea and gazing out the window into the crowded green struts of the bamboo that she remembered that today was different, today was special: *Shūbun-no-hi,* the autumnal equinox, a holiday in Japan even if it passed unnoticed here.

Her spirits lifted. She would make *ohagi,* the rice balls coated in bean paste people left at the graves of their ancestors to honor the spirits of the dead, and she'd put on one of her best kimono and burn incense too, and when Sanjuro came home they'd have a quiet celebration and neither of them would mention the fact that the graves of their ancestors were six thousand miles away. She thought about that while she was in the shower—about that distance and how long a broom she'd have to find to sweep those graves clean—then she put on the rice and went outside to the garden. If she were in Japan she would have arranged flowers on her parents' graves—red flowers, the *Higanbana* of tradition—but here the closest thing she could find was the bougainvillea that grew along the fence.

The wind rattled the bamboo as she went down the slope with her clippers and the cedar-shake roof of the house below rose to greet her. This was the boy's house, and as she bent to cut the brilliant red plumes of the flowers and lay them over one arm, she saw the cooking grill there in the yard and thought back to two nights ago, or was it three? Sanjuro had been beside himself. He'd gone out of his way to buy a plastic squeeze bottle of starter fluid for these people, the boy and his mother, thinking to help them, and then the boy had stood out there in full view, looking up at the windows and smirking as he fed the fire with long iridescent strings of fuel till the strings were fire themselves. He wasn't thankful. He wasn't respectful. He was a bad boy, a delinquent, just as Sanjuro had said all along, and the mother was worse—and a teacher, no less. They were bad people, that was all, no different from the criminals on the news every night, stabbing each other, screaming, their faces opening up in one great maw of despair.

Setsuko felt the weight of the sun. A gust flailed the bamboo and flung grit at her face. She made her way back up the hill, the wind whipping her kimono and sawing at the canes till they were like swords clashing together, and there was wind drift all over the surface of the pond and the koi moiling beneath it like pulsing flames. The mouth of the brass urn took the flowers, a spray of them, and she went down on her knees to get the arrangement just right. But then the wind shifted them and shifted them again, the papery petals flapping against the bamboo that framed the pond, and after a while she gave it up, figuring she'd rearrange them when Sanjuro came home. She was thinking of her mother when she set the incense cone in the burner and put a match to it, the face of the ceramic Buddha glowing through its eye holes as if it were alive.

But the wind, the wind. She got up and was halfway to the house when she heard the first premonitory crackle in the leaves gathered like a skirt at the ankles of the bamboo. She jerked round so violently that her kimono twisted under one foot and she very nearly tripped herself. And she might have caught the fire then, might have dug a frantic scoop of water out of the pond and flung it into the bamboo, might have dashed into the house and dialed 911, but she didn't. She just stood there motionless as the wind took the flames out of the bamboo and into the yard, rolling on across the hill away from her house and her garden and her tea things and the memory of her mother to set them down in a brilliant sparking burst that was exactly like a fireworks display, cleansing and pure and joyful, on the roof of the house below.

THIRTEEN HUNDRED RATS

There was a man in our village who never in his life had a pet of any kind until his wife died. By my calculation, Gerard Loomis was in his mid-fifties when Marietta was taken from him, but at the ceremony in the chapel he looked so scorched and stricken people mistook him for a man ten or twenty years older. He sat collapsed in the front pew, his clothes mismatched and his limbs splayed in the extremity of his grief, looking as if he'd been dropped there from a great height, like a bird stripped of its feathers in some aerial catastrophe. Once the funeral was over and we'd all offered up our condolences and gone back to our respective homes, rumors began to circulate. Gerard wasn't eating. He wouldn't leave the house or change his clothes. He'd been seen bent over a trash barrel in the front yard, burning patent leather pumps, brassieres, skirts, wigs, even the mink stole with its head and feet still attached that his late wife had worn with pride on Christmas, Easter and Columbus Day.

People began to worry about him, and understandably so. Ours is a fairly close-knit community of a hundred and twenty souls, give or take a few, distributed among some fifty-two stone-and-timber houses erected nearly a century ago in what the industrialist B.P. Newhouse hoped would be a model of Utopian living. We are not Utopians, at least not in this generation, but our village, set as it is in the midst of six hundred acres of dense forest at the end of a consummately discreet road some forty miles from the city, has fostered, we like to think, a closeness and uniformity of outlook you wouldn't find in some of the newer developments built right up to the edges of the malls, galleries and factory outlets that surround them.

He should have a dog, people said. That sounded perfectly reasonable to me. My wife and I have a pair of shelties (as well as two lorikeets, whose chatter provides a tranquil backdrop to our evenings by the fireplace, and one very fat angelfish in a tank all his own on a stand in my study). One evening, at dinner, my wife glanced at me over her reading glasses and said, "Do you know that according to this article in the paper, ninety-three percent of pet owners say their pets make them smile at least once a day?" The shelties—Tim and Tim II—gazed up from beneath the table with wondering eyes as I fed scraps of meat into their mobile and receptive mouths.

"You think I ought to speak with him?" I said. "Gerard, I mean?"

"It couldn't hurt," my wife said. And then, the corners of her mouth sinking toward her chin, she added, "The poor man."

I went to visit him the next day—a Saturday, as it happened. The dogs needed walking, so I took them both with me, by way of example, I suppose, and because when I'm home—and not away on the business that takes me all over the world, sometimes for weeks or even months at a time—I like to give them as much attention as I can. Gerard's cottage was half a mile or so from our house, and I enjoyed the briskness of the season—it was early December, the holidays coming on, a fresh breeze spanking my cheeks. I let the dogs run free ahead of me and admired the way the pine forest B.P. Newhouse had planted all those years ago framed and sculpted the sky. The first thing I noticed on coming up the walk was that Gerard hadn't bothered to rake the leaves from his lawn or cover any of his shrubs against the frost. There were other signs of neglect: the storm windows weren't up yet, garbage overspilled the two cans in the driveway, and a pine bough, casualty of the last storm, lay across the roof of the house like the severed hand of a giant. I rang the bell.

Gerard was a long time answering. When finally he did come to the door, he held it open just a crack and gazed out at me as if I were a stranger. (And I was nothing of the sort—our parents had known each other, we'd played couples bridge for years and had once taken a road trip to Hyannis Port together, not to mention the fact that we saw each other at the lake nearly every day in the summer, shared cocktails at the clubhouse and basked in an air of mutual congratulation over our separate decisions not to complicate our lives with the burden of children.) "Gerard," I said. "Hello. How are you feeling?"

He said nothing. He looked thinner than usual, haggard. I wondered if the rumors were true—that he wasn't eating, wasn't taking care of himself, that he'd given way to despair.

"I was just passing by and thought I'd stop in," I said, working up a grin though I didn't feel much in the mood for levity and had begun to wish I'd stayed home and let my neighbor suffer in peace. "And look," I said, "I've brought Tim and Tim II with me." The dogs, hearing their names, drew themselves up out of the frost-blighted bushes and pranced across the doormat, inserting the long damp tubes of their snouts in the crack of the door.

Gerard's voice was hoarse. "I'm allergic to dogs," he said.

Ten minutes later, after we'd gone through the preliminaries and I was seated on the cluttered couch in front of the dead fireplace while Tim and Tim II whined from the front porch, I said, "Well, what about a cat?" And then, because I was mortified at the state to which he'd sunk—his clothes were grubby, he smelled, the house was like the lounge in a transient hotel—I found myself quoting my wife's statistic about smiling pet owners.

"I'm allergic to cats too," he said. He was perched uncomfortably on the canted edge of a rocker and his eyes couldn't seem to find my face. "But I understand your concern, and I appreciate it. And you're not the first—half a dozen people have been by, pushing one thing or another on me: pasta salad, a baked ham, profiteroles, and pets too. Siamese fighting fish, hamsters, kittens. Mary Martinson caught me at the post office the other day, took hold of my arm and lectured me for fifteen minutes on the virtues of emus. Can you believe it?"

"I feel foolish," I said.

"No, don't. You're right, all of you—I need to snap out of it. And you're right about a pet too." He rose from the chair, which rocked crazily behind him. He was wearing a stained pair of white corduroy shorts and a sweatshirt that made him look as gaunt as the Masai my wife and I had photographed on our safari to Kenya the previous spring. "Let me show you," he said, and he wound his way through the tumbling stacks of magazines and newspapers scattered round the room and disappeared into the back hall. I sat there, feeling awkward—was this what it would be like if my wife should die before me?—but curious too. And, in a strange way, validated. Gerard Loomis had a pet to keep him company: mission accomplished.

When he came back into the room, I thought at first he'd slipped into some sort of garish jacket or cardigan, but then I saw, with a little jolt of surprise, that he was wearing a snake. Or, that is, a snake was draped over his shoulders, its extremities dangling beyond the length of his arms. "It's a python," he said. "Burmese. They get to be twenty-five feet long, though this one's just a baby."

I must have said something, but I can't really recall now what it was. I wasn't a herpetophobe or anything like that. It was just that a snake wasn't what we'd had in mind. Snakes didn't fetch, didn't bound into the car panting their joy, didn't speak when you held a rawhide bone just above shoulder level and twitched it invitingly. As far as I knew, they didn't do much of anything except exist. And bite.

"So what do you think?" he said. His voice lacked enthusiasm, as if he were trying to convince himself.

"Nice," I said.

I don't know why I'm telling this story—perhaps because what happened to Gerard could happen to any of us, I suppose, especially as we age and our spouses age and we're increasingly set adrift. But the thing is, the next part of what I'm going to relate here is a kind of fiction, really, or a fictive reconstruction of actual events, because two days after I was introduced to Gerard's python—he was thinking then of naming it either Robbie or Siddhartha—my wife and I went off to Switzerland for an account I was overseeing there and didn't return for four months. In the interval, here's what happened.

There was a heavy snowfall the week before Christmas that year and for the space of nearly two days the power lines were down. Gerard woke the first morning to a preternaturally cold house and his first thought was for the snake. The man in the pet shop at the mall had given him a long lecture before he bought the animal. "They make great pets," he'd said. "You can let them roam the house if you want and they'll find the places where they're comfortable. And the nice thing is they'll come to you and curl up on the couch or wherever, because of your body heat, you understand." The man—he wore a nametag that read Bozeman and he looked to be in his forties, with a gray-flecked goatee and his hair drawn back in a patchily dyed ponytail—clearly enjoyed dispensing advice. As well he should, seeing that he was charging some four hundred dollars for a single reptile that must have been as common as a garden worm in its own country. "But most of all, though, especially in this weather, you've got to keep him warm. This is a tropical animal we're talking about here, you understand? Never—and I mean never—let the temperature fall below eighty."

Gerard tried the light on the nightstand, but it was out. Ditto the light in the hall. Outside, the snow fell in clumps, as if it had been preformed into snowballs somewhere high in the troposphere. In the living room, the thermostat read sixty-three degrees, and when he tried to click the heat on, nothing happened. The next thing he knew he was crumpling newspaper and stacking kindling in the fireplace, and where were the matches? A quick search round the house, everything a mess (and here the absence of Marietta bit into him, down deep, like a parasitical set of teeth), the drawers stuffed with refuse, dishes piled high, nothing where it was supposed to be. Finally he retrieved an old lighter from a pair of paint-stained jeans on the floor in the back of the closet and he had the fire going. Then he went looking for Siddhartha. He found the snake curled up under the kitchen sink where the hot water pipe fed into the faucet and dishwasher, but it was all but inanimate, as cold and slick as a garden hose left out in the frost.

It was also surprisingly heavy, especially for an animal that hadn't eaten in the two weeks it had been in the house, but he dragged it, stiff and frigid, from its cachette, and laid it before the fireplace. While he was making coffee in the kitchen, he gazed out the window on the tumble of the day, and thought of all those years he'd gone in to work in weather like this, in all weathers actually, and felt a stab of nostalgia. Maybe he should go back to work—if not in his old capacity, from which he was gratefully retired, then on a part-time basis, just to keep his hand in, just to get out of the house and do something useful. On an impulse he picked up the phone, thinking to call Alex, his old boss, and sound him out, but the phone line was down too.

Back in the living room, he sank into the couch with his coffee and watched the snake as it came slowly back to itself, its muscles shivering in slow waves from head to tail like a soft breeze trailing over a still body of water. By the time he'd had a second cup of coffee and fixed himself an egg on the gas range, the crisis—if that was what it was—had passed. Siddhartha seemed fine. He never moved much even in the best of times, with the heat on high and the electric blanket Gerard had bought for him draped across the big Plexiglas terrarium he liked to curl up in, and so it was difficult to say. Gerard sat there a long while, stoking the fire, watching the snake unfurl its muscles and flick the dark fork of its tongue, until a thought came to him: maybe Siddhartha was hungry. When Gerard had asked the pet shop proprietor what to feed him, Bozeman had answered, "Rats." Gerard must have looked dubious, because the man had added, "Oh, I mean you can give him rabbits when he gets bigger, and that's a savings really, in time and energy, because you won't have to feed him as often, but you'd be surprised—snakes, reptiles in general, are a lot more efficient than we are. They don't have to feed the internal furnace all the time with filet mignon and hot fudge sundaes, and they don't need clothes or fur coats either." He paused to gaze down at the snake where it lay in its terrarium, basking under a heat lamp. "I just fed this guy his rat yesterday. You shouldn't have to give him anything for a week or two, anyway. He'll let you know."

"How?" Gerard had asked.

A shrug. "Could be a color thing, where you notice his pattern isn't as bright maybe. Or he's just, I don't know, what you'd call lethargic."

They'd both looked down at the snake then, its eyes like two pebbles, its body all but indistinguishable from the length of rough wood it was stretched out on. It was no more animate than the glass walls of the terrarium and Gerard wondered how anyone, even an expert, could tell if the thing was alive or dead. Then he wrote the check.

But now he found himself chafing at the cusp of an idea: the snake needed to be fed. Of course it did. It had been two weeks—why hadn't he thought of it before? He was neglecting the animal and that wasn't right. He got up from the couch to close off the room and build up the fire, then went out to shovel the driveway and take the car down the long winding community road to the highway and on into Newhouse and the mall. It was a harrowing journey. Trucks threw blankets of slush over the windshield and the beating of the wipers made him dizzy. When he arrived, he was relieved to see that the mall had electricity, the whole place lit up like a Las Vegas parade for the marketing and selling of all things Christmas, and with a little deft maneuvering he was able to wedge his car between a plowed drift and the handicapped space in front of the pet store.

Inside, Pets & Company smelled of nature in the raw, every creature in every cage and glassed-in compartment having defecated simultaneously, just to greet him, or so he imagined. The place was superheated. He was the only customer. Bozeman was up on a footstool, cleaning one of the aquariums with a vacuum tube. "Hey, man," he said, his voice a high sing-song, "Gerard, right? Don't tell me." He reached back in a practiced gesture to smooth down his ponytail as if he were petting a cat or a ferret. "You need a rat. Am I right?"

Gerard found himself fumbling round the answer, perhaps because the question had been put so bluntly—or was it that Bozeman had become clairvoyant in the instant? "Well," he heard himself say, and he might have made a joke, might have found something amusing or at least odd in the transaction, but he didn't because Marietta was dead and he was depressed, or so he reminded himself, "I guess so."

The rat—he didn't see it; Bozeman had gone into the back room to fetch it—came in a cardboard container with a molded carrying handle on top, the sort of thing you got if you asked for a doggie bag at a restaurant. The animal was heavier than he'd expected, shifting its weight mysteriously from one corner of the box to another as he carried it out into the snow and set the box on the seat beside him. He turned on the fan after he'd started up the engine, to give it some heat—but then it was a mammal, he figured, with fur, and it didn't have as much of a need because it could warm itself. And in any case it was dinner, or soon to be. The roads were slick. Visibility was practically zero. He crawled behind the snowplow all the way back to Newhouse Gardens and when he came in the door he was pleased to see that the fire was still going strong.

All right. He set down the box and then dragged the python's terrarium across the floor from the bedroom to the living room and set it to one side of the fireplace. Then he lifted the snake—it was noticeably warm to the touch on the side that had been closest to the fire—and laid it gently in the terrarium. For a moment it came to life, the long run of muscles tensing, the great flat slab of the head gearing round to regard him out of its stony eyes, and then it was inert again, dead weight against the Plexiglas floor. Gerard bent cautiously to the rat's box—would it spring out, bite him, scrabble away across the floor to live behind the baseboard forever as in some cartoon incarnation?—and, with his heart pounding, lowered the box into the terrarium and opened the lid.

The rat—it was white, with pink eyes, like the lab rats he'd seen arrayed in their cages in the biology building when he was a student—slid from the box like a lump of gristle, then sat up on its haunches and began cleaning itself as if it were the most natural thing in the world to be transported in a doggie bag and dumped into a glass-walled cavern in the presence of a tongue-flicking reptile. Which might or might not be hungry.

For a long while, nothing happened. Snow ticked at the windows, the fire sparked and settled. And then the snake moved ever so slightly, the faintest shifting of the bright tube of its scales, energy percolating from the deepest core of its musculature, and suddenly the rat stiffened. All at once it was aware of the danger it was in. It seemed to shrink into itself, as if by doing so it could somehow become invisible. Gerard watched, fascinated, wondering how the rat—reared in some drowsy pet warehouse, slick and pink and suckling at its mother's teats in a warm gregarious pack of its pink siblings, generations removed from the wild and any knowledge of a thing like this snake and its shining elongate bulk—could recognize the threat. Very slowly, by almost imperceptible degrees, the snake lifted its head from the Plexiglas floor, leveling on the rat like a sculpture come to life. Then it struck, so quickly Gerard nearly missed it, but the rat, as if it had trained all its life for just this moment, was equal to it. It sprang over the snake's head in a single frantic leap and shot to the farthest corner of the terrarium, where it began to emit a series of bird-like cries, all the while fastening its inflamed eyes on the white hovering face of Gerard. And what did he feel? He felt like a god, like a Roman emperor with the power of fatality in his thumb. The rat scrabbled at the Plexiglas. The snake shifted to close in on it.

And then, because he was a god, Gerard reached into the terrarium and lifted the rat up out of the reach of his python. He was surprised by how warm the animal was and how quickly it accommodated itself to his hand. It didn't struggle or try to escape but simply pressed itself against his wrist and the trailing sleeve of his sweater as if it understood, as if it were grateful. In the next moment he was cradling it against his chest, the pulse of its heart already slowing. He went to the couch and sank into it, uncertain what to do next. The rat gazed up at him, shivered the length of its body, and promptly fell asleep.

The situation was novel, to say the least. Gerard had never touched a rat in his life, let alone allowed one to curl up and sleep in the weave of his sweater. He watched its miniature chest rise and fall, studied the intricacy of its naked feet that were like hands, saw the spray of etiolated whiskers and felt the suppleness of the tail as it lay between his fingers like the suede fringe of the jacket he'd worn as a boy. The fire faltered but he didn't rise to feed it. When finally he got up to open a can of soup, the rat came with him, awake now and discovering its natural perch on his shoulder. He felt its fur like a caress on the side of his neck and then the touch of its whiskers and fevered nose. It stood on its hind legs and stretched from his lap to the edge of the table as he spooned up his soup by candlelight, and he couldn't resist the experiment of extracting a cube of potato from the rich golden broth and feeding it into the eager mincing mouth. And then another. And another. When he went to bed, the rat came with him, and if he woke in the dark of the night—and he did, twice, three times—he felt its presence beside him, its spirit, its heart, its heat, and it was no reptile, no cold thankless thing with a flicking tongue and two dead eyes, but a creature radiant with life.

The house was very cold when he woke to the seeping light of morning. He sat up in bed and looked round him. The face of the clock radio was blank, so the electricity must still have been down. He wondered about that, but when he pushed himself up and set his bare feet on the floor, it was the rat he was thinking of—and there it was, nestled in a fold of the blankets. It opened its eyes, stretched and then climbed into the palm he offered it, working its way up inside the sleeve of his pajamas until it was balanced on his shoulder. In the kitchen, he turned on all four gas burners and the oven too and shut off the room to trap the heat. It wasn't until the kettle began to boil that he thought about the fireplace—and the snake stretched out in its terrarium—but by then it was too late.

He returned to the pet store the following day, reasoning that he might as well convert the snake's lair into a rat's nest. Or no, that didn't sound right—that was what his mother used to call his boyhood room; he'd call it a rat apartment. A rat hostel. A rat—Bozemen grinned when he saw him. "Not another rat," he said, something quizzical in his eyes. "He can't want another one already, can he? But then with Burms you've got to watch for obesity—they'll eat anytime, whether they're hungry or not."

Even under the best of conditions, Gerard was not the sort to confide in people he barely knew. "Yes," was all he said, in answer to both questions. And then he added, "I may as well take a couple of them while I'm here." He looked away. "To save me the trip."

Bozeman wiped his hands on the khaki apron he wore over his jeans and came out from behind the cash register. "Sure," he said, "good idea. How many you want? They're six ninety-nine each."

Gerard shrugged. He thought of the rat at home, the snugness of it, the way it sprang across the carpet in a series of little leaps or shot along the baseboard as if blown by a hurricane wind, how it would take a nut in its hands and sit up to gnaw at it, how it loved to play with anything he gave it, a paper clip, an eraser, the ridged aluminum top of a Perrier bottle. In a moment of inspiration he decided to call it Robbie, after his brother in Tulsa. Robbie. Robbie the Rat. And Robbie needed company, needed play-mates, just like any other creature. Before he could think, he said: "Ten?"

"Ten? Whoa, man, that is going to be one fat snake."

"Is that too many?"

Bozeman slicked back his ponytail and gave him a good long look. "Hell, no—I mean, I'll sell you all I've got if that's what you want, and everything else too. You want gerbils? Parakeets? Albino toads? I'm in business, you know—pets for sale. This is a pet shop, *comprende*? But I tell you, if that Burm doesn't eat them PDQ, you're going to see how fast these things breed . . . I mean, the females can go into heat or whatever you want to call it at five weeks old. Five *weeks*." He shifted his weight and moved past Gerard, gesturing for him to follow. They stopped in front of a dis-play of packaged food and brightly colored sacks of litter. "You're going to want Rat Chow," he said, handing him a ten-pound sack, "and a bag or two of these wood shavings." Another look. "You got a place to keep them?"

By the time he left the store, Gerard had two wire cages (with cedar plank flooring so the rats wouldn't contract bumblefoot, whatever that was), twenty pounds of rat food, three bags of litter and two supersized doggie bags with five rats in each. Then he was home and shutting the door to keep out the cold even as Robbie, emerging from beneath the pil-lows of the couch, humped across the floor to greet him and all the lights flashed on simultaneously.

It was mid-April by the time my wife and I returned from Switzerland. Tim and Tim II, who'd been cared for in our absence by our housekeeper, Florencia, were there at the door to greet us, acting out their joy on the doorstep and then carrying it into the living room with such an excess of animation it was all but impossible to get our bags in the door before giv-ing them their treats, a thorough back-scratching and a cooed rehearsal of the little endearments they were used to. It was good to be home, back to a real community after all that time spent living in a sterile apartment in

Basel, and what with making the rounds of the neighbors and settling back in both at home and at work, it wasn't till some weeks later that I thought of Gerard. No one had seen him, save for Mary Martinson, who'd run into him in the parking lot at the mall, and he'd refused all invitations to dinner, casual get-togethers, ice-skating on the lake, even the annual Rites of Spring fund-raiser at the clubhouse. Mary said he'd seemed distracted and that she'd tried to engage him in conversation, thinking he was still locked in that first stage of grieving and just needed a little nudge to get him on track again, but he'd been abrupt with her. And she didn't like to mention it, but he was unkempt—and he smelled worse than ever. It was startling, she said. Even outdoors, standing over the open trunk of his car, which was entirely filled, she couldn't help noticing, with something called Rat Chow, even with a wind blowing and a lingering chill in the air, he gave off a powerful reek of sadness and body odor. Someone needed to look in on him, that was her opinion.

I waited till the weekend, and then, as I'd done back in December, I took the dogs down the wide amicable streets, through the greening woods and over the rise to Gerard's cottage. The day was glorious, the sun climbing toward its zenith, moths and butterflies spangling the flower gardens, the breeze sweetened with a scent of the south. My neighbors slowed their cars to wave as they passed and a few people stopped to chat, their engines rumbling idly. Carolyn Porterhouse thrust a bouquet of tulips at me and a mysterious wedge-shaped package wrapped in butcher's paper, which proved to be an Emmentaler—"Welcome home," she said, her grin anchored by a layer of magenta lipstick—and Ed Saperstein stopped right in the middle of the road to tell me about a trip to the Bahamas he and his wife had taken on a chartered yacht. It was past one by the time I got to Gerard's.

I noticed right off that not much had changed. The windows were streaked with dirt, and the yard, sprouting weeds along the margins of the unmowed lawn, looked as neglected as ever. The dogs bolted off after something in the deep grass and I shifted the bouquet under one arm, figuring I'd hand it to Gerard, to cheer him up a bit, and rang the bell. There was no answer. I tried a second time, then made my way along the side of the house, thinking to peer in the windows—for all anyone knew, he could be ill, or even, God forbid, dead.

The windows were nearly opaque with a scrim of some sort of pale fluff or dander. I rapped at the glass and thought I saw movement within, a kaleidoscopic shifting of shadowy forms, but couldn't be sure. It was then that I noticed the odor, saturate and bottom-heavy with ammonia, like the smell of a poorly run kennel. I mounted the back steps through a heavy accounting of discarded microwave dinner trays and a tidal drift of feed bags and knocked uselessly at the door. The wind stirred. I looked down at the refuse at my feet and saw the legend *Rat Chow* replicated over and over in neon-orange letters, and that should have been all the information I needed. Yet how was I to guess? How was anyone?

Later, after I'd presented the bouquet and the cheese to my wife, I tried Gerard's phone, and to my surprise he answered on the fourth or fifth ring. "Hello, Gerard," I said, trying to work as much heartiness into my voice as I could, "it's me, Roger, back from the embrace of the Swiss. I stopped by today to say hello, but—"

He cut me off then, his voice husky and low, almost a whisper. "Yes, I know," he said. "Robbie told me."

If I wondered who Robbie was—a roommate? a female?—I didn't linger over it. "Well," I said, "how're things? Looking up?" He didn't answer. I listened to the sound of his breathing for a moment, then added, "Would you like to get together? Maybe come over for dinner?"

There was another long pause. Finally he said, "I can't do that."

I wasn't going to let him off so lightly. We were friends. I had a responsibility. We lived in a community where people cared about one another and where the loss of a single individual was a loss to us all. I tried to inject a little jocularity into my voice: "Well, why not? Too far to travel? I'll grill you a nice steak and open a bottle of Côtes du Rhône."

"Too busy," he said. And then he said something I couldn't quite get hold of at the time. "It's nature," he said. "The force of nature."

"What are you talking about?"

"I'm overwhelmed," he said, so softly I could barely hear him, and then his breathing trailed off and the phone went dead.

. . . . . .

They found him a week later. The next-door neighbors, Paul and Peggy Bartlett, noticed the smell, which seemed to intensify as the days went on, and when there was no answer at the door they called the fire department. I'm told that when the firemen broke down the front door, a sea of rodents flooded out into the yard, fleeing in every direction. Inside, the floors were gummy with waste, and everything, from the furniture to the plaster-board walls and the oak beams of the living room ceiling, had been gnawed and whittled till the place was all but unrecognizable. In addition to the free-roaming animals, there were hundreds more rats stacked in cages, most of them starving and many cannibalized or displaying trun-cated limbs. A spokeswoman for the local ASPCA estimated that there were upwards of thirteen hundred rats in the house, most of which had to be euthanized at the shelter because they were in no condition to be sent out for adoption.

As for Gerard, he'd apparently succumbed to pneumonia, though there were rumors of hantavirus, which really put a chill into the com-munity, especially with so many of the rodents still at large. We all felt bad for him, of course, I more than anyone else. If only I'd been home through the winter, I kept thinking, if only I'd persisted when I'd stood outside his window and recognized the odor of decay, perhaps I could have saved him. But then I kept coming back to the idea that there must have been some deep character flaw in him none of us had recognized—he'd chosen a snake for a pet, for God's sake, and that low animal had somehow morphed into this horde of creatures that could only be described as pests, as vermin, as enemies of mankind that should be exterminated, not nur-tured. And that was another thing neither my wife nor I could under-stand—how could he allow even a single one of them to come near him, to fall under the caress of his hand, to sleep with him, eat with him, breathe the same air?

For the first two nights I could barely sleep, playing over that horrific scene in my mind—how could he have sunk so low? How could anyone?

The ceremony was brief, the casket closed (and there wasn't one of us who wanted to speculate on the reason, though it didn't take an especially active imagination to picture Gerard's final moments). I was very tender with my wife afterward. We went out to lunch with some of the others and when we got home I pressed her to me and held her for a long while. And though I was exhausted, I took the dogs out on the lawn to throw them their ball and watch the way the sun struck their rollicking fur as they streaked after the rumor of it, only to bring it back, again and again, and lay it in my palm, still warm from the embrace of their jaws.

ANACAPA

The boat left at eight a.m., and that wouldn't have presented a problem, or not especially, if Damian hadn't been in town. But then Damian was the whole reason for being here on this dock in the first place, the two of them hunkered over Styrofoam cups of coffee and shuffling in place with an assemblage of thirty or so males and two females (one of whom would turn out to be the deckhand), waiting in a kind of suppressed frenzy to board and lay claim to the prime spots along the rail. Hunter didn't like boats. Didn't especially like fish or fishing. But Damian did, and Damian—his roommate at college fourteen years ago and a deep well of inspiration and irritation ever since—always got his way. Which was in part why eight a.m. was such an impossible hour on this martyred morning with the sun dissolved in mist and the gulls keening and his head pounding and his stomach shrunk down to nothing. The other part of it, the complicating factor, was alcohol. Gin, to be specific.

They'd drunk gin the night before because gin was what they'd drunk in college, gin and tonic, the drink of liberation, the drink of spring break and summer vacation and the delirium of Friday and Saturday nights in the student clubs with the student bands pounding away and the girls burning like scented candles. Never mind that Hunter stuck almost exclusively to wine these days and had even become something of a snob about it ("Right over the hill in the Santa Ynez Valley? Best vineyards in the world," he'd tell anyone who would listen), last night it was gin. It had started in the airport lounge when he'd arrived an hour early for Damian's flight and heard himself say "Gin and tonic" to the bartender as if a ventriloquist were speaking for him. He'd had three by the time Damian arrived, and then for the rest of the night, wherever they went, the gin, which had managed to smell almost exactly like the scent of the jet fuel leaching in through the open window, continued to appear in neat little glasses with rectangular cubes of ice and wedges of lime till he and Damian collapsed at the apartment five short hours ago.

He stared blearily down at the blistered boards of the dock and the tired sea churning beneath them. For a long moment he watched a drift of refuse jerking to and fro in the wash beneath the pilings and then he leaned forward to drop a ball of spit into the place where, he supposed, waxing philosophical, all spit had originated. Spit to spit. The great sea. Thalassa, roll on. The water was gray here, transparent to a depth of three or four feet, imbued with a smell of fish gone bad. He spat again, watching transfixed as the glistening fluid, product of his own body, spiraled through the air to vanish in the foam. And what was spit, anyway? A secretion of the salivary glands, serving to moisten food—and women's lips. His first wife—Andrea—didn't like to kiss while they were having sex. She always turned her head away, as if lips had nothing to do with it. Cee Cee, who'd left him three weeks ago, had been different. In his wallet, imprisoned behind a layer of scratched plastic, was a picture of her, in profile, her chin elevated as if she were being stroked, her visible eye drooping with passion, the red blaze of a carnation tucked behind her ear like a heat gauge. He resisted the impulse to look at it.

Damian's voice—"Yeah, man, that's what I'm talking about, *fortification!*"—rang out behind him and Hunter turned to see him tapping his Styrofoam cup to those of a couple in matching windbreakers, toasting them, as if there were anything to celebrate at this hour and in this place. Damian had a flask with him. Hunter had already been the recipient of a judicious shot of brandy—not gin, thank god—and he presumed Damian was sharing the wealth. The woman—she was small-boned, dark, with her hair wrapped like a muffler round her throat—looked shy and sweet as she sipped her infused coffee and blinked her eyes against the burn of it. In the next moment, Damian had escorted the couple over to the rail and was making introductions. "Hey, Hunt, you ready for another?" he said, and Hunter held out his cup, hoping to deaden the pain, and then they were all four tapping the rims of the spongy white cups one against the other as if they were crystal flutes of Perrier-Jouët.

"This is Ilta's maiden voyage, can you believe it?" Damian crowed, his voice too loud, so that people had begun to stare at him.

"This is cor-rect," she said in a small voice animated by the occasion, and, he supposed, the brandy. "I do it for Mock." And here she looked to the man in the matching windbreaker, whose name seemed to be either Mack or Mark, Hunter couldn't be sure.

"I'm a regular," the man said, grinning as he tipped back his cup and then held it up for Damian to refresh, "but my wife's never been out." He looked harmless enough, one of those ubiquitous, fleshy-faced, pants-straining, good-time boys in his forties who probably sat behind a computer five days a week and dreamed in gigabytes, but Hunter would have killed him in a minute for the wife, whom he clearly didn't deserve. She was a jewel, that was what she was, and that accent—what was it? Swedish? "She eats the fish, though," Mack or Mark went on. He gave her a good-natured leer. "Don't you, dumpling?"

"Who doesn't?" Damian put in, just to say something. He was the type who needed to be at the center of things, the impresario, the star of all proceedings, and that could be charming—Hunter loved him, he did—but it could be wearing too. "I mean, fresh fish, fresh from the sea like you never get it in the store?" He paused to tip the flask over the man's cup. "I mean, come on, Ilta, what took you so long?"

"I do not like the, what do you say? The rocking." She made an undulating motion with her hands. "Of this boat."

They all looked to the boat. It was big enough, a typical party boat, seventy, eighty feet long, painted a crisp white and so immovable it might have been nailed to the dock. In that moment Hunter realized he hadn't taken his Dramamine—the label advised taking two tablets half an hour to an hour before setting out—and felt in his jeans pocket for the package. His throat was dry. His head ached. He was wondering if the little white pills would have any effect if he took them now, or if they worked at all no matter when you took them, remembering the last time he'd been talked into this particular sort of adventure and the unrelenting misery he'd experienced for the entire six and a half hours of the trip ("There's nothing more enjoyable—and tender, tender too—than seeing somebody you really admire puking over the rail," Damian had kept saying). The memory ran a hot wire through him and before he could think he had the package out and was shaking four pills into the palm of his hand and offering them to Ilta. "Want a couple of these?" he asked. "Dramamine? You know, for motion sickness?" He pantomimed the act of gagging.

"We gave her the patch," the husband said.

Ilta waved a finger back and forth, as if scolding Hunter. "I do it for Mock," she repeated. "For the anniversary. We are married today three years ago."

Hunter shrugged, cupped his palm to his mouth and threw back all four pills, figuring the double dose had to do something for him.

"In Helsinki," the husband put in, his face lit with the blandest smile of possession and satisfaction. He put an arm around his wife and drew her to him. They kissed. The gulls squalled overhead. Hunter looked away. And then suddenly everyone snapped to attention as the other woman—the deckhand in waiting—pulled back the bar to the gangplank. It was then, just as they'd begun to fumble around for their gear, that the man with the spider tattoo thrust himself into the conversation. Hunter had noticed him earlier—when they were in the office paying for their tickets and renting rods and tackle and whatnot. He was a crazy, you could see that from across the room, everything about him wired tight, his hair shaved down to a black bristle, his eyes like tracers, the tattoo of a red-and-black spider—or maybe it was a scorpion—climbing up the side of his neck. "Hey," he said now, pushing past Ilta, "can I get in on this party?" And he held out his cup.

Damian never flinched. That was his way. Mr. Cool. "Sure, man," he said, "just give me your cup."

In the next moment they were shuffling forward to the reek of diesel as the captain fired up his engines and the boat shivered beneath them. Everything smelled of long use, fishermen here yesterday and fishermen coming tomorrow. The decks were wet, the seats damp with dew. Fish scales, opalescent, dried to a crust, crunched underfoot. They found a place in the cabin, room for four at one of the tables lined up there cafeteria style, and the spider man, aced out, made his way to the galley. Hunter had a moment to think about Cee Cee, how she would have hated this—she was a downtown girl, absolutely, at home in the mall, the restaurant and the movie theater and nowhere else—and then there was a lurch, the boat slipped free of the dock and beyond the salt-streaked windows the shore broadened and dipped, and very slowly fell away into the mist.

It was an hour and a half out to the fishing grounds. Hunter settled in gingerly, his stomach in freefall, the coffee a mistake, the brandy compounding that mistake and the Dramamine a dissolve of pure nothing, not even worthy of a placebo effect. It wasn't as if it was rough—or as rough as it might have been. This was June, when the Santa Barbara Channel was entombed in a vault of fog that sometimes didn't burn off till two or three in the afternoon—June Gloom, was what they called it in the newspaper—and as far as he knew the seas were relatively calm. Still, the boat kept humping over the waves like a toboggan slamming through the moguls at the bottom of a run and the incessant dip and rise wasn't doing him any good. He glanced round him. No one else seemed much affected, the husband and wife playing cards, Damian ordering up breakfast in the galley at the front of the cabin, the others snoozing, reading the paper, scooping up their eggs over easy as if they were in a diner somewhere on upper State Street, miles from the ocean. After a while, he cradled his arms on the tabletop, put his head down and tumbled into a dark shaft of sleep.

When he woke, it was to the decelerating rhythm of the engines and a pulse of activity that rang through the cabin like a fire alarm. Everybody was rising en masse and filing through the doors to the deck. They'd arrived. He felt a hand on his shoulder and lifted his head to see Damian looming over him. "You have a nice sleep?"

"I dreamed I was in hell, the ninth circle, where there's nothing moving but the devil." The boat rolled on a long gentle swell. The engines died. "And maybe the sub-devils. With their pitchforks."

The flask appeared. Damian pressed it to his lips a moment, then held it out in offering. "You want a hit?"

Hunter waved him away. He still hadn't risen from his seat.

"Come on, man, this is it. The fish are waiting. Let's go."

There was a shout. People were backed up against the windows, clumsy with the welter of rods that waved round them like antennae. Somebody had a fish already, a silver thrashing on the boards. Despite himself, he felt a vestigial thrill steal over him. He got to his feet.

Damian was halfway to the door when he turned round. "I put our stuff out there in back on the port side—Mark said that was the best spot. Come on, come on." He waved a hand impatiently and Hunter found his balance all at once—it was as if he'd done a backflip and landed miraculously on his feet. Just then the sun broke through and everything jumped with light. Damian went flat as a silhouette. The sea slapped the hull. Someone else cried out. "And wait'll you get a load of Julie," he said under his breath.

"Julie? Who's Julie?"

The look Damian gave him was instructive, teacher to pupil. After all, as Damian had it he'd come all the way down here for the weekend—for this trip, for last night and tonight too—to cheer up his old buddy, to get him out of the house and back among the living, waxing eloquent on the subject of Hunter's failings into the small hours of the day that was just now beginning. "The deckhand, man. Where you been?"

"Sleeping."

"Yeah, well maybe it's time to wake up."

And then they were out in the light and the world opened up all the way to the big dun humps of the islands before them—he'd never seen them so close—and back round again to the boat and its serried decks and the smell of open water and Julie, the deckhand, freshly made-up and divested of the shapeless yellow slicker she'd worn back at the dock, Julie, in a neon-orange bikini and sandals with thin silver straps that climbed up her bare ankles, waiting to help each and every sportsman to his bait.

So they fished. The captain, a dark presence behind the smoked glass of the bridge that loomed over them, let his will be known through the loud-speakers on deck. *Drop your lines,* he commanded, and they dropped their lines. *Haul in,* he said, and they hauled in while he revved the engines and motored to another spot and yet another. There were long stretches of boredom after the initial excitement had passed and Hunter had an abundance of time to reflect on how much he hated fishing. At long intervals, someone would connect, his rod bent double and a mackerel or a big gape-mouthed thing variously described as either a rockfish or a sheephead would flap in over the rail, but Hunter's rod never bent or even twitched. Nor did Damian's. Before the first hour was up, Damian had left his rod propped on the rail and drifted into the cabin, emerging ten minutes later with two burgers wrapped in waxed paper and two beers in plastic cups. Hunter was hunched over his knees on one of the gray metal lockers that held the life jackets and ran along both sides of the boat, his stomach in neutral, trying all over again to get used to the idea of lateral instability. He accepted the burger and the beer.

"This sucks," Damian said, settling in beside him with a sigh. Their rods rode up and down with the waves like flagpoles stripped of their flags.

"It was your idea."

Damian gazed out across the water to where the smaller island, the one separated from the bigger by a channel still snarled in fog, seemed to swell and recede. "Yeah, but it's a ritual, it's manly. It's what buddies do together, right? And look at it, look where we are—I mean is this beautiful or what."

"You just said it sucks."

"I mean this spot. Why doesn't he move us already?" He jerked his head around to shoot a withering glare at the opaque glass of the bridge. "I mean, I haven't caught shit—what about you? Any bites?"

Hunter was unwrapping the burger as if it were crystal, thinking he'd maybe nibble at it—he didn't want to press his luck. He set it down and took the smallest sip of beer. In answer to Damian's question, he just shrugged. Then, enunciating with care, he said, "Fish are extinct."

"Bullshit. This guy on the other side got a nice-sized calico, like eight or nine pounds, and they're the best eating, you know that . . ." He took a massive bite out of the hamburger, leaning forward to catch the juices in the waxed-paper wrapping. "Plus," he added through the effort of chewing, "you better get on the stick if you want to win the pool."

Hunter had been so set on simply enduring that he'd forgotten all about the pool or even the possibility of connecting, of feeling some other force, something dark and alien, pulling back at you from a place you couldn't imagine. "What are you talking about?"

"The pool, remember? Everybody on the boat put in ten bucks when they gave you the bag with your number on it? You must really be out of it—you put in a twenty for both of us, remember, and I said I'd get the first round?"

"I'm not going to win anything." He let out a breath and it was as if the air had been sucked out of his lungs.

Mostly, the night before, they'd talked about sex. How when you didn't have it you were obsessed with it, how you came to need it more than food, more than money. "It's the testosterone clogging your brain," Damian had said, and Hunter, three weeks bereft, had nodded in agreement. "And I'll tell you another thing," Damian had added after a lengthy digression on the subject of his latest girlfriend's proclivities, "once you have it, I'm talking like five minutes later, it's like, 'Hey, let's go shoot some hoops.'" Now, because he couldn't seem to resist it, because they were in college all over again, at least for the weekend, he said, "Just keep your rod stiff, 'cause you never know."

And then Mark was there, in a pair of disc sunglasses and a baseball cap that clung like a beanie to his oversized head. He had his own burger in one hand and a beer in the other. The boat slipped into a trough and rose up again on a long debilitating swell. "Any luck?" he asked.

"Nada," Damian said, his voice tuned to the pitch of complaint. "The captain ought to move us. I mean with what we're paying you'd think he'd work his fish-finding mojo just a little bit harder, wouldn't you?"

Mark shrugged. "Give him time. I know the man. He can be a bit of a hardass, but if they're out there he'll find them. He always does. Or almost always." He looked thoughtful, his lower face arranged around his chewing. "I mean, sometimes you get skunked. It's nature, you know, the great outdoors. Nobody can control that."

"How about Ilta?" Hunter heard himself say. "She get any?"

Mark drew a face. "She's not feeling so well, I guess. She's in the head. Been in the head for the past fifteen minutes."

"Green in the gills," Damian said with a joyful grin, and Hunter felt his stomach clench around the tiniest morsel of burger and bun.

"Something like that," Mark said, gazing off into the distance. "She just needs to get her sea legs, is all."

"I shouldn't have brought her. She only did it for me—to please me, you know? The only time she's been on a boat before this was the ferry between Copenhagen and Göteborg and she said she vomited the whole time—but that was years ago and I figured, we both figured, this would be different. Plus, we got her the patch."

Hunter thought about that a moment, even as Damian started in weighing the relative merits of patch and pill as if he'd just stepped out of pharmacy school. He was feeling bitter. Bitter over the day, the place, the fish, the lack of fish, over Cee Cee and Ilta and Julie and all the rest of the unattainable women of the world. He was picturing Mark's wife in the cramped stinking head, cradling the stainless steel toilet, alone and needful while her husband gnawed his burger and guzzled beer, and he was about to say something cutting like "I guess that just proves the seas's no place for a woman," when the captain's voice droned through the speakers. *Haul in,* the captain commanded, and Hunter went to his pole and began to crank the reel, the weight of the sinker floating free, and the hook, when it was revealed, picked clean of the wriggling anchovy that Julie, in her bikini, had threaded there for him.

Mark didn't move. "I'm already in," he said, by way of explanation. "But you watch, he's going to take us southeast now, nearer the tip of the island." He paused, chewing. "That's Anacapa, you know. It's the only one of the Channel Islands with an Indian name—the rest are all Spanish."

Hunter didn't resent him showing off his knowledge, or not exactly—after all, Mark was the authority here, the regular, the veteran of scute and scale and the cold wet guts and staring eyes of the poor brainless things hauled up out of the depths for the sake of machismo, buddyhood, the fraternity of hook, line and sinker—but he didn't want to be here and his stomach was fluttering and for all he knew he'd be next in the head, like a woman, like a girl, and so he said, "Don't tell me—it means Soup-can in the Indian language, right? Or no: Microwave, Microwave Oven."

"Come on, Hunt, you know they didn't have any of that shit." Damian had set down his burger to reel in, the plastic cup clenched between his teeth so that his words were blunted. He was warning him off, but Hunter didn't care.

"It means illusion," Mark said, as the boat swung round and everybody, as one, fought for balance. "Like a mirage, you know? Because of the fog that clings to it—you can never be sure it's really there."

"Sounds like my marriage," Hunter said, and then, as casually as if he were bending over the coffee table in his own living room to pick up a magazine or the TV remote, he leaned over the rail, the sudden breeze catching his hair and fanning it across his forehead, and let it all heave out of him, the burger and bun, the beer, the coffee and brandy and Dramamine, and right there at the end of it, summoned up from the deepest recess, the metallic dregs of the gin.

The next spot, which as Mark had predicted, was closer to the island, didn't look much different from the last—waves, birds, the distant oil rigs like old men wading with their pants rolled up—but almost immediately after the captain dropped anchor, people began to hook up and a pulse of excitement beat through the crowd. One after another, the rods dipped and bent and the fish started coming over the rail. In the confusion, Hunter dropped his burger to the deck, even as Damian's rod bowed and his own began to jerk as if it were alive. "You got one!" Damian shouted, stepping back to play his own fish. "Go ahead, grab it, set the hook!"

Hunter snatched up the rod and felt something there. He pulled and it pulled back, and so what if he'd inadvertently slipped on the catsup-soaked bun with its extruded tongue of meat and very nearly pitched overboard—this was what he'd come for. A fish. A fish on the line! But it was tugging hard, moving toward the front of the boat, and he moved with it, awkwardly fumbling his way around the others crowding the rail, only to realize, finally, that this was no fish at all—he was snagged on somebody else's line. In that moment, three people up from him, the spider man was coming to the same realization.

"Jesus Christ, can't you watch your own fucking line?" the man snarled as they separately reeled in and the tangle of their conjoined rigs rose shakily from the water. "I mean you're down the other fucking end of the boat, aren't you?"

Yeah, he was. But this moron was down on his *fucking* end too. It wasn't as if it was Hunter's fault. It was nobody's fault. It was the fault of fishing and lines and the puke-green heaving ocean that should have stayed on the front of a postcard where it belonged. Still, when he'd finally made his way down the deck and was staring the guy in the face, he ducked his head and said only, "I'll get my knife."

That decision—to shuffle back alongside the glassed-in cabin and across the open area at the stern of the boat, to dig into the tackle box Damian had brought along and come up with the bare blade of the gleaming Swiss-made knife there and measure it in his hand while everyone on the boat was hooking up and the deck had turned to fish and a wave bigger than any of the others that had yet hit rocked the boat like a potato in a pot—was regrettable. Because the captain, hooded above, outraged, pressed to the very limit, let his voice of wrath tear through the speakers: "You with the knife—you, yeah, you! You trying to stab somebody's eye out?"

Hunter lurched like a drunken man. He squinted against the sun and up into the dark windows that wrapped round the wheelhouse till it seemed as if the boat were wearing a gigantic pair of sunglasses. He saw the sky reflected there. Clouds. The pale disc of the sun. "No, I'm just—" he began, but the captain's voice cut him off. "Put that goddamned thing away before I come down there and throw it in the goddamned ocean!"

Everyone was looking at him while they pumped their bent rods or hustled across the deck with one writhing fish or another suspended by the gills, and he wanted to protest, wanted to be the bad guy, wanted to throw it all right back at the dark god in his wheelhouse who could have been Darth Vader for all he knew, but he held himself back. Shamefaced, he staggered to the tackle box and slammed the knife into it, the very knife Damian had insisted on bringing along because men in the outdoors always had knives because knives were essential, for cutting, hewing, stabbing, pinning things down, and when he turned round, one hand snatching at the rail for balance—and missing—Julie was there. The wind took her hair—dark at the roots, bleached by the sun on the ends—and threw it across her face. She gave him a wary look. "What's the problem?" she asked.

"I didn't do anything," he said. "I just wanted to cut a tangle, that's all, and he—this guy up there, your precious captain, whoever he is, unloads on me . . ." He could hear the self-pity in his voice and knew it was all wrong.

"No open knives allowed on deck," she said, looking stern. Or as stern as a half-naked woman with minute fish scales glittering on her hands and feet could manage to look on the deck of a party boat in the middle of a party.

He could have blown it, could have been a jerk, but he felt the tension go out of him. He gave her a smile that was meant to be winning and apologetic at the same time. "I'm sorry, I guess I didn't know any better. I'm not a regular, but you already knew that, didn't you—just from looking at me, right? Tell you the truth, I feel a whole lot better experiencing the mighty sea from a barstool in that place back at the wharf—Spinnakers, you know Spinnakers?—with a cocktail in my hand and the fish served up on a plate, and maybe a little butter-lemon sauce? To dip? And lick off your fingers?"

When he mentioned Spinnakers, she'd nodded, and now she was smiling too. "It's all right," she said. "Here, let me help you." She took him by the sleeve then and led him across the deck to where the spider man, his face at war with itself, stood waiting.

What happened next remained a bit fuzzy, but as it turned out Hunter wasn't destined to be the bad actor, not on this trip. The spider man stepped forward to claim that role, and his transformation from bit player

to full-blown menace needed no rehearsal. There was Julie, quick and efficient, her legs flexed and breasts swaying with the motion of the boat as
she pulled in the tangle and cut the lines free with a pair of nail clippers
she'd magically produced, and in the next moment she was handing each
of them their rigs. She looked to Hunter first—and he was deep inside
himself, fixated on the question of the nail clippers and where she could
possibly have kept them given those two thin strips of cloth and the way
they seemed to grow out of her flesh—and asked if he needed help rigging
up again. Before he could say yes, because he did need her help in unraveling the mystery of the sinker so that it would swing away from the leader
instead of snarling up the minute he dropped it overboard, and because
he liked the proximity to her, liked looking at her and hearing her voice in
the desert of this floating locker room, the spider man spoke up. His voice
was ragged, jumping up the scale. "What about me?" he demanded. "This
dickhead's the one that snagged me and I'm the one losing out on fishing
time. You going to give me a refund? Huh? He can wait. He doesn't know
what the fuck he's doing, anyway."

The boat lurched and Hunter grabbed the rail to steady himself. "Go
ahead," he said, "do him first, I don't care. Really. I don't."

The spider man looked away, muttering curses, as she bent to retie his
rig. "What about bait," he said. "This clown"—he jerked a thumb at
Hunter—"fucked up my bait. I need bait. Fresh bait."

She could have told him to fetch it himself—she was there to help and
smile and show off her physique in the hope and expectation of tips, sure,
but she was nobody's slave and any five-year-old could bait a hook—and
yet she just gave him a look, padded over to the bait well and came back
with a live anchovy cradled in one hand. But he was off now and there was
no bringing him back, his harsh cracked voice running through its variations—she was wasting his time, and the whole thing, the whole fucking
boat, was a conspiracy and he wanted a refund and he was damned fucking well going to get it too and they could all kiss his ass if they thought he
was going to put up with this kind of cheat and fraud because that's what
it was, screwing over the customer, eight bucks for a goddamned burger
that tasted like warmed-over shit—and when finally she'd threaded the

anchovy on his hook he said, loud enough for everybody to hear, "Hey, thanks for nothing. But I guess you're peddling your little ass for tips, right, so here you go"—and before she could react he stabbed a rolled-up bill into the gap between her breasts.

It wasn't a happy moment. Because Julie wasn't frail and wilting, wasn't like Ilta, whose sweet suffering face stared out of the vacancy of the head every time one of the sportsmen pulled back the door in an attempt to go in and relieve himself. She was lean and muscular, knots in her calves and upper arms, her shoulders pulled tight. In a single motion she dug out the bill and threw it in his face without even looking at it, and then she slapped him, and this was no ordinary slap, but an openhanded blow that sent him back against the rail.

For a split second it looked as if he was going to go for her and Hunter braced himself because there was no way he was going to let this asshole attack a woman in front of him, even if he had to take a beating for it, and he would, he would take a beating for Julie. Gladly. But the spider man, a froth of spittle caught in the corners of his mouth, just glared at her. "All right!" he shouted. "All right, fuck it," and he swung round, whirled the rented pole over his head like a lariat and flung it out into the chop, where gravity took it down just as if it had never existed.

Later, after the captain had come down personally from his perch to restrain the spider man and the command went up to haul in and the engines revved and the boat began hammering the waves on the way back to the dock, Hunter took a seat in the cabin to get out of the wind and for the first time since the night before he felt a kind of equilibrium settle over him. Mark and Damian were at the counter, leaning back on their elbows and sipping beer out of their plastic cups. Ilta was stretched out on a bench in the far corner, her face to the wall, a blanket pulled up over her shoulders. The others milled round in a happy mob, eating sandwiches, ordering up cocktails, reliving their exploits and speculating on who was going to win the pool, because apparently it wasn't over yet. In announcing the problem that had arisen with one of the passengers, the captain had promised to make up the lost time with a little inshore fishing—an hour or so, for halibut—once they'd deposited the unhappy sportsman back at the dock. An hour more. Hunter would have preferred an hour less, but he found himself drifting up to the counter to order a gin and tonic—as a calmative, strictly as a calmative—and then taking it outside, in the breeze, to where Julie stood over a pitted slab of wood at the rear of the boat, filleting the day's catch.

Behind her, a whole squadron of gulls, interspersed with half a dozen pelicans, cried havoc over the scraps. She looked tired. Gooseflesh stippled her shoulders and upper arms. Her makeup was fading. She dipped mechanically to the burlap sacks to extract the fish, slamming them down one after another before gutting them with an expert flick of her knife, half of them alive still and feebly working their tails. Next she ran the blade against the grain to remove the scales, a whole hurricane of translucent discs suddenly animated and dancing on the breeze as if by some feat of prestidigitation, and then she teased out the fillets and shook them into plastic bags, dumping the refuse overboard with a clean sweep of the knife. A few sportsmen stood around watching her. The engines whined at full throttle, the wake unraveling from the stern as if from an infinite spool, the birds vanishing in the froth. Hunter steadied himself against the rail and lifted the plastic cup to his lips, his fingers stinking of baitfish, wishing he had a dripping sack of plunder to hand her, but he didn't. Or not yet, anyway. "You look like you've done that a time or two before," he said.

She looked up with a smile. "Yeah," she said. "One or two." Up close, he saw that her torso glittered with the thin wafers of the scales, scales everywhere, caught in the ends of her hair, fastened between her breasts, on her calves and the place where her thighs came together.

"Could I get you a drink?" he asked, and when she didn't answer, he added, "I'm having a gin and tonic. You like gin?"

The knife moved as if it had a life of its own. The fish gave in, lost their heads, ribs and tails, while the fillets, white and yielding, disappeared into ice chests, all ready for freezer or pan. And here was Damian's bag, #12, laid out before her like an offering. He could hear Damian crowing even now because Damian had hooked a lingcod that was bigger by a pound and a half than his nearest competitor's catch and he hadn't been shy about letting everybody know it—"I'm going to win that pool, you wait and see," he'd said before sidling up to the bar with Mark, "and I'm going to tip Julie a hundred and ask her to have a drink with us later, for your sake, your sake only, buddy, believe me." The thought of it made him feel queasy all over again. "Sure," Julie said. "I like gin, who doesn't? But I can't drink while I'm on duty—it's against regulations. And plus, the captain—"

"Yeah," he said, "the captain."

The boat slammed down hard and jerked back up so that he had to brace himself, but the knife never paused. After a moment he said, "Well, what about afterwards then, after we're back in, I mean? Would you like to have a drink then? Or dinner? After you get cleaned up and all?"

"That might be nice," she allowed. "But we've still got a whole lot of fishing to do. So let's not get premature here—"

He leaned back and let the gin wet his lips. He could see the way things would unfold—he was going to fish like the greatest fisherman on earth, like Lucky Jim himself, and he was going to catch a fish twice the size of Damian's. A hundred dollars? He'd tip her the whole thing, all three hundred, and she'd hold on to his arm while the spider man stalked off to haunt some other ship and Anacapa faded away in the mist and Damian went back home to sleep on the couch. That was the scenario, that was what was going to happen, he was sure of it. Of course, on the other hand, she must have had a dozen propositions a day, a girl as pretty as that, doing what she did for a living, and besides what would he do with all that fish? Was there room for it in the freezer even? Or would it just sit on a shelf in the refrigerator, turning color, till he dropped it in the trash?

"Right?" she said. "Agreed?"

He took another sip of his drink, felt the alcohol quicken in him even as his stomach sank and sank again. The gulls screeched. The knife flashed. And the shore, dense with its pavement and the clustered roof tiles and the sun caught in the solid weave of the palms, came up on him so quickly it startled him. "Yeah," he said, "yeah, sure. Agreed." He held to the rail as the captain gunned the engines and the boat leaned into an arc of exploding light, then tipped the cup back till he could feel the ice cold against his front teeth. "And just you wait," he said, grinning now. "I'm going to nail the granddaddy of all the halibut from here to Oxnard and back." _

Of course, given the vicissitudes of the day, that wasn't how it turned out. If there was a granddaddy out there cruising the murk of the bottom, he kept his whereabouts to himself. Still, Hunter took a real and expanding satisfaction in watching the spider man, his wallet lightened by the price of the rod, reel and rigging he'd tossed, slink off the boat with his head down, while the rest of them—the true sportsmen, the obedient and fully sanctioned—got their extra hour of bobbing off the coast on a sea reduced to the gentlest of swells while the sun warmed their backs and almost everybody took their shirts off to enjoy it. A few people hooked up, Damian among them, and then the captain gave the order to haul in and Damian was declared winner of the pool for his lingcod and he got his picture taken with his arm around Julie in her bikini. As it happened, Hunter and Damian were the last ones off the boat, Julie standing there at the rail in her official capacity to help people up onto the gangplank and receive her tips. "It was awesome," Damian told her, his plastic bag of fish fillets in one hand, five twenties fanned out in the other, "really awesome. Best trip we've ever had—right, Hunt?"

Hunter had dipped his head in acknowledgment, distracted by Julie and the promise he'd come so close to extracting from her out there on the rolling sea. He was about to remind her of it—he was waiting, actually, till Damian went up the ladder so he could have a moment alone with her—when Damian, with a sidelong glance at him, said, "Hey, you know, we'd really take it as an honor, Hunter and me, if you'd come out to dinner with us. To celebrate, I mean. What about champagne? Champagne sound cool?"

Julie looked first to Hunter, then Damian, and let a slow grin spread across her face. "Real nice," she said. "Spinnakers? In, say, one hour?"

Which was what had brought them to this moment, in the afterglow of the trip, the three of them seated at a table up against the faded pine panels of the back wall, looking out to the bar crowded with tourists, fishermen and locals alike, and beyond that to the harbor and the masts of the ships struck pink with the setting sun. Julie was in a sea-green cocktail dress, her legs long and bare, a silver Neptune's trident clasped round her neck on a thin silver chain. Damian was on one side of her, Hunter on the other. They'd clinked champagne glasses, made their way through a platter of fried calamari with aioli sauce. Music played faintly. From beyond the open windows, there was the sound of the gulls settling in for the night.

Gradually, as he began to feel the effects of the champagne, it occurred to Hunter that Damian was monopolizing the conversation. Or worse: that Damian had got so carried away he seemed to have forgotten the purpose of this little outing. He kept jumping from one subject to another and when he did try to draw Julie out he was so wound up he couldn't help talking right through her. "So what's it like to be a deckhand?" he asked at one point. "Pretty cool job, no? Out on the water all day, fresh air, all that? It's like a dream job, am I right?" Before she could say ten words he'd already cut her off—he loved the outdoors too, couldn't she tell? He was the one who'd wanted to come out on the boat—"I practically had to drag Hunt, here"—and it wasn't just luck that had hooked him up with that lingcod, but experience and desire and a kind of worship of nature too deep to put into words.

Hunter tried to keep up his end of the conversation, injecting sardonic asides, mimicking the tourists at the bar, even singing the first verse of a sea chantey he made up on the spot, but Julie didn't seem especially receptive. Two guys, one girl. What kind of odds were those?

Damian had shifted closer to her. The second bottle of champagne went down like soda water. Hunter nudged Damian under the table with the toe of his shoe—twice, hard—but Damian was too far gone to notice. Halfway through the main course—was he really feeding her shrimp off the tines of his fork?—Hunter pushed back his chair. "Men's room," he muttered. "I'll be right back." Julie gave him a vague smile.

To get to the men's, he had to go out on the deck and down a flight of stairs. All the tables on the deck were occupied, though the fog was rolling in and there was a chill on the air. People were leaning over their elbows, talking too loud, laughing, lifting drinks to their lips. Jewelry glinted at women's throats, fingers, ears. A girl in her teens sat at the far table, the one that gave onto the stairs, looking into the face of the boy she was with, oblivious to the fact that she was sitting at the worst table in the house. Hunter thumped down the stairs and felt a sudden flare of anger. Son of a bitch, he was thinking. He wasn't going to sleep on the couch. No way. Not tonight. Not ever.

He slammed into the men's room and locked the door behind him. The stalls were empty, the sinks dirty, the overhead light dim in its cage. He smelled bleach and air freshener and the inescapable odor they were meant to mask. It had come in on the soles of deck shoes, sandals and boots, ammoniac and potent, the lingering reek of all those failing bits of protoplasm flung up out of the waves to be beached here, on the smudged ceramic tile of the men's room beneath Spinnakers. The smell caught him unawares and he felt unsteady suddenly, the floor beneath him beginning to rise and recede. But that wasn't all—the room seemed to be fogging up all of a sudden, a seep of mist coming in under the door and tumbling through the vent as if a cloud had touched down just outside. The far wall faded. The mirror clouded over. He rubbed a palm across the smeared glass, then a paper towel, until finally he put both hands firmly down on the edge of the sink and stared into the mirror, hoping to find something solid there.

THREE QUARTERS OF THE WAY TO HELL

now he could take, but this wasn't snow, it was sleet. There was an inch of it at least in the gutters and clamped atop the cars, and the sidewalks had been worked into a kind of pocked gray paste that was hell on his shoes—and not just the shine, but the leather itself. He was thinking of last winter—or was it the winter before that?—and a pair of black-and-whites he'd worn onstage, really sharp, and how they'd got ruined in slop just like this. He'd been with a girl who'd waited through three sets for him that night, and her face was lost to him, and her name too, but she had a contour on her—that much he remembered—and by the time they left she was pretty well lit and she pranced into the street outside the club and lifted her face to the sky. *Why don't we walk?* she sang out in a pure high voice as if she wanted everybody in New York to hear her. *It's so glorious, isn't it? Can't you feel it?* And he was lit himself and instead of taking her by the wrist and flagging down a cab he found himself lurching up the street with her, one arm thrown over her shoulder to pull her to him and feel the delicious discontinuous bump of her hip against his. Within half a block his cigarette had gone out and his face was as wet as if he'd been sprayed with a squirt gun; by the time they turned the corner his shoes were gone, and there was nothing either he or the solemn *paisano* at the shoe repair could do to work the white semicircular scars out of the uppers.

He dodged a puddle, sidestepped two big-armed old ladies staring at a Christmas display as if they'd just got off the bus from Oshkosh, and pinched the last drag out of the butt of his cigarette, which hissed as he flicked it into the gutter. For a minute, staring down the length of Fifth Avenue as it faded into the beating gloom like something out of an Eskimo's nightmare, he thought of hailing a cab. But there were no cabs, not in weather like this, and the reason he was walking the thirty-odd blocks to the studio in the first place, he reminded himself bitterly, was because he didn't have money to waste on anything so frivolous as carfare. He lifted his feet gingerly and turned into the blow, cursing.

It was cold in the apartment—the landlady was a miser and a witch and she wouldn't have turned on the heat for two free tickets to Florida—and Darlene felt her body quake and revolt against the chill as she stood before the mirror plucking her eyebrows after a lukewarm shower. She couldn't muster much enthusiasm for the session. It was grim outside, the windows like old gray sheets tacked to the walls, and she just couldn't feature bundling up and going out into the storm. But then it was grimmer inside—peeling wallpaper, two bulbs out in the vanity, a lingering sweetish odor of that stuff the landlady used on the roaches—and she never missed a date, not to mention the fact that she needed the money. She was in her slip—she couldn't find her robe, though she suspected it was balled up somewhere in the depths of the laundry basket, and there was another trial she had to get through, the machine in the laundry room inoperative for two weeks now. Her upper arms were prickled with gooseflesh. There was a red blotch just to the left of her nose, tracing the indentation of the bone there. The eye above it, staring back at her like the swollen blown-up eye of a goldfish at the pet store, was bloodshot. Bloodshot. And what was she going to do about that?

On top of it all, she still wasn't feeling right. The guy she'd been seeing, the guy she'd been saving up to go to Florida with for a week at Christmas—Eddie, second trumpet with Mitch Miller—had given her a dose and her backside was still sore from where the doctor had put the needle in. The way her head ached—and her joints, her right shoulder especially, which burned now as she positioned the tweezers above the arch of her eyebrow—she began to wonder if there'd actually been penicillin in that needle. Maybe it was just water. Maybe the doctor was pinching on his overhead. Or maybe the strain of gonorrhea she'd picked up—that Eddie had picked up in Detroit or Cleveland or Buffalo—wouldn't respond to it.

That's what the doctor had told her, anyway—there was a new strain going around. His hands were warm, the dab of alcohol catching her like a quick cool breeze. *Just a little sting,* he said, as if she were nine years old. *There. Now that's better, isn't it?*

No, she'd wanted to say, it's not better, it's never better and never will be because the world stinks and the clap stinks and so do needles and prissy nurses and sour-faced condescending M.D.s and all the rest of it too, but she just opened up her smile and said *Yeah.*

She was tired of every dress in the closet. Or no, not just tired—sick to death of them. All of them. The hangers clacked like miniature freight cars as she rattled through them twice, shivering in her slip and nylons, her feet all but frozen to the linoleum. *Christ,* she said to herself, *Jesus Christ, what the hell difference does it make?* and she reached angrily for a red crepe de chine with a plunging neckline she hadn't worn in a year and pulled it over her head and smoothed it across her hips, figuring it would provide about as much protection from the cold as a swimsuit. She'd just have to keep the cloth coat buttoned up to her throat, and though it was ugly as sin, she'd wear the red-and-green checked scarf her mother had knitted her . . . what she really needed—what she deserved, and what Eddie, or somebody, should give her and give her soon—was a fur.

A gust threw pellets of ice against the windowpane. For a moment she held the picture of herself in a fur—and not some chintzy mink stole, but a full-length silver fox—and then it dissolved. A fur. Yeah, sure. She wasn't exactly holding her breath.

The hallway smelled like shit—literally—and as he stomped the slush off his shoes and bent to wipe the uppers with the paper towels he'd nicked from the men's room at Benjie's, where he'd stopped to fortify himself with two rye whiskeys and a short beer, he wondered what exactly went on on the ground floor when they weren't recording. Or maybe when they were. Neff would press just about anything anybody wanted to put out, whether it was boogie-woogie, race records or that rock and roll crap, and who knew how many junkies and pill heads came in and out of the place so stewed they couldn't bother to find the bathroom? He took off his hat, set it on the extinct radiator and ran both hands through his hair. There was a slice of broken glass in a picture frame on the wall and that at least gave him back his reflection, though it was shadowy and indistinct, as if he'd already given up the ghost. For a moment there, patting his hair back into place while he stared down the dim tunnels of his eyes, he had a fleeting intimation of his own mortality—he was thirty-eight and not getting any younger, his father ten years' dead and his mother fading fast; before long it would be just him and his sister and one old wraith-like spinster aunt, Aunt Marta, left on this earth, and then he'd be an old man in baggy pants staring at the gum spots on the sidewalk—but suddenly the door opened behind him and he turned round on a girl in a cloth coat and he was immortal all over again.

"Oh, hi, Johnny," she said, and then she gave the door a look and leaned back into it to slam it shut. "God, it's brutal out there."

At first he didn't recognize her. That sort of thing happened to him more and more lately, it seemed, and he told himself he had to cut back on the booze—and reefer, reefer was the worst, sponging your brain clean so you couldn't recognize your own face in the mirror. He'd come into some joint—a bar, a club, his manager's office—and there'd be somebody there he hadn't expected, somebody transposed from some other scene altogether, and he'd have to fumble around the greeting and give himself a minute or two to reel his brain back in. "Darlene," he said now, "Darlene Delmar. Wow. I haven't seen you in what, years? Or months, anyway, right?"

She was wearing sunglasses though it was as dark as night outside and there was some sort of welt or blemish under the left lens, right at the cheekbone. She gave him a thin smile. "Six months ago, Cincinnati. On what was that station? W-something."

"Oh, yeah," he said, faking it, "yeah. Good times, huh? But how you been keeping?"

A rueful smile. A shrug. He could smell her perfume, a faint fleeting whiff of flowers blooming in a green field under a sun that brought the sweat out on the back of your neck, spring, summer, *Florida,* but the odor of the streets drove it down. "As well as can be expected, I guess. If I could get more work—like in a warmer climate, you know what I mean?" She shook out her hair, stamped her feet to knock the slush off her heels, and he couldn't help looking at her ankles, her legs, the way the coat parted to reveal the flesh there.

"It's been tough all over," he said, just to say something.

"My manager—I've got a new manager, did I tell you that? Or how could I, since I haven't seen you in six months . . . ?" She trailed off, gave a little laugh, then dug into her purse for her cigarettes. "Anyway, he says things'll look up after the New Year, definitely. He was talking about maybe sending me out to L.A. Or Vegas maybe."

He was trying to remember what he'd heard about her—somebody had knocked her up and she'd had a back-room abortion and there'd been complications. Or no, that wasn't her, that was the girl who'd made a big splash two years back with that novelty record, the blonde, what was her name? Then it came to him, a picture he'd been holding a while, a night at a party somewhere and him walking in to get his coat and she was doing two guys at once, Darlene, Darlene Delmar. "Yeah," he said, "yeah, that'd be swell, L.A.'s the place, I mean palm trees, the ocean . . ."

She didn't answer. She'd cupped her hands to light the cigarette— which he should have lit for her, but it was nothing to him. He stood rooted to the spot, his overcoat dripping, and his eyes drifted to the murky window set in the door—there was movement there, out on the street, a tube of yellow extending suddenly to the curb. Two guys with violin cases were sliding out of a cab, sleet fastening on their shoulders and hats like confetti. He looked back to her and saw that she was staring at him over the cigarette. "Well, here come the strings," he said, unfolding an arm to usher her up the hall. "I guess we may as well get to it."

He hadn't bothered to light her cigarette for her—hadn't even moved a muscle for that matter, as if he were from someplace like Outer Mongolia where they'd never heard of women or cigarettes or just plain common courtesy. Or manners either. His mother must have been something, a fat fishwife with a mustache, and probably shoeless and illiterate on top of it. Johnny Bandon, born in Flatbush as Giancarlo Abandonado. One more wop singer: Sinatra, Como, Bennett, Bandon. She couldn't believe she'd actually thought he had talent when she was growing up, all those hours listening alone to the sweet tenor corroboration of his voice and studying his picture in the magazines until her mother came home from the diner and told her to go practice her scales. She'd known she was working with him today, that much her manager had told her, but when she'd come through the door, chilled right to the marrow, she'd barely recognized him. Rumor had it he'd been popping pills, and she knew the kind of toll that took on you—knew firsthand—but she hadn't been prepared for the way the flesh had fallen away from his face or the faraway glare of his eyes. She'd always remembered him as handsome—in a greasy sort of way—but now here he was with his cueball eyes and the hair ruffled like a duck's tail feathers on the back of his head, gesturing at her as if he thought he was the A&R man or something. Or some potentate, some potentate from Siam.

Up the hall and into the studio, a pile of coats, hats and scarves in the secretary's office, no place to sit or even turn around and the two fiddle players right on their heels, and she was thinking one more job and let's get it over with. She'd wanted to be pleasant, wanted to make the most of the opportunity—enjoy herself, and what was wrong with that?—but the little encounter in the hallway had soured her instantly, as if the pain in her backside and the weather and her bloodshot eye wasn't enough. She unwound the scarf and shrugged out of her coat, looking for a place to lay it where it wouldn't get sat on.

Harvey Neff—this was his studio and he was producing—emerged from the control booth to greet them. He was a gentleman, a real gentleman, because he came up to her first and took her hand and kissed her cheek and told her how terrific it was to be working with her again before he even looked at Johnny. Then he and Johnny embraced and exchanged a few backslaps and the usual words of greeting—*Hey, man, long time no see* and *How's it been keeping?* and *Cool, man, cool*—while she patted down her hair and smoothed her skirt and debated removing the dark glasses.

"Listen, kids," Harvey was saying, turning to her now, "I hope you're up for this, because as I say we are going to do this and do it right, one session, and I don't care how long it takes, nobody leaves till we're all satisfied, right? Because this is a Christmas record and we've got to get it out there, I mean, immediately or there's no sense in making it at all, you know what I mean?"

She said she did, but Johnny just stared—was he going to be all right for this?—until Fred Silver, the A&R man for Bluebird, came hurtling into the room with his hands held out before him in greeting and seconded everything Harvey had said, though he hadn't heard a word of it. "Johnny," he said, ignoring her, "just think if we can get this thing out there and get some airplay, because then it slips into the repertoire and from Thanksgiving to New Year's every year down the road it's there making gravy for everybody, right? I mean look at 'White Christmas.' 'Santa, Baby.' Or what was that other thing, that Burl Ives thing?"

The room was stifling. She studied the side of Fred Silver's head—bald to the ears, the skin splotched and sweating—and was glad for the dress she was wearing. But Johnny—maybe he was just a little lit, maybe that was it—came to life then, at least long enough to shrug his shoulders and give them all a deadpan look, as if to say I'm so far above this you'd better get down on your knees right now and start chanting hosannas. What he did say, after a beat, was: "Yeah, that I can dig, but really, Fred, I mean really—'Little Suzy Snowflake'?"

They walked through it twice and he thought he was going to die from boredom, the session men capable enough—he knew most of them—and the girl singer hitting the notes in a sweet, commodious way, but he was for a single take and then out for a couple drinks and a steak and some *life,* for christ's sake. He tried to remind himself that everybody did novelty records, Christmas stuff especially, and that he should be happy for the work—hell, Nat King Cole did it, Sinatra, Martin, all of them—but about midway through the arrangement he had to set down the sheet music and go find the can just to keep from exploding. *Little Suzy Snowflake.* It was

stupid. Idiotic. Demeaning. And if he'd ever had a reputation as a singer—
and he had, he did—then this was the kiss of death.

There were four walls in the can, a ceiling and a floor. He locked the
door behind him, slapped some water on his face and tried to look at himself long enough in the mirror to smooth his hair down—and what he
wouldn't have given to have been blessed with hair that would just stay in
place for ten minutes instead of this kinky, nappy mess he was forever trying to paste to the side of his head. Christ, he hated himself. Hated the
look in his eyes and the sunken cheeks and the white-hot fire of ambition
that drove him, that had driven him, to this, to make this drivel and call
it art. He was shit, that was what he was. He was washed up. He was
through.

Without thinking twice he pulled the slim tube of a reefer from the
pack of Old Golds in his jacket pocket and lit up, right there in the can,
and he wouldn't have been the first to do it, God knew. He took a deep
drag and let the smoke massage his lungs, and he felt the pall lift. Another
drag, a glance up at the ceiling and a single roach there, making its feelers
twitch. He blew smoke at it—"Get your kicks, Mr. Bug," he said aloud,
"because there's precious few of them in this life"—and then, without
realizing just when he'd slipped into it, he found he was humming a Cab
Calloway tune, biggest joke in the world, "Reefer Man."

She must have looked like the maternal type—maybe it was the dress, or
more specifically, the way it showed off her breasts—because Harvey pre-
vailed upon her to go down the hall to the restroom and mother the star
of the proceedings a little bit because the ticker was ticking and everybody, frankly, was starting to get a little hot under the collar, if she knew
what he meant. "Like pissed off? Like royally?" Darlene took a moment,
lowered her head and peeped over the sunglasses to let her eyes rove over
the room. "Poor man," she said in her sweetest little-girl-lost voice, "he
seemed a bit confused—maybe he can't find his zipper." Everybody—she
knew them all, except the strings—burst out in unison, and they should
have recorded *that*. George Withers, the trombonist, laughed so hard he

dropped his mouthpiece on the floor with a thud that sounded like a gun-shot, and that got them all laughing even harder.

There was a dim clutter of refuse in the hallway—broken music stands, half a smashed guitar, a big waist-high ashtray lifted from the Waldorf with the hotel's name etched in the chrome and a thousand extinguished butts spilling over onto the floor—and a lingering smell of stopped-up toilets. She nearly tripped over something, she didn't stop to see what, and then she was outside the restroom and a new smell came to her: he was smoking reefer in there, the moron. She'd dragged herself all the way out here in the cold to do a job, hoping for the best—hoping for a hit—and here he was, the great Johnny Bandon, the tea head, getting himself loaded in the can. Suddenly she was angry. Before she knew what she was doing she was pounding on the door like a whole van full of narcs. "Johnny!" she shouted. "Johnny, people are waiting." She tried the doorknob. "Open up, will you?"

Nothing. But she knew that smell. There was the sound of water run-ning, then the toilet flushed. "Shit," she hissed. "Damn you, open up. I don't know about you, but I need this, you hear me? Huh?" She felt some-thing rise in her, exactly like that geyser she'd seen in *Life* magazine, red-hot, white-hot. She rattled the knob.

There was the metallic click of the bolt sliding back and then he pulled open the door and told her in an even voice to keep her shirt on, only he was smiling at her, giving her the reckless grin of abandon that ten years ago had charmed half the women in the country. She was conscious of the fact that in her heels they were the same height and the crazy idea that he'd be the perfect dance partner flitted through her head as he stood there at the door and the marijuana fumes boiled round him. What he said next totally disarmed her, his voice pitched to the familiar key of se-duction: "What's with the glasses? Somebody slug you, or what?"

The world leapt out at her when she slipped the sunglasses from her eyes, three shades brighter, though the hallway was still dim as a tomb. "It's my eye," she said, touching a finger to her cheekbone at the right or-bit. "I woke up with it all bloodshot."

From down the hall came the muted sound of the band working their way through the arrangement without them, a sweeping glide of strings, the corny cluck-cluck-knock of a glockenspiel and the tinkling of a triangle, and then the horns, bright and peppy, Christmas manufactured like a canned ham. "You're nuts," he said. "Your eye's no more bloodshot than mine is—"

She couldn't help smiling. "Oh, yeah? Have you looked in the mirror?"

They were both laughing suddenly, and then he took her by the arm and pulled her into the restroom with him. "You want some of this?" he said.

There was something about the moment—the complicit look she gave him, the way she showed her teeth when she laughed, the sense he had of getting away with something, as if they were two kids ducking out of school to have a smoke under the fire escape—that just lit him up, just like that, like a firecracker. Neff could wait. They could all wait. He passed her the reefer and watched her eyes go wide with greed as she inhaled and held it in, green eyes, glassy and green as the bottom of a Chianti bottle. After a moment the smoke began to escape her nostrils in a sporadic way, as if there was something burning inside of her, and he thought first of the incinerator in the basement of the tenement he'd grown up in, and the smell of it, of cardboard and wet newspaper and everything scraped off a plate, cat litter, dead pets, fingernail parings, and then, as if that sponge had wiped his brain clean, of church. Of votary candles. Of incense. Jesus, he was high as a kite.

"What?" she said, expelling the smoke through her mouth. "What's that grin for?"

He let out a laugh—or no, a giggle. "I just had this image," he said. "Very strange. Like you were on fire inside—"

Her eyes were on him, green and unblinking. She was smiling. "Me? Little old me? On fire?"

"Listen," he said, serious suddenly, and he was so far out there he couldn't follow his own chain of thought, "did you go to church when you were a kid? I want to know. You're Catholic, right?"

Her eyes went away from him then, up to where one very stewed roach clung to the ceiling, and they came back again. "Yeah," she said, ducking her head. "If you can believe it, I was in the choir."

"You were? Wow. Me too. I mean, that was how I—"

She put a hand on his arm as if to emphasize the connection. "I know exactly what you mean—it's probably how ninety percent of the singers out there got started. At least the ones I met, anyway."

"Church."

"Church, yeah." She was grinning at him, and when she grinned her dimples showed and her face opened up for him till he had to back up a step for fear of falling right into it.

He wanted to banter with her, say something clever, charming, keep it going, but instead he said, "You ever go anymore?"

She shook her head. "Not me. Uh-uh. It's been years." Her lips were pursed now, the dimples gone. "You?"

"Nah," he said. "All that was a long time ago. When I was a kid, you know?"

An achingly slow moment revealed itself in silence. She passed him the reefer, he took a drag, passed it back. "I guess we're both about halfway to hell by now," she said.

"Oh, I don't know," he said, and everything seemed to let go of him to make way for that rush of exhilaration he'd been feeling ever since she'd stepped into the can with him, "I'd say it's more like three quarters," and they were laughing all over again, in two-part harmony.

It was Harvey himself who finally came to fetch them and when Johnny opened the door on him and the smoke flowed out into the hallway she felt shamed—this wasn't what she'd come for, this wasn't professional or even sensible. Of course, Harvey had seen it all in his day, but still he gave her a sour look and it made her feel like some runaway or delinquent caught in the act. For a moment she flashed on the one time she'd been arrested—in a hotel room in Kansas City, after a night when she'd felt the music right down in her cells, when she'd felt unbeatable—but she stopped right there amidst the clutter and shook out her hair to compose herself. Harvey was white-faced. He was furious and why wouldn't he be? But Johnny chose to ignore it, still riding the exhilaration they'd felt in the bathroom—and it wasn't the reefer, that wasn't it at all, or not all of it—and he said, "Hey, Harvey, come on, man, don't sweat it. We're ready to slay 'em, aren't we, babe?"

"Sure," she said, "sure," and then they were back in the studio, dirty looks all around, Harvey settling into the control booth with Fred Silver, and the opening strains of "Little Suzy Snowflake," replete with glockenspiel and tinkling triangle, enveloping the room.

"No, no, no, no," Johnny shouted, waving his arms through the intro, "cut, cut, cut!"

Neff's face hung suspended behind the window of the control booth. "What's the matter now?" his voice boomed, gigantic, disproportionate, sliced three ways with exasperation.

Johnny was conscious of his body, of his shoulders slipping against the pads of his jacket and the slick material of his pants grabbing at his crotch as he turned and gestured to the booth with both palms held out in offering. "It's just that Darlene and me were working something out back there—warming up, you know? I just think we need to cut the B-side first. What do you think?"

Nobody said a word. He looked at Darlene. Her eyes were blank.

There was a rumble from the control booth, Harvey with his hand over the mike conferring with Fred Silver, the session men studying the cuffs of their trousers, something, somewhere, making a dull slippery hissing sound—they were running tape, and the apprehension of it brought him back to himself.

"I think"—the voice of God from the booth, *Domine, dirige nos*—"we should just get on with it like we planned or we're going to be here all night. Know what I'm saying, Johnny?" And then Silver, a thinner voice, the Holy Ghost manifesting Himself in everything: "Keep it up, Johnny, and you're going to make me pick up the telephone." Neff's hand went back to the mike, a sound like rubbing your sleeve over a trumpet mute, and there was more conferring, the two heads hanging there behind the glass like transparencies.

He felt scared suddenly, scared and alone and vulnerable. "Okay," he said to the room, "okay, I hear you." And he heard himself shift into another mode altogether, counting off the beat, and there were the strings pouring like syrup out of the corners and the whisper of the brushes and the high hat and he was singing in the unshakable pure tenor that was Johnny Bandon's trademark, and forget Harvey, forget the asinine lyrics, he was singing here, singing: only that.

Something happened as soon as Johnny opened his mouth, and it had happened to her before, happened plenty, but it was the last thing she'd expected from a session like this. She came in on the second verse—*Little Suzy Snowflake/Came tumbling down from the sky*—and felt it, the movement inside of her, the first tick into unconsciousness, what her mother used to call opening up the soul. *You're a soul singer,* her mother used to say, *you know that, little sister? A real soul singer.* She couldn't help herself. She took Johnny's lead and she flew, and so what if it was corny, so what if the glockenspiel was a cliché out of some fluffy nostalgic place and time nobody could remember and the arrangement was pure chintz? She flew and so did he.

And then the B-side, warmer, sweeter, with some swing to it—"Let it snow, let it snow, let it snow"—and they traded off, tit for tat, call and response, *But baby it's cold outside.* When Harvey's voice came at them— "That's it, kids, you nailed that one down"—she couldn't quite believe it was over, and from the look of Johnny, his tie tugged loose, the hair hanging in his eyes, he couldn't believe it either.

The musicians were packing up, the streets and the night awaiting them, the sleet that would turn to snow by morning and the sky that fell loose over everything because there was nothing left to prop it up. "Johnny," she murmured, and they were still standing there at the mike, both of them frozen in the moment, "that was, I mean that was—"

"Yeah," he said, ducking his head, "we were really on, weren't we," and from the way he turned to her she was sure he was going to say *Let's go have a drink* or *Your place or mine?* but he didn't. Instead he just closed his eyes and began to sing, pure, sweet and high. Nobody moved. The ghostly heads in the recording booth pivoted toward them, the horn players looked up from their instrument cases and their felt rags and fragile mouthpieces. Even the strings—longhairs from the Brooklyn Academy of Music—hesitated. And then, on the third bar, she caught up to him, their two voices blended into one: *It is the night/Of our dear Savior's birth.*

The moment held. They sang the song through, then sang it again. And then, without pause, as if they were reading from the same sheet, they swept into "Ave Maria," "O Come All Ye Faithful," "What Child Is This," the sweet beat of the melody as much a part of her as the pulsing of the blood in her veins. She didn't know what time it was, didn't know when Harvey and the A&R man deserted the booth, didn't know anything but the power of two voices entwined. She knew this only—that she was in a confined space, walls and floor and ceiling, but that didn't make any sense to her, because it felt as if it opened up forever.

WILD CHILD

1

During the first hard rain of autumn, when the leaves lay like currency at the feet of the trees and the branches shone black against a diminished sky, a party of hunters from the village of Lacaune, in the Languedoc region of France, returning cold and damp and without anything tangible to show for their efforts, spotted a human figure in the gloom ahead. The figure appeared to be that of a child, a boy, and he was entirely naked, indifferent to the cold and the rain. He was preoccupied with something—cracking acorns between two rocks, as it turned out—and didn't at first see them coming. But then one of the party—Messier, the village smith, whose hands and forearms had been rendered the color of a red Indian's with the hard use of his trade—stepped in a hole and lost his balance, lurching into the boy's field of vision. It was that sudden movement that spooked him. One moment he was there, crouched over his store of raw acorns, and the next he was gone, vanishing into the undergrowth with the hypersensitivity of a stoat or weasel. None of them could be sure—the encounter had been so brief, a matter of seconds—but they unanimously claimed that the figure had fled on all fours.

A week later, the boy was spotted again, this time at the verge of a farmer's fields, digging potatoes from the ground and bolting them as they were, without benefit of cooking or even rinsing. The farmer's instinct was to chase him off, but he restrained himself—he'd heard the reports of a wild child, a child of the forest, *un enfant sauvage*, and he crept closer to better observe the phenomenon before him. He saw that the child was very young indeed, eight or nine years old, if that, and that he used only his bare hands and broken nails to dig in the sodden earth, like a dog. To all outward appearances, the child seemed normal, having the fluid use of his limbs and hands, but his emaciation was alarming and his movements were swift and autonomous—at some point, after the farmer had approached to within twenty yards of him, the child reared his head and made eye contact. It was difficult to see the child's face because of the unbarbered thatch of his hair and the way it masked his features. Nothing moved, not the flock on the hill, nor the clouds in the sky. The countryside seemed preternaturally silent, the birds in the hedgerows holding their breath, the wind stilled, the very insects mute underfoot. That look—the unblinking eyes, black as coffee poured straight from the pot, the tightening of the mouth around discolored canines—was the look of a thing out of Spiritus Mundi, deranged, alien, hateful. It was the farmer who had to turn away.

That was how it began, the legend brewing, stewing, simmering in every pot throughout the district through the fall of 1797, in the fifth year of the new French Republic, and into the year that succeeded it. The Terror was over, the King was dead, life—especially in the provinces—returning to normal. People needed a mystery to sustain them, a belief in the arcane and the miraculous, and any number of them—mushroom gatherers and truffle diggers, squirrel hunters, peasants bent under the weight of faggots or baskets of turnips and onions, kept watch in the woods, but it wasn't until the following spring that the boy was sighted again, this time by a party of three woodcutters, led by Messier, the smith, and this time they gave chase. They chased the boy without thinking, without reason, chased him because he ran from them, and they might have been chasing anything, a cat, a hind, a boar. Eventually, they ran him to tree, where he hissed and flailed the branches, flinging things down on them. Each time one of them attempted to mount into the branches and snatch for the boy's callused foot, he was pummeled and bitten, until finally they decided to smoke him out. A fire was built beneath the tree, the boy all the while watching these three bipeds, these shagged and violent and strangely habited and gibbering animals, out of the deep retreat of his eyes. Picture him there, crouched in the highest branches, his skin so nicked and abraded it was like a hide haphazardly tanned, the scar at his

throat a bleached white tear visible even from the ground, his feet dangling, arms limp, as the smoke rose about him.

Picture him, because he wasn't able to picture himself. He knew nothing but the immediate, felt only what his senses transmitted to him. When
he was a child of five, small and undernourished, the stubborn thirteenth
child of a stubborn peasant family, his mind lax and pre-lingual, he was
taken out into the forest of La Bassine by a woman he hardly knew or acknowledged, his father's second wife, and she didn't have the strength to
do what she had to do, and so when she took him by the hair and twisted
his head to expose the taut flesh of his throat she shut her eyes fast and the
kitchen knife missed its stroke. Still, it was enough. His blood drew steam
from the leaves and he lay there in a shrunken, skeletal nest, night coming
down and the woman already receding into the trees.

He had no memory of any of it, no memory of wandering and foraging
until his blouse and crude pantaloons were torn, were mesh, were string,
no memory at all. For him, there was only the moment, and in the moment he could catch things to feed his hunger, things that had no names
and no qualities except their desire to escape him, frogs, salamanders, a
mouse, a squirrel, nestling birds, the sweet and bitter sacs of the eggs
themselves. He found berries, mushrooms, ate things that sickened him
and at the same time sharpened his senses of gustation and olfaction so
that he could distinguish what was edible from what was not. Was he
lonely? Scared? Superstitious? No one can say. And he couldn't have said
himself, because he had no language, no ideas, no way of knowing he was
alive or in what place he was alive or why. He was feral—a living, breathing atavism—and his life was no different from the life of any other creature of the forest.

The smoke irritated his eyes, interrupted his breathing. Below him,
the fire built and climbed and everything was obscured. When he fell,
they caught him.

2

Fire he knew, remnants of the blazes the farmers made of last year's stalks and the stubble of the fields, and he'd learned through trial that a potato in the ashes turns to meal, savory and fragrant, but the smoke of the woodcutters' blaze overcame him so that the air was poisoned all around him and he fell into another state. Messier took him up and bound his limbs and the three men brought him back to the village of Lacaune. It was late in the afternoon, the night already gathering round the trunks of the trees and consolidating the leaves of the bushes as if they'd been tarred. All three were anxious to be home, to warm themselves at the hearth—it was cold for April and the sky spitting rain—but here was this marvel, this freak of nature, and the astonishment of what they'd done sustained them. Before they'd passed the first outlying houses, the boy flung comatose over Messier's shoulder, the whole village knew they were coming. Père Fasquelle, the oldest man in Lacaune, whose memory stretched back to the bloodline of the dead king's father's father, was out in the street, his mouth hanging open, and every child danced away from courtyards and doorways to come running in a mob even as their parents put down hoes and ladles and stirring spoons to join them.

They took the boy to the tavern—where else, but the church, and there was no sense in that, or not yet, anyway—and he seemed to come to life then, just as Messier was handing him through the door to DeFarge, the tavern keeper. The smith had a proprietary hold on the boy's legs, supporting him at the small of the back, and DeFarge took possession of the shoulders and head in his soft white taverner's hands. Behind them, Messier's two companions and the surging crush of the village, children crying out, men and women alike jostling for position and everyone focused on the open door so that a stranger coming on the scene would have thought the mayor had declared a holiday and the drinks on the house. There was a moment suspended in time, the crowd pressing, the child caught between the outdoors and the interior of that fabricated structure, the feral and the civilized in balance. That was when the child's black eyes flashed open and in a single savage movement he jerked his head forward and upward, clamping his teeth on the excess flesh beneath DeFarge's chin.

Sudden panic. DeFarge let out a scream and Messier tightened his grip even as the taverner let go in pain and terror and the child crashed to the floor, rending flesh, and those who saw it said it was just as if a swamp turtle, dredged out of the muck, had whipped round its viridian head and struck out blindly. The blood was there, instant, paralyzing, and within seconds the taverner's beard flowered with it. Those already in the room jerked away from him while the crush at the door fell back precipitately and the child, Messier gone down with him, bucked and writhed in the doorway. There were shouts and cries and two or three of the women let out with fierce draining sobs that seemed to tear the heart out of the crowd—this was a wild thing amongst them, some beast or demon, and there it was at their feet, a twisting shape in the shadow of the doorway, blood on its snout. Startled, even Messier gave up his hold and jerked to his feet, his eyes staring as if he were the one who'd been attacked.

"Stab it!" someone hissed. "Kill it!"

But then they saw that it was only a child, measuring just over four and a half feet tall and weighing no more than seventy bone-lashed pounds, and two of the men covered his face with a rag so he couldn't bite and pressed their weight into him until he stopped writhing and the claws of his hands, which had worked out of the knots, were secure again. "There's nothing to fear," Messier proclaimed. "It's a human child, that's all it is." DeFarge was led away, cursing, to be treated, and no one—not yet—had thought of rabies, and they crowded in close then, poking at the bound-up child, the *enfant sauvage* stripped from the fastness of the forest. They saw that his skin was roughened and dark as an Arab's, that the calluses of his feet were thick and horned and his teeth so yellowed they were like a goat's. The hair was grease itself and protected them from the unflinching glare of his eyes where it fell across his face and the rough corners of the cloth jammed deep in his mouth. No one thought to cover his genitals, the genitals of a child, two acorns and a twig.

The night wore on and nobody wanted to leave the room, the excess prowling round the open door, queuing up for a second and third look, the drink flowing, the darkness steeping in its post-winter chill, DeFarge's wife throwing wood at the fire and every man, woman and child thinking they'd seen the miraculous, a sight more terrifying and wonderful than the birth of the two-headed calf at Mansard's the year past or the adder that had borne a hundred adders just like it. They poked the child, prodded him with the toes of their sabots and boots—some of the more curious or courageous leaned in close to catch the scent of him, and every one of them pronounced it the smell of the wild, of the beast in its lair. At some point, the priest came to bless him, and though the wild Indians of America had been brought to the fold of God and the aborigines of Africa and Asia too, the priest thought better of it. "What's the matter, Father?" someone asked. "Is he not human?"

But the priest—a very young man with an angelic face and hardly a trace of beard—just shook his head and walked out the door.

Later, when people grew tired of the spectacle and eyelids began to collapse and chins give way to gravity, Messier—the most vocal and possessive of the group—insisted that the prodigy be locked in the back room of the tavern overnight so that news of his capture could be spread throughout the province in the morning. They'd removed the gag to enable the child to eat and drink, and a number of people, women amongst them, had attempted to coax him to taste one thing or another—a heel of bread, a scrap of stewed hare, wine, broth—but he'd twisted and spat and would take nothing. Someone speculated that he'd been raised by wolves, like Romulus and Remus, and would consume only the milk of a she-wolf, and he was given a very small quantity of the nearest simulacrum— the deposit of one of the village bitches that had just given birth—and yet that too was rejected. As were offal, eggs, butter, *boudin* and cheese. After a while, and after half the citizens in the place had stood patiently over the bound and writhing form with one thing or another dangling from tentative fingertips, they gave up and went home to their beds, excited and gratified, but weary, very weary, and bloated with drink.

Then it was quiet. Then it was dark. Traumatized, numb, the child lay there in a state between waking and sleeping. He was trembling, not from the cold because he was hardened to the weather, even to winter and the bitterest of days, but because of fear. He couldn't feel his limbs, the cords so tightly wound they were like ligatures, cutting off circulation, and he was terrified of the strangeness of the place where he was confined, a place that was enclosed on six planes and gave no sign of the stars overhead and no scent of pine or juniper or water in its flight. Animals, bigger and more powerful than he, had taken him for their pleasure, for their prey, and he had no expectation but fear because he had no word for death and no way to conceptualize it. He caught things, quick frightened things, and he killed them and ate them, but that was in a different place and a different time. Perhaps he made the connection, perhaps not. But at some point, when the moon rose and the thinnest sliver of light cut between the jointure of two stones in the near wall, he began to stir.

He had no awareness of time. Flexing, rocking, pushing off with his flexible toes and scrabbling with his nails, he shifted in space and shifted again and again till the cords began to give up their grip. When they were loose, he tore them off as if they were strips of vegetation, the vines and tendrils and entangling branches that snatched at his wrists and ankles as he perambulated through the forest, and a moment later he was stalking the room. There were two doors, but he didn't know what a door was and the rigidity of his terror had kept him from discovering its function when he was brought into this place and laid on the compacted floor in a scattering of straw. Nonetheless, he felt them, felt the wood as a texture to itself and a contrast to the stone, and thrust his weight into them. Nothing happened. The doors—the one leading back into the tavern, the other to the yard—were latched, and even if they weren't he wouldn't have been able to uncover the secret of their hinges or their method either. But above him was the roof, thatch over a frame of stripped poles laid close as fingers and toes. A single leap took him there, where he clung upside down like an oversized insect, and then it was a small thing to separate two poles and begin to dig upward toward the scent of the night.

3

For two years and more he eluded capture, hovering like a *cauchemar* at the margins of people's thoughts, and when the mistral raked the roofs and shrieked down the chimneys, they said he was stirring up the spirits of the forest. If a hen went missing, they blamed the *enfant*, though he'd never been seen to consume flesh or even to know what it was; if it rained too much or too little or if rust afflicted the grain or aphids the vines, people crossed themselves and cursed his name. He wasn't a child. He was a spirit, a demon outcast like the rebel angels, mute and staring and mad. Peasants reported seeing him capering in moonlit meadows, swimming like a rat in the rivers, basking in the sun in summer and darting through the scabs of snow that lay on the winter hills, oblivious to the cold. They called him the Naked One. *L'Animal*. Or, simply, the Savage.

For his part, he scraped and dug and followed his nose. On the primal level, he had only to feed himself, and if he raided the fields like any other creature of the forest, he took the same risks as they, to be trapped or shot or startled to immobility by the sudden flapping of a scarecrow's rags. Still, his diet was barely adequate, as might be imagined, consisting almost entirely of vegetable matter, and in winter he suffered just as the birds did. But he survived. And he grew. Haunting the barnyards, the middens and granaries, he became bolder, quicker, stronger, and farmers took to setting the dogs on him, but he was cannier than any dog and too smart to go to tree. Did he somehow come to understand that people were his tribe in the way that a bear instinctually consorts with other bears rather than foxes or wolves or goats? Did he know he was human? He must have. He had no words to form the proposition, no way of thinking beyond the present moment, but as he grew he became less a creature of the forest and more of the pasture, the garden, the dim margin where the trees and the *maquis* give way to cultivation.

Then came the winter of 1799, which was especially bitter. By this time, wary of the forest of La Bassine and wandering in search of the next trove of mushrooms or wild grapes or berries and the grubs he extracted from the pulp of decaying trees, he'd worked his way up over the mountains, across the plain between Lacaune and Roquecézière, and then down again along the bed of the Lavergne until he arrived in the environs of the village of Saint-Sernin. It was early January, just after the New Year, and the cold held a grip on everything. When night fell, he made himself a nest of pine branches, but slept fitfully because of his shivering and the hunger that clawed at his insides. At first light he was up and pawing through the scattered clods of a dormant field, looking for anything to feed into his mouth, tubers, onions, the chaff and scraps of crops long since harvested, when a ghostly drifting movement caught his eye: smoke, rising above the trees at the far end of the field. He was crouched on all fours, digging. The ground was wet. A crow mocked him from the trees. Without thinking, without knowing what he was doing or why, he rose and trotted toward the smoke and the cottage that gave rise to it.

Inside was the village dyer, François Vidal, who'd just gotten out of bed and started up the fire to warm the place and make himself a bit of porridge for breakfast. He was childless, a widower, and he lived alone. From the rafters of his one-room cottage hung the drying herbs, flowers and marsh weeds he used in his receipts—he was the only man in the region who could produce a *bon teint* of royal purple in lamb's wool, employing his own mixture and mordant, and he was of necessity extremely secretive. Did his competitors want his receipts? Yes, they did. Did they spy on him? He couldn't have said for certain, but he wouldn't have put it past them. At any rate, he went out to the yard, to the crude shed in which he kept his cow, so that he could feed and milk her, thinking to skim off the cream to complement his porridge. That was when he saw something—the dark streak of an animal—moving upright against the dun earth and the stripped backdrop of the trees.

He had no prejudices. He hadn't heard the rumors from Lacaune or even from the next village over. And when his eyes adjusted and registered the image in his brain, he saw that this was no animal, but a human child, a boy, filthy, naked to the elements and in need. He held out his hand.

What ensued was a test of wills. When the boy didn't respond, Vidal extended both his hands, palms up, to show he was unarmed, and he spoke to him in soft, coaxing tones, but the boy didn't seem to understand or even to hear. As a child, Vidal had a half-sister who was deaf, and the family had evolved its own home signs to communicate with her, though the rest of the village shunned her as a freak; it was these signs that began to come back to him as he stood there in the cold, contemplating the naked child. If the boy was a deaf-mute, as it appeared, then perhaps he would respond to the signs. The dyer's hands, stained with the residue of his trade, spoke in quick elegant patterns, but to no avail. The boy stood rooted, his eyes flitting past the dyer's face to the house, the shed, the smoke that flattened and billowed against the sky. Finally, fearful of driving him off, Vidal backed slowly to the house, made a welcoming gesture at the door, and then stepped inside, leaving the door open wide in invitation.

Eventually, with the dyer bent over the hearth and the cow—Rousa—unmilked and lowing with a sound that was like the distant intermittent report of a meteorological event in the hills, the boy came to the open door and Vidal was able to get a good look at him. Whose child was this, he wondered, to be allowed to run wild like an animal, the filth of the woods ingrained in the very pores of his skin, his hair matted with twigs and burrs and leaf mold and his knees callused like the soles of his feet? Who was he? Had he been abandoned? And then he saw the scar at the child's throat and knew the answer. When he gestured toward the fire, toward the blackened pot and the wheat porridge congealing within it, he was thinking of his dead sister.

Cautiously, one tentative step at a time, the boy was drawn to the fire. And just as cautiously, because he was afraid that any sudden movement would chase him through the door and back out into the fields, Vidal laid sticks on the hearth till the fire leapt up and he had to remove the pot, which he set on the fender to cool. The door stood open. The cow lowed. Using his hands to speak, the dyer offered the boy a bowl of porridge, fragrant with the steam rising from it, and he meant to fetch milk and pull the door shut, once he had his trust. But the boy showed no interest whatever in the food. He was in constant motion, rocking back and forth on his feet, his eyes fixed on the fire. It came to Vidal that he didn't know what porridge was, didn't know a bowl or a spoon or their function either.

And so he made gestures, pantomiming the act of eating in the way of a parent with an infant, bringing the spoon to his lips and tasting the porridge, making a show of masticating and swallowing and even going so far as to rub his abdomen in a circular fashion and smiling in satisfaction.

The boy was unmoved. He simply stood there, rocking, fascinated by the fire, and the two of them might have stayed in position all day long if it weren't for an inspiration that suddenly came to the old man. Perhaps there were simpler, ruder foods, he reasoned, foods of the forest and fields, that the child would take without prejudice, nuts and the like. He looked round him—he had no nuts. Nuts were out of season. But in a basket against the far wall there was a small quantity of potatoes he'd brought up from the root cellar to fry in lard with his evening meal. Very slowly, communicating with his body and his hands so as not to alarm the child, he got to his feet, and slowly—so slowly he might have been a child himself playing a game of statues—crossed the room to the basket. He lifted the straw lid, and still pantomiming, held up the basket to display its contents.

That was all it took. In an instant the child was there, inches away, the wild odor rising from him like musk, his hands scrabbling in the basket till he was clutching every last potato in his arms—a dozen or more—and then he was at the fire, throwing them into the flames in a single motion. His face was animated, his eyes leaping. Short, blunted, inarticulate cries escaped his lips. Within seconds, in the space of time it took Vidal to move to the door and pull it closed, the boy had reached into the coals to extract one of the uncooked potatoes, burning his fingers in the process. Immediately, as if he had no concept of what cookery involved, he began gnawing at it. When it was gone, he reached for another and then another and the same sequence of events played out, only now the potatoes were blackened on the outside and hard within and his fingers visibly scarred.

Appalled, Vidal tried to instruct him, showing him the use of the fire irons, but the boy ignored him—or worse, stared right through him as if he didn't exist. The dyer offered him cheese, bread, wine, but the child showed no interest, and it was only when he thought to pour him a cup of water from the pitcher on the table that the child responded. He tried at first to lap the water from the cup, but then he understood and held it to

his lips until it was drained and he wanted more, which Vidal, as fascinated as if a fox had got up on two legs and come to join him at table, kept
pouring until he was sated. After which, naked and filthy, the child pulled
his limbs to his chest and fell into a deep sleep on the stones of the
hearth.

For a long while, the dyer merely sat there, contemplating this appari-
tion that had blundered into his life. He got up from time to time to feed
the fire or light his pipe, but he didn't attempt to do any work, not that
day. All he could think of was his half-sister, Marie-Thérèse, an under-
sized child with a powerfully expressive face—she could say more with
her face alone than most people with their tongues. She was the product
of his father's first marriage to a woman who had died of puerperal fever
after bearing only this one damaged child, and his mother never accepted
her. She was always last to be fed and first to receive the slap to the face or
the back of the head when things went wrong, and she took to wandering
off by herself, away from the other siblings, until one night she didn't
come back. He was eight or nine at the time, and so she must have been
twelve or so. They found her body at the bottom of a ravine. People said
she must have lost her way in the dark and fallen, but even then, even as a
child, he knew better.

Just then Rousa bellowed and he started. What was he thinking, leaving her to burst like that? He got up quickly, slipped into his coat and went
out to her. When he returned, the child was pinned against the far wall,
huddled and afraid, staring at him as if they'd never encountered one
another before. Things were out of place, the table overturned, candle-
sticks on the floor, all his painstakingly gathered and hoarded plants torn
down from the rafters and scattered like drift. He tried to calm the boy,
speaking with his hands, but it did no good—every movement he made
was matched by a corresponding movement, the child keeping his back to
the wall and maintaining the distance between them, rocking on his feet,
ready to leap for the door if only he knew what the door was. And his jaws,
his jaws seemed to be working. What was it? What was he eating, another
potato? It was then that the dyer saw the naked tail of the thing dangling

like a string of saliva from the corner of the boy's mouth, and the boy's yellowed teeth, chewing round the dun wad of fur.

If he'd felt sympathy, if he'd felt kinship and pity, now all the dyer felt was disgust. He was an old man, fifty-four years on this earth, and Marie-Thérèse had been dead nearly half a century. This was none of his affair. None of it. Cautiously, warily, all his senses on alert as if he'd found himself locked in a cage with a ravening beast, he backed toward the door, slipped outside and pulled it shut behind him.

Late that afternoon, as a cold rain pelted the streets of Saint-Sernin and fell hard over the countryside, the wild child was given up to science, and through science, to celebrity. After having rolled one of his big cast-iron dye pots across the yard and up against the door to secure it, Vidal had gone directly to Jean-Jacques Constans-Saint-Estève, the government commissioner for Saint-Sernin, to make a report and give over responsibility for the creature immured in his cottage. The Commissioner, a man who traveled widely about the district, had heard the rumors from Lacaune and elsewhere, and he was eager to see this phenomenon with his own eyes. Here was a chance, he reasoned—if this creature wasn't just some bugbear or an African ape escaped from a private menagerie—to put Rousseau's notion of the Noble Savage to the test. What innate ideas did he have? Did he know of God and Creation? What was his language—the ur-language that gave rise to all the languages of the world, the language all men brought with them from Heaven? Or was it the gabble of the birds and the beasts? He could barely restrain himself. The light was fading from the sky and he'd had no dinner, but dinner was nothing compared to what this opportunity meant. He took Vidal by the arm. "Lead me to him," he said.

By the time the Commissioner had concluded his audience with Vidal and hurried with him out into the rain to see this prodigy for himself, he was surprised to see people in the street, heading in the same direction as he. "Is it true, Citizen Commissioner?" people asked. "They've captured the wild child?"

"I hear," someone else said, and there was a mob of them now, men, women and children, plodding through the rain to Vidal's cottage, "that he has six fingers on each hand—"

"And toes," another chimed in. "And he has claws like a cat to climb straight up a wall."

"He leaps fifty meters in a bound."

"Blood, he lives on blood that he sucks from the sheep at midnight."

"Nonsense, nonsense"—one of the village women, Catherine Thibo-deaux, appeared at his shoulder, hooded against the storm—"it's only an abandoned child. Where's the curé? Call out the curé."

When they approached the yard, the Commissioner swung round furiously to hush them—"Stay back," he hissed, "you'll frighten him"—but the crowd had worked itself into a frenzy of fear and wonderment and they pressed forward like a flock heading to pasture. Everyone crowded round the door, pressing their faces to the windows, and if it weren't for the impediment of the dye kettle they would have rushed into the room without thinking. Now they hesitated, their voices dropping to a whisper, while Vidal and the Commissioner shifted the kettle aside and stepped into the room, pulling the door fast behind them. The child was there, crouched before the fire, no different from how Vidal had left him, though he didn't seem to be masticating anything at the moment. Thankfully. What was strange, however, was that he didn't look up, though certainly he must have been aware of the alien presence in the room and even of the credulous faces pressed to the windows.

The Commissioner was dumbstruck. This child—this thing—was scarred, hunched, filthy, and it gave off a stench of the barnyard, as wild and forlorn as the first upright creature created by God in His own image, the man Adam who was given dominion over the animals and named them in turn. But this *was* an animal, a kind of ape, the sort of degraded thing Linnaeus must have had in mind when he placed men and apes in the same order of being. And if there was any doubt, there was the fresh coil of its dung, gleaming on the rough planks of the floor.

The fire snapped and hissed. There was a murmur from the crowd pressed up against the windows. "Good God," he exclaimed under his breath, and then, turning to the dyer, he put to him the only question he could manage, "Is it dangerous?"

Vidal, his house a shambles so that he was embarrassed in front of the Commissioner, merely shrugged. "He's just a child, Citizen Commissioner, a poor abandoned child, flesh and blood, just like anyone else. But he's unschooled. He doesn't know porridge, doesn't know a bowl, a cup, a spoon, doesn't know what to do with them—"

Constans-Saint-Estève was in his early forties and dressed in the fashion of Paris as it was before the Revolution. He had a fleshy face and the pouting lips of an epicene. His back still pressed to the door, his eyes locked on the child, he whispered, "Does he speak?"

"Only cries and whimpers. He may be—I think he's a deaf-mute."

Overcoming his initial shock, the Commissioner crossed the room and stood over the boy a moment, murmuring blandishments. His scientific curiosity had been re-aroused—this was a rare opportunity. A wonder, really. "Hello," he said finally, bending at the knees and bringing his bland face into the child's line of vision, "I am Jean-Jacques Constans-Saint-Estève, Commissioner for Saint-Sernin. And who might you be? What is your name?"

The child stared through him, as if he were insubstantial.

"Do you have a name?"

Nothing.

"Do you understand me? Do you understand French? Or perhaps some other language?" Judging from the coloration of the child's skin, he might have been Basque, Spanish, Italian. The Commissioner tried out a greeting on him in the languages of these regions, and then, frustrated, clapped his hands together as loudly as he could, right in front of the child's nose. There was no reaction whatever. The Commissioner looked to Vidal and the pale buds of the faces hung as if on a branch at the near window and pronounced, "*Sourd-muet.*"

It was then that the villagers could stand it no longer and began to push into the room, one at a time, until the place was crowded to the walls, people trampling the dried leaves and roots scattered across the floor, examining everything—trying, Vidal thought, to discover his se-

cret methods and receipts, which made him uneasy in the extreme, made
him suspicious and angry—and it was then that the child came to life and
made a bolt for the open door. A cry went up and people leapt back as if a
mad dog were amongst them; in a trice the child was out in the yard, in
the rain, galloping on all fours for the curtain of trees at the edge of the
field. And he would have made it, would have escaped again back into
nature, but for two of the strongest men in the village, men in their twenties, great runners, who brought him to ground and wrestled him back to
the open door of the dyer's cottage. The child writhed in their grip, making a repetitive sound that rattled in his windpipe—*uh-uh-uh-uh*—and
snaking his head round to bite.

It was fully dark now, the light of the fire and a single candle falling
through the open door to illuminate the scene. The Commissioner stood
there in the doorway, looking down at the child for a long moment, and
then he began to stroke the child's face, pushing the hair back from his
brow and out of his eyes so that everyone could see that he was a human
child and no dog or ape or demon, and the stroking had the effect it would
have on any sentient thing: the child's breathing slowed and his eyes went
distant. "All right," the Commissioner said, "let him go," and the men
loosened their grip on his limbs and stepped back. For a moment the child
just slumped there on the doorstep, glistening with wet and mud, his
limbs thin as a cow's shins, and then he took hold of the hand the Commissioner held out to him and rose quietly to his feet.

It was as if some switch had been turned off in the *enfant*'s inner apparatus—he came docilely, holding on to the Commissioner's hand like a
novice on the way to church, while the village followed in solemn proces-
sional. Along the way, the rain still lashing down and the streets a soup of
mud, people tried to get close enough to touch the child, and they shouted
out that he fed only on nuts and roots in the woods—and what would he
eat now, a *blanquette de veau? Boeuf bourguignon? Langouste?* The Commissioner didn't bother to answer, but he was determined to make his
own experiment. First he would clothe the boy's nakedness and then he

would offer him an array of foods to see what he would take and in the process he would try to learn something of this prodigy that would benefit society and the understanding of mankind.

Once home, he shut the door on the villagers and instructed his servant to find a garment for the child, and then, while he ordered up his own dinner, he installed the child in the room he used as his study and offices. A fire was laid and the boy went directly to it. In the room were several chairs, a desk, shelves of legal volumes and volumes of natural history and philosophy, the Commissioner's papers, a freestanding globe and a birdcage of wrought iron. Inside the cage was a gray parrot his late father had brought back from a voyage to Gambia thirty years earlier; her name was Philomène and she could ask, in penetrating tones, for grapes, cherries and nuts, comment on the weather and the state of inebriation of dinner guests and whistle the opening figure of Mozart's Piano Sonata in A minor. Excited by the prospect of examining the boy at his leisure, the Commissioner stepped out of the room only long enough to mollify his wife and give orders to have various foodstuffs brought to him; when he returned, the boy's face was pressed against the bars of the cage and Philomène was vainly serenading him with the Mozart.

He took the boy gently by the hand and led him to the desk, where a servant had laid out a selection of foods, both raw and cooked. There was meat, rye and wheat bread, apples, pears, grapes, walnuts, chestnuts, acorns, potatoes, parsnips and a solitary orange. Of all this, the child seemed only to recognize the acorns and potatoes, the latter of which he immediately threw into the fire, while cracking the acorns between his teeth and sucking the pulp from them. The potatoes he devoured almost instantly, though they were as hot as the coals themselves; bread meant nothing to him. Again, and for many patient hours, the Commissioner tried speaking to the child, first aloud and then in dumbshow, but nothing would rouse him; he seemed no more aware than a dog or cat. And no noise, not even the beating of a drum, affected him. Finally, after making sure the windows were secure and the doors latched, the Commissioner left the child in the room, snuffed the candles and went off to bed. Where his wife scolded him—what was he thinking bringing that savage thing

into their house? What if he arose in the night and murdered them all?—
and his two sons, Guillaume and Gérard, four and six respectively, informed him that they were too frightened to sleep in their own beds and
would have to share his.

In the morning, he approached his study on silent feet, though he kept
telling himself there was no need because the child was almost certainly
deaf. He lifted the latch and peered into the room, not knowing what to
expect. The first thing he saw was the child's garment, a shift of gray cloth
that had been forced over his head the previous night; it lay on the carpet
in the center of the room beside a shining loop of excrement. The next
thing was the child himself, standing in the far corner, staring at the wall
and rocking back and forth on his feet and moaning as if he'd been
wounded in some vital place. Then the Commissioner noticed several of
his volumes of Buffon's *Histoire naturelle, générale et particulière* lying
facedown on the floor, their leaves scattered to the wind. And then, finally, he noticed Philomène, or what was left of her.

That afternoon the wild child was sent to the orphanage at Saint-
Affrique.

4

He was brought to Saint-Affrique in a fiacre, the jolting and swaying of
which caused him a great deal of discomfort. Four times during the journey he became sick on the floor of the carriage and the servant Constans-
Saint-Estève had sent along to accompany him did little to relieve his
distress, other than daubing at the mess with a rag. The child was dressed
in his gray shift, which was knotted tightly at the waist to prevent his removing it, he was barefooted and he'd been provided with a small sack of
potatoes and turnips for his sustenance. The horses seemed to terrify him.
He rocked on the seat and moaned the whole way. On arriving at the orphanage, he made a bolt for the woods, down on all fours and squealing
like a rodent, but his guardian was too quick for him.

Inside the walls, it was apparent that he was no ordinary child. The director of the orphanage—Citizen R. Nougairoles—observed that he had no notion of sitting at table or of relieving himself in the pot or even the latrine, that he tore at his garment as if the very touch of the cloth seared his skin and that he refused to sleep in the bed provided for him, instead curling up in a pile of refuse in the corner. When threatened, he used his teeth. The other children, curious at first, soon learned to give him his distance. Still, in the short time he was there, a mere two weeks, he did become acculturated to the degree that he seemed to appreciate the comforts of a fire on a bitter day and he extended his dietary range to include pease soup improved with hunks of dark bread. On the other hand, he displayed no interest whatever in the other orphans (or in anyone, for that matter, unless they were in immediate possession of the simple foods he liked to eat). People might as well have been trees for all he responded to them—except when they got too close, of course—and he had no conception either of work or recreation. When he wasn't eating or sleeping, he crouched over his knees, rocking and vocalizing in a curious inarticulate way, but every moment he looked for his chance to escape and twice had to be chased down and forcibly restrained. Finally, and this was the one thing Nougairoles found most disturbing, he showed no familiarity with the forms and objects of holy devotion. The Director concluded that he was no imposter, but the real thing—Linnaeus' *Homo ferus* in the flesh— and that the orphanage could hardly be expected to contain him.

In the meanwhile, both he and Constans-Saint-Estève wrote up their observations of the child and posted them to the *Journal des débats*, and from there the other Parisian periodicals took hold of the story. Soon the entire nation was mad for news of this prodigy from Aveyron, the wild child, the animal in human form. Speculation galloped through the streets and echoed down the alleys. Was he Rousseau's Noble Savage or just another aborigine? Or perhaps—thrilling conjecture—the *loup-garou*, or werewolf, of legend? Or was he more closely related to the orangutan, the great orange ape of the Far East, an example of which, it had been proposed, should be mated to a prostitute in order to discover its issue? Two prominent and competing naturalists—Abbé Roche-Ambroise Sicard, of the Institute for Deaf-Mutes in Paris, and Abbé Pierre-Joseph Bonnaterre, professor of natural history at the Central School for Aveyron, located in Rodez—applied to take possession of the child in order to observe and record his behavior before it was further tainted by contact with society. Bonnaterre, being closer at hand, won out, at least in the short term, and he personally took charge of the boy at Saint-Affrique and transferred him to the school at Rodez. For the child, bewildered and aching only to get free of it all, it meant another fiacre, another assault of horses, another unfamiliar face. He was sick on the floor. He clutched the sack of turnips and potatoes to his side and would not let it out of his sight.

For the next several months, at least until the Minister of the Interior acted decisively in Sicard's favor, Bonnaterre had the boy to himself. He assigned a servant to see to the boy's corporal needs and then set about staging various experiments to gauge the child's reactions and store of knowledge. Since it had been assumed that the child was deaf, all contact with him thus far had been in dumbshow, but Bonnaterre laid out a number of instruments, from the triangle to the drum to the bass viol, and led the child to them, playing on each one in succession as best he could. Beyond the windows it was a clear, bright, winter's day. Bonnaterre's servant—his gardener, to whom the boy had seemed at least minimally to relate, perhaps because of the smell of the earth about him—was stationed by the door to prevent the child's escape and to discipline him if he should act out (and he did defeat all notions of modesty, pulling his smock up to the cincture at the waist in order to warm himself at the fire, for instance, and playing with his penis as if it were a toy soldier).

At any rate, Bonnaterre—a stern and imposing man with a face as flagrant as a ham against the pure white curls of his periwig—persisted for some time, beating at the drum, drawing the bow across the strings of the bass viol, clapping, shouting and singing till the gardener began to suspect he'd lost his mind. The child never reacted, never winced or smiled or turned his head at one plangent sound or another. But then the gardener, in his idleness, reached for a walnut from the bowl of them set on a sideboard at the rear of the room, out of sight of the boy, and applied the nut cracker to it with a sound barely discernible in the general racket fomented by his master, and—it was like a miracle—the boy's head jerked round. In an instant, he was at the gardener's side, snatching at the nuts; in the next, he was atop the sideboard, pounding the shells against the gleaming mahogany surface with the nearest thing that came to hand, a silver candlestick, as it turned out.

Despite the damage to the furniture, Bonnaterre was encouraged. The child was not deaf, not deaf at all, but rather his senses had been so attuned to the sounds of nature that any noise of human agency, no matter how strident or articulate, failed to impress him: there were no human voices in the wild, nor bass viols either. Creeping about the woods in an eternal search for food, he listened only for the fall of the apple or chestnut or the cry of the squirrel, or even, perhaps, on some miraculous level, for the minute vibrations sent out by the escargot as it rides along its avenue of slime. But if food was the child's exclusive focus throughout his feral life, then how would he react now that food was abundant and his for the asking? Would he begin to develop an interior life—a propositional life—rather than being exclusively fixated on exterior objects?

Bonnaterre pondered these questions, even as he observed the boy day by day and watched as he acquired rudimentary signs to make his desires understood, pointing to the water jug, for instance, when he was thirsty or taking his caretaker by the hand and leading him to the kitchen when he was hungry, there to point at one object or another. If he wasn't immediately gratified he went to the floor, moving rapidly on hands and feet and dragging his posterior across the finished boards, at the same time setting up a withering deep-throated sort of howl that peaked and fell and rose again from nothing.

When he was given what he wanted—potatoes, walnuts, broad beans, which he shelled with amazing swiftness and dexterity—he ate until it seemed he would have to burst, ate more than any five of the other children could consume at a sitting, and then gathered up the leftovers in his gown and stole away to the courtyard, where he buried them for future reference, no different from a dog with a bone. And when he was fed with others he displayed no sense of courtesy or fairness, but took all the food to himself, whether by a bold snatch or the furtive gesture, with no thought for his fellows. During the third week of observation he began to accept meat when it was offered, raw at first, and then cooked, and eventually he came to relish potatoes browned in oil in the pan—when the mood struck him he would go to the kitchen, take up the knife and the pan and point to the cabinet in which the potatoes and cooking oil were kept. It was a rude life, focused on one thing only—on food—and Bonnaterre was able to recognize in him the origins of uncivilized humanity, untouched by culture, by awareness, by human feeling. "How could he possibly be expected to have known the existence of God?" Bonnaterre wrote. "Let him be shown the heavens, the green fields, the vast expanse of the earth, the works of Nature, he does not see anything in all that if there is nothing there to eat."

For the boy's part, he began, very gradually, to adjust. His food came to him not from a hole in the earth or a chance encounter with carrion or the wild thing that was slower than he, but from these animals that had captured him, strange animals with heavy faces and snouts, with their odd white pelage and the hairless smooth second skin of their legs. He was with the one in charge of him at some point, the one all the others deferred to, and on an impulse he snatched at the man's pelt, the whiteness there, the gleam of it, and was startled to see it detached from the man's head and dangling from his own fingers. The man—the big flushed face, the veins like earthworms crawling up his neck—leapt from his seat with a cry and made to snatch the thing back, but the child was too quick for him, darting round the room and hooting over this thing, this hide that smelled of musk and the friable white substance that gave it its color. Gabbling, the man came after him, and, terrified now, the child ran, ran to a kind of stone that was transparent and gave a view of the outdoors and the courtyard. This was glass, though he had no way of knowing it, and it was an essential component of the walls that imprisoned him. The man shouted. He ran. And the stone shattered, biting into his forearm with its teeth.

They put a bandage of cloth on his wound, but he used his own teeth to tear it off. Blood was a thing he knew, and pain, and he knew to avoid brambles, the hives of the wasps, the scaled stone of the ridges that shifted underfoot and cut at his ankles with mindless ferocity, but this was different, a new phenomenon: glass. A wound of glass. It puzzled him and he took up a shard of it when no one was looking and ran it over his finger till the pain came again and the blood showed there and he squeezed and squeezed at the slit of his skin to see the brightness of it, vivid with hurt. That night, just before supper, he tugged at the other man's hand, the one who smelled of manure and mold, till the man took him out into the courtyard; the instant the door was opened he made a run for the wall and scaled it in two desperate bounds and then he was down on the far side and running, running.

They caught him again, at the foot of the woods, and he fought them with his teeth and his claws but they were bigger, stronger, and they carried him back as they always had and always would because there was no freedom, not anymore. Now he was a creature of the walls and the rooms and a slave to the food they gave him. And that night they gave him nothing, neither food nor water, and locked him in the place where he was used to sleeping at night, though he did not want to sleep, he wanted to eat. He chewed at the crack of the door till his lips bled and his gums tightened round the pain. He was wild no more.

When they took him to Paris, when the Minister of the Interior finally intervened on behalf of Sicard and gave instructions that the child should be brought north to the City of Light, he traveled through the alien countryside with Bonnaterre and the gardener who had acted as his caretaker all the while he was in Rodez. At first, he wouldn't enter the fiacre—as soon as he was led out of the gates and saw it standing there flanked by the three massive and stinking draft horses with their stupendous legs and staring eyes, he tried to bolt—but Bonnaterre had foreseen the event and placed a cornucopia of potatoes, turnips and small, hard loaves on the seat, and his weakness led him to scramble up the step and retreat inside. As a precaution against any further mischance, Bonnaterre had the gardener affix a lead to the cord round the child's waist, a simple braid of rope, the other end of which was held loosely in the abbé's hand as the public coach made its appointed stops and took on the odd passenger along the way. Was this a leash, such as might be used on a dog? It was an interesting question, one with pointed philosophical and humanitarian implications—certainly Bonnaterre didn't want to call it a leash, nor did the gardener—and as the boy rocked on the seat and made sick on the floor, the abbé kept hold of it with the lightest touch. The coach heaved on its springs, the gardener made himself small, Bonnaterre looked straight ahead. And when a blanched, imposing lady and her maid boarded the fiacre in a market town along the way, he went out of his way to assure them that the child was no threat at all and that the lead was solely for his own protection.

Nonetheless, when they stopped that evening at an inn along the way, the child (he was taller now and he'd put on weight, hardly a child any longer) did manage to create a scene. As the coachman held the door for the lady, the child gave a sly, sudden jerk at the lead, tearing it from the abbé's hand; in the next moment, using the lady's skirts as a baffle, he bounded down from the coach and lit out up the road in his curious, loping, lopsided gait, the leash trailing behind him. The lady, thinking she was being attacked, let out with a shriek that startled the horses into motion even while Bonnaterre and his servant clambered down to give chase and the hostler fought the reins. As can be imagined, the abbé was in no condition to be running footraces along the rutted dirt byways of a country lane, and he hadn't gone twenty feet before he was bent double and gasping for air.

This time, however, and to everyone's relief, the child apparently wasn't attempting an escape, but instead stopped of his own accord no more than a hundred yards off, where a ditch of stagnant water ran along the road. Before they could prevent him, he threw himself down on his stomach and began to drink. The surface of the water was discolored with duckweed, strands of algae, roadside offal. Mosquitoes settled on the child's exposed limbs. His garment was soiled in the muck. Both Bonnaterre and the gardener stood over him, remonstrating, but he paid them no mind: he was thirsty; he was drinking. When he'd done drinking, he rose and defecated on the spot (another curiosity: he defecated while standing and squatted to micturate), dirtying the skirts of his gown without a second thought. And then, as if this weren't enough, he made a snatch for something in the reeds and had it in his mouth before they could intervene—a frog, as it turned out, mashed to pulp by the time the gardener was able to pry it from his jaws.

After that, he came docilely enough to the inn, where he settled himself in the far corner of the room provided for him, gurgling and clicking over his sack of roots and tubers, to all appearances content and wanting the society of no one. But before long the villagers got wind of his arrival and crowded the inn for the rest of the night, straining to get a look at him—people clamoring at the doorway and scuffling in the halls, dogs yammering, the whole neighborhood in an uproar. He shrank into his corner, his face to the wall, and still the furor persisted till long after dark. And, of course, the closer he and his guardians got to the capital, where the influence of the newspapers was strongest, the bigger and more insistent the crowds grew. Despite himself, and despite the Minister of the Interior's strict injunction to bring the child to Paris without harm or impediment, Bonnaterre couldn't help gratifying the people along the way with at least a glimpse of the prodigy. And no, he didn't feel at all like a circus crier or a gypsy sword-swallower or anything of the kind—he was a scientist presenting the object of his study, and if the pride of possession gave him an internal glow of special privilege and authority, well, so be it.

It might have been the contact with all those people or the breathing of the night air or the miasma that hung over the roadside ditches where he liked to drink, but the child fell ill with smallpox along the way and had to be confined in the back room of an inn for a period of ten days while he broke out in spots and alternately shivered and burned with the fever. Blankets were brought, the local physician was consulted, there was talk of purging and bloodletting, and Bonnaterre was in a state—it was his head that was on the line here. Perhaps literally. The Minister of the Interior, Lucien Bonaparte, brother of Napoléon, was an exacting man, and to present him with the mere corpse of a wild child would be like bringing him the hide of some rare creature from the African jungle, its anatomical features lost, its vibrant colors already faded. The abbé got down on his knees before the writhing, bundled, sweating form of the child, and prayed.

Drifting in and out of sleep, the child watched the walls fade away and the roof dissolve to present the stars and the moon and then he was capering through a meadow while the Midi shook the trees till they bent like individual blades of grass and he was laughing aloud and running, running. He saw back in time, saw the places where he'd gorged on berries, saw the vineyard and the grapes and the cellar where a farmer had stored his crop of potatoes, new-dug from the earth. Then there were the boys, the village boys, urchins, quick-legged animals, discovering him there in the forest and giving chase, pelting him with sticks and rocks and the hard sharp stabs of their cries, and then the men and the fire and the smoke. And this room, where the walls re-erected themselves and the roof came back to obliterate the sky. He felt hunger. Thirst. He sat up and threw off the bedclothes.

Three days later, he was in Paris, though he didn't know it. All he knew was what he saw and heard and smelled. He saw confusion, heard chaos, and what he smelled was ranker than anything he'd come across in all his years of wandering the fields and forests of Aveyron, concentrated, pungent, the reek of civilization.

5

The Institute for Deaf-Mutes sprawled over several acres just across the boulevard Saint-Michel from the Luxembourg Gardens. It was formerly a Catholic seminary, which the revolutionary government had given over to Abbé Sicard for the training and advancement of the deaf and dumb. Employing a method of instruction in the language of signs he had adopted from his predecessor, De l'Epée, Sicard had become famous for the amazing transformations he'd wrought in several of his pupils, turning the all-but-hopeless into productive citizens who not only could articulate their needs and wants with perfect clarity but expound on philosophical issues as well. One of them, a well-made young man by the name of Massieu, was the cynosure of a number of Sicard's public demonstrations of his pupils' speaking and writing ability, in which the pupils answered questions written on cards by the audience, and he came to address a number of learned societies with confidence and dignity and in an accent not much worse than an educated foreigner's. Even more astonishing, this young man, who'd come to the Institute as dumb as a stone, was eventually able to dine in company and entertain people with his own original *bon mots,* memorably defining gratitude as *la mémoire du coeur* and distinguishing between desire and hope by pronouncing that "Desire is a tree in leaf, hope is a tree in bloom, enjoyment is a tree with fruit." And so, when the wild child was delivered up to Sicard by Bonnaterre, all of Paris awaited the result, the miracle that was sure to follow as the boy acquired the ability of language and the gift of civilization; it was hoped that one day he too would stand before an entranced audience and give shape to the thoughts and emotions he'd felt while living as an animal.

Unfortunately, things proved different.

After the initial flurry of excitement, after the crowds had dissipated and half the haut monde of Paris had trooped up the stairs of the Institute to observe him rocking in the corner of his room on the fifth floor, after he was brought to the chambers of the Minister of the Interior for a private interview (where he sat on his haunches in a corner and stared vacantly into the distance before relieving himself on the carpet), after the newspapers had recorded his every move and common citizens had gathered on street corners to debate his humanity, he was given over to neglect. Sicard, a man preoccupied with his more tractable pupils, the text of the book he was writing on the education of deaf-mutes and his duties as one of the founders of the Society of Observers of Man, examined the boy over the course of several days and pronounced him an incurable idiot—he wasn't about to risk his reputation on a creature that recognized no signs whatever and hadn't the sense or even the hygiene of a house cat. Thus, the child was abandoned again, but this time within the walls of the institution, where there was no one to look after him and where the other children made it their duty to chase, taunt and torment him.

He slunk about the corridors and grounds, moving from shadow to shadow as if afraid of the light, and whenever he heard the clamor of the deaf-mute students in the stairwell he ran in the opposite direction, ascending rapidly when they were below him, descending when they were above. Out of doors, he kept his back to the rough stone of the buildings, watchful and frightened, and when the others were released from their classes, he darted for the nearest tree. If he thought to escape during this period, he was frustrated not only by the fact that the keeper locked him in at night, but by the walls that delimited the grounds of the Institute—he could have scaled them in his efficient squirrel-like way, but what lay beyond the walls was the city, and he was a creature and prisoner of it now.

His only relief was in the privacy of his room, and even that was denied him more often than not because members of the scientific community continued to haunt the corridors of the Institute, one philosopher or naturalist after the other poking his head in the door or following him as he trotted the halls in his freakish sidelong gait or climbed up into the branches of the nearest tree to get away from the crush of people, people all around him where before there had been none. He took his food privately, in his room, hoarding it, and if he were to get wet—in a rainstorm or in the ornamental pond, where the other children delighted in cornering him—he had the disconcerting habit of drying himself with ashes from the hearth so that he looked like a ghoul haunting the halls. He tore the straw from his bed, refused to bathe, defecated beside the chamberpot as if in defiance. Twice, lashing out at mild Monsieur Guérin, the old man employed to maintain the grounds, he inflicted bite wounds. Sicard and all his staff gave him up for hopeless. There was even talk of sending him to the Bicêtre, where he would be locked away with the retarded and the insane, and it might have happened if it weren't for the fact that it would have reflected so poorly on Sicard, who had, after all, insisted on bringing the child to Paris. By the fall of 1800, things stood at an impasse.

It was then that a newly fledged doctor from the Val-de-Grâce Hospital came to work as medical officer at the Institute. His name was Jean-Marc Gaspard Itard, he was twenty-five years old and he'd been schooled in Marseilles prior to his internship in Paris; he was given an apartment in the main building and a modest—very modest—salary amounting to sixty-six francs per annum. The first time he encountered the wild child was after he'd bandaged a bite wound on the forearm of one of the female students and learned that the boy who'd inflicted it was even then crouched in the denuded crown of the big elm that dominated the grounds, refusing to come down. Itard had, of course, heard rumor of the child—everyone in Paris had, and Sicard had mentioned him in passing as a failed experiment—but now, angry and disturbed, he marched out of the building and into the naked wind to confront him.

The grounds were deserted; the light was fading from the sky. A cold spell had settled over the city, slops freezing in the streets, citizens wrapping up in greatcoats and scarves even as their breath steamed around them. In his haste, Itard had forgotten his own coat—he was in his jacket only—and almost immediately a chill ran through him. He hurried across the brittle grass to where the elm stood silhouetted against the faint red streaks of the sky. At first he couldn't see anything in the maze of slick black branches rattling composedly in the wind, but then a pigeon shot from the tree in a helter-skelter of wings and there was the boy, a white glow clinging like a fungus to the upper reaches of the trunk. He moved closer, his eyes fixed on the tree, until he stumbled over something, a shadow at his feet. When he bent to examine it, he saw that it was a simple shift of gray cloth, the boy's garment, flung down like an afterthought.

So he was naked, the Savage was naked, up in the tree, and he'd bitten a girl. Itard almost turned his back on him—Let him freeze, he was thinking, the animal. If that's what he wants, let him freeze. But then his eyes went to the tree again and he saw with a sudden clarity, saw the boy's neutral wedge of a face, the dark vacancy of his eyes, his pale splayed limbs, and he rode up out of his own body for a moment and inhabited the boy's. What must it have been like to be abandoned, to have your throat cut, to be captured and imprisoned and without defense except to sink your teeth into the slowest and weakest of your tormentors? To throw off your clothes, indifferent to the cold? To cower and hide and hunger? Very slowly, very deliberately, Itard lifted himself up and began to climb.

The first thing Itard did was arrange for the groundskeeper's wife, Madame Guérin, to take charge of the boy's needs, to provide a woman's touch, to mother him. Henceforth, the boy would take his meals in her apartments, along with Monsieur Guérin, whose attitude, Itard was sure, would soften toward the boy over time. Madame Guérin was then in her forties. She was a squat, uncomplaining woman, formerly of the peasantry but now, like all members of the Republic, a citizen; she was broad of bosom and hip and wore her abundant, graying hair tied up in a knot on the crown of her head. Her own children—three daughters—lived with her sister in a cottage in Chaillot and she saw them when she could.

Itard himself—unmarried, utterly devoted to his deaf-mute charges and yet ambitious and eager to prove himself—saw something in the boy the others failed to notice. High in the branches of the elm, the city spread out beneath him and the flights of birds intersecting over the rooftops, he held out his hand against the wind, murmuring blandishments, coaxing, until the boy took it. He didn't attempt to pull the child to him or to apply any force or pressure—it was far too dangerous; any sudden movement could precipitate a fall—but he just held the hand offered to him, communicating his warmth to the boy in the most elemental way. After a while, the boy's eyes settled on him, and he saw a whole world there, shuttered and excluded perhaps, but there nonetheless. He saw intelligence and need. And more: a kind of bargain in the making, a trust that sprang up automatically because they both knew that there was no one, not even the most agile of the deaf-mutes, who would have followed the Savage into that tree. When he finally let go of the boy's hand, gesturing to the ground below, the boy seemed to understand him and followed him down the trunk of the tree, each movement, each hand- and foothold synchronized to his. At the base of the tree Itard held out his hand again and the boy clasped it and allowed himself to be led back into the big stone building and up the steps to his room and the fire Itard laid there. The two of them knelt on the rough planks of the floor for a long while, warming their hands as the wind lashed at the window and night came down like an axe.

Sicard gave his permission for Itard to work with the child. What else could he do? If the neophyte failed to civilize the Savage, failed to teach him to speak and behave himself in society—and Sicard was certain he would fail—it was nothing to him. In fact, it was something of a relief, as he himself was no longer responsible, and yet if the Savage did somehow manage miraculously to acquire speech, it would reflect well on the whole enterprise; Sicard could even fleetingly envision the child, dressed in a proper suit of clothes, standing beside Massieu in an auditorium and wittily reflecting on his former life, speaking of raw tubers as *la nourriture des animaux et des Belges* or some such thing. But no, that would never happen. And it was best to lay the blame on someone else's shoulders. Still, he did manage to extract an annual stipend of five hundred francs from the government for the child's care and education and the unique experiment Itard was prepared to carry out to put to the test the thesis propounded by Locke and Condillac: Was man born a tabula rasa, unformed and without ideas, ready to be written upon by society, educable and perfectible? Or was society a corrupting influence, as Rousseau supposed, rather than the foundation of all things right and good?

For the next five years Itard would devote himself seven days a week to finding out.

The boy took to the regime warily. On the one hand, he basked in the protection Madame Guérin and Itard gave him against the mob of deaf-mutes clamoring for his destruction and he relished the unending supply of food in the Guérins' cabinet, and yet, on the other, he resisted with all his heart the doctor's attempts to control him. He'd put on weight, grown softer, paler (once he'd come in from the woods and the burning effect of the sun, his skin was seen to be as fair as any other child's), and he wanted only to crouch in a corner of his room and rock back and forth or sit by the edge of the pond and watch the light play over the water. And now, suddenly, here was this man with his insistent eyes and prodding nose haunting his every waking moment, pursuing him to his room to attack him there and even sitting down at table with him to interfere as he hoarded his food, the sausages he'd come to love and the potatoes fried in oil and the beans, the broad beans stewed into a pottage, the bread hot from the oven.

Every day, without relief, he was made to perform. And this was especially hard because for the first few weeks Itard had let him do as he pleased, taking him for long ambles in the park, allowing him to eat what and when he wanted and to hunker in his corner or curl up to sleep at any time of day or night, and that was a kind of heaven to the child because he was the leader, his whims were Itard's whims, and with Itard at his side he could defy the deaf-mutes, especially one lean, quick whipcord of a boy who was forever creeping up on him to administer wet blows with his open hands or to wrestle him to the floor and press his weight into him till he couldn't breathe. Itard was there for him now, there to watch over him, but also, very slowly and subtly, to mold him to his will. On the morning of the first snowfall, when the whole institution was clothed in slumber and every sound damped by the steady, silent accumulation, the child woke with a frantic pounding joy and darted naked down the flights of stairs to the yard where he held his face to the sky and cried out at the descending swirl of pristine crystals and burrowed into the drifts, insensible to the cold, and no one attempted to stop him. The stone buildings loomed like cliffs calling down the storm out of the sky. Shapes formed and fragmented in the air, visions playing there in the courtyard for him and him alone. And then he looked up, sensing something, a presence, and there the man was, Itard, wrapped in his greatcoat and scarf, the dark curls of his hair whitening, his lashes, his eyebrows, the sharp projection of his nose.

The next day, the regime commenced and ever so gradually heaven receded.

Itard began by taking hold of the boy immediately after breakfast and giving him a long hot bath, a bath that lasted three hours and more, Madame Guérin heating pot after pot of water, the boy frolicking, splashing, diving, spouting, at play like any other child bathed in sustaining warmth and free to express himself, but there was a purpose here, a civilizing purpose, and the fact that the child was made clean and free of offensive odors was merely the ancillary benefit. No, what Itard was doing—and these baths continued every day for the next month—was sensitizing the Savage, making him aware of his body, his self, in a way the life of the animal could never have done. After the bath each day, another hour would be spent in massage, as Itard and Madame Guérin took turns rubbing his limbs, the small of his back, soothing him, giving him pleasure, allowing him to appreciate an interaction he'd never before experienced: he was being touched by one of his fellow creatures, and there was no fear in it, no violence. Sure enough, within the month, he would fall into a tantrum if the water wasn't hot enough or the hands of his masseur sufficiently firm, and he began dressing himself without prompting, because now he felt the cold like any other domesticated creature and there was no going back. So too with his food. The Savage who had subsisted on raw roots and tubers, who had plucked potatoes from the fire and devoured insects and torn rodents with his teeth, turned up his nose at a plate of food that contained something he didn't care for or that was contaminated by a single shining example of Madame Guérin's silvered, flowing hair.

There were other things too that showed him coming awake in his senses. He learned to use a spoon to remove potatoes from a boiling pot, rather than simply thrusting in his oblivious fingers. He came to recognize himself in a hand mirror and to manipulate it so that it caught the light and tossed it from one corner of the room to the other. His fingers sought out the softness of Madame Guérin's skirts and the delicious ripple of the corduroy of Itard's suits. When he caught his first cold and sneezed, perhaps for the first time in his life, he was terrified and ran to his bed to bury himself beneath the counterpane, afraid that his own body was assaulting him. But then he sneezed again and again and before long, with Itard standing over him and murmuring reassurance, he came to anticipate the sneeze and ride its currents, exaggerating the sound of it, laughing, capering around the room as if propelled by an internal wind.

The next step—and here the boy began to chafe under his teacher's demands—was the commencement of the second stage of the regime, designed to focus his vision and sharpen his hearing in the way that his taste and tactile sensitivity had been stimulated. To this point he had engaged in a kind of selective hearing, registering only the sounds connected with eating, the rattle of spoon in bowl, the hiss of the flames under the pot, the cracking of a nut, but human speech—aside from inflection, as when either Itard or the Guérins lost patience with his tantrums or attempted to warn him away from things that might injure him—failed to register. Speech was a kind of background music, no different from the incomprehensible twitter of the birds of the forest or the lowing of the cow or bark of the dog. Itard set out to train him first by imitation, reasoning that this was how infants acquired language, miming what was said to them by their parents. He broke the language down into simple vowel and consonant sounds, and repeated them over and over, in the hope that the boy would echo him, and always he held up objects—a glass of milk, a shoe, a spoon, a bowl, a potato—and named them. The boy's eyes dodged away from his. He made no connection whatever between these rude noises and their referents and after months of study he could produce no sounds other than a kind of dull moaning and the laughter that awakened in him at the oddest and most frustrating moments. Still, he did react to the blunted speech of his deaf-mute tormenters—running from the noise of them, as he would have run from any startling sound in nature, a clap of thunder or the crash of a cataract—and one evening, when Itard had just about given up hope, he finally managed his first articulate expression.

It was in February, the sky stretched low and gray over the city, dinner stewing in a thousand pots, the eternal thumping and slamming and bellowing of the other students quietened both by the weather and the usual pre-prandial lull. Itard was seated in the kitchen of the Guérins' apartment as Madame Guérin prepared the meal, quietly smoking and observing the boy, who was always at his most alert when food was the focus. It happened that while the boy was at the stove, overseeing the boiling of his potatoes, the Guérins, husband and wife, began an animated discussion of the recent death of one of their acquaintances in an accident involving a carriage. Madame Guérin claimed it was the fault of the coachman—that he was negligent, perhaps even drunk—while her husband defended him. Each time she made a claim, he said, "Oh, but that's different," and put in a counterclaim. It was that simple exclamation, that vowel sound, that "o" that caused the boy to turn his head, as if he could distinguish it from the rest. Later, when he was preparing for bed (and, incidentally, showing a marked preference for freshly laundered sheets and a featherbed to the nest of sticks and refuse and the cold planks he'd formerly insisted upon), Itard came to him to say goodnight and drill him on his vowels, thinking that the agency of sleep might somehow help impress the sounds on the empty tablet of the boy's mind.

"Oh," Itard said, pointing to the window. "Oh," he said, pointing to the bed, to his own throat, to the round and supple sound hanging in the air.

To his amazement, from deep in the boy's throat, the same sound came back at him. The boy was in his nightgown, tugging at the blankets. There was no show of ablutions or pretense of prayers to a non-conceptualized God; when the child felt sleepy, he retired to his room and plunged into the bed. But now, as he lay there, he repeated the sound, as if struck by the novelty of it, and Itard, excited, bent over him, repeating "oh, oh, oh," until the child feel asleep.

It only seemed natural then, that in the morning, when the boy came to him, Itard called him by his new name, the one he'd suggested for himself, an august and venerable name borne proudly by any number of Frenchmen before and since, a name in which the accent fell heavily on the open second syllable: Victor. His name was Victor, and though he couldn't pronounce the first part of it and perhaps didn't even hear it and never would, he learned to respond to the second. He was Victor. Victor. After thirteen years on this earth, he was finally somebody.

6

It was around the time of his naming that Victor—or rather, Itard, on Victor's behalf—received an invitation to attend the salon of Madame Récamier. This was a great opportunity, not only for Victor, whose cause could be promoted amongst the most powerful and influential people in France, but for Itard too, who, despite himself, had unrealistic social expectations, and like any other man, yearned for recognition. Madame Récamier was then twenty-four years old, a celebrated beauty and wit, wife of a wealthy banker three times her age and doyenne of a château in Clïchy-la-Garenne, just outside the city; anyone who was anyone came there to pay her homage and to be seen. Accordingly, Itard bought himself

a new jacket and had Madame Guérin make Victor a suit of clothes replete
with a high-collared shirt, waistcoat and cravat, so that he looked like a
gentleman in miniature. For a full week before the date of the salon, Itard
devised various games and stratagems to teach Victor how to bow in the
presence of a lady, with mixed results.

On the evening of the party they hired a carriage, Victor by now having lost his fear of horses to the extent that he stuck his head out the
window and shrieked with glee the whole way, startling pedestrians, gen-
darmes and dogs alike, and proceeded through a cold rain to Clïchy-la-
Garenne. At first things seemed to go well, the *bon ton* of Paris making
way for the doctor and his charge, the former savage who was now dressed
and comporting himself like any other boy of thirteen, though Victor
failed to bow to anyone, let alone his hostess, and persisted in trotting
from one corner of the grand hall to the other, smearing his face with
whatever foods he was able to find to his liking, the beaded eggs of fish
presented on wafers of bread, fungus that had been stuffed, breaded and
fried in hot oil, the remains of songbirds skewered nose-to-anus.

Madame Récamier gave him the seat of honor beside herself and even
fussed over Itard a bit, trying to draw him out for the benefit of her guests,
hoping he might, like a circus trainer, persuade Victor to show off some
trick or another. But Victor didn't show off any tricks. Victor didn't know
any tricks. Victor was mute, unable—or unwilling—even to pronounce
his own name, and he wasn't in the least susceptible to Madame Récamier's legendary beauty and celebrated eyes. After a while she turned to the
guest seated on her other side and began to regale the table at large with
an involved story concerning the painter who had recently done her portrait in oils, how he'd made her sit frozen in a single position and wouldn't
even allow one of the servants to read aloud to her for fear of breaking her
concentration. The tedium she'd endured. The suffering. What a beast
this painter was. And at a gesture from her everyone looked up and there
it was, like a miracle, the very portrait of the inestimable Madame Récamier—couchant, her feet tantalizingly bare and her face wearing a dig-
nified yet seductive look—displayed on the wall behind them. Itard was
transported. And he was about to say something, searching for the right

words, something charming and memorable that would rise above the self-satisfied gabble of his fellow diners, when a crash, as of priceless statuary upended, silenced the table.

The sound had come from the garden, and it was followed, sharply, by a second crash. Itard looked to Madame Récamier, who looked to the vacant seat beside her even as one of the notables at the far end of the table cried out, "Look, the Savage—he's escaping!" In the next moment, the whole party was thrown into turmoil, the men springing up to burst through the doors in pursuit, the ladies gathering at the windows and fanning themselves vigorously to keep from fainting with the excitement of it all, the servants fluttering helplessly round the vacated places at the table and the hostess herself trying to look as if this were all part of the evening's entertainment. Itard, mortified, threw back his chair in confusion, the napkin clutched like a lifeline in his right hand. He was immobilized. He didn't know what to do.

By the time Itard came to his senses, Victor was zigzagging back and forth across the lawn, pursued by a dozen men in wigs, frilled shirtfronts and buckled pumps. Worse, the boy was divesting himself of his garments, flinging the jacket from his shoulders, tearing the shirt down the middle, running right out of his shoes and stockings. A moment later, despite the hot baths, the massages and the training of his senses, he was as naked to the elements as he'd been on the day he stepped out of the woods and into the life of the world—naked, and scrambling up the trunk of one of Madame Récamier's plane trees like an arboreal ape. Itard moved through the doors as if in a trance, the shouts of prominent citizens— including the august General Jean Moreau, Jean-Baptiste Bernadotte, future king of Sweden and Norway, and old Monsieur Récamier himself—ringing in his ears. With the whole party looking on, he stood at the base of the tree, pleading with Victor to come down, until finally he had to remove his own jacket and begin climbing.

The humiliation of that evening stayed with Itard for a long while, and though he wouldn't have admitted it, it played a role in his attitude toward his pupil in the ensuing weeks and months of his training. Itard cracked down. No longer would he allow Victor to get away with the tantrums that too often put an end to his lessons, no longer would he tolerate any deviance from civilized behavior, which most emphatically meant that Victor would henceforth and strictly keep his clothes on at all times. And there would be no more tree climbing—and no more forays into society. Society could wait.

At this stage in Victor's education, in addition to constantly drilling him on his vowels, Itard began to employ the method Sicard had used in training his deaf-mutes to read, write and speak. He began by having Victor attempt to match everyday objects—a shoe, a hammer, a spoon—with simple line drawings of them, the idea being that once Victor had mastered the representation, then the symbols that depicted them in language, the words, could be substituted for the drawings. On the table in Victor's room, Itard laid out a number of these objects, including the key to Madame Guérin's food closet, an article of which the boy was especially enamored, and then fastened the drawings to the opposite wall. When he pointed to the drawing of the key, for instance, or the hammer, he demonstrated to Victor that this was the object he wanted. Unfortunately, Victor was unable to make the connection, though Itard persisted, perfecting his drawings and drilling the boy over and over while simultaneously pronouncing the appropriate word: "*La clé,* Victor, bring me *la clé.*" Occasionally, Victor did bring the correct object, but just as often, despite a thousand trials, he brought the hammer when the key was wanted or the shoe when it was the spoon his teacher had requested.

Itard then hit on the idea of having his pupil manually match the objects to the drawings, a less complex task surely. He began by arranging each of the articles on a hook beneath the corresponding drawing. He and Victor sat on the bed in Victor's room and studied the arrangement—key, hammer, spoon, shoe—until Victor had had time to associate each object with the drawing above it, then he rose, gathered up the objects and handed them to Victor to put up again. For a long while, Victor merely looked at him, his eyes soft and composed, then he got to his feet and put the objects back in their proper order. He was able to do this repeatedly, without hesitation, but when Itard changed the sequence of the drawings, Victor continued to place the objects in their original order—he was relying on his spatial memory alone. Itard corrected him, over and over, and just as often, no matter how Itard arranged the drawings or the objects, Victor placed the things where they had originally been, always relying on memory. "All right," Itard said to himself, "I will complicate the task." Soon there were a dozen articles, then fifteen, eighteen, twenty, so many that Victor could no longer remember the order in which they had been arrayed. Finally, after weeks of drills, of firmness, of pleading, of insistence, Itard was gratified—or no, he was delighted, ecstatic—to see his pupil making careful comparison of drawing and object and ultimately mastering the task at hand.

Next, it was the words. Itard went back to the original four objects, set them on their hooks, printed the signifiers for each in clear block letters— LA CLÉ, LE MARTEAU, LA CUILLER, LE SOULIER—and removed the drawings. Nothing. It was just as before—Victor made no connection whatever between what must have seemed to him random markings and the tangible things on the hooks. He was able only to arrange the items from memory, and no amount of study, no number of repetitions, could enlighten him. Weeks passed. Victor began to balk at the drills. Itard persisted. Nothing happened. Puzzled, he went to Sicard.

"The boy is congenitally infirm," the abbé said, sitting behind his great mahogany desk and stroking one of the cats that roamed the Institute's grounds. "He is, I am sorry to say, an idiot—and not an idiot because he was abandoned but a true idiot, a cretin, and it was his idiocy that was the cause of his abandonment."

"He's no idiot, I can testify to that. He's making progress. I see it in his eyes."

"Yes, and imagine the parents, ignorant peasants, a succession of squalling and filthy children clinging to their knees and little or nothing in the pot and they have this child—this Victor, as you call him—who cannot speak or respond normally. Of course they abandon him. It's a sad fact of life, and I've seen it time and again with my deaf-mutes."

"With all due respect, Abbé, he is no idiot. And I'll prove it. Just give me time."

Sicard leaned down to release the cat, a spoiled fat thing which was the brother or uncle or perhaps even the father (no one could remember) of the nearly identical one Madame Guérin kept in her apartments. When he sat back up again, he leveled his eyes on Itard and observed, in a quiet voice, "Just as you did at Madame Récamier's, I suppose?"

"Well, I—" This was a low blow, and Itard wasn't prepared for it. "That was unfortunate, I admit, but—"

"Unfortunate?" The abbé tented his hands before him. "The boy is an embarrassment—to you, to me, to the Institute and all we've accomplished here. Worse: he's an insult." He lowered his voice to a whisper: "Give it up, Itard. Give it up while you can—it will destroy you, can't you see that?"

But Itard wouldn't give up. Instead, he abandoned Sicard's method and went all the way back to the beginning. As he saw it, Victor's problem was one of perception—and it went deeper, far deeper, than in any of the Institute's deaf-mutes, whose visual acuity had been honed as an adaptation to their disability so that the thing and its representation in symbols was readily apparent to them. They had little difficulty in discerning the fine gradations in contour that separate one letter from another, a printed *b* from an *h*, an *l* from a *t*, and once they recognized the system they were able to appreciate it in all its variations. Victor, on the other hand, simply did not see the letters of the words because he couldn't distinguish simple shapes. And so, Itard came up with the idea of training Victor to recognize basic figures—cardboard triangles, circles, squares, parallelograms—and to match them to the spaces from which they'd been cut. At first, Victor took the new regime as a kind of game, and he was easily able to fit the pieces back in the holes, but then Itard, excited by the boy's progress, made the drills increasingly complicated, varying the shapes, colors and sequences of the pieces until finally, predictably, Victor revolted.

Imagine him. Imagine the wild child in his suit of clothes with his new name and his newly acquired love of comfort, with the mother-figure Madame Guérin had come to represent there to comfort and caress him and the demanding father, Itard, filling his every waking moment with impossible, frustrating tasks as in some tale out of the Brothers Grimm, and it's no surprise that he broke down, that his initial spirit, his free spirit, his wild spirit, reasserted itself. He wanted only to roam in some uncontained place, to sleep in the sun, to put his head in Madame Guérin's lap and sit at the table and eat till he burst, and yet every time he looked up, there was Itard, the taskmaster, with his fierce eyes and disapproving nose. And more, and worse: there were changes coming over his body, the hormonal rush of puberty, coarse hair sprouting under his arms and between his legs, his testes descending, his appendage stiffening of its own accord, morning and night. He grew confused. Anxious. Angry.

The blowup came on a fine spring afternoon, all of Paris redolent with the perfume of lilac and lily, the southern breeze as soft and warm as a hand laid against a cheek, the pond on the Institute's grounds giving rise spontaneously to ducklings, whole fleets of them, even as the deaf-mutes capered over the lawns, squealing and whinnying in their high, strained, unnatural voices. Itard had devised an especially complex configuration of shapes and cutouts, posters nailed up on the walls and three-dimensional figures spread across the table, and he could see that Victor was growing frustrated. He was feeling frustrated himself—this morning, like a hundred others before it, offering up hope in such niggardly increments that it seemed as if the glaciers of the Alps and Pyrenees would meet before Victor could learn to perform a task any four-year-old would have mastered in a minute.

The shapes wouldn't cohere. Victor backed away, flung himself sullenly on the bed. Itard took him by the arm and forced him to stand and confront the problem, just as he'd done over and over again all morning long, the grip of his iron fingers on the yielding flesh of the boy's upper arm as familiar to both of them as breathing in and breathing out. But this time, Victor had had enough. With a violence that startled them both, he snatched his arm away and for one suspended moment made as if to attack his teacher, his teeth bared, fists raised in anger, until he turned on the hated objects—the spheres, pyramids and flat geometric figures—and tore them to pieces. He raged round the room, ducking away from his teacher with the animal dexterity that had yet to abandon him despite the weight he was putting on, heaving the scraps out the open window, then rushing to the fireplace to fling ashes round the room and ripping at the

sheets of the bed with his teeth until they were shredded, and all the while
Itard trying to wrestle him down. Finally, ululating in a new oppressive
voice that might have been the call of some carrion bird, Victor threw
himself on the floor and fell into convulsions.

The convulsions were authentic—the eyes sunk back in the boy's head,
his teeth gnashing, tongue bloodied—but they were self-generated for all
that, and Itard, who'd witnessed this scene innumerable times in the past,
lost control himself. In a flash, he was on the boy, jerking him up off the
floor and dragging him to the open window—shock treatment, that was
what he needed, a force that was greater than he, implacable, irresistible,
a single act of violence that would tame him forever. And here it was,
ready to hand. Clutching him by the ankles, Itard thrust the boy through
the frame of the open window and dangled him there, five long stories
from the ground. Victor went rigid as a board, the convulsions dissolved
in the terror of the moment. What must he have thought? That after all
the kindness and blandishments, all the food, warmth and shelter, his
captors—and this man, this man in particular who had always forced
these strange, useless labors on him—had finally shown their true colors.
That his teacher was in league with Madame Guérin, that they'd softened
him in order to destroy him as surely as the deaf-mutes would have done
if they'd had their way, and before them the merciless boys of the villages
at the edge of the forest. He'd been betrayed. The ground would rush to
meet him.

For those few minutes, Itard didn't care what the boy was feeling. All
the pain and humiliation of the scene at Madame Récamier's came rushing back to him, all the endless wasted hours, the unceasing contest of
wills, Sicard's skepticism, the sharpened blade of the world's ready judgment and failure waiting in the wings. Victor whimpered. He wet his
trousers. A pigeon, disturbed on its roost, let out a soft flutter of concern.
And then, after all the blood had rushed to Victor's face, after the sky
seemed to explode across the horizon and close back up on itself in a black
ball and the deaf-mutes began to gather below, pointing and shouting,
Itard tightened his grip and hauled the boy back into the room.

He didn't lay him on the bed. Didn't set him in the chair or back on the floor. He held him up until Victor's muscles flexed and he was able to stand on his own. Then, very firmly and without hesitation, he made the boy gather up what scraps of cardboard remained, and recommenced the lesson.

After that excoriating afternoon, Victor seemed to come round. He still balked at his lessons, but not as often—or as violently—as before, and Itard had only to motion to the window to subjugate him completely. There were no more tantrums, no convulsions. Dutifully, his shoulders slumped and head bowed, Victor did as he was told and applied himself to his lessons, gradually acquiring a modicum of skill at matching the geometric shapes to their receptacles. At this point, Itard decided to move forward, attempting to teach him the alphabet through the agency of both his tactile sense and his burgeoning ability to make visual distinctions; to this end, he created a sort of board game in which there were twenty-four compartments, each marked with a letter of the alphabet, and twenty-four corresponding metal cutouts. The idea was for Victor to remove the cutouts from the compartments and then replace them properly, which he seemed able to do right from the beginning with relative ease. It was only by observing him closely, however, that Itard saw that Victor hadn't learned the letters at all, but was instead painstakingly setting aside the cutouts and simply reversing the order in which he'd removed them. And so Itard complicated the game, as he'd done with the representational drawings, until Victor could no longer memorize the order of the letters but had to concentrate on matching the shapes. Which he finally did. Victoriously.

This led, shortly thereafter, to Victor's pronouncing his first word aloud. It came about that one late afternoon, Madame Guérin had poured out a bowl of milk for Sultan, her pampered cat, and then a glass for Victor while the metal letters of the alphabet happened to be laid out on the table in her kitchen, and Itard, always looking for an opportunity of instruction, took up the glass before Victor could reach for it and manipulated four of the cutouts to spell the word for milk: l-a-i-t. Pronouncing it simultaneously—"Lait, lait"—he scrambled the letters and pushed them back across the table to Victor, who immediately arranged them to spell: t-i-a-l. "Good, Victor, very good," he murmured, realizing his mistake— Victor had seen the word upside down—and quickly rearranging the letters. Again the exercise, and this time Victor spelled the word properly. "Lait, lait," Itard repeated, and Madame Guérin, at the stove now, took it up too, a chant, a chorus, a panegyric to that simple and nourishing liquid, all the while pointing from the letters on the table to the milk in the glass and back again to his lips and tongue. Finally, with effort, because he'd come to relish milk as much as the cat did, Victor fumbled out the word. Very faintly, with his odd intonation, but clearly and distinctly, he echoed them: "Lait."

Itard was overjoyed. Here it was, at long last, the key to unlock the boy's mind and tongue. After praising him, after losing all control of himself and pulling Victor to him for a rib-rattling hug and pouring him a second and third glass of milk till his lips shone with a white halo, Itard ran off to the abbé's office to report this *coup de foudre,* and Sicard, for all his dubiety, withheld judgment. He could have remarked that even cretins can pronounce a few simple words, that infants of eighteen months can mouth "mama" and "papa," but instead he simply said, "Congratulations, *mon frère.* Keep up the good work."

The doctor went to bed happy that night and the next night and the night after that, and he remained happy through his mornings and afternoons until he took his dinner with Victor and the Guérins on the third evening after his pupil's triumph and Victor exclaimed "Lait!" when Madame Guérin poured him a glass of water, cried "Lait!" when she sliced him a piece of lamb, and "Lait, lait, lait!" when she set his potatoes, hot in their jackets, on the plate before him.

Was the doctor disappointed? Was he crushed, annihilated in the deepest fortress of his spirit? Was he rehearsing the abbé's words—"Give it up; it will destroy you"—over and over again? Yes, of course he was— how could he not be?—and he showed it in his face, in his gestures, in his attitude toward his ward and pupil, angry at the sight of him, of his thin wrists and too-big head and the flab beginning to accrue at his waist and in his cheeks and breast and under his chin even as Victor matched the metal cutouts to their compartments, singing out "Lait!" every time he succeeded.

Itard could never be sure if it was his own antagonism and harshness in those days following his disappointment that prompted the first major crisis in Victor's sojourn at the Institute, but when he came up the five flights of stairs in the morning to find the boy's bed empty, he blamed himself. Victor was not at the Guérins', not in Sicard's offices or mooning over the pond, and a search of the deaf-mutes' dormitories and of the grounds, extending even to the farthest walls, proved futile. Once again, as if he'd been a figment of the collective imagination, the wild child had vanished.

7

Outside in the dark, beyond the gates of the Institute, Victor was adrift. There was too much noise. There were too many people. Nothing seemed familiar, nothing seemed real. The sky was jagged, unrecognizable, the city a flower carved of stone, blooming under a moonless spring night, its petals radiating out in a thousand alleys and turnings and dead ends. Something had driven him out of his bed, down the flights of stairs and then across the grounds and up through the gates and into the streets, but he couldn't remember what it was. Some slight, some injury, the continuing and immitigable frustration of trying to please this man with his fierce grip and seething eyes—yes, and something else too, something he couldn't take hold of because it was inside of him, beating with the pulse of his blood.

Earlier, just after dinner, one of the deaf-mutes (not like him, a she, a new inmate arrived that morning with hair that hung down her back and a screen of heavy folded cloth concealing her legs and the other thing that was there, the potent physical mystery he could divine in the way he could sense the presence of an animal in a silent glen or sniff out the sodden secret pocket of earth that gave up the gift of a mole or truffle) had come to him in the hallway outside his room and held out her hand. She was offering him something, a sweet thing, small and sweet from the oven, and he didn't like such things and slapped it from her hand. There it was, on the floor, between them. She drew in her breath. Her face changed. And suddenly her eyes sprang at him, her arms jerking and her elbows knifing as her fingers bent and flexed and contorted themselves in some mad show, and he backed away from her. But when she reached down to retrieve the sweet, he came at her from behind and put his hands there, in the place where her limbs joined beneath the cloth, and he didn't know what he was doing or why he did it.

And yet there were repercussions. The she jumped as if she'd been stung, whirling round at the same time to rake her nails across his face, and he didn't understand and struck back at her and suddenly she was making the noise of an animal, a rising complaint that echoed down the hallway till the man appeared, his jacket askew and his face rigid with the expression Victor knew to be dangerous, and so he shrank away even as the man took hold of him roughly and made his voice harsh and ugly till it too rang out from the stone. This booming, this racket, and what was it? The teeth clenched, the parceled sounds flung out, each syllable a blow, and why, why? There was the physical pain of that enraged grip, and any creature would have felt it, any dog grabbed by the collar, but that was as nothing to the deeper pain—this was the man who demanded everything of him and who hugged him and petted him and gave him good things to eat when he complied, and to see him transformed was a shock. Victor remembered the window—and the closet into which he'd been thrust whenever he balked in those first months of his training—and he let himself go limp even as the man dragged him through the door, across the floor of his room and into the closet. And so, when it was time for bed, when the man's footsteps approached and the key turned in the lock and the closet door was pulled open, Victor would not make it up with him, would not hold his arms out for a hug as he'd done so many times before, and when the night came he hid by the gates till he heard the stamp and shudder of the horses and the chime of the wheels and the gates swung open to release him.

At first, in the freedom of the night, he'd felt supercharged with excitement, and he stole away from the walls with a sense of urgency, something in the smell of the air, polluted as it was, bringing him back to his old life when everything was untainted and equally divided between the kingdoms of pleasure and pain. He kept to the shadows instinctively, the noise of the carriages like thunder, people everywhere, emerging from the mist like specters, shouting, crying, their clogs beating at the stones, and dogs—how he hated them—making their racket in the alleys and snarling behind the fences. This new energy, this new feeling, drove him on. He walked till his shoes nagged at his feet and then he walked out of them and left them standing there in an alley behind him, two neat leather shoes, one set in front of the other in mid-step as if he'd been carried off by some great winged thing. A light rain began to fall. He turned one way to avoid a group of men bawling in their rumbling, low, terrible voices, and then he was running and he turned another way and was lost. The rain quickened. He huddled beneath a bush and began to shiver. All the urgency had gone out of him.

When he woke, the night had gone silent but for the hiss of the rain in the trees along the street and the trill of it in the gutters. He didn't know where he was, didn't know who he was, and if someone had stooped down under the bush and called him Victor—if Madame Guérin in her apron had appeared at that moment with her soft face and pleading hands and called him to her—he wouldn't have recognized his name. He was cold, friendless, hungry. Just as he'd been before, in the woods of La Bassine and the high cold plain of Roquecézière, but it was different now because now he felt a hunger that wasn't for food alone. He shifted position, tried to draw his wet clothes around him as best he could. One side of his face was smeared with filth where he'd lain in the mud. The soles of both feet were nicked and bleeding. He shivered till his ribs ached.

At first light, a man in uniform saw him curled beneath the bush and prodded him with the glistening toe of a boot. He'd been somewhere else, dislocated in his dreams, and he sprang up in a panic. The man—the gendarme—spoke something, the quick, harsh words like a drumbeat, and when he made a snatch for Victor's arm, he was just half a beat too slow. Suddenly Victor was running, the paving stones tearing at his feet, and the gendarme ran too, till the rain and the mist intervened and Victor found himself sitting beneath a tree overlooking the rush and chop of the moving river. Somewhere else, not half a mile distant, Itard and the Guérins roamed the streets, stopping pedestrians to inquire of him—Had anyone seen him, a boy of fifteen, his sharp nose, clipped hair the color of earth, in blue shirt and jacket, the wild boy, the Savage escaped from the Institute for Deaf-Mutes? People just stared. Itard turned away from them, calling "Victor, Victor!" with a ringing insistence, even as Madame Guérin's voice grew increasingly plaintive and hollow.

The city awoke and arose. Fires were lit. Raw dough fell into hot oil, eggs cracked, pike lost their heads, civilization progressed. Victor sat there in the rain, running his hands over his body, over the stiffening thing between his legs and the heavy roll of flesh round his midsection, the miracle of it, and then he pushed himself up and followed his nose across the street to where an open doorway gave onto a courtyard blossoming with the scent of meat in a pan. The rain slackened here, caught and held fast by the eaves. There was pavement underfoot. He could see a woman moving behind a window that was cracked an inch or two to let in the air, and he went to the window and stood watching her as she tended the meat and the pan and the odor of it rose up to communicate with him. It took a moment before she saw him there, his face smeared with mud, his hair wet and hanging, his black eyes fixed on her hands that spoke to the pan on the stove and the licking of the fire and the rhythm of the long two-pronged fork. She said something then, her face flaring in anger, her voice growling out, and in the next moment she vanished, only to reappear at a door he hadn't seen. There were more words flung out into the rain, and then there was the dog, all teeth and clattering nails, and Victor was running again.

But four legs outrun two, and just as he made the street the animal's jaws closed on him, on his right leg, in the place where the buttock tapers into the long muscle beneath it. The animal held on, raging in its own language, and he knew he had to stay upright, knew he had to fight it from the vantage of his height and not give in and fall beneath its teeth. They jerked there, back and forth, the animal releasing its grip only to attack

again and again, the blood bright on the black ball of its snout, and he
beat at the anvil of its head with both fists until something fell away inside
him and his own teeth came into play, clamping down on the thing's ear.
Then the snarls turned to pleas, to a high, piping, bewildered protest that
was no domesticated sound at all, and he held tight to the furious jerking
anvil till the ear was his and the dog was gone. He tasted hair, tasted tissue, blood. People stared. A man came running. Someone called out to
God as his witness, a common-enough phrase, but Victor knew nothing
of God or of witness either. For the first time in a long buried while, he
chewed without a thought for anything else but that, and he was chewing
still as he turned on his heel and trotted up the street in his torn pants, his
own blood hot on the back of his thigh.

He thought nothing. He didn't think of Madame Guérin or the food
locker or of Itard or the she who'd offered him the sweet thing in the bleak
familiar hallway outside the door of his room, and he didn't think of the
room or the fire or his bed. Walking, he felt the pain in his feet and this
new fire burning in the flesh of his thigh, and he limped and shuffled and
stayed as close to the walls as he could. Everything that had come before
this moment had been erased. He kept walking round the same block,
over and over, his head down, shoulders slumped, in search of nothing.

Itard had fallen into a deep, exhausted sleep when one of the deaf-
mutes who'd been sent out to scour the neighborhood came to him with
a pair of scuffed leather shoes in hand. The boy—he was Victor's age,
lean, clear-eyed, his hair cut too close to the scalp by the Institute's in-
competent barber—was fluent in the manual language of the deaf-mutes
and was able to tell Itard where he'd found the shoes and to lead him there
and even demonstrate in which direction they'd been pointed. Itard felt
stricken. He felt sick. The shoes—he turned them over in his hand—were
worn unevenly along the inside seam where Victor's lurching, pigeon-
toed gait punished the leather. There was no doubt. These shoes, these
artifacts, were as familiar to him as his own boots.

It was raining, the cobblestones glistening as if they'd been polished.
Pigeons huddled on the windowsills and under the eaves. Itard bent to
touch the spot the boy indicated and then looked off down the dripping

alley to where the walls seemed to draw together in the distance. He was afraid suddenly. The experiment was over. Victor was gone for good.

Even as he got to his feet and hurried down the alley, the deaf-mute at his side, he pictured Victor passing swiftly through the city, guided by his nose and ears, throwing off his suit of clothes like a yoke, working his way up along the bank of the Seine till the fields opened around him and the trees went dense in the ravines. He didn't stop to think what the boy would eat or that he was dependent now and grown heavy with surfeit and luxury, but thought only of Victor's eyes and teeth and how he would stoop to snatch up a frog or snail and crush it between his jaws—yes, and how well had all the eternal hours of exercises, of matching shapes and letters and forming vowels deep in the larynx prepared him for that? It was nothing. Life was nothing. He—Itard—for all his grand conception of himself and his power and his immutable will, was a failure.

A moment later they emerged from the alley and were back out on a wet, twisting street crowded with people and the baggage they hauled and carried and pressed to their bodies as if each loaf or sausage or block of paraffin was as vital as life itself, no chance of finding him here, no chance, and he thought of Victor's room, empty, and in the same moment that he was struck by the pang of his loss he felt a clean swift stroke of liberation slice through him. The experiment was over. Done. Finished. No more eternal hours, no more exercises, no more failure and frustration and battling the inevitable—he could begin to live the rest of his life again. But no. No. Victor's face rose up before him, the trembling chin and retreating eyes, the narrowed shoulders and the look of pride he wore when he matched one shape to another, and he felt ashamed of himself. He could barely lift his feet as he made his way back to the Institute through the bleak, unsettled streets.

It was Madame Guérin who wouldn't give up. She searched the streets, the paths of the Luxembourg Gardens where she took Victor for his walks, the cafés and wineshops and the alleys out back of the grocer's and the baker's. She quizzed everyone she met and displayed a crude charcoal sketch she'd made of him one night as he sat rocking by the fire, tending his potatoes, and she alerted her daughters and sent old Monsieur Guérin out to limp along the river and look for the inadmissible in the slow, lethal slip of the current. Finally, on the third day after he'd gone missing, one of the women who sold produce to the Institute's kitchens came to her and said she'd seen him—or a boy like him—across the river, begging in the marketplace at Les Halles.

She set out immediately, the woman at her side, her feet chopping so swiftly she was out of breath by the time she reached the bridge, but she went on, her blood clamoring and the color come into her face. The day was warm and close, puddles in the streets, the river a flat, stony gray. She was sweating, her blouse and undergarments soaked through by the time they reached the marketplace, and then, of course, the boy was nowhere to be found. "There," the woman shouted suddenly, "over there by the flower stall, there he is!" Madame Guérin felt her heart leap up. There, sitting on the pavement beneath a wagon and gnawing at something clenched in his two fists, was a boy with a dark thatch of hair and shoulders narrowed like a mannequin's, and she hurried to him, his name on her lips. She was right there, right at his side, bent over him, when she saw her mistake—this was a wasted scrap of a boy, starved and fleshless and staring up hostilely out of eyes that were not Victor's. Her legs felt unaccountably heavy all of a sudden and she had to sit on a stool and take a glass of water before she could think to offer the woman her thanks and start back for the Institute.

She was walking slowly, deliberately, her eyes on the pavement so as to avoid stepping into a puddle and ruining her shoes, and in her mind she was trying to get hold of her loss and fight down her sense of desolation—he would turn up, she knew he would, and if he didn't, she had her daughters and her husband and her cat, and who was he anyway but a poor, hopeless, wild boy who couldn't pronounce two words to save his life—when she glanced up to avoid a skittish man with a cane and locked eyes with Victor. He was on the far side of the street, carriages rattling by, the humped shoulders and floating heads of pedestrians intervening, all of Paris moving in concerted motion as if to frustrate her, as if to take him away again, and when she stepped into the road to go to him she didn't bother to look right or left and she ignored the curses of the ham-fisted man in his wagon and the stutter of his horses' hooves, because nothing mattered now, nothing but Victor.

For one uncertain moment, he didn't react. He just stood there, pressed against the wall of the building that loomed behind him, his face small and frightened and his eyes losing their focus. She saw how he'd suffered, saw the mud layered in his hair, the torn clothes, the blood at the seat of his pants. "Victor!" she called, sharply, angrily. What was he thinking? What was he doing? "Victor!"

It was as if those two syllables had become palpable and hard, fastened to a stone that hurtled out of the sky and struck him down. He fell to his knees and sobbed aloud. He tried to speak, tried to say her name, but there was nothing there. "*Uh-uh-uh-uh*," he said, his voice ragged with emotion, "*uh-uh-uh-uh*," and he crawled the last few penitential steps to her and took hold of her skirts and wouldn't let go.

While that scene in the streets was unfolding, Itard was back in his rooms, working with a mute boy who was functionally deaf but had retained some measure of hearing. This boy—his name was Gaspard and he was Victor's age, fair-haired, well-made, with a quick smile and tractable disposition—had progressed rapidly since coming to the Institute from a remote village in Brittany the preceding year. He could communicate readily by means of signs and he quickly mastered the exercises designed to allow him to associate an object and its graphic representation and then the object and the written word assigned it. For the past month, Itard had been drilling him in the shaping of the sounds of these words with the palate, lips, tongue and teeth, and the boy was beginning to string together discrete bits of sound in a comprehensible way, something Victor had been unable to do, though two years had gone by since he'd first come to the Institute—and Victor had the advantage of normal hearing. It was a conundrum, since Itard refused to believe that Victor was mentally deficient—he'd spent too much time with him, looked too deeply into his eyes, to believe that. At any rate, he was putting Gaspard through his drills and thinking of Victor, of Victor lost and wandering somewhere out there in the city, at the mercy of common criminals and sexual inverts, when Monsieur Guérin knocked at the door with the news that he'd been found.

Itard jumped up from the desk, knocking over the lamp in his excitement, and if it weren't for Gaspard's quick thinking and active feet, the whole room might have gone up in flames. "Where?" Itard demanded. "Where is he?"

"With Madame."

A moment later, with the reek of lamp oil in his nostrils and permeating his clothes, Itard was downstairs in the Guérins' apartment, where he found Victor lying rigid in the bath while Madame Guérin tended to him with soap and washcloth. Victor wouldn't look at him. Wouldn't so much as lift his eyes. "The poor child," Madame Guérin said, swiveling her neck to gaze up at him. "He's been bitten by some animal and lying in filth." Steam rose from the bath. Two vast pots of water were heating on the stove.

"Victor, you've been bad, very bad," Itard said, letting his intonation express everything he felt except relief, because he had to be stern, had to be like his own father, who would never let a child have his way in anything. Especially this. Running off as if he didn't belong here, as if he hadn't been treated with equanimity and even affection—and if he didn't belong here, then where did he belong? "Victor!" He raised his voice. "Victor, look at me."

No response. The boy's face was a wedge driven into the surface of the water, his hair a screen, his eyes focused on nothing.

"Victor! Victor!" Itard had moved closer until he was leaning over the tub, both hands gripping the sides. He was angry suddenly, angry out of all proportion to the way he'd felt just a moment earlier when Monsieur Guérin had brought him the news. What had changed? What was wrong? He wanted to be acknowledged, that was all. Was that too much to ask? "Victor!"

He couldn't be sure, because of the bathwater and the influence of the steam, but the boy's eyelids seemed to be wet. Was he crying? Was he movable too?

Madame Guérin's voice came at him out of the silence. "Please, Monsieur le Docteur—can't you see that he's upset?"

In the morning, first thing, though it might have been perverse, though it might have been his overzealousness that had precipitated the crisis in the first place, Itard went back to work on Victor, redoubling his efforts. Some elementary principal had been re-established over that bath, a confirmation of the order of being, he the father and Victor the son, and he was determined to take advantage of it while he could. He'd seen the influence of his own and Sicard's methods on Gaspard and some of the other deaf-mutes, and so he went back to drilling Victor on the simple objects and the words, written out on cardboard, that represented them. At first, Victor was as incapable of making the connection as he'd been at an earlier stage, but as the months progressed a kind of intellectual conversion gradually occurred so that Victor was finally able to command some thirty words—not orally, but in written form. Itard would hold up a card that read BOUTEILLE or LIVRE and Victor, making a game of it, would scramble out the door, mount the stairs to his room and unfailingly fetch the correct object. It was a breakthrough. And after endless repetitions, with several bottles and several books, papers, pens and shoes, he even began to generalize, understanding that the written word did not exclusively refer to the very specific thing in his room but to a whole class of similar objects. Now, Itard reasoned, he was ready for the final stage, the leap from the written word to the spoken that would engage all his faculties and make him fully human for the first time in his life.

For the next year—an entire year, with its fleeing clouds and intermittent rains, its snows and blossomings and stirrings in the trees—Itard trained him in the way he'd trained Gaspard, staring at him face to face and working the cranio-facial muscles through their variety of expressive gestures, inserting his fingers into the boy's mouth to manipulate his tongue and in turn having the boy touch his own and feel the movement of it as speech was formed. They drilled vowels, reached for consonants, for the simplest phones. It was slow going. "Fetch *le livre*, Victor," Itard would say, and Victor would simply stare. Itard would then get up and cross the room to hold the book in his hand, simultaneously pointing to Victor. "Tell me, Victor. Tell me you want the book. The book, Victor. The book."

In the meanwhile, whenever a breeze would stir the curtains or the clouds would close over the grounds or lightning knife through the sky, Victor would go to the window, no matter what they were doing or to what crucial stage the lesson had attained, deaf to all remonstrance. He had put on weight. He was taller now, by two inches and a half. Stronger. More and more he had the bearing of a man—unnaturally short, yes, and with the unformed features of a boy, but an incipient man for all that. There was the evidence of the hair under his arms and radiating out from his pubes and even the faint translucent trace of a mustache above his upper lip. During this period he was more easily distracted and he seemed to go blank at times, staring, humming, rocking, just as he'd done when he first came out of the woods. Increasingly, he seemed agitated too, and as his body continued to change, he became more of a problem about the grounds.

In addition to the incident with the deaf-mute girl, there was further cause for worry. While Itard couldn't imagine Victor's doing serious physical harm to anyone, male or female, the boy continually overstepped the bounds of propriety so that Sicard began to regard him as an immoral influence on the other children, and with good reason. There was no more sense of shame in him than in an arctic hare or an African ape that lived in its skin, and when the mood took him he would pull out his phallus and masturbate no matter the situation or the company (though thankfully, to this point, the abbé was unaware of it). He would rub up against people inappropriately, male and female alike. Increasingly, on awakening, he would dispense with his trousers and sometimes his undergarments too. No amount of discipline or punishment could make him feel shame or even modesty.

Once, when Madame Guérin's three daughters were present and they were all of them—the Guérins, Itard and Victor—having a picnic on the grounds of the Observatory in the Gardens, Victor made a fumbling amorous approach to Julie, his favorite of the three. He was used to seeing Julie, who often came to visit her mother—"Lee, Lee!" he would cry when she came into the room—and she seemed genuinely sympathetic toward him, not simply for her mother's sake, but because she was good-hearted and compassionate. On this day, however, no sooner had they spread the blanket and opened the hamper, than Victor made a snatch at the lion's share of the sandwiches and ran off with them to hide in a cluster of trees. This was his usual behavior—he had little sense, after all his training and humanizing, of anyone outside of himself, of pity or fellow-feeling or generosity—but this time there was a twist. A few moments later he came sidling back to the group, his face smeared with fish paste and mayonnaise, and began stroking the hair first of one sister, then another, his fingers visibly trembling as he touched them; then, with each in turn, he laid his head in her lap a moment until finally he got up and seized her by the back of the neck, his grip firm and yet gentle too. When they ignored him, he seemed hurt and pushed himself awkwardly away. The last was Julie, and she was more tolerant than her sisters. The same scenario played out, but then, showing a leap Itard felt he was incapable of, the boy took Julie firmly by the hand, pulled her to her feet and then led her across the grass to the clump of trees where he'd secreted the sandwiches.

The sisters shared a glance and made a remark as suggestive as they could in the presence of their parents, and Madame Guérin gave out with a little laugh of embarrassment, while her husband, stoic, elderly, his considerable nose reddened by the sun, gave all his attention to the sandwich before him. "Our Savage has grown civilized under the spell of feminine charm, eh?" Itard observed. "And who could blame him?" All eyes, but for Monsieur Guérin's, focused on the clump of trees and the pronounced sunstruck movement there. Intrigued, and with a lifted eyebrow for the party to show that he was amused and not at all concerned on a deeper level, though he was, of course, knowing Victor's rudimentary conception of propriety, Itard went to investigate.

Victor, his face bloodless and sober, was gently squeezing Julie's knees as if they were balls of malleable wax he was trying to shape into something else altogether, and at the same time he kept gesturing to his cache of sandwiches. The sandwiches, four or five of them—all showing conspicuous marks of his teeth—lay in a bed of fresh-picked leaves. Julie tried her best to look bemused, though she was plainly uncomfortable, and after she let Victor stroke her hair and mold her knees for some minutes, she smiled brightly and said, "That's enough, Victor. I want to go back to *Maman* now."

Victor's face took on a defeated look as Julie rose in a fragrant swirl of skirts and began to retrace her steps back to the party. "Lee!" he cried piteously, patting the depression in the grass where she'd been sitting, "Lee! Lee!" And then, in a kind of desperation, he held up the remains of a half-eaten sandwich as the ultimate expression of his love.

Itard was moved by this, of course—he was only human. But he couldn't conceive of how to instruct his pupil in morals or decorum when he was unable to implant words in his head—Victor couldn't formulate his own desires, let alone express them, and each day's exercises seemed to take him further from the goal. Six months went by, then another year. Victor began to chafe under the regimen in a way that recalled the early days, and no matter how many times they worked their facial muscles and their tongues and drilled over the same words, Victor simply could not pronounce them. Itard himself, a man with the patience of the gods, came to dread their sessions, until finally, reluctantly, he had to face the truth— Victor was regressing. Gaspard came and went, working now as a shoemaker's apprentice, able to read, write and speak with some degree of fluency, and others appeared in his place and learned and developed and moved on too. Sicard was growing impatient, as was the Minister of the Interior, who had authorized the funds for Victor's care and expected some sort of tangible return on the public investment. But there was some block here, some impediment Victor just couldn't seem to overcome, and despite himself Itard was forced to admit that it was the irremediable result of those years of estrangement, those years of inhumanity and wandering without any human voice to speak to him. He began to give up hope.

Then there came a day, a bright day of spring with a scent of renewal on the warm breeze blowing up out of the south, when Sicard appeared in the doorway to the doctor's rooms. Itard had been expecting a student and had left the door ajar, and he looked up in surprise—never, in all his time at the Institute, had the abbé come to visit him in his rooms, and yet here he was, wrapped in his soutane, his features pinched round the tight disapprobation of his mouth. This was trouble, and no doubt about it.

"The Savage," Sicard spat, and he was so worked up he could barely get the words out.

Itard got up from his desk in alarm and took up the water pitcher and the glass beside it. "Abbé," he said, already pouring, "can I get you a glass of water? Would you—?"

Sicard was in the room now, swiping one open palm across the other, his robe in a riot of motion. "That animal. That—God help me, but he's incurable. That idiot. That self-polluter, that, that—"

Itard gave him a stricken look. "What's he done?"

"What's he done? He's exposed himself in the flesh before the assembled female inmates and Sister Jean-Baptiste as well. And, and manipulated himself like one of the idiots in the Bicêtre—which is where he belongs. Either there or prison." He glared at Itard. His breathing—the ratcheting of the air through his nostrils—was thunderous. His eyes looked as if they were about to dissolve.

"But we can't just abandon him."

"I will not allow him to corrupt this institution, to pollute the innocent minds of these children—our wards, doctor, our wards. And worse—what if he acts on his impulses? What then?"

From outside the open window came the cries of the children at their games, the sound of a ball thumped and bodies colliding. Laughter. Shouts. Children at play, that was all it was. Only the sound of children at play, and yet it depressed him. Victor didn't play. Victor had never played. And now he was a child no longer.

Itard had tried everything, removing meat from the boy's diet, as well as any other foods that might contribute to unnatural excitation, giving him long baths again in the hope of calming him, and when he was most worked up, bleeding him till the tension flagged. Only the bleeding seemed to work, and then only for a few hours at a time. He saw Victor's face suddenly, rising before him in his consciousness, saw the pale descending slash of it in the corner of his room as he sat rocking over his feet and jerking at himself, saw the sheen of the eyes that pulled the whole world back into that primeval pit from which the first civilized man had crawled an eon ago. "He's not like that," he said lamely.

"He's incurable. Ineducable. He must be sent away."

There was a solution that had occurred to Itard, but it was something he couldn't discuss with anyone, certainly not the abbé or Madame Guérin. If Victor were able to express himself carnally, to experience the release every healthy male needs if he's not to become mad, then maybe there was hope yet, because this regression of his, this inability to focus and absorb his lessons—to speak like a human being—was perhaps somehow tied to his natural needs. Itard thought of hiring a prostitute. For months he'd wrestled with the notion, but finally he saw that he couldn't do it—it was one thing to rescue a child from savagery, hold him up to examination as a specimen, train his senses and his mind, and it was quite another to play God. No man had that right.

"We can't do that," he insisted. "He's a ward of the state. He's our responsibility. We took him from the woods and civilized him and we can't just throw up our hands and send him back—"

"Civilized him?" Sicard had spread his feet apart as if he expected to crouch down and grapple over the issue. He'd refused a seat, refused the water. He wanted one thing and one thing only. "You have no more to say about it."

"What about the Minister of the Interior? My report to him?"

"Your report will say that you've failed." His expression softened. "But not for lack of trying. I appreciate the energy you've put into this, we all do—but I told you this years ago and I'll tell you now: give it up. He's an idiot. He's filthy. An animal. He deserves only to be locked up." He snatched up the glass of water as if to examine its clarity, then set it down again. "And more: he should be castrated."

"Castrated?"

"Like a dog. Or a bull."

"And should we put a ring through his nose too?"

The abbé was silent a long while. The breeze picked up and rustled the curtains. A shaft of sunlight, golden as butter, struck the floor at his feet. Finally—and he had to raise his voice to be heard over the cries of the children—he cleared his throat and said, "I don't see why not. Truly, I don't."

8

The report, the final report Itard prepared for the Minister of the Interior, was a trial, a kind of crucifixion of the soul that made him want to cry out every time the quill touched the page. It was an admission that he'd wasted five years of his life—and of Victor's—in assaying the impossible, and that for all his brashness and confidence, all his repeated assurances to the contrary, he had failed. Ultimately, he had come to understand that the delimiting factors of Victor's abandonment were insurmountable—that he was, as Sicard insisted, ineducable. In the interest of science and in small measure to justify his own efforts, Itard listed these factors for the official record: "(1) Because he cannot hear the speech of others and learn to speak himself, Victor's education is and will remain incomplete; (2) His 'intellectual' progress will never match that of children normally brought up in society; (3) His emotional development is blocked by profound egotism and by the impossibility of channeling his awakening sexual feeling toward any satisfactory goals."

As he wrote, the pen seemed to drag across the page as if it were made of lead, every moment of hope he'd experienced in his association with Victor—the boy's rapid progress in those first few months, his first word, his naming, the leap he'd made in distinguishing written words—rising up before him and then vaporizing in despair. It took him several days and pot after pot of coffee before he began to understand that even in his failure there had been at least a muted success. Victor shouldn't be compared to other children, he argued, but only to himself—he was no more sentient than a plant when he'd first come out of the woods, differing only from the vegetative state in that he could move and vocalize. He was then the Savage of Aveyron, an animal-man, and now he was Victor, a young man who despite his limitations had learned to make himself useful to society, or at least the society of his guardians, Monsieur and Madame Guérin, for whom he was not only able but eager to perform household tasks such as cutting wood for the fire and setting the table for meals, and in the course of his education he had developed some degree of moral sensibility.

Some degree. He had no sense of shame, but then neither did Adam and Eve before the serpent came into the Garden, and how could he be blamed for that? Perhaps the most wrenching lessons Itard had felt compelled to give him were the ones designed to make him stretch beyond himself, to understand that other people had needs and emotions too, to feel pity and its corollary, compassion. Early on, when Victor was used to stealing and hoarding food in his room, Itard had tried to teach him a version of the Golden Rule in the most direct way he could think of—each time Victor filched some choice morsel from Itard's plate or old Monsieur Guérin's, Itard would wait his opportunity and swipe something back from Victor, even going so far as to slip into his room in his absence and remove his hoard of potatoes, apples and half-gnawed crusts of bread. Victor had reacted violently at first. The minute he turned his attention to his plate and saw that his *pommes frites* or broad beans were missing—that they were now on his teacher's plate—he threw a tantrum, rolling on the floor and crying out in rage and pain. Madame Guérin made a face. Itard held firm. Over time, Victor eventually reformed—he no longer took food from others' plates or misappropriated articles he coveted, a glittering shoe buckle or the translucent ball of glass Itard used as a paperweight—but the doctor could never be sure if it was because he'd developed a rudimentary sense of justice or, simply, that he feared reprisal in the way of the common criminal.

That was what led the doctor, sometime during the third year of the boy's education, to the most difficult lesson of all. It was on a day when they'd drilled with shapes for hours and Victor had been particularly tractable and looking forward to the usual blandishments and rewards Itard customarily gave him at the end of a trying session. The sun was sinking in the sky. Beyond the windows, the clamor of the deaf-mutes in the courtyard rose toward the release of dinnertime. The scent of stewing meat hung on the air. For several minutes now Victor had been looking up expectantly, awaiting the conclusion of the exercises and anticipating his reward. But instead of reward, Itard gave him punishment. He raised his voice, told Victor that he'd been bad, very bad, that he was clumsy and stupid and impossible to work with. For a long while he continued in this vein, then rose abruptly, seized the boy's arm and led him to the closet where he'd been confined, as punishment, when he'd been particularly recalcitrant during the early days of his education.

Victor gave him a look of bewilderment. He couldn't fathom what he'd done wrong or why his teacher's face was so contorted and red and his voice so threatening. At first, mewling plaintively, he let himself be led to the door of the closet, but then, as Itard was about to force him into it, Victor turned on him in outrage, his face flushed and his eyes flashing, and for a long moment they struggled for dominance. Victor was bigger now, stronger, but still he was no match for a grown man, and Itard was able to shove him, pleading and crying, into the closet. The door wouldn't shut. Victor wouldn't allow it. He braced his feet against the inside panel and pushed with all his strength and when he felt himself losing the battle he lurched forward suddenly to sink his teeth into Itard's hand before the door slammed shut and the key turned in the lock. It was an emotional moment for the doctor. His hand throbbed—he would have to treat the wound—and the boy would hate him for weeks, but he rejoiced all the same: Victor had developed a sense of justice. The punishment was unde-served and he'd reacted as any normal human being would have. Perhaps it was a small victory—would the Savage of Aveyron, dragged down from his tree, have grasped the concept?—but it was proof of Victor's humanity and Itard included mention of it in his report. Such a child—such a young man—he argued in conclusion, was deserving of the attention of scien-tists and of the continued support and solicitude of the government.

The report ran to fifty pages. The Minister of the Interior had it pub-lished at government expense, Sicard included with it a letter praising Itard's efforts, and Itard received some measure of the recognition and celebrity he'd craved. But the experiment was over, officially, and Victor's days at the Institute were numbered. Sicard militated for the boy's removal, writing the Minister of the Interior to the effect that for all Itard's heroic efforts the boy remained in a state of incurable idiocy, and that further he was a growing menace to the other students. It took some time—months and then years of depletion and vacancy—but eventually the government agreed to continue in perpetuity Madame Guérin's annual stipend of one hundred fifty francs to care for Victor and to award her an additional five hundred francs to relocate, with her husband and the boy, to a small house around the corner from the Institute on the impasse des Feuillantines.

If Victor was at all affected by the move from the only home he'd known, from the room he'd occupied all this time and the grounds he'd roamed till he had every twig and leaf, furrow and rock memorized, he didn't show it outwardly. He was a great help in moving the Guérins' furnishings, and the new environment seemed to excite him so that he got down on all fours and sniffed at the baseboard of the walls and examined each of the rooms minutely, fascinated to see the familiar objects—his bed and counterpane, the pots and pans, the twin chairs the Guérins liked to pull up to the fire—arrayed in this new place. There wasn't much of a yard, but it was free of deaf-mutes, and it was a place where he could study the sky or apply the axe and saw to the lengths of wood Madame Guérin required for the stove, where he could lie in the sun alongside Sultan, who had grown yet fatter and more ponderous as he aged. And each day, just as she'd done for years, Madame Guérin took him for a walk in the park.

And Itard? He made an effort to visit, at least at first, and on hearing his voice, the boy would come running to him for a hug, and the reward—a bag of nuts or an orange—the doctor never failed to produce. Victor was in his twenties now, shorter than average—short as a child—but his face had broadened and he'd developed a rudimentary beard that furred his cheeks and descended as far as the scar on his throat. When he went out for his walks he still trotted along in his unique way, but around the house and the yard he began to shamble from place to place like an old man. Itard regarded the Guérins as old friends—almost as comrades in arms, as they'd all gone through a kind of war together—and Madame always insisted on cooking for him when he visited, but there was an awkwardness between him and his former pupil now, all the physical intimacy of their years together reduced to that initial hug. What was the point? What could they possibly say to each other? Victor spoke with his eyes, with certain rude gestures of his hands, but that was a vocabulary in which Itard was no longer interested. He was a busy man, in constant demand, his fame burgeoning, and with time his visits became less and less frequent until one day they stopped altogether.

At the same time, the Guérins, now effectively retired from the Institute, were aging in a way that made it seem as if the weeks were months and the months years piled atop them. Monsieur Guérin, ten years his wife's senior, fell ill. Victor hovered in the doorway of the sickroom, looking out of his neutral eyes, uncomprehending—or at least that was the way it seemed to Madame Guérin. The more her husband needed her, the more Victor seemed to regress. He demanded her attention. He tugged at her dress. Insisted that she come into the next room to fix him his *pommes frites* at any hour of the day, to pour him milk or massage his legs or simply to look and marvel at something he'd discovered, a spider making its web in the corner where the chimney met the ceiling, a bird perched on the windowsill that was gone by the time she turned her head. And then Monsieur Guérin was gone too and Victor stood bewildered over the coffin and shrank away from the strange faces gathered above it.

The day after the funeral, Madame Guérin didn't get out of bed until late in the afternoon and Victor spent the day staring out the window, beyond the projection of the building across the street, and into the view of the open lot beyond. He poured himself glass after glass of water, the original liquid, the liquid that took him back to his time of freedom and deprivation, and stared out to where the grass stood tall and the branches of the trees caught the wind. When the light shifted toward evening he moved to the cupboard and set the table as he'd been trained to do: three bowls, three mugs, three spoons and the twice-folded cloth napkins.

Ducking his head, he went into Madame Guérin's room and stood over the bed gazing at the heaviness of her face, her skin gone the color of ash, the lines of grief that dropped her chin and tugged at the corners of her eyes. He was hungry. He hadn't been fed all day. The fire was dead and the house was cold. He motioned to his mouth with his right hand and when Madame Guérin began to stir he took her arm and led her to the kitchen, pointing at the stove.

As soon as she came through the doorway, he knew that something was wrong. She pulled back, and he could feel her arm trembling against his, and there was the table, set for three. "No," she said, her voice strained and caught low in the back of her throat, "no," and it was a word he understood. Her shoulders shifted and she began to cry then, a soft wet insuck of grief and despair, and for a moment he didn't know what to do. But then, as tentatively and cautiously as he'd stalked the things he trapped in the grass a whole lifetime ago, he moved to the table and took up the bowl, the cup, the spoon and the napkin and silently put them back where they belonged.

In the years to come, Victor rarely left the house or the small square of the yard, hemmed in as it was by the walls of the surrounding buildings. Madame Guérin became too frail eventually to take him for his walks in the park and so he stood at the window instead for hours at a time or lay in the yard watching the clouds unfurl overhead. He took no pleasure in eating and yet he ate as if he were starved still, still roaming La Bassine with his stomach shrunken in disuse. The food thickened him around the middle and in the haunches. His face took on weight till he was nearly unrecognizable. No one knew. No one cared. He'd once been the sensation of Paris, but now he was forgotten, and even his name—Victor—was forgotten too. Madame Guérin no longer called him by name, no longer spoke at all except to her daughters, who rarely visited, wrapped up as they were in their own lives and passions. And the citizens of Paris, if they remembered him in passing, as they would remember the news of another generation or a tale told round the fire late at night, referred to him only as the Savage.

One morning Sultan vanished as if he'd never existed and before long there was another cat asleep in the chair or in Madame's lap as she sat and knitted or stared wearily into the pages of her Bible. Victor barely noticed. The cat was a thing of muscle and hidden organs. It stalked grasshoppers against the wall in the sun and ate from a dish in the kitchen, and with a long, languid thrust of its tongue it would probe itself all over, even to the slit beneath its tail, but mostly it lay inert, sleeping its life away. It was nothing to him. The walls, the ceiling, the glimpse of the distant trees and the sky overhead and all the power of life erupting from the earth at his feet: this was nothing. Not anymore.

He was forty years old when he died.